Home to Ohio

By Deborah E. Warr

ISBN
First Printing 2003
Cover art and design by Carla Boers

Published by:
Limitless, Dare 2 Dream Publishing

Lexington, South Carolina 29073

Find us on the World Wide Web
http://www.limitlessd2d.net

Printed in the United States of America by
Axess Purchasing Solutions
PO Box 500835
Atlanta, GA 31150

Dedication

To Richard

Acknowledgements

Special thanks to Chief of Police Michael Yates for his insights into real crime investigations and Therese McGuire for aiding with background material that added to the reality of the story.

Deborah E. Warr
March 2003

Special Notation

Sometime in the early morning hours of April 1st, 1968, in the small town of Milan, Ohio, a family was brutally murdered.

William Cassidy was 42 years old and his wife, Anna Cassidy, was 39. William was dead at the scene, having been shot at point blank range with what appeared to have been a shotgun. Anna, his wife, was taken to Fisher-Titus Hospital but died only ten minutes or so after arriving. Their daughter, Patricia, a 12 year old child, had yet to reach her teens when she was rushed to Elyria Memorial Hospital suffering from face and scalp lacerations. She was taken into emergency surgery at 10:15 that morning. It was believed at the time that Patricia had been beaten with a blunt instrument, most likely the same shotgun used to murder her parents in their upstairs bedroom, where their bodies had been discovered. Young Patricia was found in her own bedroom, nearby. She would not recover from her wounds. Their son Michael returned home after working in a nearby tavern, just after 4 that morning, to discover his parents had been murdered and his young sister barely clung to life.

Michael Cassidy was only 17 years old at the time.

The author, Deborah E. Warr, was a classmate.

Whether you were a member of the family or just from the neighborhood, it was an absolutely horrific thing to have happen and it affected everyone it touched, whether directly or indirectly.

This book was inspired by the unspeakable horrors of that night, so long ago. Neither the author nor the publishers of this book present it as anything more than a work of fiction. Sometimes something happens in our life that is so terrifying and unimaginable that it lingers, refusing to let us go. We all do the what-ifs, the I-wonders. **Home to Ohio** is truly the result of the muse at work. The characters in this story exist only on these pages and in the heart and mind of the author. No implication is made or intended with regard to the Cassidy murders or any other real event or person.

It is often said: "Write what you know." Deborah E. Warr has done exactly that. She has written about something that she actually experienced and in doing so, we hope, has chased away at least of few of the demons.

At the time of the writing of this book, the murders of the Cassidy family remain unsolved. We send our deepest regards to all who knew and loved them, trusting in the belief that justice will be found, whether it is in this life or another.

The publishers

Chapter One

How do I begin? If you passed me in a crowd, believe me, you wouldn't give me a second look. I'm on the other side of fifty, short dishwater blonde hair, thanks to my hairdresser and well, let's just say my figure has gone pretty much south. There was a time when I may have turned heads, but the years haven't been as kind to me as my Hollywood counterparts. I'm not that old. I just sort of blend in now with the rest of the so-called "baby boomers". My kids have grown up and gone their own way. I'm now the last minute babysitter and gofer if I'm in the mood, (which I'm not all the time), but enough to keep me in their good graces.

I never really thought that much about the inevitable, you know, the Big Chill, Curtains, A Visit from the Grim Reaper, or whatever else you care to call it, until my husband died playing tennis last year. One day he was the picture of health, a big strapping fellow full of life and the next, a victim of a massive coronary. We barely had time to say good-bye. His mortality forced me to think of my own. I remember how it was before. I just took life for granted. Dying was for drooling, mindless nursing home fodder. I figured I wouldn't have to think about The End for years and years. After all, my mother lived into her eighties and my grandmother her nineties. And then my husband stopped breathing forever. Seeing how quickly he was taken, I imagined life to be like a beautiful kite to which we all hold a fragile string. We need the breeze to keep it aloft, but if a storm comes along, like cancer or heart disease, the string breaks and we cease to exist. My string has seemed a little more frayed since then.

I live in Atlanta, but I didn't grow up here. In fact, I've lived here more years than I did in Ohio where I was born although I came here in my twenties. People occasionally notice that I don't speak with the drawl of a true daughter of the South, though occasionally "yawls" and "reckons" will slip into my speech. My children were all born here and I wouldn't dream of living anywhere else. But Midwestern roots run deep. It must have something to do with the black soil. It gets under the toenails or something. Georgia clay is as unyielding as it is red. Anyway, I digress. Getting back to the matter at hand.

As I was saying, my husband's untimely passing made me start thinking about my own life and where I was going with it. I had put so much of myself into him, I felt as though I had lost touch with me. So much of who I am is a result of where I came from. I realized that if I was going to give meaning to my life, I needed to get back in touch with the real me. I guess I'm a little old to "find myself", but better late than never. I decided that I needed to go back to where it all began. I needed to go home to Ohio.

Home in Ohio is a small town, close to the shores of Lake Erie. When I was a teenager, the lake was so polluted, you couldn't swim or fish in it and anyone who did was just plain crazy. They tell me that there was a time when I was really little that people actually did go in the water. In fact, I nearly drown in it at the age of three, or so I'm told; though I honestly don't remember it. They cleaned it up after I left and from all I hear it's safe again, but I wouldn't stick a toe in it on a bet.

Most of the people I grew up with moved away from Milan after we graduated. The majority gravitated to the major Ohio cities like Toledo, Cleveland and Columbus, but a few, like me, spread even further afield. Many years have passed between visits for me up there and some of my trips have even been happy occasions, but most have been because the family lost another member. Those kites have a way of slipping away no matter where you live.

Every year for the past forty years on Labor Day weekend, our little town holds its annual Melon Festival in the Town Square. The whole community turns out for it. The ladies' auxiliary hold bake sales, the high school band sells fried cheese and the farmers display their prize muskmelons. The daughters of the most prominent citizens compete for the coveted title of Melon Festival Queen. They hold a parade complete with floats, fire trucks, marching bands and local politicians in convertibles. They always have carnival rides for the kids and enough hotdogs and French-fries to give half of Ohio heartburn. Gossip is swapped among the locals as easily as the arts and crafts are sold to the tourists. They've managed to maintain the local color, but as it gains in popularity, the crowds have grown. Over 100,000 attended last year. I'm sure that in a few years, many of the vendors will be from other places if they aren't all ready.

The economy of the town is based primarily on farming and small manufacturing. Dairy and produce farms still dot the landscape although most of the small operations have been taken over by large conglomerates. As in other parts of the country the days of the small single family farm are becoming a thing of the past. For the most part things remain pretty quiet in the village of my youth. People still leave their doors unlocked and the crime and decay of the big city viewed on the evening news seems a world away. The residents are for the most part hard working, honest folk, close knit, but somewhat wary of strangers. Everybody knows everybody's business and kids are still taught the Golden Rule.

My ancestors going back at least four generations all hailed from there. The family farm used to be a few miles outside the city limits. My grandparent's home has long since been torn down and the land turned into a landfill. The once lush, fertile ground is now the repository of the detritus of modern society, its rolling hills scraped flat by bulldozers. Only to those of us who grew up there are the memories of it alive. Where once cattle grazed and corn grew, methane gas vents belch noxious fumes into the air. They say they will make it a golf course some day when the land can no longer hold another shred of debris, but I doubt it. A future golfer is just as likely to hit a tin can as he is a drive off the eighth tee. There's no telling what lies buried beneath that poisoned earth. There is little room for sentimentality in these days of planned obsolescence. It seems our family paid a higher price than most.

My brother managed to temporarily salvage my parents' home across the road from what was my grandparent's farm, but soon it too will be forfeited to the State in repayment for the years my parents spent in a nursing home before they died. I pity the man or woman assigned the task to sell it. Its location will make it nearly impossible to sell. Finding someone willing to live across from a landfill will be quite a challenge. Who knows? They will probably use the acreage for more waste disposal. My grandchildren, unfortunately, will never be able to visit the old family homestead.

As if by some quirk of fate, about a year into my widowhood, I received an invitation to my 30-year class reunion. It was the impetus I needed to convince me to make a pilgrimage back to the place I called home so many years ago. My husband's insurance had left me with enough money so that I didn't have to work, so there wasn't anything to keep me from going.

It just so happened that this year the Melon Festival corresponded with my 30-year high school class reunion. I had to change planes twice to get to Cleveland, but finally arrived with a few hours to kill before the first of the festivities got underway. I decided to drive past the site of my grandfather's farm before letting my old friends know that I was in town. I should tell you that not everything of my heritage has been obliterated. Only a mile or two away up the road from where I grew up is a tiny well-kept cemetery where the ashes of my parents are buried at the feet of my grandparents in the family plot. My grandfather's parents are there as well. Some of the gravestones date back to the early 1800's and others are so badly worn, they can't be read. Many of the interred lost their lives fighting in the Civil War. In fact, discharge papers signed by Abraham Lincoln were discovered in my grandmother's attic although they are now the property of some collector who placed the highest bid at her estate sale, the same day that the farm went on the auction block. No sense dwelling on what might have been. What's done, is done.

I came back to that spot on a glorious autumn day to lay flowers on my parents' grave. The grass growing over them was soft and fragrant, a cool breeze was blowing through the old gnarled cypress trees and the sun was warm on my back. They rest on a hill overlooking what remains of the countryside they loved. My father didn't live to see the current state of his birthplace just beyond the woods in the distance and it is just as well. He was a simple man who spent his life caring for the needs of his family and I loved him dearly.

As I stood over their grave markers, my mind drifted back over the years. I remembered how lonely I sometimes felt as a child being the last one to leave the nest and living so far out in the country. I had plenty of friends at school, of course, but there was always a sharp division between the town folk and country folk. Every so often, there would be a sleepover at a girlfriend's house, but most of my early childhood was spent playing by myself roaming the fields and woods with the family mutt, Duke. There was that one time that my best friend, Betsy rode her horse several miles from their dairy farm to my house without telling her mother. We spent the day together and had a great time. That is until her mother called mine in a panic because Betsy hadn't shown up for supper. We were probably in the fifth grade at the time and caught hell for it for weeks afterward, but it sure was fun. I looked forward to mentioning our great adventure to her at some point during my visit. We were born three days apart in the same hospital bed. Of all the kids I grew up with, she stands out as the best friend I ever had even though we drifted apart when we got older. Ah, those were such innocent days.

My reverie was interrupted by the arrival of a funeral procession. I had been so wrapped up in my own thoughts, I hadn't noticed that a tent had been erected on the far side of the cemetery over a newly opened grave and decided to give the mourners some privacy. With one last look back at the Malcolm monument, I trudged to my rental car and headed into town anxious to reconnect with my history.

It was Monday and the Melon Festival wasn't set to begin until Saturday, but preparations were already well underway. The shop windows around the Square were plastered with crepe paper and posters and a crew with a boom truck was hanging red, white and blue bunting on the lampposts. A couple of kids were mowing the grass and a couple more were busy adding a fresh coat of paint to the vintage bandstand. The air was filled with anticipation and everywhere I looked, I saw familiar sights, from the old Carnegie Library where my aunt used to work to my teenage hangout the Dairy Bar. I remember to this day how the paper bags from there used to smell like old hamburger grease and the time I dropped an ice cream cone on the sidewalk and refused to go back for another out of embarrassment much to my father's consternation. Milan looks pretty much the same as it did all those years ago thanks to some savvy local planners. They have managed to keep it small and quaint though I noticed on the ride in that some of the old houses have been turned into bed and breakfast establishments. I was surprised to see that my old hometown somehow became a tourist stop in my absence.

It was still too early to check into the Milan Inn, so I decided to grab a hamburger from the Dairy Bar for old times sake. I had hardly sat down in the newly upholstered booth before a woman a few years older than me approached my table.

"Well, as I live and breathe!" she gushed, "Aren't you a Malcolm? I'm Kay Cornwall, my maiden name was Pennington. You probably don't remember me, but I went to school with your brother. Is he here with you?" she asked looking hopefully around, "I haven't seen him in, gosh, twenty-five years. Are you all here for the Melon Festival?"

It took me a second to place her. The name was certainly familiar, but the face was not. As I recall, she and my brother were quite an item in school. The girl I remembered had been one of the most popular girls in my brother's class, you know, cheerleader, the whole bit and if my memory serves me correctly, I was looking at the 1962 Homecoming Queen. When she and my brother were dating, she had barely said two words to me. She had always done her best to ignore me. I guess you could say my memories of her were not fond ones. She had put on a more than a few pounds and she seemed to be wearing an awful lot of make-up for such a casual setting. She was dressed in an expensive-looking yellow pants outfit with white high-heeled sandals and wide-brimmed hat. Her perfume wafted my way and it's cloying scent combined with the smell of grilled onions made my stomach turn a flip.

"Oh, yeah," I said, trying my best not to gag, "I remember you. I'm Chip's little sister. Just up from Georgia for the Festival. Plus we're having our thirty-year class reunion. And no, regrettably my brother won't be coming this year. He's on vacation with his wife and family and couldn't make it. He's got three grandchildren now," I added just for spite, surprised to discover an unexpected animosity bubbling to the surface.

"Well, that's just wonderful!" she enthused, but I could tell her heart wasn't in it. Her original smile had dropped considerably.

"So, what have you been up to all these years, Kay?" I asked conversationally, knowing full well that she had learned all she wanted to know. "Do you still live around here or are you just visiting like me?"

"Oh, I went to Ohio State for a couple of years. Got married, moved to Cleveland for a while, but things didn't work out, so I moved back here when my mother passed away. We never had any kids and I've never remarried. As you can imagine, there aren't that many single men left around here anymore. All the good ones have moved away. Now I sell real estate. I've got an office over by the police station. This area is really growing. You'd be surprised how many people that moved away are coming back. You wouldn't be in the market for a house around here, would you?"

"No," I laughed, "I'm really happy where I am. I think about this place a lot, but I'm afraid my heart's in the south now."

"Well, if you change your mind," she said, fishing a business card from her handbag and sliding it across the table, "give me a call. And do tell your brother I said hello. I'd really love to see him."

"Oh don't you worry. I'll give him the message. You take care now, Kay. It was nice seeing you again."

"Same here. Well, I've got a client waiting. Have a nice time at the Festival. Maybe I'll see you there."

"Sure thing, Kay," I smiled as she glided away. It probably never dawned on her that I'd noticed that she never called me by name or asked about my life. As far as she was concerned, I was still just my brother's little sister. She had barely acknowledged my existence in the past, so why should I care now? I guess in all fairness, she at least recognized me. I can't explain why it bothered me, but it did. Of all the people I was looking forward to seeing again, she was definitely not one of them.

My food had still not arrived, so I wandered over to the jukebox and began scanning the titles. To my delight, it was packed with oldies. I made a few selections and returned to my booth to the beginning chords of the Beach Boys' Little Deuce Coupe. My good mood restored, I started humming along. My burger, fries and cherry Coke arrived, just as good as I remembered. I was immediately transported back to the sixties. I felt sixteen again. The only thing that was missing was a carload of my friends making silly jokes and hassling the waitress and it would have been perfect. Boy, we sure had some good times back then.

I sopped up the last of the ketchup and drained my Coke. I would have ordered some hand-dipped ice cream but resisted the temptation, reminding myself that while I was feeling like a sixteen year old, my stomach was still in its fifties. I am embarrassed to admit that I had tried to crash diet in order to lose weight for the reunion, but had failed miserably. I decided my old friends would have to take me just the way I was. Who would care anyway? We're all the same age, so it wouldn't come as any surprise that waistlines had expanded and hair had fallen out. I laughed. Who was I trying to kid? I am a grandmother for goodness sake!

Enough time had passed so that I could check into my hotel room. I paid my tab and walked to my rental car. I felt a little guilty that I hadn't called Betsy to let her know I was in town, but needed some time alone. I knew that if I had called her, she would have insisted that I stay with her and her husband as I have on previous occasions. I figured that we'd have plenty of time to get reacquainted later in the week. For now, I wanted to recapture my youth on my own. I hoped she would understand.

It only took a few minutes to reach the Inn. One of the beauties of Milan is that just about everything is within walking distance. I guess I forgot to mention that the town's claim to fame is that it is the birthplace of Thomas Edison. He only lived there for a few years, but his home has been made into a national landmark and there is now a bronze statue of him and his mother in the Square. People from all over the country come each year for tours led by local volunteers. It's a tiny little brick house lovingly restored and filled with memorabilia. It holds a special place in my heart not only because it's a part of my heritage, but also because my father was a third cousin of the inventor. I have cherished memories of my dad telling us about the time when he was a just a boy that Edison visited my grandfather's farm, the same farm that now lies buried under the town's garbage. The inventor was in his eighties at the time and my dad said it was a day that left a lasting impression. I promised myself that I would stop in at some point during my stay.

I was checked in and unpacked in short order. There was still plenty of daylight left and the weather was balmy, so I decided to take a walk. I wandered along the shaded sidewalks with no particular destination in mind, letting my footsteps lead me where they would. I passed what had been the homes of people I grew up with, looking for a familiar face, but disappointed to see from the names on the mailboxes that they were now filled with new families. I hoped they appreciated how lucky they were to live in such a beautiful place filled with so much history.

Without really thinking about it, I was inextricably drawn to the library where I had spent so many hours as a child. Unlike its sleek modern equivalents, all concrete, glass and steel, the Milan Library is a grand old lady. Built of solid red brick and granite, its steep stone steps and heavy brass doors led me back to a time I had almost forgotten. As soon as I caught that special scent of dusty paper, glue and bindings, I knew I had come home. This was the place that nurtured my love for books. Here I had dreamed of becoming a nurse like Sue Barton or a solver of mysteries like Nancy Drew and began my childhood love affair with horses through the pages of Black Beauty.

This was also the place where I got my first inkling of the scandalous from the pages of the forbidden Peyton Place, which I had accidentally found hidden under the front desk while lending a hand to my librarian aunt one winter's evening. That's when I learned that there were "special" books never meant to fall into the hands of children. The head librarian had been horrified when she found out, of course, but to me it was like found gold. The incident remains to this day a treasured memory. The library seemed so big back then, as though the stacks went on forever. I remember feeling as though the whole world was at my fingertips.

I stood just inside the entry vacantly gazing around and the white-haired lady behind the counter asked if I needed any help. She had a rather puzzled look on her face. I suddenly realized that I had been standing there for quite some time and must have looked like a lost soul, so I hurried over.

"As a matter of fact, you can," I stammered, bringing myself back to the present, "I grew up around here and spent a lot of time at this library when I was a kid. I'd be interested in anything you could suggest that would give me some information about Milan around the time that I lived here. My 30-year class reunion is this week and it would be fun to see if

17

there was anything happening then that I may have forgotten. Do you have any suggestions?"

"I thought you looked familiar!" she smiled. "I couldn't be sure until you said something. You're a Malcolm, aren't you?"

"Yes, that was my maiden name. I'm a Richardson, now. Why? Do I know you?"

"I went to school with Carolyn Malcolm back in the fifties. You look and sound just like her. Are the two of you related?"

"She's my oldest sister. She lives near Akron now. She's married with four grown kids and a bunch of grandkids. I'd be glad to tell her I saw you, if you'll give me your name."

"I remember that she had a baby sister. As I recall she missed out on a lot of activities because she had to baby-sit. My how time flies," she said, shaking her head, "you tell her that Connie Peterson said hello. I was a couple of years ahead of her, but you are the spitting image of her. Will she be coming for the Festival?"

"I don't think so, but if she does, I'll have her look you up," I offered, slightly embarrassed that I had no clue who she was.

"Oh please do! I'm sorry, I didn't mean to go on so. Of course you don't remember me. You were just a toddler then. Now, what was it you wanted?" she said, getting back to the matter at hand.

"I'm interested in anything concerning Milan during the mid-sixties through the early seventies. Do you have anything covering that period?"

"I think I have just what you're looking for," she said pushing her glasses up the bridge of her nose, "there used to be a local paper called The Milan Ledger. It went out of business years ago, but we still have all the back issues on microfilm. Would you like to start there?"

"Sounds good to me," I replied, anxious to get started.

She led me to a small backroom with an old fashioned viewer on a table facing the rear windows. The walls were lined with shelves full of microfilm boxes all carefully marked with the names of various periodicals, some of them dating back to before I was born. There was also a computer in the corner, which she said they used for imaging these days, but what I wanted was on microfilm. She showed me how to work the machine and where The Milan Ledger films were located. As she left the room, she told me to just leave the films on the table when I finished and she would put them away. I got the feeling she didn't trust me to return them to their proper place. I guess she thought of me as Carolyn's baby sister. I couldn't help but smile at the thought.

I soon found what I was looking for and before long I was browsing through articles filled with familiar names and events from my teenage years. The Ledger came out on Thursdays and there was lots of space devoted to the Milan High School Indians football and basketball teams. We rarely won any games, but the sports reporter was always upbeat and hopeful. Some of the boys in the photos were as familiar to me as members of my family. I even found an old picture of me from 1965 working on an art club project with some classmates tucked between an article about how the weather was affecting seed corn production and the Henderson's trip to Europe. I'm sure I have a copy of it in a scrapbook somewhere back home, though I couldn't put my hands on it to save me.

As the images flashed past I was struck by how very little actually happened in the community from week to week. The pages were filled with high school sports and articles of interest to farmers with a little gossip thrown in. There wasn't much crime to speak of unless you counted the occasional drunk and disorderly arrest notices. That is until I came to February 1968.

I almost missed it. I was starting to feel a little nauseated and my eyes hurt. Try staring into the kaleidoscopic images of a microfilm reader for a couple of hours and you'll know what I mean. Anyway, just as I was about to switch off the machine and take a break, I spotted the headlines of the February 3, 1968 issue:

"THREE FOUND SLAIN IN LOCAL RESIDENCE, POLICE BAFFLED".

"Chief of Police, Arthur Talbot reports that he and Officer John Miller responded

to a call they received concerning a disturbance at 747 Dixon Road around 3:00 a.m.

Tuesday morning. Upon arrival, they discovered the bodies of Patrick McCoy, his

19

wife Loretta and their 10-year old daughter Becky. The deceased are currently being
examined by the Erie County Coroner, Dr. Maxwell Snow to determine the cause of
death. Chief Talbot refused to speculate on the deaths other than to indicate that foul
play was suspected and that the investigation into the matter is ongoing. No further
details are available at this time.

The day I first learned of the incident is as burned in my memory as the day that John F. Kennedy was assassinated. I remember I was dressing for first period gym class when I overheard some girls talking about it. They said that the parents and sister of one of the boys in our class had been killed in a furnace explosion during the night. At first, I thought they were playing some kind of sick joke or if true, must have heard wrong and it turns out that they had, but at the time, it was just too unbelievable.

By that afternoon more information leaked out and we heard that there had not been an explosion, but that the parents died of shotgun blasts and the little girl had been bludgeoned to death. (Where the story about the furnace blowing up came from, I don't know.) I just remember everyone walking around in shock for days after. For the rest of the week the halls were unusually quiet, the students subdued. The teachers could be seen huddling outside their classrooms speaking in hushed tones. Their quiet conversations would immediately stop when the kids got close enough to hear. People started locking their doors at night and keeping a closer eye on their kids. Things like that just didn't happen in our little village. For all we knew there was some kind of deranged killer out there prowling the area.

I scanned the following issues for more details of the crime, but there was precious little information. The police were obviously keeping a tight lid on their investigation during the weeks that followed. The reports in the Ledger were sketchy at best, saying only that the investigation was continuing. The paper never mentioned who actually found the bodies. Most of what I remember came from the school rumor mill.

Here's what I was told, whether it's true or not, is anybody's guess. Around midnight, Mark McCoy, a boy we had all known since kindergarten and who lived a couple of miles from me, came home from his part time job sweeping floors at the local tavern. He walked upstairs to his parent's room to let them know he was home. Their bedroom door was closed, but the lights were on. When he knocked on their door, there was no answer, which seemed odd, so he opened the door a crack, thinking that they must have fallen asleep with the lights on. He called out to them and when they didn't answer, he walked to the side of the bed to rouse them and that's when he made the grisly discovery. They were both dead, unrecognizable, blood and brain tissue spattered on the bed linens, headboard and wall. He rushed to his sister's room where he found her also in her bed covered in blood. He didn't call the police, but drove to a friend's house. He was disoriented and acting very strangely, his behavior convincing the family that something terrible had happened to him. Some said he was covered in blood while others insisted that he had changed his clothes before he left the scene. The friend's father supposedly is the one who placed the call to the police.

There had never been any plausible explanation as to why he said he came home shortly after midnight and the bodies were not discovered until several hours later. The gossipmongers insisted it was because he was the killer, but lots of people defended him, saying he was so distraught, he must have just gone crazy from what he had seen and couldn't be held responsible for his actions.

All I know is that he wasn't in school for a couple of months after his folks were killed and when he did come back, he wasn't the same easygoing boy we knew from before. He was downright spooky. He had this vacant look in his eyes, rarely spoke and for the most part kept entirely to himself. As I look back on it, I have to wonder what the heck we expected. The kid had lost his entire family in a ghastly murder, but we were young and didn't know any better. Anyway, a few days after his return, we were in Civics class and the teacher having completed the day's lesson a little early, asked if anyone had any questions. Several of us raised our hands including Mark. The teacher called on a couple of students and then Mark stunned everyone by asking in this weird monotone voice if it was possible for someone to do something really horrible and have no memory of it.

The room went deathly still and everyone held their breath. We all expected him to blurt out that he had murdered his folks. The poor teacher, his face a brilliant crimson, choked out that Civics class was not the proper place to discuss his question and quickly tried to direct everyone's attention back to the subject at hand, but Mark was not to be deterred. He repeated his question and the teacher mumbled something to the effect that he really didn't know, but it was definitely not the time or place to talk about it. All of us sat there goggle-eyed and couldn't have been more shocked than if the teacher had suddenly grown two heads. Mercifully the bell rang before he could ask a third time and everyone hustled from the room as fast as their legs could carry them, including the teacher. The next day Mark wasn't at school and he never came back. To everyone's surprise, we heard that he was shipped off to the Army shortly thereafter and never charged with the crime.

From time to time over the years I have asked several people if anyone was ever arrested and the answer has always been no. My dad told me once that he was well acquainted with Patrick McCoy and knew him as a foul-mouthed drunken wife-beater and could name any number of people that would have been less than sad to see him gone. So who knows? To many locals the finger will always point in Mark's direction, but the case, as far as I know, is still officially unsolved.

My head was throbbing and it was getting late. My stroll down memory lane had proved to be a little less pleasant than I had hoped. If I hurried I would be able to get back to my hotel room before dark. I switched off the machine, and walked out past the front desk. Connie nodded my way and I stepped outside. As my eyes swept the Square from the top of the steps, my pretty little town looked a lot less innocent than it had just a few hours earlier. I could swear I felt as though I was being watched as I strode back toward the Inn. Once I closed and locked the door behind me, the feeling passed and I spent the rest of the evening reading and soaking in the tub feeling positively foolish for letting my imagination get the better of me.

Chapter Two

I spent a restless night, my heart jumping in my chest at every unfamiliar sound. I finally drifted off at some point after hours of tossing and turning and woke around 10:00. Berating myself for letting something that happened over thirty years ago get to me, I decided to put the unpleasant thoughts behind me and do a little more sightseeing. I grabbed a paper cup of the complementary coffee and a stale doughnut from the hotel lobby and headed back towards the Square. It was going to be another glorious day. There was a slight snap in the air and the sun was shining.

As I walked along the same path I had traveled the night before, I reminded myself that this really was a great place to grow up. A block from the center of town, I passed a lady working in her immaculately manicured lawn. She was pulling weeds from her flowerbed and when she waved hello, I complimented her on her roses. She smiled and thanked me, saying it was a lot a work, but well worth the effort. Our friendly exchange lifted my spirits, making me feel foolish for thinking there was anything sinister lurking in the shadows and chalked it up to my overly active imagination.

I walked past the library and up the north side of the Square past the Town Hall and several antique and gift shops towards the Edison birthplace. I knew that if I planned to take a tour, I would need to do it before the crowds starting arriving for the weekend. As I turned the corner, I glanced through the windows of the bank where my folks used to have their accounts, remembering the time when I was little that the bank president had let me play with their collection of antique coin banks and wondering if it was still there. From the look of things, there wasn't room for such sentimentality. The whole place had been modernized and sold to a big chain. It had lost its charm to the latest drive for technology. I decided not to stop in. I knew it wouldn't be the same and wanted to keep that special memory just the way that it was.

I passed the Milan Museum on the right and came to the birthplace on the left. A group of children were lined up in front of the little house, the tour guide giving them their final instructions before allowing them to enter the building. They all turned at my approach and the guide asked if I wished to join them. She said I was welcome, but if I preferred, I could come back in an hour for the next tour. I told her that I didn't mind as long as the kids and their teacher were okay with it. A precious little blonde-haired girl walked over to me, looked up at me solemnly, took my hand and led me to the group, so the decision was made for me. That done, the elderly volunteer resumed her stern warning that everyone would be required to stay on the plastic runners and there was to be no touching of any of the artifacts. I winked at my little companion and we filed inside.

The guide was extremely well versed on the history of the house and the Edison family, pointing out different points of interest and describing their significance. We all got a lesson on the history of the founding of Milan and I was proud that I could claim a piece of it. I would have mentioned to her that I was distantly related to the inventor, but I doubt she would have been impressed. She was the expert on the subject and I was merely another outsider among thousands who visit each year.

When the tour was over, we waved good-bye and I watched with some envy as the kids trouped back in the direction of the school with their teacher close behind. I longed for the time when it would have been me. The old school house used to house all twelve grades, but was now an elementary school. The year after I graduated, our high school merged with a neighboring town and a sprawling new building called Edison High was built halfway between. Nothing remains of our beloved Milan High except in the memories of old fogies like me.

I continued my trip down memory lane by stopping in to the Milan Museum. My great aunt had bequeathed an old horsehair settee to the Museum and I wanted to be sure that it was still there. As soon as I entered, someone called out to me.

"Ellen! Ellen Malcolm! I'd know you anywhere! You haven't changed a bit!"

An older woman in a print dress and sensible shoes rushed over and patted my arm affectionately. I had no earthly idea who she was.

"Oh, hello," I stammered, "it's so good to see you again."

She noticed my hesitancy and quickly identified herself as the mother of one of my classmates, Bobby Bertram.

"Why I haven't seen you since you kids graduated from high school! Where are you living now?"

I explained that I was from Atlanta, etc., etc. She told me all about what her son was doing, etc., etc. She said she helped out at the Museum just to have something to do and gave me the grand tour. I felt like a celebrity as she introduced me to her co-workers though I can't exactly say why.

My stomach told me that it was well past lunchtime by the time I finished looking around, so I took a shortcut back to the Square around the block past the Methodist Church, thinking I would indulge in the ice cream I had passed up the day before and worry about the calories later.

The route took me past the police station, a tiny brick building behind the Town Hall that looks as though it belongs on the siding of a child's train set. No big changes here. I meant to just pass on by, I honestly did, but I just couldn't resist going in and talking to someone about the McCoy murders. I still couldn't believe that nothing had ever been done about finding the person responsible. A chunky girl in her early twenties looked up from her computer screen as I entered and asked if she could help me. I asked to speak with the current Chief of Police if he was available. She looked me over, I guess to assure herself that I wasn't there for anything urgent and asked me to wait. She went into the office behind her and I could hear some quiet conversation. A few moments later she returned, followed by a big guy around thirty or so with a crewcut and startlingly blue eyes. He introduced himself as Chief Andy Taylor, shook my hand and asked me to follow him into the office.

As I took a seat in front of his desk, I chuckled and asked him if anyone ever said anything about the fact that he had the same name as the fictional character Sheriff Andy Taylor from the Andy Griffin Show. I must have touched a nerve because he didn't share my humor and I immediately apologized.

With my foot squarely implanted in my mouth, I quickly explained who I was, why I was in town and how I had become interested in any information he could give me about the murders back in 1968.

25

"So, Chief Taylor, can you tell me anything I couldn't get from the reports I found at the library?" I asked, hoping I hadn't blown it with my stupid comment about his name.

"I've only been Chief for the past five years," he said, tilting back in his chair and crossing his beefy arms across his chest, "but I'm sure that case would have gone cold years and years ago. If there was a file on it, it's probably with the old dead files that were put into cold storage right after I came on board. As you can see we don't exactly have a lot of room in here. I didn't have the time to go over all the old stuff. Cases had been piling up for years. It took me weeks to dig through it all. The Chief before me wasn't exactly the most organized guy in the world. We had uncollected speeding tickets going back fifteen years. Matter of fact, I had to practically beg the City Council for the funds to hire an assistant. Thank heavens for Lucy! If it weren't for her, I'd still be buried under the paperwork. We've only had a computer to work with for two years! Just because this is a small town doesn't mean you can't do things properly!"

"I can certainly understand your frustration," I agreed, but was determined to get anything I could. I continued, "I may have gotten my information from the TV cop shows, but I was under the impression that there is no statute of limitations on murder and no matter how much time has passed, the perpetrator could still be charged with the crime."

"Yes, I suppose that's true. Why? Do you have anything new to offer?" he asked, the front legs of his chair banging back to the floor, leaning over his desk and looking at me with renewed interest.

"Oh, ah, no," I said, feeling my face get hot, "no, I was just curious. It's just that everyone I've ever talked to about it just sort of assumed that Mark McCoy killed his sister and his folks and well," I hesitated, "well, got away with it!"

Just then his eyes narrowed and the patronizing expression he had been giving me vanished like raindrops on hot cement. His face flushed and his hands curled into white-knuckled fists.

"Did you say, Mark McCoy?" he asked, his mouth a thin hard line.

"Why yes," I squeaked, his reaction making me feel extremely uncomfortable, "he was in my class back in the sixties. He and his sister used to ride the same school bus with me. Do you know him?"

"Oh you could say that!" he growled. "He just happens to own one of Erie County's biggest car dealerships. I bought my Blazer from him a couple of years ago! Gave me a super deal! He supplies our police force with squad cars at cost! He is very well respected in this town. He's a goddamn war hero for chrissakes! There's no way the man I know would have had anything to do with what you're talking about! Lady, I don't know what kind of game you're playing, but I'm going to have to ask you to leave. I've got to prepare for the biggest event of the year this weekend. I'm a very busy man!"

He jumped to his feet and just like that, the interview was over. I felt his icy blue eyes boring into my back as I left his office. His assistant, Lucy, who I am sure, heard the whole thing, looked at me with scorn. I barely got out of the door before I heard him shouting for her to get her butt in his office, expletives deleted. I felt as though I had been slapped in the face. My shock must have been pretty obvious, because a couple I passed on the steps stared at me as if I needed assistance. I had opened a can of worms and had a feeling I was going to pay for it.

Suddenly I wasn't hungry anymore. I felt as though I might start bawling right there, so I made a beeline back to the hotel. I promised myself that I would call Betsy just as soon as I got there and put the whole humiliating experience out of my mind. What I thought had been solid ground had turned into quicksand. If I had been a drinking woman, I would have probably headed to the nearest tavern and drunk myself silly, but sanity prevailed and by the time I got to my room, my hands had stopped shaking.

The exertion had calmed me considerably and as I reached for the phone to call my friend, a thought struck me. Why was I feeling so intimidated? I had told the truth! Didn't the public have a right to know who was responsible for three brutal murders? Just because that pig-headed Chief of Police, Andy Freaking Taylor, didn't believe me, didn't give him the right to treat me like some kind of idiot! The more I thought about it, the madder I got. Of course, he would defend Mark McCoy! He probably owes the man! He doesn't want some outsider coming in and upsetting the apple cart! And there was another possibility. Maybe Mark really didn't have anything to do with the slaughter of his family. The real killer could be out there somewhere living a normal life and he had lived under a cloud of suspicion for nothing!

I made up my mind that come hell or high water, I would get the truth out of somebody, but it was time I let Betsy know I was in town. She answered on the third ring and immediately insisted that I drop everything and hurry over. She said she would get on the phone in the meantime and invite some of our old friends for an impromptu gabfest.

As I drove out towards her restored farmhouse just up the road from her family's dairy farm, I thought about how good it was to hear the warmth in her voice. Years would pass between our contact with one another, but she was always the same sweet person I remember. She would forever be a pony-tailed tomboy in my heart, though she was now getting on in years just like me. When I arrived, we embraced and the years melted away. There was never any pressure on either side to keep in touch. We both had our separate lives now, but the bond that had been forged would never be broken.

We spent the next couple of hours catching up on our lives, swapping information on our kids and grandkids. Her husband, her high school sweetheart whom she had married right after graduation, came home from his successful electronics business and joined in. He had been quite a cutup in school and had us in stitches regaling us with tales of his own.

Soon after that another old friend, Emily Johnson stopped by. She and her husband own a charter fishing boat on Lake Erie. Other than for a few creases around her eyes, she looked exactly the way she did as a teenager. She invited Betsy and me out for a short jaunt to the lake islands for the following day. Betsy said she had too much to do since she was in charge of one of the fundraising concessions at the Melon Festival, but I eagerly accepted. I felt as though the fresh air would do me good, maybe chase away the dark mood that had come over me after my encounter with Chief Taylor.

The rest of the evening was spent reminiscing about the good old days and I found myself basking in the glow of people I knew as well as members of my own family.

Chapter Three

Betsy, as I expected, wanted me to spend the night at her house, but I had already settled in at the hotel, so over her protestations, I returned there. The next morning I awoke refreshed and looking forward to the day out on the lake with Emily and her husband. When I peeked through the curtains, the weather had taken a turn for the worse. The sky was overcast and the wind had picked up considerably. Emily called to say that I was to meet them at the pier and we would decide then if it would be safe to go out in the boat. She suggested that I bring along a jacket just in case. The lake swells were cresting at three feet and if it didn't get any rougher we would go for it. She said that their boat was a 25-foot cabin cruiser and could handle just about anything the lake threw at it, but they believed in playing it safe and I whole hearted agreed.

By the time I arrived at their dock, a few sprinkles of rain had started to fall, but the weather report was improving. Emily asked if I was prone to seasickness and offered me a patch. Not wanting to seem like a wimp, I refused. A couple of hours later I would regret my bravado.

The first leg of the trip took us out to Put-in-Bay, a small island community that can only be reached by boat or by air. It's a quaint little place filled with small vacation homes and a few permanent residences. It was the last week of the summer season and the marina was packed with every sort of watercraft. We had lunch in the only café on the island. They had the freshly caught fried fish, but I had the soup and salad. They assured me that the fish was perfectly safe to eat, but I couldn't. I simply couldn't shake the images of raw sewerage I had seen floating by on my trips to the lake when I was a kid, though I had to admit the lake water was a whole lot cleaner than I remember it.

During the course of our conversation, I casually mentioned my interest in the mystery surrounding the McCoy murders. Emily said that it was ancient history and preferred not to dwell on such an unpleasant subject, but her husband, Jeff, was intrigued. He had grown up in Cleveland and had never heard the story. I kept it brief out of deference to

Emily's wishes, but when I mentioned Sheriff Talbot's name from the newspaper article, she joined in. She said that Talbot had died sometime in the 80's and was replaced as Chief of Police by John Miller. Miller, she said, had been Chief until a few years ago when Taylor took over. She said that Miller had been paralyzed from the neck down in a hunting accident and was confined to a nursing home on the outskirts of town. She confirmed that as far as she knew, no one had ever been charged with the murders. It was a closed subject and Mark had gone on with his life, even though most everyone from back then figured he probably did it.

Not wanting to bring everybody down, we changed the subject and nothing more was said about it. Anyway, we hadn't been back on the boat for more than a few minutes heading back out into deep water when the waves increased. The ups and downs also increased and I got unpleasantly reacquainted with my soup and salad over the side. I had never been seasick before and believe me, it is not something I ever care to experience again.

Jeff got us safely back to shore and once my feet touched land, the queasy feeling passed. They decided to go back out, so I thanked them and I wished them well assuring them that I had had quite enough fun for one day. We promised to get together again at the reunion dinner and I waved good-bye as they backed away from the mooring.

As I walked to my car, I thought back on our conversation over lunch. Emily had said that John Miller was still in town, though a bedridden invalid. I wondered if he could answer some of my questions. My day of sailing cut short, I had the whole afternoon ahead of me, so I figured it was worth a shot. At the very worst, he could refuse to speak to me or even unable to speak to me, but the paper said that he was there when the bodies were discovered. He must have taken part in the ensuing investigation. Once again, my curiosity got the better of me and I drove to the Shady Oaks Nursing Home.

The convalescent center was a single-story building, clean and modern with well-kept grounds and gravel pathways heading off in all directions. Flowers were everywhere. When I entered the reception area, I expected to be assaulted by the smell of old urine and antiseptic like most of the human warehouses of my experience, but to my surprise, it was actually rather pleasant. The entire place had been tastefully furnished with antiques and artwork, and if not for the few old folks sleeping in their wheelchairs and toddling down the hall on the railings, it could have been someone's home. The receptionist was friendly and more than happy to show me to Miller's room. She said he didn't get many visitors and would appreciate having someone to talk to.

When we reached his doorway, she went in first. He was in the bed by the windows; the bed closest to the door was unoccupied. He had been asleep, but turned his head our way when she spoke his name. His face was gaunt and deeply lined; his body barely making a bump under the blankets, but his eyes were lively and full of intelligence. I approached the side of the bed and introduced myself. I was rewarded with an incredibly attractive smile, which I knew instantly must have melted more than a few hearts before his accident. To my surprise, he lifted his right hand and shook mine quite firmly. Seeing that all was in order, my escort excused herself and I took a seat by the window where he could see me.

"So, what's a pretty lady like you doing in a place like this?" he asked with a sly twinkle in the corner of his eye.

"Well, Mr. Miller, I was hoping you might help me with something," I began.

"If it requires any heavy lifting, I'm afraid you've come to the wrong place," he laughed. "And please, call me Jack."

"Okay, Jack. Actually, I understand that you once worked on the Milan Police force and wanted to know if you could tell me about the murders that took place here in Milan back in 1968."

His friendly expression turned to one of suspicion, the tone of his voice chilly, "are you some kind of reporter or something? If you are, you can just move it on out of here. I've got nothing to say to any nosey rag peddlers."

"Jack, Mr. Miller, I promise you I am definitely not a reporter!" I cried, afraid I had blown it once again. "I grew up here in town from the time I was born until I got married. I live in Georgia now, but went to school with the boy whose family was killed. I was doing a little research at the library to reconnect with my past, you know, looking for people I once knew and events to jog my memory so that I would get some sense of who I was back then, you know. I thought it would help break the ice with people at my 30-year class reunion this weekend. That's when I came across the reports from the old Milan Ledgers about the killings. As far as I could tell, the killer had never been caught and it made me curious. I tried to get some information from your replacement, Chief Taylor, but I'm afraid we didn't exactly hit it off and he refused to speak to me. He practically tossed me out on my ear and told me to mind my own business."

The friendly expression returned to his face. "Taylor can be a real hard ass when he wants to. So you're playing amateur detective, is it?"

"Well," I blushed, "I never thought of it that way, but I guess I am. I just can't get it out of my mind that three people lost their lives and nothing was ever done about it, at least as far as I've been able to tell. It just doesn't seem right somehow."

"I'll agree with you there," he sighed, laying his head back on his pillows and gazing out the window. "You know I was one of the cops who responded to the call that night."

"I know. You were mentioned in the Ledger articles."

"Yeah, in all my years as a cop, that was the worst. I'm not ashamed to say that I tossed my cookies that night and I wasn't alone. Seasoned officers lost it right along with me. I guess the worst part wasn't the parents, although that was pretty bad, but the little girl, well, suffice it to say that there was very little left of her face. Whoever hit her did a real number on her."

"What about their son, Mark? Did you ever suspect him?"

"Well, you always suspect family members first. Most murders are committed against family members. That's standard procedure. Question the ones closest to the victims."

"Was the rumor that he waited several hours to report the murders true?" I asked treading as lightly as I could, afraid I would ask the wrong question and get rebuffed yet again.

"I hadn't heard that one," he admitted with a frown, "but then I wasn't the one who questioned him. I wasn't the senior officer on the case. Chief Talbot and some state boys he called in handled the interrogation. We'd never had a triple homicide before. About the closest thing to it was when old Archie Witherspoon threw himself into his combine in 1963 because he couldn't take it anymore. Now that was one for the books.

We just weren't equipped back then to handle anything of that magnitude."

"But there must have been some theories tossed about," I said, "I can't believe there wasn't talk going around the police station or something! It just doesn't make any sense!"

"Well sure, we talked about it, but the Chief ordered that we weren't to discuss it with anyone outside the force. We all figured that it was just a matter of time before somebody either confessed or talked about it to their friends and whoever did it would get caught. We were told that the kid's story checked out and that he didn't do it, so the investigation was back to square one. Eventually, they gave up trying."

"But I thought murder investigations never completely go away. I've heard of people in the news being convicted of murders from years and years ago. There was a woman just the other day in her sixties that got convicted of poisoning her kids when they were babies! They exhumed the bodies and everything!"

"Yeah, well that does happen every now and again, but believe me, once a case goes cold, it's nearly impossible to solve it. People get older, memories fade. There are always new cases that come along, so nobody has time to spend on old ones. Matter of fact, when Chief Talbot died and I took his place, I tried to do a little digging into it myself, you know, trying to make a name for myself, but couldn't turn up anything new. Then some yahoo shot me in the back on opening day of deer season and I landed here. I'm afraid you may be wasting your time. I don't mean any disrespect, but you're not exactly equipped for the job. Why don't you just get together with your friends this weekend, enjoy the Melon Festival and forget about it. I quit trying to solve the world's problems a long time ago."

"You're probably right," I sighed, "I don't know a thing about this sort of thing. Nobody else seems to be concerned, so maybe I should just drop it. According to Chief Taylor, Mark has moved on with his life inspite of what happened. He's been quite successful so I'm told. Maybe all I'm doing is opening up old wounds that need to be kept in the past where they belong."

"I think you may be right. There was time when I would have been tempted to encourage you to find out what you can, but as you can see, I'm in no shape to be of help to anybody. It's better to leave any investigating to the experts. Besides, you've been away for a long time. I'm sure you won't be very popular if you go around stirring things up. You may feel that you still belong here, but to most folks, you're an outsider."

"I suppose so, although it seems that I can't go anywhere without somebody recognizing me. You know my family all lived here back four generations. My parents both passed away and my brother and sister have moved away. My grandparent's farm has been plowed under and made into a landfill, so that's gone, not to mention the fact that the house I grew up in has been turned over to the state. I can't explain why the McCoy murder bothers me so, maybe it's because it left such a stain on my nearly perfect childhood memories."

"You said your name was Richardson, is that your married name?"

"Oh, right! I'm sorry, my maiden name was Malcolm. I used to be Ellen Malcolm. I guess I forgot to mention that. Why? Does the name sound familiar?"

"Did your family live out on Truman Road?"

"Uh huh."

"I know exactly where you mean! I remember your dad! He was a real nice guy! I met him when your brother was in that roll over accident out on Route 299! Your brother's lucky he wasn't killed. I'm sorry to hear he's gone."

"Yeah, me too. Well, I guess I'll take your advice and quit playing junior detective. But while we're on the subject, if you don't mind my asking, did they ever find out who shot you?"

"Nope. There were so many hunters in the woods that day; there was no way to tell. There were guns blazing all over the place. I just happened to be in wrong place at the wrong time. You can call it just another unsolved Milan mystery," he grinned, giving me a mischievous wink, then more seriously, "why do you ask?"

"A thought just occurred to me. Didn't you say you had been doing some investigating on the McCoy murders just before your accident?"

"Yes. It was after I became Chief of Police. I thought I could score points with the Mayor and City Council if I could solve the crime, something my predecessor had been unable to do. I was really gung-ho back then," he said, his face turning wistful. Then his eyes popped open, "Hey, wait a minute! I know where you're going with this! You're thinking that my accident was no accident!"

"It does seem a little coincidental, wouldn't you say? I could be wrong, but who knows? Maybe you were getting a little too close to finding out the truth and whoever did it, wanted you out of the picture. Surely that must have occurred to you at the time!"

"Oh come on! That stuff only happens in the movies! It was an accident, plain and simple! People get shot every year in hunting accidents. Guys who don't know the first thing about hunting go out in the woods, get liquored up and shoot at anything that moves. It happens all the time. I just happened to be one of the unlucky ones!"

"If you say so, Jack. I hope you're right. You'd certainly know a whole lot more about it than I would. I'm sorry if I upset you. I should have just kept my lame theories to myself."

"Hey, that's okay," he said kindly, "Really, I think you're just trying to read something into it that isn't there. I made peace with my situation a long time ago. There was a thorough investigation into it and it was ruled an accident. I seriously doubt that anybody was trying to, quote bump me off unquote," he said, waving his one good hand dismissively.

"You're right. I'm just a woman who's getting on in years sticking my nose where it doesn't belong. I think I'll do everybody a favor, pack up my magnifying glass and quit playing Sherlock Holmes. It was really a pleasure to meet you, Jack. Thanks for your kind words about my father. That means a lot to me. If I get a chance, I'll stop back by before I go back home, if that's all right with you."

"I would appreciate that, Ellen. I get pretty lonely lying around this place. Everybody's too busy to come visit an old crippled guy like me."

"You take care now, Jack," I said patting his hand and turned to go.

He took hold of my hand before I could take it away and held it. "I'm probably going to hate myself for saying this," he whispered, "but I never really thought about the timing between my snooping around and the accident. What if there was some connection?"

"Then whoever did it, is still out there, Jack," I said quietly. "But there's nothing we can do about it now. Right?"

"Right. Somehow I have the feeling you're not going to let this thing drop, are you?"

"I'll have to get back to you on that, Jack," I said, and carefully removed my hand from his grasp. "I'm here to catch up on old times with my classmates and enjoy the Festival, remember? You just hang in there, okay?"

"Okay," he sighed.

I walked from his bedside then and looked back at him through the doorway to wave good-bye. He had turned his head back toward the windows, and I assumed he was going to take the nap I had interrupted. That's when I noticed his one good hand curled into a fist. He muttered something I didn't catch and pounded it on the mattress. The gesture made me wonder if maybe Jack was having some doubts about his so-called accident. I felt immediately guilty for bringing up such an uncomfortable subject to a man who was so helpless and had accepted his lot in life. Once again, what I had assumed was solid ground, had turned into quicksand. For what seemed the umpteenth time, I pushed the whole thing to the back of my mind. I had lost my lunch to seasickness and was in need of some food. I drove towards town in search of a decent restaurant. I would worry about sleuthing another time. The town's mysteries would just have to take a backseat to my growling stomach.

Chapter Four

The storm that had threatened to cancel my ill-fated boat ride arrived later that evening. The rain slashed against the hotel room windows all night and I woke up several times to the sound of thunder. The Festival was set to open the day after next, so I'm sure I wasn't the only one losing sleep that Thursday night. People had been preparing for the big event for months and the last thing they needed was rain.

Thankfully, Friday dawned clear, but there was a distinct chill in the air when I stepped on the veranda. Having spent the majority of my life in the south where summer can last well into October, I realized that the dress I had brought along for the reunion dinner later that evening was much too thin. It was sleeveless and with my thin Georgia blood, I knew I'd regret wearing it, not to mention the fact that I had been somewhat optimistic as to the success of my crash diet and it was decidedly too tight. The last thing I needed was to show up at the reunion looking like a stuffed sausage.

I spent the rest of day searching the dress shops at the mall in nearby Sandusky. After hours of looking, I finally settled on a long-sleeved black number with a plunging neckline that I hoped would draw attention away from my hips. As my grandmother used to say, you can't make a silk purse out of a sow's ear, but I was determined to give it a shot. I had brought along my pearl necklace and earrings and figured I couldn't go wrong with pearls and basic black. At least that's what I'd read in the fashion magazines.

I made it back to the hotel with just enough time to shower and change. I wished I had been able to get my hair done, but there hadn't been time, so I did the best I could on my own. One last glance in the mirror told me I had probably put on way too much make-up, but it was getting late, so I went with it. I reminded myself that we were all in the same boat. I wasn't a kid anymore and nothing I did could make me into one.

I arrived at the restaurant a few minutes early. Only a handful of people had gotten there ahead of me and although I knew I was in the right place, I didn't recognize any of them. To my dismay, I realized that I was decidedly overdressed judging from what the women were wearing. While the men were in suits, the women all seemed to be wearing outfits more suitable for church and there I was with my boobs hanging out, with too much make-up on, feeling like an idiot. It was all I could do not to just turn on my heels and head back to my car. I had just about done so, when someone called out to me.

"Ellen! Ellen Malcolm! Is that you? My God! It's been thirty years! Look, everyone, it's Ellen!"

All the heads swiveled in my direction and the woman who had recognized me rushed over. She threw her arms around me and crushed me against her abundant breasts. When she finally released me, I got a better look at her and realized with a gasp that I did indeed know her. It was Linda Ericson. But nothing like the Linda I remember. The Linda I remember had been a flat chested, waif of a girl, who everyone teased because she had been caught stuffing Kleenexes in her bra in gym class. The kids had been merciless, calling her the queen of the itty-bitty titty committee. Linda had obviously taken their ridicule to heart, because either nature had eventually intervened, so else she had discovered the wonders of plastic surgery. Either way, she was an entirely different person.

"So, if it isn't Linda Ericson!" I cried, "How have you been?" I was dying to know if her new figure was natural or artificial but had the presence of mind not to ask. I figured I would find out eventually because reunions are a great source of the latest gossip. I felt sure the subject would come up sooner or later.

"I'm doing great!" she enthused, "How about you? I heard you had moved to Georgia. I've got four kids and a grandchild on the way. What have you been up to all these years?"

I gave her a quick rundown of my life, about how I was a widow and grandmother, etc. and the next thing I knew she was leading me back to her table where three members of her old crowd and their respective spouses and her husband were sitting.

Linda and I had never really been that close in school. She had been the part of another group of girls that, as I recall, where mad for the Beatles. They each had their favorite Beatle and would talk for hours about how great they were. I never was much into fads back then. I always looked at that sort of thing as a little too juvenile for my tastes. I never could see the point to all the screaming over a bunch of guys in a band, who couldn't care less about their fans. I guess I was pretty snobbish even back then, and I regretted it, considering the warm welcome she had just given me.

The conversation continued around the table and before long, I was caught up on what life had dished out to everyone. The final tally was three divorces, thirteen kids and a few grandchildren. Everyone at the table lived somewhere other than Milan, but had all stayed in Ohio. Linda worked for the telephone company, another was a registered nurse at the Cleveland Clinic and another bragged of her successful career as an insurance agent. I don't remember what the other one said she did, but I guess it doesn't really matter. She was more interested in bashing her ex-husband's reputation anyway. Just about the time we ran out of things to talk about, I spotted Betsy and her husband talking to Emily and Jeff across the room.

I excused myself with the usual half-hearted promise to keep in touch and walked towards the table where Betsy and the others were sitting. On the way I passed several more people I knew and stopped briefly to chat. Most of the guys looked pretty much the same except for the deficiency in the hair department and the expansion around the midsections. There was more gray hair and wrinkles than I had hoped to see, but the majority of these folks came from good Midwestern stock like me and didn't feel the need for such foolishness. I finally saw a couple women in cocktail dresses over by the bar, but they seemed to be a good bit younger than the rest of us. I noticed that they were clinging to the arms of the more successful men in the class with fake smiles pasted on their faces. I assumed that they were either the new wives or girlfriends who had been coerced into coming to a party for a bunch of us old folks. Call me catty, but I couldn't wait to find out and I knew somebody would fill me in.

Betsy and the others made room for me at the table and we soon were lost in the conversation that can only be shared with old friends. Everyone got a laugh at my expense when Emily insisted on telling about my lack of seaworthiness and I got the scoop on Linda's amazing bust line. According to Betsy, she had dated a plastic surgeon from Cincinnati after her first divorce and they had been his parting gift. We all howled with laughter and I nearly choked on my drink.

As I was wiping tears from my eyes, sure that I must have mascara dripping off my chin, someone tapped me on the shoulder. I turned and looked up to see the face that had nearly made me swoon all through high school. He looked even better than he had back then. He was one of the lucky ones who still had his hair though a little gray at the temples and had managed to keep his athletic build. As the saying goes, men grow distinguished, while women just grow old.

His name was Bill Hamilton and I had loved him from afar for as long as I can remember. He had been a star on the basketball team and one of the most popular boys in school. He had always been nice to me, although the closest I ever came to dating him was on the few occasions when he would ask me about my thoughts on his latest conquest. He always had his pick of the girls and I, being a little pudgy and an egghead to boot, was not one of them. I can't count the times I had gazed all doe-eyed at him while he talked about his dates, knowing that he didn't have a clue that I would have given my eyeteeth to go out with him.

And there he was; all glorious six feet of him. And there I was, wearing an outlandish outfit bulging at the seams with mascara streaks on my cheeks. I'm sure I must have turned at least three shades of scarlet before I could choke out a hello.

"Ellen! I thought that was you!" he grinned and gave me a hug. "I was hoping you would be here tonight! How have you been?"

"Bill!" I hollered, feeling so flustered, I wished I could just suddenly vanish like a magician's assistant, "I've been just great! But you, you look fantastic!"

Betsy and Emily knew about my secret crush and I could feel their eyes taking it all in with amusement. I knew they couldn't wait to razz me about it, but at that moment, I didn't care. One look into his big brown eyes and I was transported back to our study hall days, when our shoulders would accidentally touch as I helped him with his homework. Or when he would lean in close to ask my opinion of his latest cologne. Or the time we all piled into his car and I got to sit all scrunched up next to him.

I got so wrapped up reminiscing that I realized he had said something that I missed.

"I'm sorry, what did you say?" I asked, bringing myself back to the present.

"I asked you if you'd like to dance. That is unless you think your husband would mind?"

"Husband? Oh, of course, you'd have no way of knowing. I'm a widow. My husband died last year," I said.

He was immediately embarrassed, and expressed his sympathy, but I assured him that I had adjusted to the loss and had gone on with my life.

"Look Bill, we were very happily married for 25 years. It was rough at first, but I'm doing okay now. We're all here to have a good time, right?" I reminded him, "not to get all maudlin. What about you? Are you here with your wife?"

"Nope. I'm divorced, but I'm living with someone. So, what do you say? Care to join me?" he asked.

I turned to tell Betsy and the others where I was going, and when I caught Betsy's eye, she grinned and gave me a mischievous wink. I stuck my tongue out at her and graciously accepted his invitation.

I wish I could say he swept me off my feet, we chucked it all and rode off into the sunset together, but that only happens in romance novels. As I was gliding around the dance floor in his arms, swirling in a mist of unrequited love, he started telling me how he had discovered that he preferred men to women and had decided to be open about it. He said he was contemplating a move to San Francisco where people were a lot more tolerant of alternative lifestyles. He said he had been looking forward to seeing me because I had always been such a good listener and given him such good advice when we were kids. Not to mention the fact that he probably wouldn't have graduated if it weren't for all the times I let him copy my homework.

Suffice it to say that our encounter left a lot to be desired and by the time he escorted me back to the table I was relieved.

I didn't ask him to join us. He seemed a little offended at first, but took it like a man and made a beeline for the bar where he remained for the rest of the evening, tossing back what appeared to be straight vodka. The last I saw of him, he was leaning on the bar with his arm draped over one of the waiters, whispering drunkenly in his ear. When I told Betsy and Emily about it, they both laughed so hard they nearly peed their pants. So much for unrequited love.

I saw Mark McCoy that night. He was one of the men I had seen earlier with the younger women although I hadn't recognized him. He was surrounded by the guys he had hung out with in school and seemed to be having a good time. He was heavier than I remember him, but definitely looked the part of a prosperous car salesman. I wanted to go say hello to him, but something told me it was probably better if I didn't. He and his buddies were far enough away and the restaurant crowded enough so that no one noticed that I didn't speak to him.

The party continued into the night and I was having a great time. Shortly after my disastrous reunion with Bill, Earl Henderson showed up. Now Earl was one of those kids that never really fit in anywhere. Every class has one. He lived down in the flats by the river. Every spring his family's house would get flooded, but they were too poor to move. He always came to school in torn sneakers and worn-out clothes and was the butt of jokes. Kids can be so cruel.

He arrived at the restaurant with his hair slicked straight back in a wrinkled old suit that he had probably gotten off the rack at the Salvation Army. He got a beer from the bar and sat in the corner by himself, but it wasn't long before the class bully, (every class has one of them, too) Gary Yarborough noticed him and started giving him a hard time, teasing him and jabbing him in the ribs.

I tried to ignore what was happening, hoping one of the men would come to his rescue, but of course, none of them did. When I couldn't take it anymore, I walked over and told Gary his wife was looking for him. You see; it seems big, bad Gary had married a woman even meaner than he was, so the mere mention of her name was all it took to send him scurrying.

I took a seat next to Earl, who to my surprise did not appreciate my interference.

"Look you, I can take care of myself. I sure don't need any help with the likes of him from no goddamned woman!" he snarled, taking a big swig of his beer.

"Hey, take it easy, Earl! I didn't mean to offend you! I just get a kick out of pulling old Gary's chain," I explained. "I just wanted to say hi and see how you're doing! You do remember me, don't you?"

He squinted in my direction. I knew he was my age, but the years had not been so kind to Earl. His face was a mass of wrinkles and his slicked back hair was streaked with gray. I noticed that the first two fingers of his right hand were yellow from nicotine, an unfiltered Camel was smoldering in the ashtray. Slowly, a look of recognition washed over his face and his smiled, revealing teeth even more stained than his fingers.

"Well I'll be damned! I remember you! You're Ellen Malcolm! You were one of the few kids that treated me half-decent! I was hoping I'd get a chance to see you tonight."

"Yep, you're right on the money, Earl. So what have you been up to all these years?" I asked, fanning away the smoke from his cigarette, which had drifted into my face.

He noticed my gesture and stubbed it out, "sorry about that," he mumbled, "these things are going to be the death of me. The doc at the VA hospital says I need to quit, but I been doing it since I was twelve. I figure I'm going to die of something, it might as well be something I enjoy!" he laughed, laughter which turned into a coughing fit.

When he was finally able to catch his breath, he continued, "I guess I really shouldn't have come to this thing. Lord knows; these people never gave a hoot about me in school. Most of 'em wouldn't give me the time of day if their life depended on it," he grunted, picking a fleck of tobacco from the tip of his tongue.

"Well, Earl. I care and I'm really glad you came. You belong here just as much as anyone else!" I declared, waving a hand at the crowded room. He was such a pitiful sight; I couldn't help but feel sorry for him. I could only imagine how hard his life must have been.

"Well thanks for saying that, Ellen. Like I said, you always were one of the good ones."

"I appreciate that, Earl. So, you said something about the VA, were you in the service?"

"You bet your ass, I was! Spent six months in 'Nam. I enlisted right out of school like a damn fool. I was a pretty good shot, so they made me a sniper and I guess I went a little crazy, because I got caught taking a bead on some snot-nosed candy-assed lieutenant who wouldn't quit riding my case. I guess I must have snapped or something, because the next thing I know, I was back stateside, locked up in the psyche ward. They pumped me full of Thorazine, made me yack all day to some therapist guy and finally let me go. I came back home and lived with my momma until she died and I've been here ever since. Not a happy story, but you have to take what you get."

"I'm sorry to hear about your momma, Earl. I know that must have been hard on you," I said, feeling guilty for how easy my own life had been.

"It was. She died of stomach cancer and she didn't go quick. It was a blessing when she passed. If anybody deserved to go to heaven, I know my momma did."

"So, what are you doing now?" I asked, trying to steer the conversation to less painful subjects.

"I live by myself. I never found a woman that would have me, so I never got married. I got a pretty good job with the Township, though. I haul trash, help out with street repairs and clean up the municipal buildings."

"That's good to hear, Earl. So what do you do for fun? You can't work all the time."

"Not much time for fun, Ellen. I guess about the only thing I really like to do is hunting. I'm still a mighty good shot. I bagged a 12-pointer last fall. I got the head mounted and everything!"

"That's great, Earl" I said, trying to think of some polite way to leave without hurting his feelings.

"So what about you, Ellen?" he asked, "you're still in pretty good shape. You married?"

"I was, but my husband passed away last year of a heart attack. I'm living in Georgia now. I've got three grown kids and two grandchildren! Can you believe that?" I laughed.

"No! You don't look old enough to have grandchildren!"

"Come on, Earl," I teased, glancing back over my shoulder towards the bar, thinking I'd like a glass of wine, "you know perfectly well how old I am! We're the same age for goodness sakes!"

"Yeah, I forgot about that," he smiled, then turning serious, "say Ellen, there's word going around town that you've been asking questions about what happened to Mark McCoy's folks. You really ought to be careful about that. There's people in town who don't like people sticking their nose into stuff that's none of their business."

"How'd you know about that, Earl?" I asked, snapping to attention. I felt a little flutter in my chest.

"Actually, you're the reason I got dressed up in this monkey suit and came here tonight. You don't really think I came because I missed all my good old friends, do you? I don't exactly have fond memories of my days at dear old Milan High! When I heard you were in town and what you'd been up to, I remembered that you had always been nice to me. I figured nobody else would tell you to back off, so I would. I'd sure hate to see anything bad happen to you, Ellen. You're a really nice lady."

"Thanks for that, Earl. But you still didn't say how you knew I was asking questions. Who told you?" I asked, feeling increasingly uncomfortable.

"Nobody told me, Ellen. Like I said, part of my job is cleaning up. I was sweeping up around the police station and I heard Lucy, the Chief's secretary talking on the phone. She was telling somebody about what she overheard the day you and the Chief were talking. She was saying that her boss was in a really foul mood over it and was taking it out on her. I didn't pay any attention to it until she mentioned your name."

"I don't know why he should have gotten upset," I said defensibly, "I was merely curious about an unsolved crime. What's the big deal?"

"Come on, Ellen! You made him look bad! It's his job to see that the bad guys get caught. You practically accused him of not doing his job!" he said, a genuine look of concern on his face, "I've had some run-ins with him, he's not somebody you want for an enemy! Trust me on this!"

"There's no law that says you can't ask questions, Earl," I insisted, "I think he was just mad because he's friends with

Mark and doesn't want me stirring up the past. He talked as though Mark walks on water or something. I think you're making too much of this, Earl."

"Ellen, let it go! There are things in this town that you know nothing about. It's all in the past and believe me, you'll be a lot safer if you just drop the whole thing. I've been keeping an eye on you, but I can't follow you around the rest of your life. Tell me you'll give up on this thing!"

"What do you mean, you've been following me? Come on, Earl. What did you mean by that?" I asked, startled by what he had said.

"Okay, I admit it. I found out you were staying at the Milan Inn. I followed you out to Betsy Lambert's house the day after your meeting with the Chief. You passed me the next day on 299 coming back from the lake. I know you went to talk to Jack Miller, because I followed you to Shady Oaks and the lady at the desk told me so. I would have followed you today, but I had to work. You're here, so I guess wherever you were today, you didn't get into any trouble."

"Oh for crying out loud, Earl!" I said, angry with him for spying on me and thinking he had the right to follow me around, "this is nuts! I don't need a keeper! I'm perfectly capable of taking care of myself!" It was all I could do to keep from yelling at him, but one look at the sincerity in his eyes made me stop.

"Look, Earl," I said, regaining my composure, "I'm sorry I snapped at you, and I really appreciate your concern, but you really don't need to keep tabs on my comings and goings while I'm in town. I'm a big girl, I can take care of myself!"

"Ellen, there's something that you don't know and I'm not going to get into it here, but promise me you'll let it go. Just because you used to live here, doesn't mean nothing can happen to you."

"What do you mean, you know something that I don't? Do you know who killed the McCoy's? If you know something, you need to report it, Earl!" I cried.

"For Pete's sake, keep your voice down, Ellen!" he whispered hoarsely, his eyes casting about the room with suspicion. "I told you, not here! People with a whole lot more experience in what you're trying to do have been hurt. Believe me, I know!"

"Come on, Earl. Aren't you being just a tiny bit paranoid here?" I asked and immediately regretted saying it, when I remembered his history.

"You're just like everybody else around here after all, aren't you, Ellen?" he sneered, "crazy old Earl, that's what they all call me! Why should I have thought that you would be any different? I knew I was making a mistake coming here. I'm sorry I said anything! Look, I gotta get going. Don't worry about me. I'll leave you alone! Maybe one day soon you'll wish you'd listened to me!"

He pushed back his chair and stood to leave. I reached out and took hold of his sleeve. He looked down at my hand and then at my face. A look of betrayal was plainly etched on his weathered face.

"Earl, I didn't mean to insult you. Please, sit down for just a few more minutes. I shouldn't have said what I did. Please don't be angry!" I said, afraid I had completely alienated the only person in town who knew anything about what was fast becoming my obsession.

He searched my face to be sure I was being sincere and grudgingly returned to his seat. He refused to look at me at first, concentrating instead on downing the last of his beer and then lighting another Camel with his stainless steel Zippo lighter.

"Earl, I'm sorry. I should be thanking you for caring about me. Come to think of it, I should be flattered that you felt you had to protect me. I think that was a very sweet thing for you to do."

"Oh all right!" he growled, blowing a plume of smoke from his nose, "I ain't no hero. Don't be getting all mushy on me. Maybe I'm just sick and tired of all the damn lies and secrets in this town and wanted to do something good for a change. I should have just minded my own business!"

"Earl, you obviously know more than you're willing to tell me tonight. You may be right, maybe I should have been a little more discreet. I've been away for over 30 years and you've been here right in the middle of things. What do you say we get together in a couple of days and talk about it some more, somewhere private where we don't have to worry about being overheard? You could meet me at my hotel. I'll even chip in for a six-pack, what do you say?"

He didn't respond at first, but sat twirling the empty beer bottle between his hands as if he were trying to make up his mind. He took so long to speak that I thought that I had lost him, but he finally looked at me. There was a single tear in the corner of his eye.

"Okay, I'll do it. Just remember, Ellen, it's your funeral," he said softly, "and probably mine."

Chapter Five

I kissed his cheek and he left. Several people saw it and I could feel their curious stares all the way back to Betsy's table.

"What the heck was that all about?" she whispered as soon as I sat down.

"Don't worry, Betsy, Earl and I aren't going to run off together! I felt sorry for him is all. I sure didn't see anybody else going out of their way to be nice to him. I don't think he has a friend in the world."

"Ellen, you always were the champion of the down trodden. How'd you get Gary to leave him alone?" she asked.

"I told him Marie was looking for him!" I said with a sly smile, "he took off like the hounds of Hell were after him!"

We both got a chuckle out of that, but the fun had gone out of the party for me. I just couldn't get what Earl had said out of my mind. I was tempted to discuss it with Betsy, but I thought better of it. If there really was someone out there that meant me harm, I didn't want to involve my dearest friend in it.

When the reunion finally broke up, I drove back to my hotel alone. I caught myself sneaking peeks in the rearview mirror to see if I was being followed and I wasn't, at least as far as I could tell. I almost wished that I had seen Earl tailing me, because I was feeling distinctly uneasy. I told myself that I had probably been taken in by the ranting of a disturbed man, but I have to admit I was relieved when I got back to my room without incident.

The next day was Saturday, opening day of the Melon Festival. By the time I reached the Square, the crowds had already started to fill the streets. Craft tents and concession stands had sprung up overnight like mushrooms. The whole sleepy little town had taken on a carnival atmosphere. The warm weather had returned and in the light of day, my reaction to the strange conversation with Earl lost its hold on me. I wandered up and down the paths that had been laid out, weaving my way through the throng, shopping for souvenirs for my family back in Georgia. I finally came to Betsy's booth and found her knee deep in preparing the hundreds of hotdogs, buns and cups of lemonade her women's group were selling to raise money for charity. It was obvious that they needed help, so I spent the rest of the morning taking a turn at the barbecue grill and setting up the food to sell to the visitors. We were so busy; I didn't have time to think about anything else.

By the time the lunchtime crowd had thinned, a Dixieland band had begun to play in the gazebo in preparation for the annual crowning of the Melon Queen later that afternoon. According to Betsy, Mayor Dan Albertson's granddaughter, Cathy was the predicted winner. She was a tall, dark-eyed beauty whose entry in the contest had been sponsored by Mark McCoy's car dealership. She added that although Cathy was certainly a pretty girl, it didn't hurt that Mark was providing the convertibles that would be used in the parade scheduled for Labor Day. As in all the previous years, it was more a contest based on political influence than looks and poise alone.

More members of Betsy's club arrived to take over the stand for the evening, so Betsy and I took the lawn chairs she had brought and set them up over by the bandstand where we could watch the Melon Queen competition. One by one the girls paraded across the stage dressed in evening gowns, with upswept hairdos and false smiles pasted on their painted faces. Each girl had her own supporters in the crowd as demonstrated by the hoots and whistles that broke out after each took her turn. All of the finery couldn't help some of the girls, who looked awkward and nervous. A couple of them were decidedly a little too heavy to be in a beauty contest, but I had to give them credit. They all did the best with what they had, but it was painfully obvious that they couldn't hold a candle to Cathy Albertson. She was a vision of elegance amidst a group of country bumpkins.

They had saved her stroll across the stage past the table of judges for last and I could see why. All the other girls paled in comparison. She had flawless olive skin and long, shiny dark brown hair that flowed around her shoulders. She wore a pale cream silk sheath dress, strapless and split up one side just far enough to show off her long slim legs. Where the other girls had opted for rhinestones and glitter, Cathy chose simplicity. Her graceful moves would have been right at home

50

on a New York fashion runway. Her only adornment was a bright red rose artfully tucked behind one ear. Pandemonium broke out when she resumed her place at the end of line of contest hopefuls. She, of course, was crowned the winner to no one's surprise and I had a feeling that she was destined to go on to bigger and better things.

The contest completed, workers began roping off the area for the street dance scheduled later that evening. We folded up our chairs and walked back to the hotdog stand. More ladies had taken over, so our help wasn't needed. From all reports, they had sold more than expected. Betsy said she needed to go pick up some additional supplies and asked me to join her.

I still hadn't bought anything to take home for the kids, so I declined her invitation. I wanted to do a little more shopping at the craft tents before they shut down for the night. I also hoped that I might run into Earl again to reassure myself that I hadn't imagined the whole weird encounter from the previous night. If I did run into him, I wanted to be alone. I was determined that I would not involve Betsy in my problems if they even existed.

I saw a group of people that I had seen at the reunion across the Square in front of the Town Hall and worked my way through the stalls in their direction. They had their heads together, engrossed in conversation, which instantly stopped as soon as I approached. I got the impression that I must have been the topic of discussion from the sheepish looks they gave me. No one was smiling.

"Hi guys," I said, searching their faces for an explanation, "so what's going on? You all look like you were having a pretty heavy conversation there. What's up?"

I tried to keep my tone upbeat, but no one responded. They exchanged glances as if to decide who would speak for the group. Finally, Linda Ericson, the breast implants recipient that had caused us such mirth at the reunion stepped over to me and put her arm across my shoulders. I felt a chill because her action told me that whatever they had been discussing was definitely bad news.

"Okay, Linda, come on tell me. What's wrong? You're all scaring me here," I said, feeling a little weak in the knees.

"Ellen, I don't know how to tell you this, especially since you just saw him last night, but we just heard the news," she said with a look that said she wished someone else had been elected the bearer of bad tidings, "but there was a terrible accident last night."

"What? What are you talking about, Linda?" I demanded, feeling the blood drain from my face, "what accident? Was somebody hurt? Who had an accident? Come on, you guys. This isn't funny. Somebody better tell me right now!"

"It was Earl Henderson, Ellen," she said softly, "he went off the road and hit a tree. He was killed instantly. We all saw you talking to him last night and well, didn't know how to tell you. We were all just feeling kind of guilty that we didn't speak to him when we had the chance. He was always so, you know, different! You were the last person to see him alive. I just don't know what to say. I'm sorry, Ellen."

I'm not sure that I can describe what passed over me then. All I can remember is feeling suddenly dizzy. My entire body broke out in a cold sweat and my legs got rubbery. A couple of the guys rushed over and helped Linda get me to a nearby park bench, where I put my head down between my knees to keep from fainting.

Linda crouched down and put her arms around me. "Ellen, I'm sorry," she cried, panic rising in her voice, "I didn't know any other way to tell you! I had no idea you would react this way! Can I get you something to drink or something? God, I'm sorry! Ellen, are you going to be all right?"

I could hear her shouting to her husband to run get some water and eventually the faintness started to recede. He brought me a cup of water and I sat up to drink it. A crowd had started to form around us. Somebody asked if we needed an ambulance. When I could speak, I assured everyone that I was okay and thankfully, they moved on.

Linda hovered over me until I finally convinced her that I wasn't going to fall out again. I demanded to know the details of Earl's so-called accident.

"I don't know any of the details," she said, giving me a quizzical look, "what do you mean so-called accident?"

"Never mind, Linda," I told her, realizing what I had said. "I must still be a little out of it. Where did you hear about it?"

"We overheard Chief Taylor talking to the Mayor about it, just a little while ago" she said, "but he wouldn't tell us anything. He just said that Earl was discovered dead in his pick-up truck wrapped around a tree and they were looking into it. We all saw him drinking at the reunion, Ellen. Word has it that he'd been arrested for drunk driving before."

"Where was Chief Taylor when you last saw him?" I asked, knowing full well that I only saw Earl drink one beer. He had definitely not been drunk when I last saw him. I kept that piece of information to myself.

"They were over by the bandstand. The Mayor was with his granddaughter Cathy talking with us. We were congratulating her on winning Melon Queen, when Chief Taylor interrupted us. The music was so loud, he had to shout and we couldn't help but hear what he said," she explained.

I knew I had to speak to the Chief right away, so I took off in that direction over Linda's protests. I assured her I was feeling better and promised I would go back to my hotel and rest, just as soon as I talked to the police. I could tell she was dying of curiosity, but was grateful that she didn't insist on coming with me.

The Mayor and his party were still by the gazebo, but the Chief wasn't with them. When I asked, they told me he had just left on his way back to the police station. I spotted him through the crowd and ran to catch up with him.

When I got closer, I called out to him, but he couldn't hear me over the noise and kept walking. I finally caught up with him when he stopped to speak to some tourists. I stood a little way off, panting from my chase after him.

"What the hell do you want?" he growled when he finished, his hands planted at his hips.

"Chief Taylor, I really need to speak to you. There's something you need to know!" I answered, wincing at his display of hostility.

"Look, Ms. Richardson, I told you the other day to mind your own business! If you don't quit, I'm going to have to run you in for disturbing the peace or some other damn thing! I've had about all I can take from you!"

"You don't understand, Chief, I just heard about Earl Henderson. I was told that he was killed last night. I was just talking to him at that class reunion I told you about. I have some information you need for the investigation into the wreck."

I expected him to show some interest in what I had to say, but instead, he crossed his arms and scowled at me.

"Would that be the same class reunion where there was lots of alcohol served and everyone got a little carried away talking about the good old days and had more than a few too many? I've been to class reunions, Ms. Richardson. I know how those things are. Maybe you had a drink or two yourself. Did you drink and drive last night?"

My face gave him his answer and he turned on his heel dismissively. I shook off my embarrassment and ran after him.

"Wait, Chief!" I insisted, grabbing hold of his sleeve. He stopped and looked at me accusingly.

"Okay, I admit, I did have a glass or two of wine when I got there, but I quit early in the evening. I was not drunk when I got in my car, I assure you."

"If I had a nickel for every time I've heard that, I could retire," he huffed.

"Look, regardless of what you think, that's the truth. What I wanted to tell you was that I spent quite a long time talking to Earl and I only saw him drink one beer. And when he left, he definitely was not drunk. I don't think what happened to him was an accident. I just think you ought to look into it some more," I finished lamely, but could tell he wasn't interested in anything I had to say.

"Let me explain something to you, Ms. Richardson," he said, his eyes narrowing as he glared into mine, "our police force is perfectly capable of handling the investigation into traffic accidents or anything else without your assistance. Earl Henderson was a notorious drunk. I was at the scene and my nose told me all I need to know. What was left of him reeked of alcohol. I have dragged enough idiots like him from wrecks to know. Just because you only saw him drink one beer doesn't mean he didn't go someplace else after he left you and got plastered. It wouldn't be the first time old crazy Earl did that. Now I'm telling you for the last time. Keep your theories to yourself and let us handle the police work. Good-bye, Ms. Richardson," he said with finality and stormed away.

I don't ever remember feeling so helpless as I did at that moment. I hoped he was right, that Earl had died in a crash caused from drunk driving. Because if he didn't, I was in terrible danger.

Chapter Six

I stood rooted to the spot where the Chief had reprimanded me. I was humiliated, my ears still ringing from his harangue. It seemed that no matter where I turned, somebody was always slamming the door in my face. There weren't any people nearby, because the sun had begun to set and everyone was either heading for their cars or the street dance area. I felt shaky and weak and terribly alone. It suddenly occurred to me that the person who may have run Earl off the road could be watching me that very instant. I decided that there was safety in numbers and dashed off in the direction of the dance. I searched the faces of the people around me to assure myself that no one was paying particular attention to me. If anyone was, they weren't being obvious about it.

I queued up behind a large group of locals to purchase a ticket to the dance. I planned to hook up with Linda Ericson and her friends or anyone else I knew, so I wouldn't be by myself. I thought I might be able to get someone to walk with me back to the hotel. It was only a few blocks, but the thought of walking through the shadows between the streetlights terrified me. I was so focused on my search for a familiar face, that when someone tapped me on the shoulder; I let out a little yelp. I whirled around; ready to either fight or flee and there stood Bill Hamilton my girlhood man of my dreams looking decidedly puzzled at my unexpected reaction.

"Whoa! Take it easy, killer!" he grinned, "you look like you're about to take somebody's head off!"

When I didn't share his attempt at humor, he became concerned.

"Ellen, what's wrong? You're as white as a sheet!"

"Good heavens, Bill!" I gasped, my heart hammering in my chest, "you about scared me out of my wits!"

"I'm sorry, Ellen. I didn't mean to startle you. I couldn't leave town until I saw you again. I just wanted to apologize for last night. Things didn't go very smoothly between us. I guess I was hoping we could be friends again and it didn't work out that way. You know, like me not knowing about your husband and then, well, dumping my news on you out of the blue and then to top it all off, acting like an idiot in the bar. You must think I'm a real jerk!" he said miserably.

"No. No, it's okay, Bill. Really! I'm touched that you would be worried about what I think. People change! I live in Atlanta, for crying out loud. It's not like I don't know any gay people. You are who you are! It isn't my place to pass judgement on anybody!"

"Ellen, I don't think you understand what you meant to me back in school, is all. I wanted to tell you last night, but it came out all wrong. Hey, would you like to go somewhere and get a cup of coffee or something? I'll understand if you don't want to."

"Actually, I would love to go have some coffee with you," I said, taking his arm, "I wasn't really feeling up to going to the dance anyway."

I felt better having him close by and we walked back up the street towards the Dairy Bar. I glanced behind us several times along the way to be sure we weren't being followed.

"Okay, Ellen, out with it," he said as soon as we slid into the booth, "You practically jumped out of your skin back there. Why are you so nervous? It isn't like you. Has somebody been giving you a hard time?"

"I guess you haven't heard about Earl Henderson, have you?" I asked, wondering how much I wanted him to know.

"What about Earl? Did he make a pass at you or something? I saw you talking to him last night, but you both seemed pretty friendly. Is he the reason you're acting this way?"

"I don't think Earl will be making any passes at me or anybody else for that matter," I quipped, "he died in a car wreck last night!"

"What! You're kidding! What happened? Was he drunk?"

"Why does everybody always ask that?" I snapped, "the poor guy's dead and everyone immediately assumes he did it to himself!"

"Hey, I'm sorry. Don't get your panties in a twist! The guy was an alcoholic and he died in a car crash. It isn't such a long stretch to assume it was due to drinking and driving!" he snapped back.

"No, I'm sorry," I sighed, putting my head in my hands, "I guess I'm just a little shook up that I finally reached out to him after all these years and now he's dead! He had been through so much in his life and nobody cared about him. The whole thing has just got me upset. I'm sorry I yelled at you."

"Don't worry about it. It's no big deal. It's just that I had no idea that you cared one way or the other about Earl! Jeez, there I go again! Here you are, feeling bad about somebody who died, and I yell at you. Some friend I am!"

"Don't beat yourself up, Bill," I said, patting his hand, "matter of fact, you have no idea how glad I am to see you. You'll never know how good it is to see a friendly face just now. Can I ask you to do me a favor?"

"Sure, name it."

"I'm still feeling a little out of it. After we finish here, would you mind walking me back to my hotel? I'm staying at the Inn and I'd really appreciate the company. And no, in case you're wondering, this is not an invitation to spend the night," I added, allowing myself a little smile, "I won't try to seduce you!"

"Oh my!" he twittered in a falsetto voice, "thank goodness for that! Women can be such animals!"

We shared a laugh at that. It was such a relief to be with him. I felt safe again. I knew it wouldn't last, but I wanted to savor it for as long as I could. As we talked about the past over our coffee, I found myself drawn to him again, just like I was in high school. We talked and laughed at our shared memories as only two old friends can do. I even started wishing that something more could come between us. But of course, that was out of the question. He had moved on to a life that was completely foreign to me. No matter what happened to either of us, my bittersweet memories of those first womanly stirrings were mine alone to cherish. I had loved him from afar and would continue to do so. Nobody could ever take that away from me.

An hour had passed and it was getting late. We finished our coffee and stepped out of the diner into the blaring rock and roll music from the dance going full tilt down the street. People of all ages were out under the street lamps gyrating to the Golden Oldies blasting from the DJ's speakers, but I declined his invitation to go. I felt drained from all that had happened that day and needed to get away from the commotion. His solid presence as he walked beside me made me almost forget that I had anything to fear. I wanted to fill him in on my troubles, but decided to spare him. We had just spent a delightful evening together getting reacquainted and I didn't want to ruin it.

When we arrived at my door, he gave me a hug and a brotherly peck my cheek. I watched him walk away with a profound sense of sadness. I hadn't asked him in, because I knew that if I had, I would have gone back on my promise not to try to dissuade him from his sexual preference. As I look back on it now, it was the best decision I could ever have made. He died of AIDS the following year. Another beautiful kite had slipped away.

Chapter Seven

I was so exhausted I fell asleep in my clothes. I awoke the next morning bleary-eyed and rumpled, with a horrible taste in my mouth from all the coffee I had drunk. I dragged myself to the shower, where I stayed with the hot water pounding down on my head until I finally came back to the land of the living.

I was faced with a dilemma. I needed help, but refused to involve the people I loved. With Earl dead, I would never learn what he could have told me. Chief Taylor had thrown up roadblocks at every turn and had as much as threatened to toss me in jail. I knew I wouldn't be getting any help there.

As I dressed, I mulled over my situation and then it hit me. There was at least one person in town who might be willing to give me some advice as to what my next move should be. Someone who might be willing to listen and give me some perspective. Someone who had a personal stake in the whole mess. Before I had a chance to change my mind, I grabbed my car keys and hopped in my rental car. It was time for another visit with ex-chief of police Jack Miller.

On the way out to Shady Oaks, I swung by a doughnut shop drive-through and picked up an assortment of pastries. I needed his friendship and figured it wouldn't hurt to bring him a treat. I kept an eye out for any suspicious cars following me, but as far as I could tell, there weren't any.

When I arrived at the facility, I went straight to his room, and from the look on his face, it was as if he had been expecting me.

"If that's what I think it is," he grinned, pointing at my offering, "you are a woman after my own heart! I was just thinking how long it has been since I had anything sweet. You wouldn't believe the slop they give us around here!"

I pulled the wheeled food tray across his lap and emptied the sugary treasure on a paper napkin. He made his selection and took a huge bite. A look of pure pleasure washed over his face. I took one as well and dragged the chair from the window up close to his bedside.

"So, what made you think you had to come back bearing gifts?" he asked with a mischievous glint in his eye. When I didn't immediately respond, his expression turned serious, and said flatly, "you didn't take my advice, did you?"

"Actually, I did, Jack," I assured him, "I did just like you told me. I went to the reunion and put the whole McCoy murder thing out of my mind."

"So why the long face? Didn't you have a good time?"

"I had a great time!" I asserted, "that is, until my conversation with Earl Henderson."

"Crazy Earl was there? Was he in your class? I never would have figured he'd be into that sort of thing. Old Earl never struck me as the sentimental type. He's about as antisocial as they come."

"Yeah, he was definitely uncomfortable being there. He didn't have any friends in school. He was pretty much the butt of the other kid's jokes, so I was surprised that he came, too. But I felt sorry for him, sitting all by himself, so I got him to talk to me. He told me about his life, about his problems, you know, we just sort of shared information about our lives. I felt guilty that I never had taken the time to get to know him."

"So, what did he say that's got you all worked up again?" he asked as he reached for another treat.

"He said he had come specifically to speak to me. He said he heard talk in town about my visit to Chief Taylor and wanted to warn me to back off. He said that there were people who weren't very happy about me dredging up the past, especially Chief Taylor."

"So Earl wasn't so dumb after all," he sniffed, "you ought to be grateful. I told you as much myself!"

"But that's not all he said, Jack," I continued, "he also said he knew some things about the McCoy murders that I didn't."

"Did you tell him to report this so-called information to the authorities?" he asked sternly.

"Of course, I did! But he said he couldn't, because other people had been hurt when they tried to reopen the case. Jack, I think he may have been referring to your accident!"

"I hardly think Earl Henderson knows anything at all! He probably had a crush on you in school and thought the reunion was the perfect opportunity to get you to notice him!

Come on, Ellen. You're obviously a very intelligent woman. Don't tell me you fell for it!"

"I probably would agree with you, except that there's more to the story."

He tucked his chin and gave me a patronizing glance, but I ignored it and went on, "I know what you're thinking, but he sounded so sincere, I tried to get him to tell me what he knew. He refused, saying that he was afraid we would be overheard."

"And someone suggested that the two of you get together someplace private. Am I right?" he asked interrupting me. "Heavens to Betsy, Ellen, how gullible can you get!" he scoffed.

"Okay, wise guy, yes I did. But the meeting never took place. He was killed in a car accident a few hours later. His pick-up smashed into a tree and he was killed instantly. There were no witnesses. Don't you find that the least bit coincidental? One minute he's telling me he knows something about the McCoy murders and he's dead the next?"

"Not necessarily. Everybody in town knows that Crazy Earl had a drinking problem. I locked him up on Drunk and Disorderly's several times myself! He probably just got himself all liquored up in celebration of his success in wooing the charming Ellen Malcolm into going on a date with him!" he teased. "So what did Chief Taylor say about it, because I know you must have gone to him with this!"

"As a matter of fact, I did." I admitted, becoming more impressed with his intuition by the minute, "yesterday afternoon. He said the same thing everyone else in town is saying. Earl was drunk and hit a tree, end of story."

"See? At least somebody has some common sense around here!" he laughed and when he saw my hurt expression, sobered. "Ellen, honey, come on! Don't get your feelings hurt! You're obviously a very caring person who is trying to make things right for three people who died a long time ago! But face it, there is no big conspiracy here. Earl's death was just an unfortunate coincidence. Quit looking for things that just aren't there!"

"There is one other thing that Earl said that should be of interest to you," I said, determined to get him to listen.

"Okay, lay it on me!" he said rolling his eyes.

"Earl's hobby was deer hunting. He told me all about how he had killed a 12 point buck and had the head mounted. He bragged about what a great shot he was. He even said he had been a sniper in Vietnam. Doesn't that make you wonder if maybe Earl was in the woods the day you were shot?"

"So now you think poor old dead Earl shot me? Is that what this is all about?" he laughed heartily and shook his head.

"I'm not saying anything of the sort, Jack!" I growled, "I'm glad you're getting such a kick out of this, I might add!"

"Sorry," he said, drying his eyes on the sheet. "Okay, go on."

"What I was about to say before you started laughing like a hyena, is that there is a possibility, however remote, that Earl was in the woods the day you were shot and maybe he saw who shot you. Maybe that's why he was afraid for me. Maybe he thought that whoever shot you might take a shot at me and cared enough to warn me! You have to admit that it's plausible!"

"Except for the fact that the police talked to everyone in the woods that day and nobody saw anything!" he countered.

"So who's to say that they did ask Earl and he lied because he was afraid? I'm not so sure I would have spilled my guts if I witnessed a shooting and knew the attacker was at large. Think whom we're talking about here! Crazy old Earl Henderson! The town laughingstock! What chance would he have getting police protection? Especially if the shooter was somebody that everybody in town knew and respected! You have to admit, Jack, it makes a lot of sense!" I said reasonably.

"Okay, I see your point! Lord knows, you've raised questions in my mind, but I'm having a really hard time buying into your conspiracy theory. There was a thorough investigation into my shooting and it was ruled an accident, pure and simple.'

"Then why were you so upset when I brought it up the last time I was here?" I asked innocently, just to show him that he wasn't the only one with intuition.

His sallow cheeks blushed crimson, "okay, young lady, you're pretty observant yourself! I did wonder about it and put a call into a friend of mine who retired from the force a couple of months ago. He was one of the officers that investigated the shooting. He assured me that everything was done properly. I believe him. He is a good friend of mine and he wouldn't lie."

"Did you happen to mention my name to this friend of yours?"

"No I didn't. And no, I'm not going to tell you who he is. You'd be wasting your time. He wouldn't talk to you, believe me. If you think Chief Taylor is a hard ass, this guy is even worse."

"So I'm back to square one. I'm beginning to feel like the little boy who cried wolf. Only there really may be a wolf out there stalking me and nobody will listen until I'm dead and buried," I cried, wishing I had never heard of the McCoys, Earl Henderson or anyone else in this godforsaken town.

"Now take it easy," Jack soothed, "I seriously doubt that there is anybody out to get you, but there may be a way to do some discreet digging into it that will put the whole thing to rest once and for all."

"What do you mean, Jack," I asked hopefully. "Are you saying you'll help me?"

"Don't get your hopes up just yet, Ellen. There's a chance I may be able to get my hands on the old records and see what they indicate. That friend of mine might be willing to get them for me if I handle it just right. I'm not making any promises here, but if I can, I would need you to help me. My eyesight isn't so good anymore and all I got is this one good hand. Would that make you feel better?"

I was so relieved, grateful and overwhelmed at his offer, I jumped up and threw my arms around him. He was unable to return my hug in full, but he patted my back with his good right hand.

When I released him, he winked at me. "Better watch out, young lady, or I'll be asking you out on a date myself!" he said with a chuckle.

"You got yourself a date, Mr. Miller!" I laughed, "and the doughnuts are on me!"

Chapter Eight

I tidied up the leftovers and brushed the crumbs from his bed. A nurse knocked on the door and pointedly informed me in no uncertain terms that it was time for Mr. Miller's bath and I needed to leave. When she noticed the bakery bag on his tray table, she shot me a look. I guess I must have broken some rule, but I chose to ignore her. Regardless of his medical condition, I couldn't see what harm a couple of doughnuts would do. I hated to leave when we had just made such a positive connection, but the nurse started laying out towels and clean linens, indicating she had no intention of leaving.

Jack asked for my telephone number, so I jotted it down. He promised to call me just as soon as he got what we needed. I told him I probably wouldn't be in my room until later in the evening, but said I would pick up any messages he left. I moved the telephone where he could reach it and when the nurse glared at me again, I told Jack good-bye and went back to my car.

It was Sunday, the second day of the Melon Festival, so I drove back into town. I decided I would drive to the Square this time, since I couldn't be sure I would have someone to walk with me like I had the night before. I simply felt safer in the car. The crowds were even heavier than they had been on Saturday and it took me a while to find a place to park.

I joined the throng and went directly to Betsy's booth. She immediately wanted all the details about my "date" with Bill Hamilton. I should have known that word would get around that we were seen walking together on our way to the Inn. I assured her that nothing untoward had happened and that my virtue and his were still unsullied, but she insisted on teasing me about it for the rest of the afternoon. The friendly banter was just what I needed to keep me from thinking about Jack and what we might discover. The subject of Earl's accident never came up and for that, I was grateful.

I still hadn't done any shopping, so Betsy and I spent the rest of the afternoon perusing the arts and craft booths for souvenirs and tee shirts. We sampled some muskmelon ice cream, which was surprisingly good. Everywhere we went, we met old friends and classmates, who invariably made some crack about seeing me with Bill. The fact that he had come out of the closet and then was seen walking me back to my hotel after dark was the cause of a great deal of speculation and idle curiosity. I'm sure Bill would have gotten a kick out of it had he been there. He was comfortable with his choice and didn't care what anybody had to say about it. For a town with so many secrets, I was surprised that he and I would stir up such interest.

I finally found what I had been looking for and Betsy helped me carry it all to my car. I felt sweaty and tired and begged off from joining her and her husband for dinner. Plus I was anxious to get back to my room and see if Jack had left me any messages as well, but of course, I didn't tell Betsy. She said she needed to get back to the hotdog stand anyway and I rushed back to my room as the sun was setting.

To my disappointment, there were no messages waiting for me there, so I called up some room service and took a long hot bath to settle my frayed nerves. I emerged so relaxed, I called it a day and slipped into my nightgown. I planned to watch some television in bed, but I fell asleep almost instantly.

During the night I had a vivid dream in which a little girl kept calling out to me to help her and no matter how hard I tried, I couldn't reach her. Every time I would get close, a faceless man would snatch her away. She was screaming in terror, but no matter how hard I ran she was always off in the distance. I startled awake in a cold sweat to discover that the lights were still on and an old horror movie was blaring on the TV set. I decided the sounds from the show must have merged with my dream, but I couldn't ignore its significance. I shivered, feeling as though Becky McCoy had reached out from her grave and touched me. I prayed that Jack and I would be able to turn up something soon. I didn't relish the thought of any more ghostly visitors, real or imagined.

I switched off the TV with the remote and turned off the lights. I'm happy to say that the rest of the night passed peacefully.

Chapter Nine

Labor Day dawned bright and clear, which I knew would make the parade goers happy. I had spent a restless night and wanted to sleep late, but woke up to the sound of kids running and shouting outside my hotel room door. I started to call the front desk to complain, but thought better of it when I saw by the bedside clock that it was already after 9:00 a.m. The parade started at 11:00, so I was going to have to hurry if we had any hope of getting a decent spot on the parade route. Betsy and I hadn't arranged for a place to hook up, so I knew it would take a while to find her.

There were plenty of people filling the sidewalks from the Inn to the Square, so I left the car where it was and joined them. It only took a few minutes to locate Betsy and her husband. They had bought a sackful of sausage biscuits and orange juice which they shared with me as we walked to the far side of Main Street. Bleachers had been set up and we found room on the top row. The parade lasted until noon. It was just as I remembered from when I was a child. There were marching bands, baton twirling troupes, firetrucks and an assortment of floats. The Melon Queen, Cathy Albertson looked regal with her scepter and crown atop the biggest one that was covered with ads for Mark McCoy's car dealership. The Mayor rode perched like a peacock on the convertible that immediately followed driven by Mark himself, smiling and waving at the crowd as he passed by. It was plain to see that Mayor Albertson was more than a little proud of his granddaughter's victory.

Two police cars with their lights flashing were last in line to signal the end of the parade and the street immediately filled with people making their way back to the festivities in the Square as soon as they passed.

I spent the rest of day with Betsy and several other old friends, including Emily and Jeff Johnson who had taken the day off from their charter business. I had such a good time, I never once thought about Jack or anything unpleasant. The day turned out to be what I had hoped my trip back home would be, filled with laughter and fun with the best friends I have ever had in my life.

By late afternoon, the vendors began packing up their wares and the crowds dispersed. By nightfall, only the trash and trampled grass remained. All of us piled into Emily and Jeff's minivan and drove out to Betsy's place for an impromptu cookout and I'm a little ashamed to say, I never made it back to my hotel room that night. We stopped on the way and picked up a couple of cases of beer and to be honest, I don't remember what happened later. The only thing I can say is I woke up in a spare bedroom in my clothes with a killer hangover. From the looks of my fellow revelers, we must have certainly had a good time.

Betsy made us all bacon and eggs, being raised on the farm, but I think she secretly hoped it would make us all sick and teach us a lesson. She wasn't much of a drinker and wanted to prove a point, but was much too gracious to be obvious about it. At least that's what I figured. She is a good hearted, church-going lady. I could only hope that I hadn't said or done anything to embarrass her.

I thanked her profusely for letting me spend the night and caught a ride back to my hotel with Emily and Jeff. I fell into bed and slept off the rest of my headache until late afternoon. I hadn't taken the time to check for messages when I came in, so as soon as I woke up I called the front desk. There was still nothing from Jack. I spent the rest of that evening in a haze, staring at the tube and trying to read. It wasn't long before I got sleepy again, and couldn't keep my eyes open, so I switched off the light. Thankfully, I slept like a log that night with no ghostly visitors haunting my dreams.

Chapter Ten

I was awakened early the next morning by the jangling phone. I dragged the handset to my ear and mumbled hello. It was the call I had been expecting.

"What the hell are you doing still in bed!" Jack wanted to know, his voice entirely too chipper for the time of day, "we've got work to do!"

"Good morning to you too, Chief," I said, swinging my legs over the side of the bed, "I take it your buddy came through for us."

"I'm sitting here looking at a stack of file boxes as we speak. Why don't you drag your lazy butt out of bed and get over here. I'm dying to see what he found!"

"I'm on my way, Jack. In case I didn't tell you before, I really appreciate what you're doing for me."

"Well, there is one thing you can do to demonstrate your gratitude."

"What's that, Jack?" I asked, knowing what he was about to say.

"I like the ones with chocolate icing! And this time, bring along some coffee. You wouldn't believe the crap they call coffee around here."

"You got it, Chief!"

On the way to Shady Oaks I thought about how he had sounded on the phone. His voice had been so full of enthusiasm and energy; it was easy to picture the vibrant man he must have been before he lost the use of his body. He reminded me of an old fire horse set out to pasture who bolts at the first scent of smoke. Whether our efforts bore fruit or not, I had the feeling that the attempt would breathe life back into him. He was a cop to the bone and I was glad that I had played a part in reawakening that part of him.

As soon as I entered his room, I had to look twice to be sure I was seeing the same man. He sat propped up on pillows; half glasses perched on the end of his nose with an open file in front of him on his tray table. When I approached, he peered up at me over the top of the glasses and gave me the once over.

"Sorry, but I couldn't wait. I talked the nurse into getting me started. She gave me this big lecture about how she wasn't a secretary and had the other patients to bathe and feed and blah, blah, blah, but as you can see, I won the argument. So, I see you got the good stuff," he said, nodding in the direction of my packages, "I take mine black. You can put the doughnuts over there."

He went immediately back to his perusal of the file's contents dismissively and I started to laugh. He looked up at me quizzically.

"And just what is so funny?" he asked.

"You sly old dog!" I laughed, handing him his coffee, "here I was thinking you were so helpless and you've got us all jumping at your commands. I'll bet you ran a pretty tight ship before you landed in that bed!"

"You're damn right I did!" he replied with a deadpan look on his face, and then grinned. "But don't worry, my bark is a whole lot worse than my bite! Now, if you don't mind, Ms. Richardson, we don't have time to stand here yammering. Grab that box over there and start putting the files in chronological order. The dumb nurse gave me one from the middle. I need to start with the earliest."

"Yes sir!" I said, a trace of a smile crossing my lips. He had turned the tables on me. I had been expecting to do most of the investigating, but it soon became apparent who was in charge. He reminded me of my late husband who was also a take-charge kind of man and if the circumstances had been different, I could have easily fallen for him.

One glance at the contents of the files squashed my romantic fantasies. The first that I came to was filled with gristly photographs of the crime scene from the McCoy murders. My stomach flipped at the sight of them and I began to regret that I had eaten anything before seeing them. I had seen plenty of movie special effects and make-up, just like anyone else, but these were pictures of real people, bloodied and battered, captured in the cold viewfinder of a crime scene technician's camera. The sight of them made me wish I had never opened this Pandora's box. The violence of the attack was more than I could have possibly imagined.

Jack, on the other hand, gave no indication that they had any effect on him. His expression never changed as he casually flipped through them. He had, after all, seen it all in person.

I had to sit down. My search for the truth was leading me down a path I had never anticipated. Jack continued his review of the file I had given him, oblivious to my distress and after several moments had ticked by, removed his glasses and looked up at me as if he had forgotten that I was there.

"Ellen? Are you all right? You look a little green around the gills," he said quietly, "you don't have to do this if you're not up to it. Like I told you before, it wasn't a pretty sight. I puked like the greenest rookie when I saw them. We could just forget the whole thing, and let whoever did this to these people walk. Is that what you want?"

I knew what he was doing. He knew I had come too far to wimp out on him.

"No," I said softly, "it just sort of hit me when I wasn't expecting it. You were trained to handle this sort of thing, Jack. I just wasn't prepared for the impact those pictures would have on me. I'll be all right."

He looked at me kindly and nodded, "let me tell you something, Ellen. You are one of the nicest women I have ever met. Most women in your shoes would have quit a long time ago. You even managed to talk this old man into finishing something I started before I wound up here. Before you came, I was feeling pretty damn sorry for myself. You've given me something to focus on. I haven't felt this alive in years."

"Thanks, Jack. I'm glad I met you, too."

"Let me offer a suggestion," he said, "why don't you step outside and get some fresh air? When you get back, we'll look at those pictures again, together. Only this time, I want you to really look! I want those images burned into your head. If they make you sick, it's okay, you won't be the first. If you feel anything, it should be anger. Anger at the son of a bitch that did that to those people. Do you think you can do that?"

I nodded and did as he suggested. The sunshine and fresh air cleared my head and eased my queasiness. I dreaded returning to his room, but I forced myself to go back in.

"Feeling better?" he asked, looking up from the file.

"Yeah, so far so good," I said weakly, "let's get this over with before I change my mind."

He spread the photos out on his tray table and I walked closer to where I could see them over his shoulder, but I kept my eyes straight ahead. I really didn't want to see them again, but forced myself to look down at them.

"This is the kitchen," he pointed out, his tone professionally neutral, "see those dark spots there on the linoleum and smeared by the door handle? That's blood. Drops were found leading away from the hallway outside the master bedroom and down the stairs across the kitchen floor to the back door. The killer must have been covered in blood. There was no such thing as DNA tests back then. But through blood type analysis it was determined that the blood drops came from a combination of all three victims."

I found I was soon so engrossed in his commentary that I forgot about my head and queasy stomach. I followed his advice and concentrated on my outrage that someone had done such a horrible thing and gotten away with it. Even when he came to the pictures of the bodies, I kept looking.

"Now see the fingers that are missing on Patrick McCoy's right hand there. Those are defensive wounds. That means that he saw his killer and threw up his hands to protect his face. As you can see, there was very little left of his head. See the hole that the blast left in the headboard and wall behind it. The position of the body and the fact that he is still partially covered by the blankets says he was in bed at the time of the attack. But he was sitting up. There must have been some sort of confrontation with his attacker. The ballistics report on the pattern indicates that the shooter was approximately three to four feet away."

"Pattern? What do you mean by that?" I asked.

"I'm sorry, I forgot you're new at this," he said, "do you know anything about guns?'

"Only that they kill things, including people" I replied, letting my personal feelings about guns color my response.

"I guess we won't have to worry about you joining the NRA anytime soon," he quipped. "Don't you know that guns don't kill people, people kill people?"

"Yeah, yeah, whatever," I sniffed, "you were saying?"

"Okay. Patrick was shot in the face with a shotgun. Now shotguns don't shoot bullets like a rifle or pistol does. Surely you've seen shotgun shells before!"

"Yes, Chief, I know what shotgun shells look like! My dad used to go pheasant hunting every fall when I was a kid! I remember we had to pick out the little pellets sometimes."

"Well, then you know what a spray pattern is! The closer you are to the target, the smaller and tighter the pattern. The farther away you are, the bigger and less dense the pattern becomes. His wife's body isn't shown in this photograph. This one shows her. She was found slumped over behind the dresser in the corner. She was obviously trying to get away, but the killer stood between her and the door. She was turned toward the wall when she was hit. She got it in the side and around to the back. She was standing when she was shot, see how the blood streaks above her point downward? There's also a hole in the wall above her. She was standing, got hit and then slid down the wall into the crouching position she was found in. This tells me that the killer's main target was Patrick. He must have got it first. His wife tried to escape, but there was no place to run. She was eliminated as a potential witness."

"Was the gun ever found?"

"Not according to the report. The killer must have taken it with him."

"Does it say if Patrick McCoy owned a shotgun?" I asked.

"Before I answer that, tell me why you ask?" Jack demanded.

"Because it would help identify the killer. If his own gun killed Patrick McCoy, it could point the finger at someone who was familiar with the house, someone from the inside, like his son, Mark. If he didn't own a gun, that means someone had to bring one along with him, not necessarily eliminating Mark as a suspect, but increasing the likelihood of it being someone from outside the home. That person would have gone there purposely to kill the family. In Mark's case, using his father's gun, it could be ruled a crime of passion. In the other case, it would clearly have been premeditated. How am I doing so far, professor?" I asked.

"Very good, Ms. Richardson!" he beamed, "I am impressed! As a matter of fact, they were never able to determine if anyone in the house owned a shotgun or not. They asked Mark about it, but he never gave them a straight answer. I have a feeling you are a natural at this!"

"Either that or I been watching too much television," I said dryly.

I knew he was only being kind, but his words made me feel better about my initial reaction. There was a lot more material to go over, so we plunged ahead.

"Now we get to the second attack," he continued, "the bludgeoning of Becky McCoy. These are pretty graphic, do you think you can handle it?"

"I hope so," I said, "I'm already going to have nightmares, so what's the difference?"

"Here is how the little girl was found. She was in the hallway outside her parent's room. As you can see she was face down pointing away from the door. We assume from her position that she came to investigate the noise, saw the attacker and tried to escape. Plus the wounds to her head all came from the rear. Now why do you suppose she wasn't shot like the parents?"

"I haven't a clue. Sorry, I guess I've used up all my natural ability on the shotgun ownership question."

"Okay, let's put it another way. The coroner's report said she died of blunt trauma. What do you suppose he used to hit her with?"

"Whatever was handy, I guess. From the way her head is all bashed in, he sure didn't use his fists."

"And...."

"And I guess that would mean he used the shotgun as a club to beat her with?"

"Bingo! The coroner's report states that the wounds were consistent with the butt of a gun! Which tells us something about that gun."

"And that would be?"

"That it was probably and I say probably because it was never found, a double barrel shotgun that only held two shells! He would have been able to shoot the parents in rapid succession, but wouldn't have had time enough to reload in order to shoot the girl. If he had a pump action shotgun, he would have had sufficient ammo to shoot her as well. Of course, there is the possibility that he only had two shells loaded in a pump action, but since it was never found, it's all conjecture. Either way, he chased her down and hit her with the butt of the gun!"

"So that means that the police were looking for what was possibly a double barrel shotgun with damage to the stock, am I right?"

"Yep, but they never found it. There was a pond a few hundred yards from the house, which they dragged, but it never turned up, so the murder weapon was gone."

The next picture was a close up of an interior door. The caption indicated that it was the door leading into the master bedroom.

"Why did they take this picture?" I asked.

"Look closer at the lower third of the door. What do you see?"

"Oh, I see what you're talking about," I said, holding it up to the light, "the door is cracked. There is some kind of smudge there in the middle of the lower panel. What do you think that means?"

"The technician's report says they thought it looked like someone had kicked the door in. There was an indentation in the plaster on the inside wall that matched up with the door handle plus the wood around the striker plate was damaged. There were fragments of wood found in the carpet just inside the door. It looks as though the attacker kicked in the door with his foot before entering the room to confront Patrick McCoy. It indicates to me that whoever did this was filled with rage. He certainly didn't sneak up on them."

I soon lost all track of time as Jack continued my first lesson in forensic investigation with him as the headmaster and me his wide-eyed pupil. We had just started going over the transcript of Mark's interrogation, when the orderly interrupted us by bringing Jack his lunch. I needed a break and some time to absorb what we had found out so far, so I swept the pictures back into the folder and put it back with the others in the box. I left Jack to his lunch with a promise to return and walked to my car. I sat behind the wheel for a few minutes before starting it. I guess I was suffering from sensory overload, because it was all I could do to keep from bursting into tears. I just couldn't get the horrible images out of my head.

Out of the corner of my eye I noticed a black and white squad car come wheeling into the parking lot and pull into a slot at the other end of the row. The occupant of the car didn't look my way, but when he got out and walked toward the entrance, I recognized him instantly. It was my good pal, Chief Taylor and from the scowl on his face, I knew it was anything but a social call. My first thought was to hurry back in and find out what he was doing there, but thought better of it. I was already in enough hot water with him and the last thing I needed was to be found in possession of some "borrowed" records. I hoped Jack would be able to handle the situation.

I backed out and drove to a nearby hamburger stand where I ate in my car. I was nearly too nervous to eat, but I took my time and managed to choke it all down. I decided I would drive by Shady Oaks and if his car was still there, I would go back to the hotel and wait for Jack to call me and let me know that it was safe to return.

I needn't have worried, because when I approached the parking lot entrance, his police car was gone. I whipped into an empty spot, rushed up to the door and down the hallway to Jack's room fully expecting to see that the boxes had been confiscated. To my surprise, they were still there.

"I had a visitor right after you left," Jack said calmly.

"Yeah, I know. I saw him. What did he want?" I asked, feeling a flutter in my chest.

"It seems that he found out about you coming to see me and wanted to make sure I wasn't giving you any encouragement. Boy, I don't know what you said to him, but he's madder than a wet hen! You better steer clear of him as best you can while you're in town. He says you're a real pain in the ass!" he laughed.

"Yeah, well he's a real sweetheart himself," I snapped indignantly, "maybe if he gave a damn about solving the murders instead of strutting around like a big cheese for the tourists, I wouldn't have to do what I'm doing!"

"Now, don't be so hard on him, Ellen. He's a very competent police officer. It's just that he has more on his plate than he can say grace over and the last thing he needs is a rank amateur detective running all over town stirring things up!"

"Well you are certainly no amateur and you seem to be taking me seriously! What did he say when he saw all the boxes?"

"Oh, you mean these boxes of used books that the library was throwing out and distributing to us poor shut-ins?" he said innocently.

"Jack! You are something else!" I laughed, relief washing over me. "I am so glad you came into my life! Even if we never solve the crime, you make it all worthwhile!"

"Well, just because we've made it this far, doesn't mean he won't be back with guns blazing when he discovers that these files are missing. Bring me the next file, will you, we've got a lot of ground to cover!"

The next file contained transcripts of witness statements. The first of Mark's transcripts only contained a couple of pages. The preliminary report indicated that he was taken to the police station during the early morning hours on the night of the crime for questioning. Chief Talbot's report indicated that Mark was displaying signs of severe emotional trauma and was either unwilling or unable to speak. When it became obvious that they would be unable to continue the interview, they sent him home with an uncle. He was called back in a couple of days later only this time he was accompanied by a lawyer, who advised them that his client would not be making any statements relating to the actual killings citing the Fifth Amendment.

When I read what it said about the Fifth Amendment, I asked, "doesn't that mean he did it? If he was unwilling to answer their questions on the grounds that it might incriminate him, isn't that an admission of guilt?"

"Not necessarily," Jack said, "he may have just had a savvy lawyer. You have to remember that the kid was probably still in a state of shock. Maybe he had been talking out of his head to the lawyer and the guy was just trying to protect him from himself. It happens all the time."

"So how are the police supposed to get to the truth? It almost seems as if he was interfering with the investigation by withholding evidence!"

"There's no law that says a person is required to make a confession, Ellen! It's up to the police to gather sufficient evidence to prove their case. The prisons are full of people who refused to cooperate with the police. There are plenty of other ways to get at the truth!"

We read on and learned that while Mark's attorney wouldn't let him answer any questions concerning the murders, he did allow him to answer their questions concerning his whereabouts before, during and after the estimated time of death of his parents and sister. The questions and answers went something like this:

C. of P. Arthur Talbot: So, Mark, why don't you tell us where you were on the evening of February 1, 1968?

Mark: You mean before I, you know, found them?

Talbot: Yes, before you came home.

Mark: I was at work at Dick's Tavern over in Huron. The dishwasher had broken down again and I stayed late to help Tommy wash the glasses and sweep up.

Talbot: Tommy? What is this Tommy's last name?

Mark: Tommy? I can't remember. We just all call him Tommy. He works in the kitchen, you know, making burgers and stuff. He doesn't speak very good English. He's not very friendly. I haven't worked there long enough to know everybody's name.

Talbot: That's okay, Mark. We'll check him out later. Go ahead. You were at work and you stayed after hours. Monday was a school night. Were your folks okay with you being out late with school the next day?

Mark: They aren't exactly thrilled, but they don't hassle me about it too much. Mostly my mom because she doesn't like drinking, because of my dad and says she doesn't want me hanging around a bunch of drunks.

Talbot: So your dad liked to drink?

Mark: Yeah, he ties one on now and then. That's how I got my job. I had to go pick him up one night that he got so loaded they wouldn't let him drive. The bartender had taken away his keys. Said they could use some help around the place. I guess they thought I was an okay guy, looking out for my dad and all.

Talbot: So, Mark, when your dad got drunk, how did he act? Was he all mellow and silly or did he get mean, like some guys do?

Mark: Sometimes he's silly, but mostly he gets mean.

Talbot: Did he ever hit you or your mom?

Mark: Maybe a couple of times, I guess. Mostly he just yells at my mom. Calls her dirty names and stuff.

Talbot: You said his anger was directed mostly at your mom. What about you or your little sister, Mark, did he ever hit either of you?

80

Mark: I never saw him hit Becky.

Talbot: What about you, Mark? Your dad ever knock you around? You know, when he was drunk?

Mark: Yes, maybe once or twice. It wasn't like he did it every night or nothing.

Talbot: How'd that make you feel? You know, those times when he came after you?

Mark: I don't know. I just tried to stay out of his way when he got like that.

Talbot: Did it make you mad? Maybe make you wish you could make it stop?

The interview was interrupted at this point by Mark's attorney. Then resuming:

Talbot: So Mark, getting back to that night. You finished up your chores. Can you tell me about what time it was when you left?

Mark: We closed at midnight. I probably stayed for about another hour helping in the kitchen.

Talbot: But you don't know exactly what time it was?

Mark: No, I just know it was a while after closing.

Talbot: Did you lock up or was somebody there with you?

Mark: Everybody left shortly after we closed. It was just me and Tommy. The boss gave the keys to Tommy to lock up when we left.

Talbot: So you and Tommy left together?

Mark: Yes, we walked out together.

Talbot: Where did you go from there?

Mark: No where. I just went home.

Talbot: How did you get there? Did this Tommy give you a ride?

Mark: No. I drove myself. I got this old Rambler that I'm buying from Mr. Swartz, one of the guys that hangs out at the bar. Everybody calls him Silky. He's one of my dad's drinking buddies. That's why I went to work, to pay for a car. My folks won't let me drive theirs.

Talbot: Okay. So you drove directly home. Did you notice anything unusual about your house when you got there?

Mark: No.

Talbot: Were there any cars in the driveway, other than the one your folks drive?

Mark: No.

Talbot: What about the lights? Were they on or off?

Mark: I don't remember. I didn't pay any attention.

Talbot: Which door did you go into?

Mark: The back, through the kitchen.

Talbot: Was the door locked or unlocked?

Mark: I don't remember.

Talbot: Do your folks usually lock their doors at night?

Mark: I guess they do, sometimes.

Talbot: So if the door was unlocked, that wouldn't have been unusual. Right?

Mark: I guess so.

Talbot: Okay. Now, let's talk about what you did after you entered the house. Okay?

Mark: I don't want to talk about what I saw.

Talbot: What about the inside of the house? Let's start with the downstairs. Was there anything that made you think something was wrong? Anything out of place? Items moved around, that sort of thing?

Mark: No. I don't remember anything unusual.

Talbot: What about sounds? Did you hear anything that made you think something was wrong?

Mark: No. Everything was quiet.

Talbot: So what did you do next?

Mark: I went upstairs.

Talbot: What did you see upstairs?

Mark: I don't remember.

Talbot: It's okay, Mark. We already know what you found up there. We just need to hear your version of it.

Mark: I'm telling you I don't remember.

Talbot: But you do remember climbing the stairs, right?

Mark: I guess so.

Talbot: So you got to the top of the stairs. What happened then?

Mark: I don't remember, I said.

Talbot: Was your sister in bed when you got to the top of the stairs?

Mark: I don't know.

Talbot: What about your folks? Were they in bed?

Mark: I don't know. I don't remember.

Talbot: Do you remember if you said anything, maybe called out to let your folks know you were home?

Mark: Maybe. I don't remember.

Talbot: So did you and your dad have a fight before you went to work that night?

Mark: I don't remember.

Talbot: You said your dad liked to drink. Was he drinking that night?

Mark: I don't remember.

Talbot: Come on, Mark. You can tell me. We already know there was alcohol in your dad's blood. Nobody's going to hurt you. You'll feel a lot better if you just talk to me.

Mark: I said, I don't remember.

Talbot: I'm going to tell you what I think happened and you tell me if it jogs your memory. Okay?

Mark: Okay.

Talbot: Here's what I think happened. I think that maybe your dad was drinking that night. And he got into one of his mean moods. Maybe you and he had an argument. I think you were pretty mad at your dad when you left to go to work that night. Are you with me so far?

Mark: I told you I don't remember.

Talbot: You don't remember what happened before you left to go to work?

Mark: No.

Talbot: So everything was just fine between you and your folks when you left to go to work?

Mark: I don't remember. I just went to work.

Talbot: Okay. But just for argument's sake, let's assume that I'm right. You had an argument with your folks and you were pretty upset when you left. Okay?

Mark: Whatever you say, I don't remember.

Talbot: Well, maybe this will help you remember. Here's what I think happened. You were angry at your dad, because the two of you got into it before you went to your job. Maybe something happened at work that upset you even more. The more you thought about your argument with your dad, the madder you got. You came home and went up the stairs. Maybe your dad shouted something from his bedroom. Something that made you even madder. The two of you

83

exchanged words. He was drunk after all. Maybe he called you some dirty names like he did your mother. And maybe, something just snapped inside. Maybe you decided you just couldn't take it anymore. Maybe you ran and got your dad's gun. Maybe you didn't mean to shoot anybody, maybe you just meant to scare him. Maybe the gun just went off accidentally. And then your mom started screaming, so you had to shut her up. So you had no choice. You were on auto-pilot. So you pointed the gun at her and it went off again. Does this sound like what happened, Mark?

Mark: No, no, I don't remember anything like that.

Talbot: And then, your little sister Becky came in the room. She started screaming and running away. Maybe she was going to tell somebody about what happened. And you couldn't let that happen, could you, Mark? You were in a lot of trouble. You couldn't let your little sister go telling on you, now could you? So you ran after her, but the gun was empty. So you grabbed her and she wouldn't quit screaming, so you took the gun and you hit her. Just to make her stop screaming, but she wouldn't, so you hit her again and again until she quit screaming. Does that refresh your memory, Mark? Isn't that what really happened?

Mark: No, no. That's not what happened!

Talbot: Then you tell me what happened, Mark.

Mark: I swear, that's not what happened. I just don't remember anything. I'm telling you the truth.

The attorney terminated the interview at this point.

"Whew, so what do you think, Jack?" I asked, "did he do it?"

"That remains to be seen, Ellen," he said, removing his glasses and pinching the bridge of his nose between his finger and thumb, "we have only just scratched the surface."

Chapter Eleven

As far as I was concerned, there was no doubt that Mark had killed his family. The description of what happened that night by Chief Talbot was almost exactly what I had been told. I said as much to Jack, but he didn't share my opinion.

"But, Jack," I said, "Mark admitted that he and his father didn't get along! Not to mention the fact that Patrick McCoy had been drinking that night! You said yourself that most murders are committed by members of the victim's family!"

"I said that's who you suspect first," he reminded me. "Just because Chief Talbot said that's what happened didn't make it so. Mark stated that he didn't remember what happened."

"Well of course he said that," I argued, "he wasn't about to admit to what he did. He was obviously lying!"

"Maybe, maybe not. Think about it, Ellen. Put yourself in Mark's place. He's just a kid. Let's assume that he didn't do it. He comes home, and walks into anyone's worst nightmare. There are the people he loves, dead. There's blood and gore everywhere he turns. How much of that scene would you want to remember? The sight was enough to drive him straight out of his mind!"

"But if he didn't do it, why didn't he just call the police right away? That would be the most logical thing to do!" I insisted.

"Yes, to a rational person, that would seem logical. But maybe he wasn't rational at that point in time. It isn't too hard to understand that his actions may have seemed irrational to a sane person. Just because he says he can't remember, doesn't mean he's guilty! And, you are forgetting the basic concept of the law."

"What's that?"

"Everyone is innocent, until proven guilty! Without proof beyond a reasonable doubt, a person cannot be convicted of a crime."

"Okay! I guess I am jumping to conclusions. Your point is well taken," I admitted, though I was anything but convinced.

"Don't forget that there were no witnesses to the murder other than the killer himself," he said. "Now I'm not saying that he didn't do it, but without a confession, or any direct evidence to link him to the crime, the police simply had nothing to go on at that point in the investigation."

"So what you're saying is that we've got our work cut out for us."

"Oh, I'd say that about says it all!" he said. "Let's see what Mark had to say the next time he talked to the police."

The next few pages of transcript covered the second of Mark's meetings with Chief Talbot. As before, his attorney was present. The questions and answers went something like this:

Talbot: So, Mark, you've had some time to think over what we talked about the last time we got together. Is there anything you want to tell me? Maybe get this whole thing cleared up.

Mark: I already told you. I don't know anything about what happened.

Talbot: Come on, Mark. You know you'll feel a lot better if you get this thing off your chest. It'll go a lot easier on you if you just tell me what happened.

Mark: I'm telling you I don't remember. Nothing has changed.

Talbot: Okay, just remember that we're going to find out eventually. I'm just trying to save us all a lot of grief here.

Mark: I'm trying to give you what you want. I promise I am. I keep telling you I don't remember, but you just won't listen.

Talbot: Okay, take it easy, son. We'll get back to that. Let's talk about what happened after you came home. You went upstairs and saw what had happened. Did you touch anything?

Mark: I don't think so, I don't know.

Talbot: Did you check to see if there was anybody alive? You know, did you feel for a heartbeat or anything?

Mark: No, I don't know, I don't remember.

Talbot: Did you do anything else after you found them?

Mark: I don't know. It's all just a blank. I swear.

Talbot: Okay, so you left the house at some point. Do you remember where you went when you left the scene?

Mark: I guess I just got in my car and started driving.

Talbot: Did you have some destination in mind? Where were you going to go?

Mark: I don't remember. I guess I just had to get away from there. I don't remember having any place in mind. I just started driving.

Talbot: Now according to our information, your folks were killed between 10:45 p.m. and 2:00 a.m. We know they were alive at 10:45, because your neighbor, Mrs. Anderson, says she called your house around that time and spoke to your mom. You told us you left the bar sometime after midnight, but you couldn't say for sure exactly when, correct?

Mark: I just remember we had to clean up, I don't know how long it took.

Talbot: That's okay, Mark. We'll be talking to Tommy the cook. Maybe he'll be able to tell us the exact time you left there. Now it takes about 15 minutes for you to get home, right?

Mark: Yes, more or less.

Talbot: So let's assume you stayed an hour after closing, which means you left the bar around 1:00 a.m. That puts you home at 1:15 a.m. You didn't get to the Yarborough's house until 2:45. They live less than 10 miles from you. If you went straight there it would have taken about 15 minutes. Does that sound about right?

Mark: I guess so.

Talbot: Okay, here's the way I see it. With an hour and a half between 1:15 and 2.45, if we allow 15 minutes to drive to the Yarborough's, that leaves an hour and fifteen minutes of time unaccounted for between 1:15 and 2:30. Do you see the problem I have here, Mark?

Mark: I don't know. I must have just driven around before I went to Gary's house.

Talbot: Let's say you got home at 1:15. Maybe it took you, lets say, 15 minutes to discover the bodies, but that's being generous. That still leaves an hour that you can't account for. Where did you drive that would have taken an hour?

Mark: I don't know. I just know I got in my car and ended up at Gary's house. I can't tell you any more than that.

Talbot: Now, Mark, we searched your house for the weapon. And you know what? We couldn't find it. You know what that means?

Mark: No.

Talbot: That means that the guy that murdered your folks got rid of it. It probably took that person a while to find a good place to hide it. Like, say, it wouldn't be surprising if it took him an hour to get rid of the gun. Does that sound reasonable to you, Mark?

Mark: I guess if you say so.

Talbot: So where's the gun, Mark?

Mark: I don't know what you're talking about. I don't want to answer any more of your questions.

Mark's attorney intervened at this point in the interrogation, saying that his client had no further statements at this time.

"So, Jack, what do you say now?" I asked, "it seems to me that he's covering up. He had a whole hour to do what? It was the middle of the night. Where was he if he wasn't either killing his family or ditching the murder weapon somewhere?"

"It was too early in the investigation to assume anything, Ellen. Remember that at this point, he wasn't admitting to anything. It was Talbot who made the assumption that he did it. Unless there was some physical evidence, or a witness or a confession, they had nothing. See here? They checked him for powder residue when he came in for his first interrogation right after it happened and there was no antimony or barium present on his hands, which they would have found if he had fired the gun."

"What are you talking about, Jack?"

"Here's the deal. When a gun discharges, it causes a small explosion when the firing pin hits the charge in the back of the shell. A person firing the gun would have traces of the residue on their hands. Mark didn't. Now that doesn't necessarily mean he didn't do it, because he may have washed his hands before they tested him or he may have been wearing gloves. But it eliminates that one piece of evidence that could point to him as being the perpetrator."

"Well, I guess I should have known that if they had what they needed, they would have done something back then."

"We've got lots more statements to cover, so let's quit jumping to the obvious and see if we can't find something that they might have overlooked. I just have this feeling that the real killer is in one of these boxes if we just keep looking. Remember we are looking for something that just doesn't fit. We'll know it when we see it," he assured me, although I was having difficulty sharing his confidence.

The next section we came to was the next of Mark's meetings with Chief Talbot, which took place the following day. It isn't verbatim, but went something like this:

Talbot: So Mark, are you feeling a little better?

Mark: I guess so. I think I may be remembering some things now. Just flashes of stuff, you know?

Talbot: That's great, Mark. Why don't you just tell me anything that comes to you?

Mark: Like I said, I came home and got a bottle of pop out of the refrigerator. It was late, so everybody was in bed. The lights were on in the kitchen and living room, but I didn't think anything about it, because I figured my mom probably left them on for me.

Talbot: That's great, Mark. Take your time, we've got all the time in the world. You'll feel a lot better if you talk to someone about it.

Mark: Well, I was feeling kind of tired, so I started up the stairs and I saw something on the floor. It was dark up there and it looked like a pile of clothes or something, so I walked over to pick them up, you know, because my mom is always yelling at me to pick up after myself and that's when I saw my little sister. I thought she was asleep out there in the hall and I walked over to wake her up. I didn't want her to get in trouble with my dad, because I figured that maybe she had wet the bed again and that makes him really mad. That's when I got a good look at her and she was all bloody and stuff, you know. I just, I

89

couldn't move. I was yelling in my head, but nothing was coming out. I was afraid to move and then I saw the light coming out from under the door to my folks' room and I went in to tell them, and they were all bloody too and I got really scared because I was afraid that whoever did it might still be in the house. So I ran down the stairs and out the back door to my car.

Talbot: Why didn't you call the police?

Mark: I don't know, I guess I was afraid the guy was still in the house. I wasn't thinking, I just knew I had to get away. I drove my car and kept on driving. After a while it all just seemed like a really bad dream and I just put it out of my mind. I just couldn't think about it any more. I didn't want to think about again, ever, and I didn't at first. But now the pictures have started flashing in my head, like a movie, you know. I can't make them stop. They're all dead and now you think I killed them, but I swear, I didn't. I didn't do it, you have to believe me Chief Talbot; I didn't kill them. I didn't.

Talbot: Do you remember now if you touched anything upstairs?

Mark: I don't know. I don't think so. There was just so much blood.

Talbot: Mark we found a fingerprint in blood on the back door. It was your fingerprint, son. How do you suppose it got there?

Mark: I don't know.

Talbot: Are you sure you don't know?

Mark: I just remember seeing her all covered in blood, that's all. I can't think about anything else.

The interview continued from this point, but Mark's statement remained basically the same. He still insisted that he had no recollection of what he did during the missing time after he came home and then arrived at Gary's house an hour later.

"Now I'm not so sure he did it," I said, "his story sounds like it could have happened that way. What do you think, Jack? Was he telling the truth this time?"

"We obviously can't get inside his head, but it certainly has a truthful ring to it, doesn't it? Notice his use of the word 'I' all throughout his statement. If he were trying to distance himself from the experience out of guilt, he would have avoided saying 'I did this,' or 'I did that.' Using the words 'I', 'me' or 'mine' makes it personal. Plus, he doesn't throw in a bunch of unrelated information in an attempt to draw attention away from the subject at hand. It's a pretty simple and up front narrative. I'm beginning to wonder if he really did just block out the whole thing as some sort of self defense mechanism."

We had spent the better part of the day reading and sorting through the files. It was getting late and I could tell that we both needed a break. One close look at the dark circles that had developed under Jack's eyes told me that he wasn't as strong as he pretended to be. There certainly wasn't any weakness in his mind, but his body was something else. I couldn't afford to let him overdo it. I knew that without him, I had no hope of even coming close to the truth, so we called it a night. I promised to return early the next morning. He was asleep before I made it out of the door.

I envied his ability to put everything aside so easily later when I tried to get to sleep at my hotel. I spent the remainder of the night bombarded by questions. Was Mark telling the truth? And if he was, who had killed the McCoy's? Could that person still be out there somewhere, determined to stop us? Had that same person shot Jack when he tried to reopen the case? Was this person also responsible for Earl's death? And worst of all, was my own life in danger as well? Or even worse, maybe Mark was responsible for all of it. I drew upon the outrage that I had felt at the sight of those poor victims and swore that I would do everything I could to finally bring an end to it once and for all. The blood of the McCoys demanded it.

Chapter Twelve

The next morning when I arrived at Shady Oaks, I passed Jack's nurse coming out of his room with his empty breakfast tray. She stopped me in the hall and asked if she could speak with me before I saw him. I was immediately alarmed that something was wrong, but couldn't tell from her expression. I followed her to the tray trolley where she slid the tray onto one of the shelves.

"Is something wrong with Jack?" I demanded. Her attitude towards me up until that point had been anything but friendly. I prepared myself for a lecture about disrupting schedules and tiring out her patient, but to my surprise, she smiled at me.

"Oh, I'm sorry, I didn't mean to cause you concern," she said, "I just wanted to tell you how much we all appreciate what you're doing for Mr. Miller. The poor thing was just withering away before you showed up. He had almost lost his will to live and now, look at this tray! He hasn't had an appetite like this since I've been taking care of him and that's been over four years. I haven't seen him so, I don't know how to describe it, lively! Whatever you two have been doing has done him a world of good. He's even got a little surprise for you. He absolutely insisted!"

"What do you mean surprise?" I asked, totally unprepared for her change in attitude.

"You'll see!" she laughed and started pushing the trolley down the hall.

I rushed to Jack's room and there he was, sitting propped up with pillows in a wheelchair by the window.

"My God! Look at you!" I cried and hurried over to give him a hug. "What in the world is going on around here?"

"Now don't make a big thing of it, Ellen," he said sheepishly, "I just decided I was tired of feeling sorry for myself. It practically took an act of congress to get the nurses to drag my sorry butt into this contraption. I guess I decided it was time to rejoin the human race."

"Are you sure you're able to do this, Jack? You don't need to be a hero to impress me, you know."

"Who said I'm doing it to impress you, Ms. Richardson?" he asked with a mischievous glint in his eye. "Maybe all I needed was a reminder that this washed up old war horse has something to contribute after all. I just needed some incentive!"

"Well, I'm going to take credit for it anyway! You look mighty handsome sitting there, Chief. Are you ready to plunge in again?"

"Bring it on!" he grinned.

I dragged the other chair over, set up the tray table between us and handed him the file containing the statements of others that were questioned by the police.

The first was that of Tommy Czerwinski, the cook from Dick's Tavern. He said that Mark had arrived at the bar around 7:00 that evening. His statement confirmed that Mark had stayed for his entire shift and had indeed left work around 1:00 a.m., but didn't make a point of checking the time on the night in question. When asked if he knew the victims, he stated that he was familiar with Patrick McCoy from seeing him at the bar, though he knew him as Pat. He said he felt sorry for Mark because his father was not a very nice man. He said he liked Mark okay, but didn't really know a lot about him, since the boy didn't do a lot of talking. To him, he seemed to be a pretty reliable worker, though he didn't really think a bar was such a good place for a young man to work, but it wasn't his place to say. He didn't offer any opinion as to whether he thought Mark capable of committing the crime, saying he minded his own business and Mark did the same. He further stated that Mark didn't seem particularly upset that night. He was asked if he knew anyone that would want to do the McCoy family harm. He stated that he had been called upon to break up a fight that Pat McCoy had been involved in during one of his visits to the bar, but didn't know any of the others involved. He repeated that he just worked there and spent most of his time in the kitchen, not mingling with the customers.

"Well, so much for Tommy the cook," I said, feeling a little let down by his statement.

"Now don't sell Mr. Czerwinski short," Jack said with a sniff, "he has given some information that might prove useful later on. He confirms that Mark must have left the bar around 1:00. He obviously didn't have a very high opinion of Patrick McCoy, but seems to think that Mark was a pretty good kid. He has also opened up the possibility of the elder McCoy having enemies. People have been known to take a bar fight to the next level. Maybe Mark wasn't the only one with reason to kill his old man."

The next statement was that of the neighbor, Julia Anderson about the phone call she placed to Mrs. McCoy on the night of the murder. She stated that she talked to the mother at approximately 10:45 p.m. She said she had called about their dog dumping over her trashcans and was pretty upset. She said she had called the McCoy's on three other occasions for the same reason and that Mrs. McCoy promised to come over the next day and clean up the mess as she had done in the past. She indicated that Mrs. McCoy sounded calm, but irritated that she had called so late in the evening. As far as she could tell from the conversation, everything seemed normal and she didn't have any sense that something out of the ordinary was happening at the McCoy residence. She stated that she had not heard any gunshots coming from the house, which wasn't surprising in view of the distance between the two houses. She said she went to bed around 11:30 after the evening news and did not wake up until she heard the sirens from the police cars that passed her house around 3:00 a.m.

"The McCoy's were still alive at 10:45. Mark is confirmed as being at the bar when Mrs. Anderson made the call. Since it is nearly impossible to determine the exact time of death, there is still an awful lot of time for the killer to get in and out without being seen," Jack said, rubbing his chin.

"Why wasn't the coroner able to be more exact about that?" I wanted to know.

"Back then they didn't have nearly as many sophisticated ways of determining time of death as we have now. And even today, it is still very difficult to prove time of death accurately. There are just so many factors involved. The temperature of the room, the location and position of the bodies all play a part. Some people have spent their entire careers trying to figure it out. Once a body has cooled, there is no way to tell how long the person has been dead. If they got to the body, say within an hour of death, they could use the temperature of the body to determine how long it had been dead. After that, it would simply be guesswork. There was some indication of lividity found, which says that they had been dead for at least a couple of hours when they were found."

"What do you mean by lividity?" I asked, being unfamiliar with the term.

"Okay, I'm no expert, but this is what I understand about it. You see, while your heart is pumping, the blood circulates all around your body. When the heart stops, the blood has no where to go so it pools into the lowest areas of the body by the force of gravity. This forms dark patches that look like bruises. It takes a while for these marks to show up, so the coroner looks for them as a way to tell how long the body has been dead. The method was used back then, and even though they still use it, it still isn't an exact science."

"Okay, but what about rigor mortis? I heard once that they can use that as a means to determine time of death."

"Again, there are other factors that can vary the speed that rigor sets in. It still is just an indicator, not proof positive. Sorry, Ellen, but that is just the way it is. There was simply no way to tell exactly when the McCoys were killed. We're just going to have to keep looking."

The next statement was that of Mark's uncle, James Patterson, brother of Loretta McCoy with whom Mark had been staying after the death of his family. He stated that he was at home with his wife on the night of the murders and his wife confirmed that he was home all evening. He stated that he was unaware of his sister's death until he was awakened by the call by the police to come to the police station and get his nephew Mark. He further stated that he and his sister did not have a close relationship because he did not get along with her husband Pat. He said he had attempted on several occasions to persuade his sister to leave her abusive husband, but had been unsuccessful thus leading to the estrangement. While he had not personally witnessed any abuse directed towards his nephew, he would not have been surprised to learn that it may have occurred in view of his brother-in-law's temperament and drinking problem. He said he did not feel that Mark was capable of committing the crime suggesting that the assailant was more likely an acquaintance of Pat McCoy. He stated that his sister's husband was an embarrassment to the family and had probably been the cause of the attack on his sister and niece.

"We can probably discount the uncle's statement, since he was obviously biased towards Mark. The kid was all he had left of his sister and he certainly wasn't shedding any tears over the loss of his brother-in-law. He was naturally going to protect his sister's son out of guilt that he had turned his back on her," Jack commented. "It was his sister that had been killed after all."

"He does seem to think that Pat may have had enemies though," I added. "And the cook Tommy said he had witnessed a fight between Pat and some other guys. It does open up the possibility of other suspects, don't you think?"

"So far no one has named any names, so we'll just have to keep digging," Jack reminded me as he pulled yet another statement from the file.

The next statement was that of Dick Chance, the owner of Dick's Tavern where Mark was employed. He stated that Mark was a reliable employee and never gave any indication of violence. He was also well acquainted with the deceased, Pat McCoy, who frequented his establishment. He indicated that on the night in question he did not observe anything unusual in Mark's behavior. He said he left the bar shortly after midnight confirming that he did in fact give Tommy the keys to lock up. He also stated that he had witnessed the altercation between Pat McCoy and another man a few weeks earlier. The same fight to which Tommy had referred in his statement. He said he didn't know what they were arguing about, only that things got out of hand because the man tipped over a table, Pat took a swing at him and they both had to be restrained. He said he, Tommy and another regular, Homer "Silky" Swartz broke up the fight and the man he could not identify left the bar while Pat McCoy stayed on until closing. The fight took place before Mark came to work for him.

"So now we have another person who says that Pat McCoy may have had someone out to get him," I observed. "I don't know, Jack. It's not beyond the realm of possibility that Mark may not have had anything to do with it."

"Yeah, too bad he didn't know the guy. Let's see if there's a statement in here from this Silky person. Maybe he knew who the other guy was," Jack said as he riffled through the remaining statements.

The police did in fact take a statement from Homer "Silky" Swartz. He indicated that his friend Pat had told him about a man who had been hassling him, the same man with whom he had the fight, but had never told him the man's name or the nature of their dispute. He assumed that it had something to do with either a woman or some money Pat owed the man, but couldn't say for sure. When asked why he would make such an assumption, he responded that Pat often made passes at women he met at the bar and liked to gamble. McCoy had come to Silky requesting loans to cover his losses on several occasions though Swartz said he never made him a loan. As to his knowledge of Pat's son, Mark, he said he felt sorry for the young man and had sold him an old car. He said that Mark was making weekly payments to him and had not missed any up until the death of his parents. He said Mark was a quiet kid, who never talked much, but showed a lot of maturity for someone his age.

"There is definitely a common theme running through all these statements. Pat McCoy was not a very nice man. He drank, gambled, played around with other women and abused his family. Is it any wonder that somebody wanted him dead?" I asked, "it sounds as though whoever did it was doing everybody a favor, except for Loretta and Becky, of course. It sounds as though Pat was as much responsible for their deaths as the killer was!"

"I'm beginning to think that as well, but don't lose sight of the fact that no matter what Pat did, he didn't deserve to have his head blown off. The evidence still points directly at the son no matter what these other people thought. All we have so far is a lot of conjecture, no hard facts."

"No wonder they weren't able to find the killer. I'm beginning to think we'll never get to the truth, Jack. Without a confession, they really had nothing to go on."

"Don't give up so quickly," Jack said, "I still think there is something that was overlooked. We just have to keep looking. Nobody said this was going to be easy!"

Of course he was right, but I felt sick at heart from what I had learned. My image of the perfect little village was unraveling. I had grown up thinking that my hometown was beyond all the cruelty and immorality associated with big city life. Not all of my cherished memories were shattered, but just like the soil of my grandfather's farm that now covered the decaying refuse of a modern society, someone from my birthplace had covered over a terrible crime. That someone needed to pay the price. The bones of Pat, Loretta and Becky McCoy would never truly rest in peace until their killer was brought to justice. I could only hope that Jack and I would uncover the truth.

Chapter Thirteen

It was getting late and I could tell that Jack's newfound strength was beginning to flag. His upright posture in the wheelchair had deteriorated over the course of the day until he was slumped over and obviously in pain. He insisted that he was fine, but I knew better and went out to the nurse's station and got them to come back to his room and get him back into bed. Over his protests, they got him settled as I gathered up the materials we had been reading and put them back in the box. I said good-bye and returned to my hotel.

I was determined to put the whole matter out of my mind temporarily, so I ordered room service, ate, took a hot bath, and spent the rest of the evening lounging around in my night clothes watching sitcoms on the television. I simply could not take any more awful revelations of the lives of Pat, Loretta, Mark and Becky McCoy, although subconsciously they never left me completely. Their demands for retribution haunted my dreams when I finally switched off the lights and nodded off to sleep.

The next morning as I made my way out to the nursing home for the next session with Jack, I came to the realization that our search for the truth was going to take longer than I expected. While I certainly had plenty of money to live comfortably thanks to my husband's life insurance, I couldn't afford to stay at the hotel indefinitely. I had already stayed several days beyond what I had originally planned and if I intended to stay for any extended period of time; I needed less expensive accommodations. I wondered if there might be a house for rent in town. I thought I might be able to find something furnished that I could lease month to month. It would be even better if I could find one in close proximity to Jack. That's when I remembered my conversation at the Dairy Bar with my brother's old flame, Kay Cornwall.

Telling myself that it was at least worth a try, I turned around and headed back into town towards her office. I wasn't exactly thrilled at the prospect of seeing her again, but she was a real estate agent and the only one I knew. There was a little brass bell attached the door that tinkled when I swung open the door and when I entered the tiny storefront, I was once again assaulted by the cloying scent of her perfume, so I knew she had to be in. I stepped up to the counter just as she came out of the back office.

"Well, hello again!" she said, reaching across to shake my hand. "I'm surprised to see you again so soon! I thought you were only here for a few days. I looked for your brother at the Festival, but didn't see him. What brings you by?"

Once again she was dressed to impress. This time her outfit was a fuchsia pantsuit that must have cost a week's salary. Her outfit made me feel distinctly out of place in my jeans, sneakers and tee shirt. I started having second thoughts about having anything to do with her. I can't explain why she had such an effect on me, other than the fact that she had always made a point of treating me like I was invisible. To be honest, I have to admit I remember feeling jealous of her when she and my brother were dating and all these years later, those feelings resurfaced.

She was staring at me with a puzzled expression and I finally found my voice, "I'm sorry," I stammered, "something's come up and I find myself in need of a place to stay that's a little less expensive than the Inn. I'm interested in something small, inexpensive and furnished that I can rent with a month to month lease. Would you know of anything that's available right away?"

At the mention of business, her eyes lighted up. "How much can you afford to pay? I've got several listings that might be what you're looking for. Come on back to my office and we'll take a look."

She led me to her office and after offering me a cup of coffee, began showing me rental properties. I told her what I felt I could afford to pay and the desired location. She had two that sounded like what I had in mind. She said she was free to show them to me if I wanted and I agreed. I called Jack from her office to tell him what I was doing. He was anxious to get back into the files, but promised to wait until I got there. I could tell that Kay was curious to know whom I had called, but I didn't offer any explanations. I wanted to keep a low profile as long as I was in town and couldn't be sure that she wouldn't talk to her friends about what I was doing.

She drove me out to the first house, but it was in such bad shape, I began to wonder if I could afford anything suitable. I think she showed me that one first on purpose, because the second house was just what I wanted although the rent was slightly higher than I wanted to pay though a lot less than the hotel would cost if I stayed there. It must have been an old real estate agent's trick to show the client what they can afford and then show them what they really want at a higher price. But whatever it was, I took the bait and Ms. Cornwall was only too happy to seal the deal.

As soon as the papers were signed, I returned to my room, gathered up my belongings, checked out of the hotel and moved into the little bungalow. The whole process probably took less time that it took for the ink to dry on the lease, but I was relieved that I had made the decision. I had grown weary of living out of a suitcase and eating fast food. The house was within walking distance of both the nursing home and a small mom and pop grocery store and I looked forward to having some home cooked meals. I planned to stock the cupboards on my way home after spending the afternoon with Jack.

It was after lunch by the time I got to his room, but he had waited for me to arrive before having the staff put him in the wheelchair. I waited in the hall until he was situated.

"So did you get settled in?" he asked absently as he started flipping through the file containing the remaining statements.

"I did. It's the little yellow house next to that big brick with the white shutters up the street. It's costing me an arm and a leg, but it's cheaper than the hotel."

"Oh yeah, I know which one you mean. I used to know the people that lived there, but I can't recall their names right off hand. You sure are serious about seeing this thing through to the end, aren't you?"

"Jack, you know as well as I do that this is not something that can be done in a day or two. I've made up my mind that I'm not going back without some answers. This way I don't feel so pressured to rush the process. Besides, there's nothing going on back home anyway. My kids are all grown up and out on their own. There's no job or husband waiting for me, so what's to stop me?"

"Okay, don't get defensive," he cried, "you don't need to convince me! I'm just sorry you can't stay here permanently, case or no case."

"Why Chief Miller," I laughed, "if I didn't know better I'd think you were getting sweet on this lowly field hand!"

"Very funny, Ms. Richardson," he muttered blushing, "we are just two people who happen to be working towards the same goal! I just meant that you have been a big help to me!"

"Whatever you say, Chief," I said feeling my own cheeks redden and then letting him off the hook. "What's next?"

The next statement was by Gary Yarborough and his father, Gerald. Mark had gone to their home on the night of the murders. I told Jack what I knew of Gary and his being the class bully. I found it rather hard to understand why Mark would have chosen Gary for a friend. Gary was a loud-mouthed braggart and Mark as I recall, was quiet and retiring. The two of them seemed a very unlikely pair.

Their joint statement was taken at the Yarborough home the day after the murders. Gerald expressed his displeasure that his son had gotten involved in the matter. Gary stated he was awakened the night of the crime by someone tapping on his bedroom window. He said that he raised the window and was surprised to see Mark there, especially at that hour of the morning. He said Mark asked if he could come in and he went around to the back door and let him in. He said that Mark was babbling incoherently and pacing around the kitchen but wouldn't say what was bothering him. Gerald said he heard the noise and got out of bed to see what was going on. They both described Mark's demeanor as alarming. He was crying and wringing his hands, but gave no indication as to the cause of his extreme agitation. They were asked if they noticed any blood on his hands or clothes. Gerald stated that there had been a little blood on his hands, but that he had him rinse it off in the kitchen sink, thinking that he was injured. When Gerald realized that the blood wasn't Mark's, he became suspicious and demanded an explanation from the boy. At first Mark refused to speak, but Gerald said he kept talking quietly to the boy and eventually he told him that something horrible had happened at his house, but refused to say what. It was at this point that Gerald contacted the police, who discovered the bodies. Gerald and Gary were asked what time Mark arrived at

104

their home, but neither had checked the time. When asked for an estimate of the time that had elapsed between his arrival and the call to the police, both said that it took about a half an hour, but were so upset by his strange behavior, could not be sure. When asked, Gary said that he had seen Mark at school that day and that he didn't seem out of the ordinary to him. There was nothing to indicate that Mark was angry with his family.

"Okay, the fact that Gerald had him wash his hands may explain why there wasn't any blood or gunshot residue found on him. It does beg the question, though, as to why there wasn't any blood on his clothes. The killer would have been covered in blood. Remember the drops that trailed towards the back door," Jack commented.

"Not to mention the fact that it may have taken longer for him to tell them what was bothering him. Maybe it took longer than they estimated. It was the middle of the night and there had to have been a lot of excitement going on. Maybe Mark got there earlier than the police thought he did. That could explain the missing time when he was supposedly hiding the murder weapon."

"Maybe," Jack agreed, "it never fails to amaze me how people never seem to know what time things occur."

"Jack, what's so surprising about it? I couldn't tell you what I was doing at any particular time just yesterday. Unless there is something to specifically draw attention to the time, nobody pays attention to what happened when!"

"Well, we are running out of statements and we are no closer than we were before. I guess we'll just have to go back over what we've already covered. I still think we are overlooking something obvious, but can't imagine what it could be."

"What with my new digs, we've got all the time in the world," I laughed.

"I have a feeling we're going to need it," Jack grunted.

"There's something I've been meaning to ask, Jack," I said as I sorted through the remaining contents of the box.

"What's that?" he asked.

"You were on the force when this happened. I would have thought that you would have at least taken some of these statements. How come you didn't participate in the investigation?"

"I'm surprised you didn't ask that before this," he said. "I wanted to, believe me. I fully expected to work on it, but the Chief wouldn't let me. I was just a rookie back then, fresh out of training. Remember, Ellen, this was a really big case. Nothing like it had ever happened in Milan before. That's why the state police were called in to investigate. This went way beyond our capabilities. Oh, a couple of the older guys were assigned to the state boys to drive them around and all, but I was kept out of the loop. They kept me busy with routine traffic duty. They didn't need someone as green as me getting in their way."

"I guess that makes sense. But I have to ask if the state did the majority of the investigation, does that mean that they would have taken files and evidence with them? There really isn't that much material here. Could there be more information sitting in a state warehouse somewhere gathering dust that might contain what we're looking for?"

"I'm sure there is. I had hoped we would be able to find something in these files, but they are really incomplete. All the physical evidence is missing as well as the original crime lab reports. All we have are the communications between the state and the local police department discussing the findings. If we could get our hands on what the state's investigation turned up, we would at least stand a chance of flushing out the truth. I beginning to feel that we are only seeing the tip of the iceberg with what we've got here."

"So how do we get our hands on the rest of it, Jack? I can't just walk up the state capitol and tell them to hand it over! They'd laugh me right out of town!" I grumbled.

"Now don't be so quick to throw in the towel! I've been out of commission for a few years, but there may still be some of my contacts left on the state police. If you'll hand me the phone, I'll see what I can do about getting what they've got on it sent here. There's nothing more we can get done today anyway. Why don't you go get your supplies for the new house? We can get together in the morning and go back over the files we have. Who knows? We might just get lucky!"

I handed him the phone and he began his inquiry. He had basically dismissed me for the day, so I departed feeling disappointed. I doubted that he would be able to get the state's cooperation, but tried not to dwell on it. I walked back to the house and looked around.   While it was certainly more comfortable than the hotel room, it just didn't seem like home. As I inspected the rooms, I came to the conclusion that it definitely needed a personal touch.   I found a scrap of paper and started making a list of all the things I would need to set up housekeeping. The list went way beyond anything I would be able to find at the local grocery, so I drove to a large discount store outside of town.   I found everything I needed there. There hadn't been any stores of its kind around when I was a kid. The concept of one-stop shopping had worked its magic here just like everywhere else in America.

By the time I returned to the house loaded down with purchases, it was getting late. I settled for a microwave frozen dinner promising myself that I would cook something the next day and settled in for the night. I was feeling a little lonely and wished I had called Betsy to let her know I was still in town, but decided it was better that I not involve her in my troubles. I was on a mission and didn't need any distractions.

I went to bed early and slept soundly with the little house folded around me like an old friend.   After all the ugliness I had been discovering, I felt warm and comforted in its tender embrace.

Chapter Fourteen

I awoke refreshed. All the doubts that had been plaguing me vanished with the rising sun. I had a couple more errands to run in order to make my move complete, so I stopped by Jack's room on the way to the telephone and utilities companies to check on his progress with the state police. When I arrived, he was in bed with the telephone cradled next to his ear. He waved me off and told me to check back later in the day. I left him in deep conversation with someone on the phone, but from his expression, I got the impression that he was making progress. My positive feelings continued as I got set up with a new telephone and all the other necessities for my extended stay in my new location.

I returned home and spent the rest of day cleaning and rearranging furniture, adding my own personality to the little house. For the first time since my arrival, I felt grounded. I found that I was tempted to make my move permanent, but when I placed a call to my daughter back home in Georgia, I was brought back to reality. Hearing her voice and that of my grandchildren was all it took to remind me that my true home was there with them. I could tell she was concerned, but I assured her that I would be home just as soon as I could. We have a close relationship, but trust one another enough not to pry. I think she probably thought I had found a new man because she dropped a few hints and I decided to let her assume that. My past was in Ohio, but my future was firmly established in the deep South. I didn't tell her why I had decided to stay on, but promised to keep in touch.

The second call I made was to Jack. He refused to say whether he had been successful or not, saying only that I had the day off and to make good use of my time. I got the feeling that he was covering up, but didn't push. He held all the cards and wasn't ready to reveal them. For a man with his insurmountable disabilities, he wielded more strength of character than anyone I had ever met. If circumstances had been different, I could have easily imagined myself falling in love with him. I thought back to my conversation with my daughter and admitted that maybe her instincts had been right after all. Maybe I was staying on for Jack's sake as much as the McCoy mystery. He was certainly becoming more important to me than I ever expected, but my romantic fantasies quickly faded when I thought about our mission. We simply had to do whatever we could to bring the murderer into the light of day and put our personal feelings aside.

The next morning after an extravagant homemade breakfast, I walked to the convalescent center. My heart skipped a beat when I saw a State of Ohio van in the parking lot. I rushed down the hall to Jack's room and nearly collided with a man pushing an empty dolly coming out. Jack was in his wheelchair with his back to the door, trying to open the top carton with his one good hand. I slipped in beside him and hugged him.

"I don't even want to know how you managed this, Jack," I grinned, "why don't you let me get that open for you?"

"It's about time you showed up," he grumbled, "I'm about to scream here. I would give anything to make this stupid body of mine do what I want it to!"

"Now settle down there, Chief," I said pulling his wheelchair back so that I could get at the carton, "you can't be getting yourself all worked up here. Save your strength for the cerebral stuff and let me do the grunt work. Okay?"

"Okay! Just get the damn thing open and let's see what they sent. I practically had to promise my last drop of blood to get this stuff!"

The entire state investigation was contained in three large cartons. One contained files and the others held physical evidence gathered from the crime scene. These items were all in plastic bags with labels describing the contents. I could see brown stains on the articles of clothing through the plastic and felt my stomach flip. I folded the top of that one back down, focusing instead on the one containing the files. I knew we would have to look at them eventually, but I wanted to hold off as long as I could. Seeing those personal belongings just made it all the more real.

A list of the box's contents was attached to the first file with a rubber band that had gotten brittle over the years and snapped in two when I tried to remove it. I handed the list to Jack.

"Well, at least they had some method to their madness. We won't have to waste time rummaging around like we did with the local files," Jack noted.

He handed the list back to me. On it was listed a coroner's report, photos, diagrams, ballistics report, shoe print evidence report, blood analysis, additional copies of witness interviews and one item that surprised me. It was a psychological report by a psychiatrist who examined Mark shortly after the murders.

I gave him the file containing the coroner's original report. Each of the victim's report had a drawing of a human figure with various wounds drawn in and labeled by the pathologist that conducted the autopsies. The upper two thirds of Pat McCoy's head had been shaded out as missing. There were also photos of the autopsies as they were in progress. Jack was as stoical as before, but it was all I could do to look at them. Seeing those poor people laid out like hunks of meat was almost more than I could take.

"Well, they seemed to do a pretty thorough job with the bodies," Jack commented. "According to this, there is no doubt that Pat McCoy was a drinker. His liver was in the first stages of cirrhosis not to mention the fact that the serology report indicates a blood alcohol content of 0.2%. There was also an indication of heart and lung disease. The guy was killing himself."

"Yeah, until somebody blew his head off! Geez, Jack, look at the damage to his head. About all that's left is his lower jaw. The rest is just gone!"

"Yeah, poor bastard! Let's see what it says about Loretta and Becky."

The diagram of Loretta's body showed massive damage to her left side and around to the middle of her back. A full shot of the body had been taken from both sides. She was a small woman with dark hair and from the right side looked as if she were sleeping. From the left side, it appeared that she had nearly been shot in two. There was no way to associate her serene expression with the horror that had been inflicted on her body. The damage to her torso was so extensive there was no way she could have survived the attack.

There were some old bruises on the side of her face and upper arms noted by the pathologist. His report stated that in his opinion they were at least a week old at the time of her death.

"So, I wonder where Loretta got those bruises," Jack muttered, "care to take a guess?"

"You know as well as I do, Jack! That poor woman! There's no telling what kind of hell her life must have been married to Patrick McCoy! No wonder somebody took him out. He really was a piece of work, wasn't he?"

"Just because he may have punched his wife doesn't mean he deserved to die the way he did, Ellen. She could have left him. Her brother would have taken her in. She stayed with him because she wanted to."

"Maybe, but she had two kids and no job skills. There's no indication that she worked outside of the house. Back then it wasn't so easy to leave an abusive husband. Divorce had a stigma to it back then that it doesn't now. Now people get divorces faster than they get married. I hope you're not suggesting she asked for whatever happened to her!"

"Okay, simmer down, Ms. Woman's Liberation!" Jack quipped, "I am merely saying that if she had left the son of a bitch she might be enjoying her golden years now instead of rotting away in her grave!"

"Yeah, well she died because of him and it just makes me mad! Sorry, I'll get down off my soapbox now."

"We assume that Pat was the primary target, but we don't know that for sure. Let's not make any assumptions until we have the proof, deal?"

"Deal."

The last report was that of the child, Becky McCoy. From the gruesome photographs taken at autopsy it didn't take an expert to see what had caused her death. The right posterior of her skull was smashed in. They had taken a close up of the wound with a technician's gloved hand holding a ruler to indicate its dimensions. The report stated that it was consistent with the size and shape of a gunstock. There were some wood fragments imbedded in the tissue as well, which led them to believe that the gun had been damaged in the attack. The report contained x-rays of Becky's skull that showed cracks radiating out from the area of impact. Their conclusion was that she had only been hit once, but with enough force to kill her instantly.

"Well, if their assumption was correct, at least she didn't suffer," I noted. "She was such a pretty little girl, what kind of animal would do such a horrible thing?"

"That does seem to be the question of the hour, doesn't it?" Jack replied, closing the file and gazing out the window.

"Jack, what about the people who knew Pat McCoy? What if they were covering up something? Maybe it's time we talked to them, you know, see if their stories have changed over time? What do you think?" I asked.

"You're forgetting that this thing happened over thirty years ago. There's the possibility that a lot of them are dead and gone now. Pat was forty-two when he was killed. If his associates were close in age, they'd be in their seventies now. I doubt that you'd be able to get much out of them. If there was a cover-up, they've kept their mouths shut for a mighty long time."

"But maybe the killer is dead now or too old to be a threat to them," I insisted. "Or maybe they think it's too late to do anything about it. What's the harm in checking it out? Maybe there's somebody that the police never interviewed. There's the bar owner, the cook, and that Silky Swartz guy. They all said they didn't know the man who had the bar fight with Pat. Maybe they found out who that man was later, but decided they don't want to get involved. The police never followed up. Who knows? Swartz said that Pat had girlfriends, but they were never named. If I could locate those women, they may know something. I know I'm grasping at straws, but we're getting nowhere with what we have so far."

"So now you're convinced that Mark didn't do it?"

"No, all I'm saying is that he apparently wasn't the only one who didn't get along with Pat. Maybe he did just find them after the real killer left the scene. It is possible, wouldn't you say?"

"At this point, anything is possible. I guess it wouldn't hurt to look for any other potential witnesses that were overlooked in the original investigation. What about the risk? You were the one, who came up with the theory that Earl's death and my accident are somehow connected to this thing," he reminded me.

"Okay, I did think that at first. But you were the one who insisted that there was no indication of foul play related to your shooting, and Earl may have simply gotten liquored up and killed himself like everyone seems to believe. Both events could be merely coincidences. It's a little late for me to be worrying about someone being after me. I'm sure half the town knows what I've been up to by now!"

"Things do have a way of getting around. You're probably not going to find anything new anyway. If you're going to insist on pursuing this, all I can say is that you better watch your back. I'm not in a position to protect you."

"Well, what a nice thing to say, Chief! Don't worry, I'll be careful."

We spent the rest of the afternoon rereading the transcripts and making a list of potential witnesses. I noticed Jack watching me with worry on his face when he thought I wasn't looking. It felt good to know that I had someone who cared about me that way. There had only been one other man who showed such concern for my welfare and he was dead. I found that I missed my husband more than I had realized. The task that lay ahead of me loomed in my thoughts. I wished that I didn't have to do it alone, but there was nothing I could do about it. We plunged ahead. I would just have to face whatever I was able to flush out of the bushes. I was like a woman possessed.

Chapter Fifteen

Later, as I reread Mark's statement, something occurred to me. "Jack, there's something about this that puzzles me."

"What's that? We've gone over his statement several times. He really didn't say much. What's your question."

"I don't know why we didn't notice it before. It isn't his statement, it's his attorney."

"What about him. The guy seemed to do a pretty good job, actually better than I would have expected back then. Most of the local lawyers were pretty lame."

"That's just it. The guy was more than adequate, he was really good. It just doesn't make sense. Mark was a kid from a family whose only source of income was an alcoholic father. I know where they lived, Jack, they were hardly wealthy people. He was under suspicion for committing the murders, so any insurance he may have had coming would have been tied up pending the investigation. Where would someone like that come up with the money to hire a really good attorney? Who do you suppose paid for it?"

"I just assumed it was his uncle, Jim Patterson. Why?"

"Does it say in there what Patterson did for a living?"

"According to this he was a long distance truck driver," Jack noted when he had found the report. "So?"

"I may be wrong here, but truck drivers back in 1968 weren't exactly rolling in dough. What if someone else paid for Mark's attorney? Maybe someone who killed his parents and wanted to help the son out of guilt over it. Maybe that person didn't mean to kill Loretta and Becky and didn't want to see Mark get blamed for it. What do you think?"

"And maybe Jim Patterson took out a second mortgage to pay for his nephew's lawyer. Geez, Ellen! That's a pretty long stretch!"

"Jack, I thought you police types acted on hunches all the time! That's what all the good TV cops do!" I countered, disappointed that he had dismissed my idea out of hand.

"Okay, Sherlock! Don't get your feelings hurt. It probably wouldn't hurt to see if the law firm is still in existence, though I doubt that even if they are they would have records going back that far, but if it will make you feel better, you may was well add them to your list."

"I already have, thank you," I sniffed. "If it's okay with you, I've got a lot of calling to do. How about I leave you to continue going through this stuff while I run home and get on the phone?"

"Okay, how about dragging those boxes over here where I can reach them. You be careful, now, you hear?" he said over his reading glasses that had slipped to the end of his nose.

"Don't worry, Chief. I will be the picture of discretion!" I assured him grabbing my purse and heading out the door.

When I reached the house, I immediately went to the phone book. I was only able to find listings in the local directory for Mark's uncle, Jim Patterson and Gerald Yarborough, father of Gary, Mark's friend. Tommy Czerwinski the cook, Dick Chance the bar owner and Homer Swartz weren't listed, which wasn't surprising since they had lived in Huron where the bar was. I tried directory assistance and got a number for Richard Chance and Homer Swartz, but there was no listing for any Czerwinski's. It took longer to find the law firm. The attorney's name was Lawrence Moore and according to my notes, he had been located in Cleveland. There were three law firms in the Cleveland area that had Moore's, but I finally found someone who heard of him at the firm of Erickson, Moore & Lieberman in Shaker Heights. The receptionist told me that Lawrence Moore was one of the founding partners, but had retired a few years ago. She wouldn't give me his home phone number, but said she would call him and see if he would return my call.

With my list in hand, I began making phone calls. I had just tried the number for Richard Chance when I was startled by a knock on the front door. I whipped open the door, angry at the interruption and thinking that it was someone selling something and was shocked to see Chief Taylor on the stoop. With my heart hammering in my chest, I managed to choke out, "Chief Taylor! You're the last person I would expect to see! What are you doing here?"

"Hello, Ms. Richardson. May I come in?" he asked quietly.

I mutely stepped out of his way and he took a seat on the couch, removing his cap and resting it on his knee.

"So, what can I do for you, Chief?" I asked, still reeling from his unexpected appearance and afraid he had come about the files we had "borrowed".

"I understand you have been spending a lot of time with Chief Miller lately," he began, gesturing for me to take a seat in the chair across from him. I hadn't moved from my spot by the door where I had been rooted since he arrived. I walked over on shaky legs, sat and faced him.

"Uh huh," I answered cautiously.

"You know I warned him about you," he said accusingly.

"I wasn't aware that it is against the law to visit patients in nursing homes," I countered defiantly then biting my tongue at my stupidity, but unable to control myself.

"Nope, no laws against that!" he laughed, irritating me even more at his arrogant tone. "Actually, I have a great deal of respect for the man."

"I'm sure there's a lot you could learn from a man with his experience," I added, knowing I was just antagonizing him, but powerless to stop. A vision of me falling through the ice came unbidden into my mind. Why couldn't I just keep my big mouth shut?

Instead of taking offense, he smiled and nodded. "Yes, you're probably right about that," he agreed to my amazement.

"So how did you know to find me here?" I asked, figuring I may as well find out as much as I could while he was in such a congenial mood.

"It was purely by accident, I assure you," he said, "I was talking to Pat Cornwall this morning and she said you had rented this place. I thought you would have gone back home right after the Festival. That was what you led me to believe anyway."

"So? I changed my plans. Are you telling me I can't stay around town if I want to? What exactly do you want from me, Chief Taylor?" I demanded, angry that Pat Cornwall obviously couldn't keep her mouth shut either.

"Relax, Ms. Richardson, I'm not here to give you a hard time! You're welcome to stay as long as you like!" he assured me.

"Okay, whatever you say, Chief Taylor," I said, rising to my feet, "thank you for playing the welcome wagon lady, now if you don't mind, I'm in the middle of something and if you don't mind, I'd like to get back to it!"

"You're still trying to find out who killed the McCoy's, aren't you?" he said staring into my eyes pointedly without making any indication that he intended to end our conversation anytime soon.

I sank back down on my chair without a word and waited for him to lower the boom.

"Look, Ms. Richardson, I know you don't like me and to be perfectly honest, I don't blame you. I came down pretty hard on you," he admitted to my surprise, "and I meant what I said. I didn't come here to cause you any trouble, although I could in light of some files that have mysteriously disappeared from storage."

"So you know about that, huh?" I managed to choke out.

"I am not as inept as you apparently think I am, Ms. Richardson. I knew it was just a matter of time once you got together with Jack Miller before it happened. I didn't buy his line about those boxes in his room containing old library books for a second. He's a wily old fox, but he's not a very good liar."

"So what happens now, Chief? Are you going to haul me off to jail? You've been wanting to do that since I set foot in this god forsaken town!"

"Oh, believe me, if you'd have asked me that question a few days ago, I would have liked nothing better! But I've had some time to think about it. Our personality clashes aside, I have to admit I admire your tenacity. There are not many people that would have kept it up like you have. You're like a dog with a rag, you know that, Ms. Richardson?" he laughed.

"Well, thanks for the compliment, I think," I said, still having no clue where this was going. "So you've decided to spare me the indignity of arresting me, what is it that you want? Are you going to confiscate the files or what?"

"To the contrary, I've come to offer my assistance to you and Chief Miller. If you are determined to do this thing, you might as well have some help. You know you are in need of some professional help, Ms. Richardson. You are certainly a well-meaning lady, but trust me, you won't get anywhere without official authority. You'd just be spinning your wheels, and Jack, well, he is as smart as they come, but he is an invalid after all. Admit it, you both need me!"

"Wait just a minute, Chief Taylor!" I cried, not willing to believe his sudden reversal in attitude, "there's more to this than you're telling me. I simply refuse to believe that there isn't something else that has caused this miraculous change of heart. Have I stepped on the wrong toes and you've been sent to keep an eye on me or something?" I asked suspiciously.

"There's no conspiracy afoot here, Ms. Richardson. I assure you. Actually I wasn't going to mention this to you, because I didn't want to alarm you, but after our conversation at the Festival about Earl Henderson's car wreck, I looked a little closer at it."

"You have got to be kidding! I got the impression that I didn't make a dent in that thick wall you threw up between us! Are you telling me you actually listened to me?" I said incredulously.

"Well, I didn't at first. But we sent out some guys from the Department of Transportation to take some pictures of the skid marks so that we could close the file on it the same way we do with all fatalities and you know what they indicated?"

"Don't tell me, let me guess," I said with a feeling of dread creeping into my heart, "there were two sets of skid marks, weren't there?"

"Yep, somebody forced Earl's truck off the road. There's no doubt about it. His death has been ruled a possible homicide. I'm afraid you were right. Somebody didn't want him talking to you about the McCoy murders. I think it's time to let the experts take over, Ms. Richardson."

"Now just a damn minute, Chief Taylor! I'm the one who started this whole mess and I'm going to see it through to its conclusion! So if you think I'm going to turn tail and run, you are wrong!"

"I figured you'd say that. That's why I didn't suggest that you leave, even though you really should. I can't protect you 24 hours a day!"

"I am sick to death of all the intrigue going on around here!" I yelled shaking with rage and fear. "This used to be my town too, damn it! I've seen what was done to those people and by God, I'm going to find out who did it! You hear me, Andy?"

"Okay, settle down, there's no need to yell. I'm on your side, okay? I'm just saying that we need to be really careful going forward. That's all."

"Well, since we're on the subject, I happen to think that maybe the same person put a bullet in Jack's back to shut him up too, if you must know!" I grumbled.

"So that's why he's gotten involved!" he said, "I knew there was some reason he would stick his neck out with the state police!"

"What? You mean you know about that too?" I asked, stunned at his admission.

"Did you think I wouldn't find out about it? The state police commissioner called me this morning to let me know Jack was nosing around one of our old cases. You really are a babe in the woods aren't you?" he said shaking his head.

"So why are you willing to let me stay on? You've now got an active case in Earl Henderson. You certainly don't need a rank amateur like me mucking up the works!" I said, stung by his last comment.

"I think you may have something to bring to the table, Ms. Richardson, in a strictly unofficial capacity. Call it feminine intuition, whatever. Lots of people have looked into the matter, but they have all been men. Who knows, maybe something was overlooked that only could be noticed from a woman's perspective. It's worth a try, don't you think?"

"Well, thank you for that," I said somewhat mollified.

"So what were you doing when I showed up unannounced? Doing a little research perhaps?"

"As a matter of fact, I was trying to get in touch with some of the people that talked to the police back then. I thought that maybe something new would turn up. Jack says I'm wasting my time, but it's my time to waste. Why? Do you think I'm doing the wrong thing?"

"Actually, I think that's an excellent idea! Why don't you show me what you've got so far? I may know something about those people and save you some time."

I hesitated to show him, not sure if he could be trusted, but he seemed so sincere, I walked into the kitchen and got my list. I brought it back to him and he looked it over with a scowl.

"It's going to take us a while to cover all this, Ms. Richardson. Would it be too much trouble for you to fix us a little something to eat? I skipped lunch and could sure use a sandwich."

I caught myself feeling resentful of his assumption that I, being a woman, would immediately be relegated to kitchen duty, but stifled the thought. He had agreed to include me in the investigation and I knew I needed him.

"Sure, Chief," I said forcing a smile, "and please, call me Ellen."

"I like lots of mayo, Ellen," he grinned, "and please, call me Andy!"

Chapter Sixteen

"So, why don't you tell me what you've got so far," Andy said around a bite of the ham sandwich I had made for him.

"Nothing new unfortunately. We've just basically been going over the statements of the people the police talked to. So far all the evidence points to Mark, but there's nothing to link him directly to the crime. There's the matter of the missing time between when he discovered the bodies and arrived at the Yarborough home. But like Jack says, without evidence, witnesses or a confession, we've got nothing."

"Why is his lawyer on the list? I hope you know that even if he's still practicing, he's not going to tell you anything Mark may have said to him. You know how lawyers are about client confidentiality."

"I not a total idiot, Andy! I have no intention of asking him about that! Actually, I was going to ask him who paid his retainer. Mark's family wasn't in a position to pay a high priced defense attorney, so I thought that maybe someone involved in the murder may have paid him. Maybe that person wanted to make up for not coming forward by helping out the son. I know it's a long shot, but it can't hurt to check. Jack thinks I'm barking up the wrong tree, but I've already got a call into the guy, so I'll just have to see what he says."

"So you are willing to accept that there may have been someone other than Mark that committed the crime? You know how I feel about that. I've known Mark for a long time and he just never struck me as a violent person. I figured you were out to crucify the guy."

"Well, you were wrong! I'm interested in the truth. I have nothing against Mark McCoy. In fact nothing would make me happier than to find the person who did it. I'd be doing him a favor! This has had to be weighing on him his whole life!"

"I glad to hear you say that, Ellen. It's best to go into something like this with an open mind. Do you want me to talk to the guy when he calls? He might say more to me. I've had a lot more experience talking to lawyers."

I felt as though he was stealing my thunder, but he was probably right. Men seem better equipped to get cooperation from people than women are. It's just one of those irritating facts of life.

"Yeah, you're probably right. I hope this doesn't mean you plan to leave me out of everything!" I said defensively.

"I promise not to cut you out, Ellen. As soon as the call comes in, you can call these other people and set up the interviews. Does that make you feel better?"

"I'm sorry I'm being so difficult, but I've been working on this for a while now and I guess I'm afraid you will take over completely. I've put my life on hold for this, Andy!"

"I know that, Ellen. I may have been a jerk about this before, but I happen to think you're pretty special, so let's try to work together on this. I have a feeling that we both have a lot to offer. Okay?"

"Okay!" I replied, relieved that we had reached an understanding.

The phone rang and I handed the phone to Andy. He answered my unspoken question with a nod. It was Lawrence Moore. Andy introduced himself as Chief of Police, telling Moore that he was reviewing the McCoy case. I gathered from Andy's end of the conversation that Moore was refusing to discuss anything Mark had said. When Andy asked about the payment of his retainer, he covered the receiver with his hand.

"He's pretty sharp for an old guy," he said to me softly, "he's going to go see if he has a record. We may be in luck. He says he's kept all his old files at his house. Says he just can't throw anything out and it drives his wife crazy."

Moore came back on the line and Andy responded with 'yes', 'I see', 'are you sure?' and 'thanks' and hung up.

He didn't say anything at first. He just sat there staring at the phone with a strange look on his face. I was about to burst with curiosity.

"Come on, Andy! What did he say? You look like you didn't expect the answer he gave you!"

"Oh that puts it mildly," he said, shaking his head, "if I hadn't heard it myself, I would never have believed it."

"Andy! I'm dying here! Who did he say paid him?"

"Dan Albertson! The mayor! I know he and Mark are business associates. He's a partner in Mark's car business, but I had no idea the friendship went back that far."

"They aren't related or anything are they?" I asked.

"Not that I'm aware of," he replied.

"Now why would a man like Mayor Albertson pay for an expensive attorney for a poor kid like Mark McCoy? Do you have any ideas?"

"Maybe it was a loan. Maybe he figured he'd get his money back when Mark was cleared of the crime from the insurance money or something," he suggested.

"That's a pretty flimsy reason to shell out big bucks, Andy! He would have no way of knowing whether Mark did it or not! If he had been charged and convicted, Albertson would never have gotten his money back. Call me cynical, but most people with money are a little more careful than that! I know he's your boss, Andy, but there's something about this that doesn't smell right! You know that as well as I do!"

"Damn it, Ellen, Dan Albertson is one of the nicest people I know! He's practically built this town single-handedly. Sometimes I hate my job!" he cried.

"You were the one who said we need to keep an open mind, Andy," I reminded him, "that means that we have to consider everybody a suspect. Maybe he was covering up for the real killer, but didn't have the heart to let Mark take the blame. Who knows, maybe he knew something or maybe he is just a real saint, we won't know until we talk to him. You know we are going to have to talk to him, Andy!"

"I know that, Ellen! I'm not going to let my personal feelings get in the way of doing my duty. It's just that this puts a whole different spin on things!"

"Maybe this thing goes a lot deeper than anyone ever suspected. Who's to say that maybe Chief Talbot was involved in some kind of cover up and the Mayor was involved. Of course we'll never know, because Talbot's dead."

"Yeah, but Dan Albertson is very much alive. Man, I wish there was some other way to do this without going to him!"

"Well, there are still the other surviving witnesses that we haven't interviewed. This thing has been stewing for over thirty years. There's no reason we have to tip our hand just yet. Maybe we'll learn something from them that will point the finger away from him. Look on the bright side, we may be able to clear him of any wrong doing without his ever being aware of it. I'm willing to wait if you are," I offered.

"Okay, I guess it couldn't hurt to do a little more digging before going to Dan. Why don't you start calling the other people on your list?"

He handed me the phone and I began calling. I was able to reach Mark's uncle, Jim Patterson and Gary Yarborough's father Gerald. Both agreed to speak with us. It took a couple of calls to reach Dick Chance. His wife answered and said that even though his son had taken over the bar, he still went down there to keep an eye on things. There was no answer at the Swartz residence, but I left a message on the answering machine.

"Okay, everything's set. Jim Patterson sounded like he would be happy to talk to us, but Gerald Yarborough was not very pleased about it. I guess he still wishes he'd never gotten involved. Are you still having second thoughts about talking to the Mayor? I'm game if you are," I said.

"No, let's just talk to these other guys and see what they have to say. I'm just not ready to put my job on the line just yet."

"You mean you think you may get fired for doing what you're paid to do?" I asked incredulously.

"Ellen, you really are naïve, aren't you? I better have a pretty good reason to go accusing the Mayor of covering up a murder. That is just reality!"

"Then I say, let's get to it! I want to stop by the nursing home first and let Jack know what's going on. You ready?"

We drove to Shady Oaks in Andy's squad car. I wondered what Jack's reaction would be when he found out about Andy's change of heart. I hoped he would see it as a step in the right direction. I wasn't disappointed.

"Man, you two are an unlikely pair!" he commented as soon as we entered his room. "How's it going there, Chief?"

The two men shook hands. I stood back feeling a little awkward in case things didn't go as well as I hoped.

"So what brings you by, Andy? Ellen here giving you a hard time?" Jack said glancing in my direction and searching my face for an explanation.

"Actually, Ellen and I have kissed and made up, Jack," he laughed and then more seriously, "but there's been some developments that have convinced me that you two could use a hand with what you've been doing. I see the library sent over some of our old files. I wonder how they got those?" he asked, gesturing at the open file on Jack's tray table.

"Okay, you got me," Jack said, guiltily flipping it shut, "are you going to take them away?"

"On the contrary, Jack. I'm offering my assistance, at least with the McCoy deal. There may have been a recent homicide related to it and frankly, we can use all the help we can get. I can't reopen the McCoy case unless I get some new evidence. Your protégé here has convinced me that there may be some new information out there."

"What's the new case, Andy?" Jack asked, his eyes lighting up at the mention of something a little more recent than thirty years ago.

"You know Earl Henderson?"

"Not personally, but Ellen told me about him. She seems to think he may have known something and got killed by someone involved. Why, did you turn up something suspicious about his accident?"

"Yeah, it looks like someone helped him run into that tree, just like Ellen suspected. So far, we've got zilch, but it sure makes you wonder."

"That makes her theory about my so-called accidental shooting sound like it may hold water."

"Okay, you guys," I interrupted what was fast becoming a good old boy's reunion and tiring of being talked about as if I weren't in the room, "now that we are all on the same team, can we get on with it? I told Jim Patterson we would be out to his house in 15 minutes. Andy, we need to get going! Jack, is there anything you need while we're out?"

"I wouldn't holler if you brought me a burger and fries," he smiled, "you look out for my girl here, Andy."

"You got it, Chief," Andy smiled pointing a finger in Jack's direction.

We left him rummaging around in the box containing the physical evidence from the state crime lab. I was glad I had an excuse not to be present when he pulled out the bloody contents. I had seen more carnage than I had ever seen or hoped to ever see again. I felt better knowing that we had two experts now, instead of one.

We arrived at the Patterson's house a few minutes late, but were met at the door by Mark's Uncle Jim. He was a wiry old gentleman with a shock of short white hair and ruddy complexion. I could see a family resemblance to Mark in him. He escorted us to the living room and offered us something to drink, which we both refused.

"So you want to talk about the murders," he said, getting right to the point.

"Yes sir," Andy replied, taking the lead, "Ms. Richardson and I are interested in anything you may remember about events that happened back then. I realize it's been an awfully long time and memories fade, but anything you can tell us would be helpful."

"Memories fade, you say? Hah! That's a laugh! I remember it like it was yesterday! That son of a bitch Pat McCoy got my sister and niece killed!" he cried, "and you people brushed it under the rug! I bet if they'd have been rich, you'd have fallen all over yourselves trying to find out who did it! Nobody gives a damn about poor people!"

"I can only say that the police did what they could at the time, Mr. Patterson," Andy said soothingly, "I was just a little kid in 1968. I assure you that had I been Chief back then, I would have left no stone unturned, no matter who was killed."

"Yeah, well Art Talbot couldn't find his butt with both hands! All he wanted was to pin it on Mark and when he couldn't, he gave up. I wouldn't be surprised if his buddies in City Hall had something to do with it. The whole lot of 'em didn't look past their noses!"

"Were you aware that Mayor Albertson paid for the services of Lawrence Moore, Mark's attorney?" I asked.

"Oh yeah, he's a peach, ain't he?" the old man snapped.

Andy and I exchanged glances.

"So how did that happen? Did you approach Mr. Albertson for a loan?" Andy asked.

"Loan? Mister, I couldn't have borrowed a dime to make a phone call back then! Nah, he came to me! He kept going on about what a terrible thing it was for a boy to be suspected of such a horrible thing! Said he would pay for everything! I told him we didn't need his damn charity! The next thing I know, Mark's got some slick city defense lawyer calling the shots. I never asked for nothing from this town. Mark thinks he's the best thing to come down the pike, but I think he's as dirty as the rest of 'em! I think he was covering his ass. Rich folks don't just up and do stuff like that!"

"I see," Andy said quietly, "do you have any idea who he may have been covering up for? Is there someone you may have suspected, other than your nephew?"

"Look, Chief. Pat McCoy was as rotten as they come. He was into all kinds of dirty business. I think he pissed off the wrong person and they blew his Goddamn head off! My sister just had the dumb luck of being married to the son of a bitch and paid the price for her stupidity."

"What kind of 'dirty business' are you referring to, Mr. Patterson?" I asked.

"Ma'am, you look like a real upstanding lady, but if you'll pardon my language, he couldn't keep his dick in his pants. He was constantly chasing skirts down at that damn tavern he hung out at. He probably messed with the wrong man's woman and got killed for it. I told my sister to leave him, but she just wouldn't listen. Every time she caught him, she'd take him back. Then, he'd beat her up and she'd come crying to me. I washed my hands of her after a while. Course, now I wish I hadn't, because she's gone! I feel like I should have been there for her and I wasn't! You have no idea how this has weighed on my conscience all these years!"

"I'm sure you did the best you could at the time, Mr. Patterson," I said, "there was no way you could have known something like that was going to happen."

"Well, I tried my best to do the right thing by Mark. That is until Dan Albertson got a hold of him. He got him to enlist in the army. I figured I'd lose him too when he got sent to Vietnam."

129

"So it was Dan Albertson's idea that he join the army?"

"That's what I said."

"How did he manage that when the police were still in the middle of the investigation? I was one of Mark's classmates. I remember he disappeared right after the murders," I said. "The investigation must still have been going on."

"Yeah, makes you wonder, don't it. I figured old Dan just pulled some strings and made it happen. I was against it from the beginning, but like I said, Mark did anything Dan told him to do!"

"And when Mark came back, he invested in his car business," Andy interjected.

"Oh, he did more than that! He practically bought the dealership for him! We sure didn't have the money to set him up! Dan Albertson owns Mark lock, stock and barrel!"

"Well, you've certainly been very helpful, Mr. Patterson," Andy said, rising to leave.

"I personally don't think you two have got a dog's chance to find the guy that killed my sister and her little girl, but I appreciate your trying," he said, tears welling up in his eyes.

"Thanks for talking to us, Mr. Patterson," I said patting his arm, "I promise we will do everything we can to find out who killed your family."

"Thanks, I sure would like to get this thing out in the open. It wouldn't bring them back, but at least somebody would finally have to pay."

We left him and walked in silence to Andy's squad car. When we got inside, I turned to Andy, "so, what do you think? It isn't looking very good for your boss. At least as far as Uncle Jim is concerned."

"He is certainly a bitter old man, but he doesn't have any more proof than we do. I think we need to check out the next person on the list. Maybe somebody will give us something concrete to go on."

The next stop was the home of Gerald Yarborough. It was on the outskirts of town in a semi-rural area. Two snarling German Shepherds escorted our car up the long gravel driveway.

"Let's hope Mr. Yarborough is friendlier than his dogs," I said, warily eyeing their raised hackles and bared teeth.

"I hadn't counted on having to wade through a forest of fangs," Andy grunted, bringing the squad car to a halt a short distance from the front porch.

"Screw this!" he muttered and tapped on the horn.

The noise sent the dogs into a renewed paroxysm of barking. The screen door flew open and Gerald Yarborough came to the edge of the porch and began yelling at them. They didn't immediately back off, so he ducked into the house and came back out with a couple of dog chains in his hands. When he got close to them they broke off the attack and cowered on the ground at his feet. He snapped the chains to the collar of each dog in turn and dragged them around to the back of the house. When he came back around without them, Andy and I stepped from the car.

"I'll bet you don't have to worry about any prowlers with those guys around!" I laughed nervously, over the top of the car hoping to break the ice with him.

"You bet your ass!" he spat. "They keep the salesmen and Bible thumpers away, just the way I like it!"

With all the excitement over, I got a better look at him. He was in his late sixties or early seventies, but still a bear of a man. He was nearly bald except for a ring of short gray hair around the sides and back of his head. He was dressed in old tattered work pants and a stained undershirt that stretched over the expanse of his ample belly. He wore the expression of someone that was angry at the world in general and certainly was not pleased that we had interrupted his day.

"May we come in, Mr. Yarborough? It will only take a few minutes." I said politely as I exchanged a glance with Andy.

"I guess I can't stop you, seeing as how you brought the law along with you," he grumbled, gesturing in Andy's direction. "I already talked to the police about the McCoy business years ago. I don't see what more I can say that I haven't said already. Nobody's been able to come up with anything new and it's been over thirty years! They are dead and buried. What's the point in rehashing it now?"

"I went to school with your son, Gary, Mr. Yarborough. You probably don't remember me, but I used to be Ellen Malcolm. I was also in the same class as Mark McCoy. I always assumed that Mark killed his folks, but I've uncovered some information that might point in another direction. I thought that since he was a friend of your son's, you might be willing to talk to us about your impressions from that night. Maybe you can remember something that Mark may have said or done that would support what we've found so far."

"So who do you think did it?" he asked, halting on his return to the porch his impatience mollified temporarily.

"I'm afraid it's still too early for us to name name's, Mr. Yarborough," Andy responded quickly interrupting me. I shot him an irritated look; angry that he would think I would just blurt out such confidential information.

"That's what I figured," he snapped and turned on his heel and continued on his way.

We hustled after him, but he ignored us, went in the front door and let the screen door slam in our faces.

"Please talk to us, Mr. Yarborough," I cried through the mesh, "don't you want to help us find out who killed those people?"

He came back to the door, pushed it open and essentially blocked the entry with his body, making it plain that he did not intend to invite us in.

"I'm going to tell you this just this once," he growled, "I never wanted to get involved in that mess in the first place. Why my idiot son had to let that kid into the house that night, I'll never know. I should have booted him out when I had the chance! The old Chief, Talbot, raked me over the coals for tampering with evidence, when I cleaned the blood off that kid's hands and practically accused me of aiding and abetting a felon. I tried to be a good neighbor, against my better judgement, I might add and got slammed for it. If you think you can find out who did it, more power to you! I washed my hands of the whole thing thirty years ago and have no intention of getting involved again. Now if you don't mind, I got work to do!"

With that, he let the screen door slam shut and closed the wooden door on us.

I started to knock on the door to try and reason with him, but Andy stopped me.

"Come on, Ellen, let's go. He made it pretty plain he has no intention of talking to us. He probably doesn't have anything to add anyway!"

I was disappointed, but had to agree. We had no authority to make him talk to us. We'd just have to keep looking.

We weren't expected for our appointment with Dick Chance for another hour since our interview with Gerald had been cut short, so Andy drove me back home to check my new answering machine for a message from Silky Swartz. He still hadn't called, so we got a couple of soft drinks and updated our notes on what we wanted to ask the bar owner when we met with him.

Later, when we walked into Dick's Tavern, it took a while for our eyes to adjust to the gloom. It was like walking into a cave. Although the sun was shining outside, all the windows on the front had been blacked out and the interior of the bar was dark. The walls and ceiling were painted black and the only illumination were the small wall sconces on the wall over the bar and the red and blue neon beer signs. The air was laced with the smell of stale cigarette smoke, mold and old grease.

A long mahogany bar ran the length of the room with battered bar stools in front. There was a mirror centrally positioned between the shelves of liquor bottles on the wall behind it. Several small tables and chairs were scattered around the remaining space with a row of high-backed red plastic covered booths along the opposite wall.

The bartender had his back to us when we approached. He was washing glasses in the small sink behind the bar. The place was essentially deserted except for two old men seated in one of the booths nursing a couple of beers.

Andy noisily cleared his throat and the bartender turned his head at the sound.

"Oh, sorry! I didn't hear you come in. What can I do for you folks?" he asked drying his hands on a towel.

I knew at once that this couldn't be Dick Chance. This man was in his late thirties or early forties. He was short with slicked back black hair and a pasty complexion.

"We have an appointment with Mr. Chance," I said.

"I'm Chance," he responded quizzically, "I don't remember making any appointments with anybody."

"I meant to say, Dick Chance. Are you his son?"

"Oh, yeah. Hey, Pop! There's some people hear to see you," he shouted in the direction of the two men seated at the rear of the room.

One of them looked in our direction, said something to his companion and walked over.

"Mr. Chance? I'm Ellen Richardson, we spoke on the phone earlier. This is Chief Taylor with the Milan police department."

We all shook hands and I got right to the point, "Is there somewhere we could go that's a little more private? We'd rather keep our conversation confidential if that's all right with you."

He nodded and led us through the flip up section of the bar through the swinging doors that led into the kitchen area. There was a tiny office in the corner and we squeezed into the wooden chairs on one side of the cluttered desk, while Chance took the swivel chair behind it.

"So what can I do for you, Ms. Richardson?" he asked brushing the stacks of receipts out of his way.

"First of all, let me say how much we appreciate your talking to us, Mr. Chance," I began, praying that he would be more cooperative than our last interviewee had been.

"Hey, I got nothing but time," he smiled, "my boy runs the place now. I just come here and get in his way. Old habits are hard to break!"

We laughed politely and I felt relieved that his reception was so friendly. He was a small man with red cheeks and lively green eyes surrounded by a mass of wrinkles. I got the feeling that he had been a hit with the ladies in his prime.

"As I said on the phone, we are looking into the murder of Pat McCoy and his family back in 1968. I understand you were acquainted with him and his son, Mark. Is that right, Mr. Chance?" I began.

"Yep. Pat was a regular. I wouldn't say he was a friend of mine, but his boy, Mark, seemed like a fairly decent kid. He worked for me before it happened, you know. I understand he's made quite a name for himself in Milan. Got himself a big car

134

dealership and everything. I'm glad he was able to put it behind him. It was a terrible thing that happened to his family."

"So you never suspected him of killing his folks?" I asked.

"Mark? Naw, he just didn't seem like the type to do something like that! That Pat was a real asshole, oops, sorry, Miss. I mean he was a real mean son of a gun. He was okay when he was sober, but nobody dared cross him when he was drinking. Thought he was God's gift to the ladies, too. Though what they saw in the likes of him, I never could figure out."

"That's sort of what we wanted to ask you, Mr. Chance," I said, "the police files contain statements that indicate that there was a confrontation here in your bar between Pat McCoy and an unidentified man a few weeks before the attack. Do you by any chance know what that argument was about?"

"They didn't exactly invite me to take part in the discussion, if that's what you mean! I didn't know there was a problem until the other fella tipped over Pat's table. He grabbed Pat by the shirt and screamed in his face, calling him a son of a bitch and telling him he would pay for whatever it was. I was behind the bar and ran into the kitchen to get Tommy to help me break it up before they tore the place up. I grabbed Pat and Tommy and Silky Swartz grabbed the other guy and pushed him out the door. I told Pat I wanted him to leave as well, but he promised to behave, so I let him stay. He basically just sulked over his beer the rest of the night and didn't give me any more trouble. I never saw the guy in here again. I figured he got over it or else they settled it somewhere else. Why? Do you think that guy might have been the one that killed Pat and his family?"

"We don't know anything for sure, Mr. Chance," Andy said. "But it would help if you could tell us who that man was. We thought maybe you saw him around later somewhere else and just forgot about the incident. There was no reason for you to associate the fight with what happened later."

"I don't think I saw him again, but Silky might know who he was. Do you want me to ask him?" he offered.

"Actually, I have a call in to Mr. Swartz. We'll be talking to him soon if he'll agree to meeting with us," I explained.

"Why wait? That was him I was with when you came in. If you'll sit tight, I'll go see if he'll talk to you," he said and left the room.

"This is great! We'll kill two birds with one stone!" I said to Andy when he was out of earshot.

"Don't get too excited, Ellen. He may refuse to see us."

He had barely said the words, when Dick Chance returned followed by Homer "Silky" Swartz. The years had not been kind to Silky. He looked sickly with stooped shoulders and the wizened old face of a chronic alcoholic. Chance offered his friend his seat behind the desk and leaned against the doorjamb. There simply wasn't enough room in the small space for another chair.

"Thank you, Mr. Swartz, for agreeing to talk to us," I said, "I guess you know from Mr. Chance why we're here."

His eyes darted between Andy and me and he licked his lips nervously.

"I'm not real comfortable around cops, Miss. They have a way to using what you say against you."

"I can assure you, Mr. Swartz, this is not an official inquiry," Andy assured him, "you're not in any trouble here. You may have some information that will help us with a murder investigation. Anything you can tell us will be held in the strictest confidence."

"I don't know! I've had some run-ins with you guys and somehow I always got in trouble. Maybe I better just mind my own business!" he cried, getting up from his chair.

"Please, Mr. Swartz, we really need your help. Like Chief Taylor said, we're just trying to get some information, not make any accusations," I said soothingly.

"Well, I don't know what you think I know!" he said, easing back down into his chair, "I told the police everything I knew back then. Why are you bringing it all up again? It won't bring 'em back, you know!"

"No, it won't. But don't you think it's time the truth came out? Somebody killed the McCoys and got away with it. Wouldn't you feel good to know that you might be able to help us catch this person?" I asked.

"Well, I guess so. But I still don't know what you want from me. Yeah, I knew Pat McCoy. I guess you could say we were friends, sort of. I sold his kid an old car, cheap! You know, just to be a good guy, not that I got one word of thanks from Pat!" he grumbled.

"What about Pat's habit of cheating on his wife? Did you know about that?" I asked.

"Yeah, he had women on the side. So what?"

"Do you know if any of these women may have been married or had steady boyfriends?"

"You asking me if Pat McCoy messed around with other guy's women? Hah! Pat never let a little thing like a husband or boyfriend stand in his way!" he chuckled.

"Tell me, Mr. Swartz, do you by any chance remember the names of any of these women? We'd really like to contact them and ask them some questions. I promise we'll keep your name out of it," I said, crossing my fingers in my lap where he couldn't see them.

He scratched his chin and rolled his bloodshot eyes to the ceiling in thought. I held my breath.

After several moments of silence, his eyes rolled back in my direction and he snapped his fingers.

"Yeah! I think I might know a couple, but you have to promise me that you won't tell them who told you. They're probably married now and wouldn't like to be reminded of what went on back then, if you know what I mean. I sure wouldn't want to cause anybody any trouble!"

"Was McCoy ever seen in public with any of these women, Mr. Swartz?" Andy asked.

"Sure! He didn't make it a secret! He didn't give a shit who saw him! Why?"

"Well, then they won't know who identified them. We could have gotten their names from anybody who had seen them. What do you say, Mr. Swartz? You'd be helping us do the right thing by your friend, Pat!"

He thought about it for a beat and then gave us the names of two women who had associated with Pat McCoy. I jotted down their names and we thanked them both for their cooperation and started to leave.

Just as I stepped through the door on my way out of the little office, a thought occurred to me. I stuck my head back in and addressed Silky.

"Say, Mr. Swartz, I almost forgot! Did you ever find out who that man was that had that fight with Pat McCoy? You know, the one that you, Mr. Chance and Tommy broke up?"

His red face paled. I could tell my question had hit a nerve. He coughed nervously and locked eyes with Chance. Something unspoken passed between them.

"Nope, never did see the guy again!" he said between coughs.

"Well, if a name comes to you, you'll let us know, won't you?" I said, knowing he was lying.

"You betcha, Miss! But my memory ain't so good any more!" he choked.

"Thanks for all your help, gentlemen," I said softly, nodding to each in turn and followed Andy to the car.

"They know, Andy," I said when we reached the car. "They know!"

We drove back to my house in silence.

Chapter Seventeen

Andy had some police business he needed to attend to, so he didn't come in when we reached my house. I promised to call him in the morning as soon as I was able to set up meetings with the women that Silky mentioned. I hadn't spoken with Jack since seeing him that morning, so I called to check in. He reminded me of his request for fast food, so I changed into jeans and tee shirt, hopped into the rental car and made a detour to the burger stand on the way to Shady Oaks.

When I arrived at his room, I expected to see him in his wheelchair, but the staff had put him back in bed. He was lying back on the pillows and his eyes were closed, but there was an open file on the tray table. When I reached out to remove it, his eyes opened and he gave me a smile.

"Did I mention that I like onions?" he said.

"No, but they come with them. Are you all right? You don't look so hot!" I said as I closed the file and placed the bag of food in its place. He looked worn out.

"Aw, the nurse is afraid I'll get sores on my butt if I sit too long. I can't feel anything down there, but they call the shots around here. Hand me some ketchup, will you?" he asked to change the subject.

I squeezed some out from the little plastic pouch from the bag onto his French fries and tucked a paper napkin under his chin.

"Jack, I worry about you overdoing it," I said softly not willing to let the subject drop, "I hope you know that I consider you a friend whether we find the McCoy killer or not!"

"That's probably the nicest thing anybody has said to this old codger in years!" he replied. "But I'm doing just fine. There's no need to go into a panic just because I take a nap now and then!"

"Okay, I'll drop it. Just remember you need to take care of yourself."

"Yes, ma'am," he said rolling his eyes, and then more seriously, "so, what did you and the Chief find out? How'd the interviews go?"

"Actually, all in all, pretty well. Andy talked to Mark's lawyer, Lawrence Moore. I was right about Mark not being able to pay his retainer, but I won't say I told you so. You'll never guess who footed the bill!"

"Okay! I'll give you this one. So lay it on me, who paid?"

"His Honor the Mayor Daniel Albertson! Pretty amazing, wouldn't you say?"

"I knew they were business partners, but Mark was just a kid back then! Yeah, I'd say that's pretty amazing. What did Jim Patterson have to say about it?"

"Uncle Jim doesn't have much use for the Mayor. Andy asked him if it was a loan and he laughed in his face. He said the Mayor just sort of took over everything, including Mark. He said it was the Mayor's idea to ship Mark off to the army. He thinks it was to cover up the real killer."

"I don't suppose he has any idea who that may have been," Jack sniffed popping a French fry in his mouth.

"No, he didn't know any of the same people that Pat did, but he seems to think it had something to do with the husband or boyfriend of one of Pat's girlfriends."

"I suppose that's possible. Of course, it could just as well have had something to do with his gambling habit. Maybe he owned the wrong people big money and couldn't pay. We need to keep that possibility open as well. So, when are you going to broach the subject with Albertson?"

"Andy wants to wait until we get something a little more conclusive before we talk to him," I explained.

"He's probably right. No sense upsetting the apple cart until you have to. I'd probably do the same thing if I were in his shoes. So, were you able to find the bar owner and that other guy, Swartz?"

"As a matter of fact, we met with them both at the same time! They both said pretty much the same thing that they did before. I was able to get a couple of names of women that associated with Pat back then. I figured I'd try to set something up with them in the morning."

"I doubt you'll get much out of them even if they will talk to you. They'd be up in years by now and not thrilled to be reminded of their less than stellar past. I hope you won't be disappointed."

"Well, like my husband used to say, if you don't ask, the answer's no. I'm going to give it a shot, so we'll see if anything new turns up. By the way, something rather curious happened just as I was leaving the interview with Dick Chance and Silky Swartz."

"What's that?"

"Well, Chance insisted that he didn't know the name of the man who had the bar fight with Pat McCoy. Then after we talked to Swartz, we were walking out the door and I realized that I had forgotten to ask him if he knew the man's name. So I did and Jack, I wish you could have seen the look on his face! I thought he was going to choke to death. I think he knows who it was, and I may be wrong, but I think he's scared of the guy. Nothing was said, but I got the impression that Chance knows too, but they are covering it up."

"Huh, that is something, isn't it? If that guy did kill Pat and his family, it would make sense that they'd be afraid of him. That tells us something though doesn't it?"

"What's that?" I asked.

"That means whoever it is, he or she is still alive and a possible threat."

"Why did you say 'she'?"

"Hey, as unlikely as it is that the killer was a woman, we have to keep all our options open, right? Remember the old saying, 'hell hath no fury like a woman scorned'!"

"You know, you're right, Jack!" I said, "I never even considered that the killer could be a woman! You really are sharp for 'an old codger'!" I teased.

"And don't you forget it!" he grinned back, "now hand me something to drink, I need something to wash down these fries."

It was getting dark by the time we finished eating and I could tell that Jack's newfound strength was flagging, so I tidied up his room and pulled the covers up under his chin. I was tempted to kiss his cheek goodnight, but resisted. We had a lot of work ahead of us and it wouldn't do to muddy up the waters by getting too emotionally attached. Maybe we could explore those possibilities when the case reached some sort of resolution. In the meantime, I would just have to keep my heart in check. But I have to admit; it wasn't easy.

When I left the facility and approached my car, I noticed that there was something stuck under the windshield wiper blade. I looked to see if any of the other cars had any under theirs, assuming it was some sort of promotional flyer, but mine was the only one. On closer inspection, it was an envelope with my name printed on the front. I plucked it out from under the wiper and got in my car. I switched on the dome light and tore it open. It contained a single sheet of paper with a message scrawled in big block letters written with a red marker pen. As soon as I read it, my hands began to shake and my body went cold. It said, "IF YOU KNOW WHAT IS GOOD FOR YOU, YOU WILL GO BACK WHERE YOU CAME FROM! YOU DON'T BELONG HERE! THIS TOWN DOES NOT NEED YOU POKING YOUR NOSE INTO THINGS THAT DO NOT CONCERN YOU!"

I sat staring at it in shock. The red letters may as well have been written in blood. I flung it away from me and whipped my head around to be sure that no one was crouching out of sight in the back seat of the car. Thankfully, the rear of the car was empty, but I quickly locked all the doors. Suddenly, I realized that the shadows beneath the bushes around the parking lot could very well be concealing a person watching me. It took a couple of tries to get the key into the ignition with my shaky fingers, but I managed to start the car and flip on the headlights. The light illuminated the area beneath the foliage and to my relief; no one was there. Except for the few cars that belonged to the staff, the parking lot was deserted.

Feeling terribly exposed and alone, I jammed the gearshift into reverse, stomped on the gas, skidded to a halt, put the car in drive and sped out toward the exit in a panic. I flew past my house and continued toward the police station on the other side of town. I hoped that Andy would still be there, since I didn't want anyone else to know about it and I didn't have a clue as to where he lived.

About half way there, I eased off the gas pedal and slowly started to come to my senses. I pulled off to the side of the road and rolled to a stop. I leaned down and picked the note up from the floor where I had thrown it and read it again. Whoever had written it, obviously thought I was getting a little too close to the truth and meant to scare me off. I realized with a start that if I showed it to the Chief, he would take me off the case and make me go home to Georgia just as I was beginning to make some progress. Looking back on it now, I probably should have followed my first instinct and shown it to him, but for some inexplicable reason, I decided against it.

I made a U-turn and drove back to my house. It took all the courage I could muster to enter its darkened interior, but I went through the rooms quickly, switching on lights and checking the closets and under the bed for any intruders. When I had satisfied myself that the house was truly empty, I made sure the doors and windows were secured and turned on the television to mask the silence. I changed into my nightgown and robe, opened a bottle of wine from the refrigerator and poured myself a glassful. After a few sips, I decided I would feel better in the living room with the noise from the TV for company, so I brought my pillows and blanket from the bedroom and arranged them on the couch. When the wine finally started to take effect, my jangled nerves settled down and I was able to relax.

I spent the rest of night there in a state of semi-consciousness, jumping at the slightest unidentified sound. I didn't fall asleep until the sun had started to come up the next morning. I was awakened around mid-morning by the sound of the telephone ringing.

"Hullo," I croaked into the receiver.

"Ellen? Is that you?" Andy wanted to know, "you sound like you just woke up. Did you and Jack burn the midnight oil or something?"

"Huh? Yeah, something like that. What time is it anyway?" I managed to say, throwing off the covers and getting my tired body into an upright position. Not only was I exhausted, but the wine had given me a horrendous headache.

"It's after 10:00! I had some paperwork that I had to get done and figured you would have called those women to set up our interviews by now. I've got some free time this afternoon if they'll see us. Do you want me to call them?"

"No, that's okay, Andy. I'll call them. Why don't you stop by after lunch and we'll get our game plan together then."

"Sounds good to me. Hey, Ellen? You don't sound so good. You aren't getting sick or anything are you?"

"No, I'm not sick!" I snapped, "unless you call it being sick of all the lies and conspiracies that seem to be plaguing this town!"

"Wow! Sorry I asked," he muttered, "what's got you so uptight?"

"I'm sorry, Chief," I quickly replied, "I just didn't get much sleep last night and I am definitely not a morning person!"

"Oh, okay. I'll see you around 1:00."

"See you then."

As soon as I hung up the phone, I started to call him back and tell him about the note that had frightened me so, but returned the handset to its place. I simply refused to let it get in the way of my involvement in the case. I decided I would just have to take extra precautions and make sure that I didn't go anywhere by myself. As long as Andy was close by, I knew no one would dare lay a hand on me.

I dragged my aching body to the shower and by lunchtime, started feeling human again. I was able to locate the women's telephone numbers through directory assistance, amazed that they were listed under the same names and still in the area. As Jack had predicted, neither of them was anxious to meet with us, but when I suggested that we meet them outside of their homes in a place of their choosing, they reluctantly agreed.

Rosemary Willowby said she would meet us at the Rye Beach State Park on Lake Erie at 2:30 and Alice Martinez agreed to meet us at her cousin's house in Sandusky at 4:00. I counted on Andy to be able to get us there, since I didn't know my way around

As promised, he arrived promptly at 1:00, giving us plenty of time to prepare for the interviews and get to the park ahead of time. We stationed ourselves at a picnic table close to the water and waited for her to arrive. She was late, but we knew it was she when she walked over.

"Ms. Willowby?" I asked as she warily approached and nodded, "this is Chief Taylor of the Milan police department."

Andy stood and they shook hands. She took the bench across from us with her back to the water. She was an attractive woman despite her age and carried herself like a woman of exceptional confidence. Her hair was strawberry blonde and she was dressed in a pale blue sweater and slacks outfit that showed off her trim figure. She had long graceful hands, which she rubbed up and down her arms as if she felt a chill. I was admiring her manicure, when I noticed that she had on an expensive wedding set with a large diamond setting.

"I wasn't aware that you were married," I commented, gesturing at the ring, "you are listed in the phonebook under Willowby. I assumed that was your maiden name."

"No, my maiden name was Liedermann," she responded. "My husband and I will have been married for 35 years this Christmas. Why?"

"Well," I stammered, "as you know we are looking into the McCoy murders and well, since you and Patrick McCoy, um, were seen together, I guess I just assumed you were single at the time."

Her eyes narrowed and her tone became hostile.

"Who told you that?" she demanded hotly.

"I'm sorry, Ms. Willowby," Andy interjected, "we're not at liberty to give out that information. Anything you can tell us will be held in the strictest confidence. We would only ask you to make your relationship with Mr. McCoy public if and when someone is ever charged with the crime and it had any bearing on the case."

"Listen, I came here on good faith to answer your questions, but as I told this lady on the phone, I really don't have anything new to offer. Yes, I knew Pat McCoy. I was sorry when I heard he'd been killed, but as to my relationship with him, I wouldn't really call it that. My husband and I separated a few years into our marriage and I have to admit, I started going the bars and flirting with the men I met there. That's when I met Pat McCoy. You see, my husband and I got married right out of high school and I guess I needed to sow some wild oats or something. I don't know! I went a little crazy for a while. When Pat was killed, I finally came to my senses and thankfully, over time my husband took me back. We've had a wonderful marriage and three beautiful children since then and that is a part of my life that I would prefer to forget. That's why I had you meet me here. I don't want all this dredged up and hurting my husband all over again!"

"I know this is unpleasant for you, Ms. Willowby, but we need to talk to as many of Pat McCoy's known associates as we can. We are trying to find out who committed that horrible attack on him, his wife and child even if it is embarrassing. I'm sure you can understand our position."

"You think this is just an embarrassment! You have no idea the kind of hell I went through to convince my husband to take me back! That episode nearly ruined the only chance I had for a life with a man who loves me! It took me years to prove to him that I could be trusted. I simply will not put my family through that again!" she cried, banging her fist on the table.

"Did your husband know about you and Pat McCoy?" I asked softly, but refusing to let her off the hook.

She glared at me and then tears welled up in her eyes.

"Yes," she sniffled, "he knew about Pat."

She dug around in her purse for a Kleenex and blew her nose.

"How did he find out?" I asked quietly.

"Oh the usual way. He followed me to the bar. Saw us leave together. It was horrible."

"Did he confront the two of you that night?" Andy asked.

"No, it was a few days later when we were arguing. Out of the blue, he told me what he had seen and demanded to know the man's name with whom he had seen me."

"And did you tell him?" I asked.

"Not at first. I didn't want him making any trouble with Pat. Pat had a terrible temper and I was afraid he might get hurt. A few weeks later, when things had calmed down and we were talking about getting back together, I told him."

"Do you remember when you had this conversation with your husband?" Andy asked.

"That was over thirty years ago! Of course I don't remember the exact date! What difference does it make now? It's all water over the dam! Pat McCoy is dead and I have moved on! I think I have answered about enough of your questions! I need to get home. I've got a meal to prepare for my family!"

With that she slid along the bench and rose to her feet. Her air of confidence was a thing of the past. She looked 10 years older.

"Wait, Ms. Willowby!" I cried, reaching out to take hold of her arm. "Just one more question and we will leave you alone!"

"What more do you want from me!" she cried. "I had put this all behind me and now you're bringing it up all over again! Go ahead. Ask your question, and then I am leaving!"

"Do you know if your husband ever confronted Pat McCoy about the affair?"

"No, I don't," she said with finality. "And whoever said he did, is a God damned liar!"

She pulled away from me and stomped off to her car. She wheeled away in a shower of gravel.

"Did you just hear what I heard? I think we may have just found out who tried to punch out Pat McCoy's lights. What do you think, Andy?"

"Could be! Let's add Mr. Willowby to our list. I think we may have to pay him a visit before this is all over."

"That's one interview I am definitely not looking forward to," I agreed.

Chapter Eighteen

On the drive to Sandusky to meet Alice Martinez, I couldn't help but ponder the implications of Rosemary Willowby's revelations.

"Andy, jealousy is a pretty powerful motive for murder. We obviously touched a nerve when we asked about a confrontation between her husband and Pat McCoy. What do you think?"

"It certainly is something that merits some more digging. If he were the guilty party, why would Mayor Albertson have gotten involved? For the life of me, I just can't see the connection."

"Maybe they were friends. You're the one who knows Albertson; maybe Willowby came to the Mayor for help. Maybe the Mayor just couldn't stand to see Mark take the fall and wanted to help Mark, but couldn't betray his friend. Jim Patterson said it was the Mayor that got Mark hustled out of town into the Army. Andy, remember I was there. Mark left town under a cloud of suspicion and the investigation just sort of went away. Who knows, maybe Albertson got to Chief Talbot somehow. You have to admit the whole thing just got swept under the rug after Mark was out of the picture. It is definitely a possibility," I argued.

"Jeez, I don't know, Ellen. That's a pretty long stretch. Don't forget that Talbot called in the state police. If he was involved in some kind of cover up, why would he bring in outsiders?"

"Andy, come on! It would have looked suspicious if he hadn't. Everyone knew he wasn't qualified to investigate a crime of that magnitude. I've seen what the state had. You know as well as I do that they did a pretty superficial job. Look how much we've learned in just a few days! Doesn't it make you wonder why no one ever talked to Rosemary Willowby or Alice Martinez? They went into it with blinders on, Andy. Maybe Talbot orchestrated the whole thing, convincing the investigators that Mark had done it, but they couldn't prove it, so they had to let him go."

"All I know is that Dan Albertson is a very influential man. You're making some pretty wild accusations about him that are based on a bunch of hearsay and speculation. Besides, even if he did what you say he did for Willowby, he was taking an awfully big risk of being charged with criminal conspiracy to cover up the commission of a capital offense himself. Why would he do that for the sake of a friendship? It just doesn't make sense! Not to mention the fact that too many other people may have been involved. How could he be sure somebody wouldn't talk?"

"Okay, I know it sounds pretty farfetched. But he was a wealthy man! It wouldn't be the first time that money exchanged hands to keep people from talking! Think about it! If he had Talbot in his back pocket, the Chief could have misdirected the state investigators away from any potentially damaging witnesses against Willowby!"

"I don't know, Ellen," he said dismissively, "It's going to take a lot more than what we have so far to convince me that Dan Albertson and Art Talbot were a part of some monumental cover up!"

Our discussion was cut short because we had arrived at the home of Alice Martinez's cousin. The house was one of a hundred others that were all the same except for minor cosmetic differences. The entire neighborhood was comprised of tiny track homes probably built during the housing glut of the 1950's after World War II.

Alice met us at the door. She was a heavyset woman with long jet-black hair, painted eyebrows that arched above her natural brow line and bright red lipstick. She was dressed in tight black stretch pants and a brilliant orange peasant blouse that dipped low in the front exposing her expansive bosom. She struck me as a woman who refused to accept the passage of time and was clinging desperately to a past that had long since passed her by. After handshakes all around, she escorted us to seats in the cluttered living room.

"I just want to thank you again for agreeing to meet with us, Ms. Martinez," I began, "as I told you on the phone, we're interested in any information you might have that will help us regarding the death of Patrick, Loretta and Becky McCoy."

"Please, call me Alice," she said, her voice raspy and deep like that of a lifelong smoker. "I'm sorry you had to meet me here, but I live with my daughter and her kids and I'd rather keep them out of this. She doesn't know about me and Pat and I'd just like to keep it that way."

"So you did have a relationship with Patrick McCoy?" Andy asked.

"What did you say your name was, honey?" she asked giving Andy the once over, flipping her hair back over her shoulder coquettishly and adjusting her bra strap.

"Chief of Police Taylor, Andrew Taylor, ma'am," Andy replied with an official tone, ignoring her preposterous attempt at flirting. The woman was not only garish in appearance, but old enough to be his mother.

"Well, Andrew, let me just say that there was a time when I might have been able to attract a big healthy specimen like you and I always have had a thing for men in uniform," she sighed. "But in answer to your question, yes, me and Pat had some good times together. Just for laughs, you know. Nothing heavy, not that I wouldn't have been willing to take things a little farther. He was a married man, although in my prime, that never fazed me. I was pretty broken up when I heard he'd been killed. I never met his wife, although she sounded like a pretty mousy little thing, may she rest in peace. Pat said she wasn't much in the bedroom. I guess that's why he liked me. I never had any problem giving a man what he needed," she smiled, giving Andy a meaningful glance.

"Did you love him?" I asked, drawing her attention away from Andy.

"Love?" she asked turning back to me. "I guess I might have loved him if circumstances had been different. I never considered myself a home wrecker although if he had left his wife I might have been willing. There was just something, I don't know, dangerous about him. He didn't give a shit what anybody thought. I liked that about him. We even talked about getting together, but there were his kids to think of and all. Who knows? He died before we ever got the chance, so there's no sense whining about it now!"

151

"So, to your knowledge, were you the only woman he associated with, outside of his wife?" I prompted.

Her expression darkened. I felt I must have touched on a sensitive area.

"That's the one thing that we fought about. Pat had this thing for this skinny little blonde snob who used to come slumming in the bar. Just about the time he and I started to really make a connection, she showed up, swinging her puny little ass in his face. I'll never forget the first time she came in. He and I were sitting in the booth in the back of the bar, having a couple of beers, all cozy and close. He had his hand on my thigh and was about to reach pay dirt, if you know what I mean, and then Miss High Society walked in. All of a sudden, I might have just as well have been last week's leftovers, because he couldn't take his eyes off her, just like all the other guys. They were all panting after her like a bunch of dogs in heat!"

"Who was this woman?" I asked, already having a good idea what her answer would be.

"Rosemary Willowby!" she spat. "Oh when she wasn't around, he was all mine, but when she came in, I didn't stand a chance. She was married, but she and her old man had some sort of falling out and Pat just couldn't keep his hands off her. I can't tell you the times he left me hanging and left the bar with her. Course, her husband put a stop to it when he found out!"

"And how did he do that, Alice?" I asked, holding my breath.

"Well, this one night, she hadn't come in and I was finally getting his attention and this guy came in looking for him. He was dressed in a suit and looked really out of place, you know, because the guys that came to the bar were mostly construction workers and the like, so he stood out like a sore thumb, you know. He just walked up to the table, knocked it over and started screaming at Pat to leave his wife alone. Well, Pat wasn't one to take it, so he jumped up and took a swing at the guy. The next thing I know, all hell broke loose and Dick Chance and a couple of the other guys rushed over and pulled them apart."

"And you're sure the man that came after Pat was Rosemary's husband?" I asked.

152

"Yeah, I'm sure. I'd never met the man, but it was pretty obvious who he was. Rosemary never came back after that, and I certainly didn't miss her!"

"Later, when you learned of Pat's death, did you ever associate that confrontation with Rosemary Willowby's husband with the murders?" I asked.

"I'm not stupid!" she cried. "Of course, I did!" I was stunned by her candor.

"I have to ask, why didn't you say anything to the police about it?" I had to know.

"Are you kidding? I did. As soon as I heard about Pat, I made a beeline for Chief Talbot's office! He told me that they already had identified the killer. End of story. He practically threw me out of his office! Told me I was nothing but a sorry whore and to mind my own business! Said I was just trying to stir up trouble for decent people and if I didn't quit running my mouth, he would run me in for soliciting! I'll have you know I never got paid for sex in my entire life! It was all I could do to keep from decking the bastard! I was so mad. I just cussed him out and went home. It was later that I found out I was pregnant, so I just kept my mouth shut!"

"What! Why would your being pregnant make you feel you had to keep quiet?" I asked incredulously.

"Because I thought the baby might be Pat's!" she confessed. "If Talbot ever found out I was carrying Pat's baby, he would have been on me like flypaper! He would have looked at me as having a mighty good reason to kill Pat and his family. You know how people's minds work. Here's me knocked up by a married man! He won't leave his family, so I kill his ass!"

Her tough exterior cracked and streaks of mascara began dribbling down her cheeks. I was so taken back, I was speechless. All I could think to do was pat her hand until she stopped sobbing.

"Does your daughter know that Pat McCoy was her father?" I asked softly.

"No," she said miserably, "and she can never find out! That's why I couldn't let her know I was talking to you. This whole thing has been buried in the past. I just couldn't bear for it to come out now, just when her life is finally getting better.

She's a good girl, got a good job and is raising her kids on her own! I help out some, but this could ruin her life!"

"There's a chance you may be called upon to testify against Mr. Willowby if it comes to that, Ms. Martinez," Andy said, "and we'll do our best to keep your daughter's paternity out of it, but I can't promise it won't come out."

"I knew it was a mistake to talk to you!" she moaned, a fresh torrent of tears streaming down her face, "it's all that damn Rosemary's fault. If she had just left us alone, we might have been able to work things out. She may as well have pulled the trigger herself! I should have just kept my big mouth shut!"

"So you truly believe that Pat, Loretta and Becky McCoy were killed by Rosemary Willowby's husband?" I asked, just to hear her say it.

"As surely as I am sitting here," she said.

"Thanks for your help, Ms. Martinez," Andy said, rising to his feet. "We'll be in touch."

"I'm sorry, Alice," I said touching her heaving shoulders and followed him out. We left her sitting alone on the couch with her face in her hands.

Chapter Nineteen

"Still think my theory doesn't hold water?" I asked as soon as we reached the car. "Alice obviously thinks there's some merit to it!"

"Hey, I never said your theory was impossible!" Andy replied defensively, pulling out into the street. "All we got is the word of a burned out old woman with an axe to grind! Maybe she killed them. If her daughter really were Pat's, she'd sure have plenty of reason to do it! Not to mention the fact that Rosemary was beating her time with her boyfriend. Those are two pretty good reasons to kill someone!"

"You sure you're not just reacting to the fact that she came on to you?" I asked half jokingly.

"Ellen! I would never let my personal feelings color my judgement about something this serious, and I resent your implication!" he declared hotly.

"Okay! Okay! Simmer down, Chief! I was just joking. Trying to lighten things up a little. I'm sorry if I offended you!"

"Yeah, whatever. She has to be the most disgusting woman I have ever encountered. Imagine her thinking any one could be attracted to a hag like her!" he swore under his breath.

"Well, I can't help but feel sorry for her. I guess I have a little more empathy for her than a man would. No matter what she said, I think she was in love with Pat McCoy and I think she took his death a whole lot harder than she was willing to admit. She got stuck raising his child on her own. It sounds like she's done the best she could by their daughter."

"Okay, she's a regular Mother Teresa! Can we talk about something else?" Andy said, cutting in front of an oncoming car making me grab the dashboard in alarm.

"She really got to you, didn't she?" I said, surprised at his vehemence.

"I mean it, Ellen. I don't want to talk about it!" he spat.

"Okay!" I agreed, "but will you at least listen to my observation of this for just a second without biting my head off or getting us killed?"

"You're going to anyway no matter what I say, so go ahead. Say what you've got to say. I can't stop you!"

"I know why she got to you," I said quietly, turning to look out of the window at the passing scenery.

"Oh you do, do you? Well, by all means, please share your wisdom, Ms. Richardson," he said snidely, the muscles in his cheeks bunching as he gritted his teeth.

"Because she scared you!" I declared.

"What! That is such bullshit!" he scoffed hotly. "That will be the day when I'm scared of a pathetic old woman like her!" he cried, his face blushing scarlet.

"I didn't say you were scared of what she did, Andy!" I insisted.

"Well, then what was I so scared of?" he demanded.

"It wasn't what she did, it was what she said! You're mad because she may have hit the nail on the head when she said Willowby killed Pat McCoy! And it follows that your good friend Dan Albertson may have had something to do with a cover up! And that scares the hell out of you! Your precious little town may be rotten to the core right under your nose!"

When he didn't respond but stared straight ahead with his hands locked on the wheel, I continued with a little less intensity, "Andy, if it's any consolation, I'm scared too! Do you think it makes me feel good to know that everything I thought I knew about my hometown may have been a big lie? Why do you think I made the trip back here? I wanted to get back the good feelings I had as a child. So far, all I've found is heartache, death and misery! You're not the only one who might be losing something precious here!"

We drove for several miles in silence. I was afraid I had lost what had been becoming a friendship. I wished I had just kept my opinions to myself. Just when I thought he would never speak to me again, he reached out and laid his hand on my arm.

"Ellen, I'm sorry I yelled at you," he sighed. "You are probably right. I did overreact and I'm sorry. Can we still be friends?"

I was still smarting from what he had said, but swallowed my pride.

"Of course I'm your friend, Andy. Why don't you let me make it up to you by cooking you dinner? That is, if your wife won't mind. You're welcome to invite her too if you like!"

"Ellen, I don't have a wife," he said, "I'm just surprised you didn't ask sooner!"

"Well, if you think I'm coming on to you, you're dead wrong, Chief Taylor!" I insisted, my own cheeks flaming. "I'm old enough to be your mother and I'll thank you to keep that in mind!"

"Oh come on, Ellen!" he laughed, "older women dream of getting a stud like me in bed! Look at old Alice! She sure didn't let a little thing like age stop her!"

We both had to laugh at that and before long we were back on friendly terms. I was relieved that the storm that had threatened our budding friendship was so quickly forgotten. As we talked, I realized that there were more facets to Andy's character than I had ever imagined. Maybe he wasn't made of stone after all.

When we pulled into the driveway at my house, he asked if I needed anything from the store. He offered to pick up some steaks from the grocery, saying he wanted to check in at the station before going off duty for the evening. It was obvious that he intended to just drop me off and come back later, but my heart thumped at the thought of entering my house alone. He gave me a puzzled look when I didn't immediately get out of the car.

"Ellen, what's wrong? You've got a funny look on your face. You aren't having second thoughts about the invitation are you? I was just kidding with that crack about older women!"

"Huh? No, of course not!" I insisted, trying to come up with a plausible reason to ask him to check out the house for me without tipping my hand about the hate mail I had received.

He kept looking at me for an explanation, so I burst out, "Andy, would you do me a huge favor?"

"Sure, what?" he asked hesitantly.

"Would you mind terribly if you went in the house with me and sort of checked things out?"

"Okay," he said giving me a puzzled look, "is there some reason you don't feel comfortable going in by yourself that you haven't told me?"

"I, um, just haven't quite gotten used to the house yet," I hedged, "I know I'm just being silly, but it would make me feel better, if it isn't too much trouble."

"Okay, Ellen. Out with it! You don't strike me as being a weak kneed female, what's going on?" he demanded.

"Nothing," I insisted, opening the car door and exiting the car. "Forget I said anything! I'll see you in a few minutes!"

I hurried up the walk and put the key in the lock. As I pulled the door open, Andy reached out from behind me where I hadn't seen him and held it shut.

"Okay," he growled, "I'll go in first. Something has got you spooked and as soon as I get back with those steaks, you're going to tell me what it is! You got that?"

"Okay," I sighed knowing he wasn't going to take no for an answer.

While I waited by the front door, he made a quick sweep of the house. He told me to lock the door behind him and reminded me again that he expected an explanation upon his return. While I waited, I tried to come up with something that he would believe, but knew I couldn't pull it off. I never have been very good at telling lies. Somehow I always get caught. It must be something in the eyes.

Anyway, I went ahead and started preparing the salad for dinner, feeling weak and foolish for being so transparent. Some great detective I was turning out to be. I felt like a scared rabbit.

It was almost an hour before he returned. I had just about given up on him, relieved that I wouldn't have to face him for at least another day, when the doorbell rang. I peeked through the peephole and saw him on the front stoop, in street clothes with a bag of groceries in his arms.

I drew back the deadbolt and held the door for him. He had showered and along with the groceries was carrying a six-pack of beer.

"Well, my goodness, Chief Taylor," I laughed, "I've never seen you out of uniform. I figured you never took it off. You almost look like a regular guy!"

"Well, don't let the look fool you," he muttered, pointing to the beeper on his belt and the pistol tucked in the back of his pants, "I'm never really off duty. I haven't had any real time off in I can't remember when, and I intend to do my best to enjoy myself! Everything seems to be pretty quiet down at the station, so maybe my deputies can handle things for a few hours. Where do you want me to put this stuff?"

I took him into the kitchen and we unpacked the groceries. He had bought a bag of charcoal and I helped him drag out the old barbecue grill I had found out back. He was soon busy cooking the meat, while I got the rest of the meal together. I took him a beer and poured myself a glass of wine. I set the table with the cracked dishes that had come with the house, wishing I had something a little nicer for my first houseguest, but he didn't seem to notice.

When we finally sat down to eat, we started talking about ordinary things and I found myself telling him all about my kids and things that had happened back home in Georgia. I surprised myself by sharing some stories about my life with my husband before he died. He told me about his divorce from his wife of three years. He said she couldn't stand being married to a cop because of the hours he kept and was now happily married to an accountant in Cleveland.

When I started to clear the table after dinner, I thought I had escaped answering his questions about my reluctance to enter my house earlier, but he took the plates from me, put them in the sink, took my hand and silently led me into the living room. I took a seat on the couch and to my surprise he sat down next to me. I started to feel a little uncomfortable at his close proximity, but decided to wait and see what he had in mind.

"Okay, Ellen," he began, taking my hand in his for the second time, "I told you I would want an explanation. We've had our nice dinner conversation and the meal was great, by the way, but it's time to pay the piper."

"Andy," I insisted, looking at anything but him, "I told you before, I've just let this whole murder thing get the best of me. I'm just a Georgia widow woman who has seen things I wouldn't want to see in my darkest nightmares and I got a little spooked! That's all there is to it. I'm sorry if I've caused you any concern!"

"Ellen, look at me," he said and I forced myself to keep my expression neutral when I looked into his eyes.

"Yes, Andy?" I said innocently, doing my utmost to hold his gaze.

"You're not a very good liar, you know that?"

"Why, Andy! That's a rotten thing to say!" I fumed, snatching my hand out of his. He took it back, ignoring my outburst as one would a child.

"Ellen, you are forgetting that first and foremost, I am a cop. It's my job to know when people aren't telling the truth and you, dear lady, are lying through your teeth!"

He held my hand a little tighter and continued searching my face, waiting for me to respond.

I glanced down at his hand and tried to pull mine away.

"You can put away the thumbscrews, officer!" I cried, "Okay! You can let go of my hand now!"

"Not until you tell me what's got you jumping at shadows! I mean it, Ellen!" he said sternly, refusing to release the pressure he was exerting on my hand.

"Okay, it's in the other room in the drawer. If you'll let go, I promise not to leave the state!" I snapped angrily.

He was still sitting in the middle of the couch when I returned with the note. I started to take a seat in a chair across the room, but he patted the place beside him indicating where he wanted me. I held the envelope against my chest and sank into the cushions. He held out his hand for it.

"Before I show you this, you have to promise me something," I said, holding it tight against me.

"Yeah, what's that?" he said raising an eyebrow.

"Promise that nothing changes. Promise that you'll keep me on the case!"

"Just what is that, Ellen? Did you get some kind of death threat or something?" he said with alarm.

"I said, promise. I mean it, Andy. You have to promise me," I insisted. "You know how I am. I'll keep looking for the killer with or without your help!"

"Okay, okay. I'll keep you on the case! Now hand it over, Ellen," he demanded.

I checked his eyes for sincerity one more time and placed the envelope on his outstretched hand. I watched his expression as he read it and could see the vein in his forehead begin pulsing.

"Where did you get this?" he asked evenly.

"I found it under my windshield wiper at Shady Oaks when I left Jack last night," I said softly; goose bumps started raising the hair on the back of my arms. "It scared me so badly, I didn't sleep a wink last night. I started to show it to you last night, but I changed my mind."

"Why was that?" he asked with a frown.

"Because I was afraid you'd get all worked up just like you're doing now and make me stop! Andy, you promised you wouldn't let some crackpot interfere with what we're trying to accomplish! You promised!" I felt like a fool, but couldn't help myself. "I just get a little nervous coming into the house by myself! If that person knows what kind of car I drive, they probably know where I live! I thought I could handle it on my own, you know! As long as I stay close to you and Jack, I'll be safe!"

I knew I sounded like a babbling idiot, but I couldn't stop. He simply sat there looking at me with an angry look on his face, crumpling the edge of the note in with his fingers.

"Shouldn't you be preserving that for fingerprints or something?" I asked, breaking his silence.

"Oh, believe me, that's the first thing I intend to do!" he snapped, tossing it onto the coffee table. "Not that it will probably do any good! The sick-o that wrote that note probably knew enough to wear gloves! Ellen, I am extremely disappointed in you! Why in heavens name didn't you tell me! How the hell am I supposed to look out for you if you keep something like that from me!"

"I'm sorry, Andy! You've got so much going on, I didn't want to add to your problems, I guess! I don't know, I was just afraid you'd tell me to leave, and well, I'm just not ready to throw in the towel!" I said miserably.

To my total shock, he put his arms around me and crushed me to his chest.

"Don't you know I care what happens to you, you idiot!" he said, stroking my hair. "I don't care if you're a hundred and ten, I care. And in case you're wondering, I have no intention of getting you into the bedroom. Not all men are pigs, you know!"

"Nobody ever said you were a pig," I sniffled against his collar, "but if you don't let me go, I might start thinking you've got a thing for me," I said teasingly to ease the tension, extricating myself from his embrace and wiping my cheeks with my hands.

"So what happens now, Chief," I said pulling myself together determined to steer clear of thoughts of what had just transpired between us.

"Well, I don't really know," he said, getting up and walking to the other side of the room as if he felt to need to put some distance between us just as I did.

"I guess for starters, I'll just have to make sure that you don't go anywhere by yourself for a while. I'll check all the locks on the windows and doors. You know not to open the door to strangers, so I don't have to tell you about that!" he said, more to himself than to me.

"See? I knew you'd know what to do!" I cried, relieved that he seemed to be taking the situation in stride.

"Hey, don't think you're going to weasel your way out of this by flattery. I'm still pretty pissed at you for keeping this from me!" he growled.

He seemed to come to some decision and walked out the front door to his squad car. I could see him speaking on the radio through the drapes. When he came back in, he began going from window to window checking the locks and muttering to himself. I decided it was best if I stayed out of his way and went into the kitchen and finished clearing the table and loading the dishwasher. When I finished, he was back on the couch watching television.

"So, what was the radio call about," I asked nonchalantly.

"I've asked the night guys to make a few extras swings by here starting tomorrow night. I think I'll bunk here on the couch tonight, if you don't mind. I think that maybe whoever wrote that note might up the ante when he finds out you went to see those women today. It's just for tonight until I have a chance to think about it some more! You okay with that?"

"Sure, if you think it's necessary. Andy, thanks for what you're doing! You have no idea how much better I feel with you here!"

"Just doing my job, ma'am," he said with the ghost of a smile, "just doing my job!"

Chapter Twenty

I expected to find Andy asleep on the couch when I got up the next morning, but he was gone, the pillow and blanket neatly folded on the couch. The note that he had tossed on the coffee table was also gone, but another was in its place. It said:

Ellen,
I'm sorry but I got a page during the night. Something came up at the station.
I'll call you as soon as I can break free. Wait for me at the house and keep the doors locked. We will go see Jack and tell him what we've got so far.
Andy

I don't know why, but with the daylight, I didn't feel so vulnerable. I felt foolish for making such a fuss. I almost wished I'd been a better liar. Andy's involvement would only restrict my movements and having lived on my own for a while, I wasn't used to being told what to do. As I sipped my morning coffee, I caught myself thinking about how he had made me feel with his arms around me. It had been a long time since a man had done that. As much as I hated to admit it, it had felt awfully good.

"Ellen! Stop this!" I muttered to myself, tossing the dregs into the sink, "the man was simply being kind! Don't be reading anything into it! He's not that much older than your kids, for crying out loud!"

With my ridiculous fantasies firmly suppressed, I went about making the bed and getting showered and dressed. I had just about decided to go on the Shady Oaks without him, when the doorbell rang. As instructed, I made sure it was he before I opened the door.

"Morning, Chief," I said. "Is everything okay down at the station?"

"Yeah, some knucklehead kid plowed into a family out on Route 71 and killed himself and the girl that was with him. The man and woman in the other car were busted up pretty bad and not expected to live. They had their kids in the back, and for once, had them strapped in, so I think they're going to make it. Course, they'll probably be orphans. It wasn't a pretty scene!"

"I'm so sorry! Have you had anything to eat? You look like you could use something!"

"Actually, I could use a cup of coffee," he said and followed me into the kitchen.

He had dark circles under his eyes and I felt worse for adding to his troubles. He took his coffee black and I handed him a cup.

"Andy, you really don't need to baby-sit me! Why don't you go get some sleep? I'll just spend the day with Jack going over what we have so far," I offered.

"I wish I could, I feel like hell, but I've got a deputy that called in sick and I need to get to the hospital so I can get some kind of statement from those people about the wreck if they're able. Plus, I need to send that note off to the state crime lab for testing, not that it will probably do any good. If you're ready, I'll drop you off at the nursing home. I'll stop by there as soon as I can. Promise me you won't leave there until you hear from me!"

"Whatever you say." I replied trying my best not to antagonize him. "You know we're probably overreacting about that note. Nothing happened last night. The person is obviously a coward. If he or she meant to harm me, they would just do it, not hide behind a stupid letter!"

"Maybe, but I'm not willing to take that chance! I know I can't watch you 24 hours a day, but I intend to do what I can. Why don't you let me decide what's best? I am the professional here, you know!"

"Okay! You're the boss!" I said in defeat. "I'm just not used to having anyone make such a big deal over me. I just hate feeling so, I don't know, intimidated. I'm not a baby, you know!"

"Yeah, well you might change your tune if someone decides to take a potshot at you! Now go get your stuff and let's get going. I've got a lot I need to get done before I can even think about the case."

From his expression, I knew he was in no mood to argue, so I grabbed my notes from the previous day's interviews and my purse and followed him to his car. He waited in the parking lot of the convalescent center until I was safely inside and drove away.

Jack wasn't in his room when I arrived. His bed was neatly made, but he was nowhere in sight. I rushed to the nurse's station in a panic.

"Where is Jack Miller? Has something happened to him?" I demanded, my heart thumping in my chest.

"Take it easy!" the nurse laughed, "he's down the hall in the solarium. He kept complaining that he didn't have room to spread out all those papers he's been messing around with, so I set him up at one of the visitor's tables! Jeez, that is some pretty gruesome stuff he's got! What in the world is he doing?"

"It's just an old case from when he was Chief of Police," I told her tersely. It took a second or two for me to catch my breath and let my heart rate slow.

She started to say something else, but I pretended not to hear and proceeded down to the hall. I could feel her curious eyes following me until I turned the corner.

I found Jack in the sunroom, his head barely visible behind a couple of cartons and a stack of papers.

"Well, what have we here?" I laughed, "the nurse says you've outgrown your room!"

"Yeah, she kept giving me grief about the mess; so I told her it wouldn't be so bad if I had more than a couple of inches of maneuvering room, so she parked me here. What do you think?" he grinned.

"Looks like you've done pretty good for yourself!" I grinned back. It did my heart good to see him so energetic and enthusiastic.

"Course, I have to keep some of the other patients from touching things. Some of these people have got Alzheimer's disease and wander up and down the halls. So far I've managed to keep them away!"

"Well, I'm sure from the look of you, you've done a pretty good job of keeping them at bay!" I chuckled pulling up a chair beside him. "So, how's it going? Have you found anything we overlooked?"

"I have gone over everything again and again," he complained, "but I keep coming up empty-handed. What about you? Did you get anything out of those women?"

"Oh, I guess you could say that." I said noncommittally picking up a sheet of paper from the table and pretending to read it.

"Come on! I can tell by that 'cat that ate the canary' expression on your face you found out a lot! Don't leave me hanging here! Tell me!"

"Okay!" I said, deciding I was just being silly making him drag it out of me, "we met with Rosemary Willowby and Alice Martinez yesterday afternoon, just as we planned."

"And?"

"Well, it seems that Rosemary was married at the time that she was having her little fling with Pat McCoy!"

"So?"

"So, it turns out that hubby found out about it and he wasn't exactly thrilled."

"Did she tell you that her husband was the man in the bar fight with McCoy?"

"Oh, no! She says it never happened, but Jack, she was cool as a cucumber until the subject came up and then she just lost it! I thought she was going to fall all over herself trying to get away from us!"

"It sounds like the lady protested too much!" Jack sniffed.

"No kidding! She's a pretty classy lady and I think she would rather we didn't air any of her dirty laundry, if you know what I mean!"

"Do you think she suspects that her husband killed Pat McCoy?" he asked.

"That's a good question! Looking back on it, I don't think she does. I think she was more concerned with bringing up her infidelity with her husband again. She said he gave her a pretty hard time before he took her back. I think she's just worried that it will stir things up with him all over again."

"Interesting. Anything else?"

"Not really, like I said, as soon as we started talking about what might have happened between her husband and Pat, she took off like a scalded dog. We weren't going to get anything more out of her."

"So what about the other lady? Was she any help?"

"Oh, Jack! That is putting it mildly. Alice Martinez is something else!" I laughed. "I think you would have gotten a kick out of her!"

"Why? What about her?"

"Well, first of all, you've got to promise you won't say anything to Andy!"

"What do you mean? Of course I plan to discuss anything she may have said that has bearing on the case with him!" he said seriously.

"No, I don't mean that! I'm talking about something else. Something outside of the case!"

"Okay! Whatever! I promise not to say anything to Andy! What was it about the woman that has got you so worked up that you don't want me mentioning it to Andy?"

"Well, first of all, you have to get a picture of the woman. She is this big-breasted old woman with long dyed black hair, penciled eyebrows halfway up her forehead and wearing an outfit that would look outlandish on a woman half her age. We had hardly sat down before she started putting the make on Andy! Said she had a thing for men in uniform! God, you should have seen his face! I thought he was going to have a cow!" I laughed.

"I take it he didn't share your hilarity!" he scowled.

"Hardly," I said, "he nearly bit my head off when I commented on it!" I noticed that he wasn't laughing so I added more seriously, "I guess you had be there to see the humor in it!"

"No wonder you don't want me ribbing Andy about it! The poor guy was probably embarrassed no end!"

"Oh come on, Jack! Lighten up! If you don't keep your sense of humor in this thing, you'll go nuts! He's a big guy. I'm sure he wasn't traumatized by the experience!"

"I guess it would be kind of funny to see him get flustered. He's such a gung-ho kind of cop!"

"There you go! But he is extremely sensitive about it, so let's just keep that to ourselves, okay?"

"You got it. Now, tell me what she had to say about the case."

"She said that she and Pat were quite an item back in the day. He told her he wasn't getting any, you know, from his wife, so she sort of filled in, if you know what I mean. I got the impression that she really cared about him and would have married him if he had left his wife. Anyway, things were moving right along for the two of them and then, in walks 'Ms. High Society', her words, and steals away her man."

"This other woman the one that you met before?"

"Bingo! Apparently, Mrs. Willowby was the other, other woman. Our painted lady didn't have much good to say about her. She said as soon as Pat laid eyes on her, it was all over but the shouting."

"And then her husband got wind of it and brought it all to a screeching halt, am I right?"

"You got that right! Alice was there the night that Mr. Willowby came after Pat! She saw the whole thing and she's not afraid to name names."

"So why didn't she go to the cops?" Jack asked.

"That's where the story gets even better! She did!" I cried.

"What? I've been over the witness statements a dozen times. There's nothing in there from her!"

"I told you it gets better! Apparently, she went to Chief Talbot about what she had seen and get this, he accused her of being a prostitute and threatened to run her in if she didn't quit trying to disparage decent people. He practically kicked her out of his office!"

"Oh, come on! I worked with Art Talbot. I seriously doubt he would have dismissed a potential witness to a capital crime so cavalierly! Do you really think she was telling the truth? Maybe she just has it in for the Willowby woman and her husband for causing trouble between her and Pat!"

"I would have thought that too if it weren't for another little piece of information that she shared with us!"

"And what would that be" he asked.

"Right after her supposed meeting with Talbot, she found out she was pregnant!"

"So?"

"Don't you see? The baby was Pat's! How could she press the issue when she was carrying the perfect motive for murder in her belly? She's kept the secret all these years, because she was afraid she would be blamed for the murder!"

"So why do you suppose she came clean at this late date?" he asked skeptically.

"I don't know! Maybe she just had to get it off her chest! It all rings pretty true to me. What do you think, Jack?"

"Well, it definitely puts a whole new spin on things. What does Andy say? Did he believe her?"

"Andy is upset, because it puts credence to the idea that Dan Albertson and Art Talbot may have had something to do with covering it up. He still thinks my theory is unfounded, but I think he may be ready to admit that it is a possibility."

"Well, we can't very well ignore this new information. I wonder why Dick Chance and Silky Swartz still maintain that they didn't know the identity of the man who attacked Pat that night?"

"Who knows? Maybe Willowby threatened them or paid them off. All I know is, I got the distinct impression that they knew a whole lot more than they were willing to tell Andy and me."

"When are you going to talk to this Willowby? I don't think it would be a good idea for you to go see him by yourself. If he is the killer, he might be dangerous. You better make sure that Andy goes with you, you hear? Don't you be going off half-cocked!" he said and gave me a stern look over the top of his reading glasses.

"Oh, don't worry. Andy barely lets me out of his sight!" I grumbled.

"Well, at least somebody has some common sense around here! You know you could be making some people mighty uncomfortable if what that woman said is true!" he warned.

"Boy, don't I know it!" I said under my breath.

"And what is that supposed to mean? Has somebody been hassling you?" he demanded.

I started to explain but at the last minute changed my mind. Jack was making such remarkable progress; I didn't want to upset him. There wasn't anything he could do about it anyway.

"Oh, you of all people know how cops are, Jack! He thinks I'll go blundering in and screw things up. Trust me, he will see to it that he is present for any future interviews!"

"Well, I'm glad. You are entirely too inexperienced. You need somebody with a little healthy skepticism along. You're not used to dealing with liars and criminals like a cop does every day of the week. Andy's a fine fella, I don't worry about you when he's around!"

"Well, thanks, Jack!" Andy said from the doorway where he had slipped up on us unseen and overheard Jack's comment. He walked over and the two men shook hands.

"You're looking pretty perky there, Chief," Andy grinned gesturing at Jack's new setting.

"Yep, you can't keep a good man down," Jack quipped, "pull up a chair and sit a while. How's it going out in the real world?"

Jack and Andy fell into their usual comfortable conversation one cop to another and as usual I was ignored. To a casual observer, they could easily have been father and son and in a way they were, at least as far as their chosen profession. It was obvious that they had a great deal of respect for one another. I couldn't have asked for two more caring men for my protectors. Watching them made me miss my husband and kids. I knew my husband would have liked them both. I was sorry he never got a chance to meet them.

My thoughts were interrupted when I realized they had stopped talking and were both looking at me.

"What? Did I miss something?" I stammered.

"Earth to Ellen! Where'd you go just then?" Andy asked.

"Oh, sorry! It's just that when you two put your heads together, I may as well as fade into the woodwork! What did you ask me?"

"I asked you to come over here and take a look at these two photographs that Jack found," he repeated, giving me a puzzled look.

I walked around to their side of the table and looked over their shoulders at a snapshot of the McCoy living room that I had seen before. Actually there were two depicting the same basic area of the room only taken from slightly different angles.

"So? What am I supposed to be looking for?" I asked.

"I'm not sure," Jack said hesitantly. "There's something about them that seems different, but I can't quite put my finger on it. I thought maybe you could see what I'm missing."

I picked them up and carried them over by the window where the light was better. According to the label on the backs, they both were pictures of the north end of the room opposite the staircase. There was a table and chairs and a curio cabinet off to the side. They were nearly identical although one had been taken by the local police photographer immediately after the bodies had been found, and the other by the state photographer the following day.

"Other than the fact that they were taken a day apart by different cameras, I can't see any difference," I said doubtfully, but just to be sure I checked again.

Then it hit me. "Hey, wait a minute! In the first one, the table looks like it has been polished. See the reflection of the lights right there? But in the one taken later, it's all covered in dust and there looks like there are some kind of marks in the dust! The marks almost look like shoe prints. It's really hard to tell from the camera angle. They were shooting across the surface of the table instead of straight down on it. Other than that, the pictures look just the same!" I said, handing them back to Andy.

He looked at it, shrugged and handed it to Jack.

"Yeah! I should have known it would take a woman to notice something like that!" Jack said. "I have been staring at these pictures for hours and just didn't see it!"

"Let me see those, Jack!" Andy said, taking them from him and holding them up side by side. "That's probably nothing but fingerprint compound! The place would have been covered in the stuff!"

"But a shoe print! Why would there be a shoe print on the dining table? What kind of sense does that make?" Jack insisted.

"Where do you see a shoe print?" Andy asked, squinting at the photos.

"Right there!" I said, pointing.

He finally saw what Jack and I had seen.

"Okay, it could possibly be a shoe print, if you really stretch your imagination," he admitted, "but what would it be doing there?"

"Well, obviously, somebody stood up on the table!" I observed, surprised that he hadn't come to the same conclusion.

"Okay, but for what purpose?" he asked. "It doesn't make any sense!"

"It makes perfect sense to me!" I said.

"Really? And why is that?" he asked.

"Because somebody needed to reach the ceiling! Maybe they needed to change a light bulb or something! I nearly broke my neck doing the same thing!" I replied.

"But why on earth would somebody feel the need to suddenly change a light bulb in the middle of a murder scene investigation? That's crazy!" Andy said.

"Let me see that picture again," Jack said, reaching out toward Andy. "There is a chandelier over the table," he observed, "a person wouldn't have to climb up on the table to change a bulb in it. Stand on a side chair, maybe, but all the way up on the table? No way!"

"What else could they have been doing?" I asked.

Andy snapped his fingers and Jack and I both looked up. "What if there was something hidden under the ceiling tiles? Whenever you disturb ceiling tiles, dust falls out of the opening and you couldn't help but step in it. Maybe someone was looking for something that was in the ceiling!"

"Andy, I have gone over the crime scene notations a hundred times!" Jack said, "there is nothing in there that said anything about the technicians checking out the ceiling tiles!"

"Who said it had to be anyone connected to the investigation? Maybe someone slipped in there after the first picture was taken, got whatever it was and left before the state people arrived!" Andy suggested, warming to his theory.

"You forget that the place was sealed, Andy," Jack reminded him, "there's no way somebody off the street could just waltz in there and help themselves to whatever. I just can't see it happening!"

"Why would it have to be someone outside the investigation?" I asked reasonably, "we are talking about the possibility of a cover up. Maybe it was Art Talbot or someone else on the force. If it was someone from the inside, I'm sure no one would have batted an eye if he or she went inside that house alone. It could happen, you know!"

"At this point, the whole thing is moot anyway," Andy sighed. "I'm sure there's been plenty of changes made to that old house over the last thirty years. The ceiling's probably been replaced a couple times over by now."

"Probably," I agreed, "but you know I have an inside track with a real estate agent!"

"You mean Kay Cornwall?" Andy asked.

"Yeah, Kay. She was dying to sell me a house! Maybe she could talk the current owners into letting us take a look around. You never know, maybe there's still something left of the old ceiling."

"You can try if you want, but I have a feeling you're going to be disappointed. The family living in the McCoy house has been there for years. I doubt they would be interested in selling it," Jack said.

"Well, I'm going to give it a shot anyway!" I said, "it sure beats sitting around here getting nowhere fast!"

I used Andy's cell phone to call Kay's real estate office. Her answering machine message said she was out of the office showing some property and to please leave a message at the tone. I left my name and Andy's cell phone number.

"So what's next?" I asked, snapping the phone shut and handing it back to Andy.

"What do you think, Andy? Ellen seems to think you need to go have a talk with Rosemary Willowby's husband. Do you want to tip our cards to him or what?" Jack asked.

"Well, so far all we got is the Martinez woman's word that he was there, I'd kind of like to get someone else's corroboration on it before we go to him. It's her word against his as it stands at the moment."

"How about Chance and Swartz? What if we put a little pressure on them? You know, tell them that the secret's out. Alice told all, etc.?" I offered. "They might be willing to change their story if they think it's already out."

"Yeah, we might be able to get something out of them. This time, let's not give them any advance warning, you know, just sort of show up. It might shake them up a little!"

"I'm ready when you are!" I agreed. "Jack, can we get you anything?"

"Yeah, bring me a magnifying glass. I want to get a better look at those marks on the table."

"You got it!"

I followed Andy down the hall and out to his car.

"Did you say anything to Jack about your hate mail?" he asked as he backed out.

"No, I didn't want to upset him. He'd only worry and there's nothing he can do about it."

"Good. The less he knows about that the better. He sure seems to be in good spirits. I guess he has you to thank for that!"

"Oh, I don't know about that!" I said, "he is a very strong-willed man. I'm sure he would have found something to bring him back to life. Like he said, you can't keep a good man down!"

"Yeah, he is that all right! It's just such a shame that a great cop like him is in such bad shape!"

"You really admire him don't you?" I asked.

"You bet I do! I don't know that I would be able to overcome his disability like he has."

"Andy, do you think there is any chance that somebody like Willowby shot him?"

"I don't know, Ellen. Unless somebody confesses, we may never know. Earl Henderson may have known, but he's conveniently out of the picture."

"Yeah, I meant to ask, how's that coming? Any leads on the other car tracks?"

"Nothing yet. I'm still waiting to hear from the experts at the state crime lab. They've got people that can sometimes tell what kind of tire made the marks, so until then, it's at a stand still."

We spent the rest of ride back to Dick's Tavern discussing his visit with the injured people at the hospital. He told me that the driver was still in critical condition, but the passenger in the front had died. He had talked to the relatives, but was not allowed in to see the survivor. The man was unconscious, so it had been a wasted trip.

When we entered the bar, it looked and smelled exactly the same as before. The current owner was in his place behind the bar, although there were a couple of scruffy looking biker types seated on the stools that hadn't been there on our previous visit. They both turned at our approach and gave Andy a hostile stare.

"Hey, Mr. Chance!" Andy said, ignoring the bikers, "is your dad around?"

"He's in the back," he said warily, wiping a glass with a towel, "was he expecting you again so soon?"

"No, my friend and I would like to talk to him for just a second. Would you mind telling him we're here?" Andy said, glancing at the guys at the bar and nodding dismissively their way. They turned back to their beers taking the hint to mind their own business. I have to admit, I was glad he was there. They looked like trouble to me.

Chance's son made a big show of holding the glass up, giving it a final swipe and carefully placing it on the shelf with the others. I guess he wanted to impress the bikers with his bravado, but his act was wasted on Andy, who just leaned against the bar patiently watching him. I guess he wanted to let us know that he wasn't pleased that we had come back. He took his sweet time walking down the length of the bar to the swinging doors to the kitchen. He was gone a lot longer than it should have taken him, but eventually he walked to the end of the bar and raised the hinged section for us to pass through.

We went directly to the tiny office and Dick Chance was sitting behind the desk. We each took a seat across from him and his eyes darted back and forth between us. I kept waiting for Andy to start, but he just sat there until the silence started getting uncomfortable. I felt as though I was witnessing some kind of power struggle and Dick Chance blinked first.

"So, what is it you want?" he said, licking his lips.

"Look, Dick," Andy said quietly, "the last time we were here, the little lady here, seemed to think that maybe you weren't completely honest with her. You know how women are, always looking for things that aren't there."

I whipped my head around at him. I had never heard him talk like that before.

"I don't know what you mean!" he insisted, glancing in my direction and nervously fiddling with the papers on the desk. "I certainly didn't mean any disrespect!"

"Now, calm down, Dick. I'm on your side! But you know something? She just won't leave me alone! She's been running all over the place talking to people about that fight you broke up between Pat McCoy and that other fella and guess what?"

"What?" he asked, blinking sweat out of his eyes.

"She seems to think that the other guy was the husband of one of your regulars. A guy by the name of Willowby! Seems his wife was quite a looker. Now Dick, you're not as young as you used to be, but I'd say that back then you would have noticed this Rosemary. She's still a might fine looking woman, so I'm sure she wasn't somebody a man would soon forget. You with me so far, Dick?" he smiled.

"Hey, that was over thirty years ago! I've seen plenty of pretty women since then. I can't be expected to remember their names!" he cried, wiping his forehead on the sleeve of his shirt. It was so obvious that he was lying that it was almost laughable.

"Hey, like I said, I only here because of Ms. Richardson. I'm telling you, she is like a dog with a bone! She just keeps riding my ass about this thing. I guess she's afraid you might get in trouble for withholding information regarding a capital offense. You know there's no statute of limitations on murder, don't you, Dick?"

"Listen you, I don't have to say nothing else! I know my rights. I don't have to answer any more of your damn questions without a lawyer present! Now why don't the two of you just get the hell off my property and don't come back without a search warrant or something!" he yelled, leaping to his feet.

Andy kept his seat, calmly gazing up at him. "Did Willowby threaten you, Dick?"

"I don't know what the hell you're talking about! I told you I'm not answering any more questions!"

"Or did somebody pay you to keep your mouth shut?" Andy suggested in the same soft tone.

"I've got nothing more to say, mister. Now unless you plan to arrest me, get the hell out of my bar!" he screamed.

I reached out my hand to Andy. Things were getting a little too intense for me. He looked at me, shrugged and rose to his feet. I really admired the way he had kept his cool. In my eyes he was a credit to the uniform. He stopped for just a second looking down at the old man who was trembling with rage and calmly walked out of the room without another word. I followed mutely. The bikers were still at the bar and stared at us all the way to the door. I didn't take a breath until we were safely in the car.

"Well, what do you think about police work now, Ellen?" he chuckled, "I thought you were going to faint on me. You should see your face! You're as white as a sheet!" he said, pulling the car into gear.

"You might have given me a little warning, Andy!" I fumed. "I thought that guy would have a stroke!"

"Naw, he's been a barkeep for most of his life. That little interview was a walk in the park for a guy like that!"

"Well he sure didn't look like he was having fun to me!"

"That's the point, Ellen. I knew he wouldn't fess up. The whole point of that exercise was to shake him up, get him thinking, you know? All of a sudden, he's not so sure that somebody didn't rat him out! I bet he's on the phone right now to all his buddies trying to find out who talked!"

"Boy, when you decide to do something, you do it in a big way, Chief Taylor!" I said, realizing just how good he was at his job.

"Well, thank you, Ms. Richardson!" he grinned, "I'm starving! You want a greasy burger and some fries? I'm buying!"

"I can't think of anything I'd rather have!" I laughed, realizing with a jolt how handsome he was at that moment. Oh, if I had only been a little younger!

Chapter Twenty-One

Andy's cell phone rang during our impromptu lunch date. Kay was surprised to hear from me so soon after moving in to the rental house, but true to form, was excited at the prospect of a potential sale. She was even further surprised when I expressed an interest in the McCoy house.

"What in world would you want with a dump like that?" she said, "I doubt any bank would be willing to finance a place in that condition. Wouldn't you like to see something a little newer? There are some really cute houses in the Firelands Manor Subdivision. I've got some contacts at the bank. We could get you in with very little money down!"

"No, Kay, I'm looking for something to fix up, you know, something not too far from where I used to live. Even if the current owners aren't willing to sell, maybe you could ask them to let me take a look around. It might give me some ideas for any other similar house that you might have listed. I just really like the style of that house. It's got a lot of potential!" I said with enthusiasm. I was glad she couldn't see my face, because she would have known I was lying through my teeth. I almost hated to lead her on, but desperate times call for desperate measures.

"Now if you'd rather not work with me on this, I guess I could try another real estate agent. But I'd really rather work with someone I know," I said, laying it on thick. "You just seem to be so tuned in to the area. I just thought you'd be willing to help me out on this."

"Of course I'll help you!" she enthused. "I wouldn't dream of letting such a good customer get away! I'll call the owners as soon as I hang up. Will you be at this number?"

I assured her that I would be hovering near the phone and snapped Andy's cell phone shut.

"I feel kind of badly about that," I said handing the phone back to Andy. "She really has been helpful."

"Don't worry about it. I'm hoping you'll decide you really do want to come back here to live. I've gotten pretty used to having you around!"

"Thanks, Andy! I wish I could, but I've got my family to think about. I would hate to miss seeing my grandkids grow up. Besides, when this is all over, I don't think I'll be very popular in this town. I may have a lynch mob chase me all the way back to Georgia!"

"I doubt that, but you're right. Things could get pretty uncomfortable around here."

"So you're starting to come around to my conspiracy theory, Chief?" I asked hopefully.

"I'm not one hundred percent certain, but I'm leaning in that direction. Just remember, we've got a long way to go before we can say for sure."

I settled for that. I knew he was having a hard time coming to grips with the idea that his boss could be a part of it, but admired his putting his personal feelings aside. It spoke volumes as to the quality of his character.

When we finished eating, we stopped by a discount store and picked up a magnifying glass for Jack. We dropped it off to him and gave him an update on the encounter with Dick Chance. Andy said he needed to get back to the police station, so he took me home with instructions to stay inside until he came back. I called Kay to see if she had been able to contact the owners of the McCoy house, but she said there had been no answer, but she would keep trying. I gave her my home phone number and she promised to call just as soon as she heard something.

I was still keyed up from the confrontation with Dick Chance, so I spent the next few hours rearranging things and giving the entire house a thorough cleaning. I knew I would go crazy without something to keep me busy. About an hour into it, the phone rang and I rushed to pick it up, assuming it would be Kay with my answer, but it was Andy, saying he was going to be tied up at the station longer than he expected. I asked him if he wanted to have dinner with me again. He said he did, but not to count on it. I used the invitation as an excuse to prepare some of my favorite recipes. Even if he didn't make it, cooking helped me pass the time.

As it turned out, I ended up eating alone. I spent the rest of the evening with the television for company. I still slept fitfully, jumping at unidentified sounds, but managed to make it through the night on my own without the reassuring presence of my self-appointed body guard.

The next morning I got the call I had been hoping for from Kay. She said that the new owners of the McCoy house were not interested in selling their property, but were willing to let me take a look. She asked if I wanted her to go out to the house with me. I figured that Andy wouldn't mind as long as I had someone with me, so I agreed. She said she had some clients coming in to see her, but would pick me up later in the day.

I still hadn't heard anything from Andy. When I tried to call him at work to let him know what I was doing, his assistant Lucy told me he had gone to the courthouse and would probably be tied up for most of the day. I decided that having the Chief of Police with me when I toured the house might raise more questions from the homeowners than I was willing to answer. I really needed to keep up the pretense of looking for a house to buy with Kay. I hoped Andy wouldn't be upset with me for not following his instructions, but made up my mind that I would cross that bridge when I came to it.

Kay arrived shortly thereafter and was her usual well-appointed self. At least this time I didn't feel so outclassed by her expensive appearance, because I had put on make-up and my best black suit and white silk blouse I had luckily thrown into my suitcase just in case I needed something nice to wear out during my visit up North. It wasn't the greatest, but at least I wasn't in tee shirt and jeans.

When I answered the door, as before, her perfume entered the living room before she did. I wondered why no one ever bothered to tell her that she needed to tone it down, but decided it wasn't my place to offer her any unwanted advice. She looked me up and down and seemed satisfied that she wouldn't be embarrassed to be seen with me. I grabbed my purse and followed her to her car.

"You really ought to let me show some of those houses out at Firelands," she said as we pulled away. "Have you ever restored an older home? You know that takes a ton of money and work! I mean, why would you want to go to all the trouble, when you can get anything you want in a new home?"

"I don't know, Kay! Just because something is new, doesn't mean it's better! I just prefer taking something that's got some history to it and making it my own. Some people like new stuff, I just prefer old. I'm really into nostalgia," I lied.

She sniffed dismissively and changed the subject by pointing out all the homes we passed that she had sold or was in the process of selling. As she rambled on, I realized that I missed female companionship and wished she could take off her real estate hat and just be a friend, but her job was the love of her life, so I let her go on and on. I guess to be fair, I was with her under false pretenses, so I really couldn't complain if she put me under a little sales pressure. I promised myself that just as soon as the case was resolved, I would give Betsy a call. She would kill me if she knew I had stayed in town and not kept in touch.

My mind had wandered away from the wonderful world of real estate, but Kay drew me back in with another long tale about her first sale. I wondered how long it would be before she brought up her other favorite subject, my brother. Luckily, she didn't get the chance, because we had arrived at the house.

The owners, Fred and Martha Fisher, met us at the door. They were a cute little elderly couple. Fred didn't say much, but stood back and let his wife do all the talking. She and Kay hugged like old friends. While Kay worked her magic on Martha, I glanced around the living room and discovered to my disappointment, that the room had been remodeled. It was completely different than the photographs I had seen. The living room now featured a modern stippled plaster ceiling. Kay and the wife continued on around the corner into the kitchen, but I lagged behind and turned to see that Fred was watching me.

"Has this room been remodeled? Somehow it doesn't seem original to the house." I said, trying to keep the disappointment out of my voice.

"Funny you should ask. That section over there used to be used as a dining room, but there's just the two of us and Martha wanted a bigger living room. There was a chandelier over by the windows, meant to hang over the table at one time. When we took it down, we had to replace the whole ceiling."

"Huh, well I bet that was quite a job!" I said just for something to say. The remodeling had destroyed any chance I might have had to see what had been above the table.

"Tell me about it! What a mess! Course, that was years ago. We could never afford to do it now the way things cost these days!"

"Yeah, I know what you mean. You must have lived in this place for quite a while."

"Yep, we got a real good deal on it. Finally paid off the mortgage just last year," he declared proudly. "You know there was a murder in this house," he whispered, glancing nervously toward the kitchen. From his expression, I got the impression that he didn't want the others to overhear.

"You don't say!" I whispered back. "What happened?"

"Martha don't like me talking about it. An entire family got wiped out. Somebody just broke in and killed them all!" he said softly.

"Good heavens!" I could tell that Fred was really enjoying having someone listen and warmed to his subject.

"And the place is haunted! Why I've seen 'em floating up and down those stairs many a night! Martha says I'm just a crazy old man, but I've seen 'em plain as day!"

"And that doesn't bother you? Having ghosts in the house, I mean?" I asked fascinated.

"Naw, they don't bother me and I don't bother them. No spirits are going to run me out of my own home!" he declared.

"Well, you are a brave man, Mr. Fisher! I don't think I'd like sharing my home with visitors from the other side!" I said, figuring a little flattery might keep him talking.

"Fred!" his wife called out from the kitchen, "I hope you're not wasting that lady's time with your wild tales. She came to see the house, not listen to you flapping your gums!"

"I ain't wasting her time, Martha! She asked me a question and I was answering it! Why don't you just mind your own business!"

"Fred! These cookies are getting cold, you know they aren't any good cold. Might as well eat store bought if you're going to eat 'em cold!" she yelled.

"I'll be there in a minute, Martha! I don't give a damn whether the cookies are hot, cold or frozen. You know I don't like raisins! You put raisins in 'em just to spite me!" he shouted.

"I most certainly did not! These are chocolate chip cookies! There aren't any raisins in these. Sometimes you can make me so mad!" she hollered back.

"Just hold your horses! I'll be there in a minute!" he yelled back. I felt as though I was witnessing what was surely a running battle for control that had been going on for years.

He walked over to an antique chest in the corner and wordlessly signaled to me that he wanted to show me something without his wife knowing. He slowly and carefully pulled out the drawer, obviously trying to keep it as quiet as possible. Just as he reached in the drawer, his wife shouted again and we both jumped.

"Fred! You better not be showing that poor woman that box! Lord knows, you just won't leave it be! You know it's nothing but a bunch of junk! I swear you can drive a woman insane!"

He put his finger to his lips indicating that I keep it quiet and withdrew a rusty old metal lock box about the size of a shoebox. It had a handle on the hinged top and the lock was missing.

"I'm going to take the lady upstairs," he yelled to his wife, tucking the box under his arm and giving me an unspoken signal to play along, "we'll be there in a minute."

I followed him up the stairs and into the master bedroom. Knowing what had taken place in that room sort of gave me the creeps, but I tiptoed along behind him anyway. He went directly to the long low dresser at the side of the room and set his treasure on it.

"What have you got there, Mr. Fisher?" I asked. I was mystified by his odd behavior. Then my heart began to pound. I wondered if there was any chance that he might actually have something that was related to our investigation.

"As you can probably tell, Martha would have a fit if she knew I was showing you this." He seemed to be debating whether I could be trusted not to tell on him.

"Hey, don't you worry! I won't say a word to your wife," I assured him. I knew I was probably getting excited for nothing, but the suspense was killing me.

He stood looking at me for what seemed like forever. It was all I could do not to snatch it away from him and open it myself, but I simply gave him my most trustworthy look and held my breath as I waited for him to make up his mind whether to show it to me or not.

He seemed to reach the decision that I could be trusted. He crossed the room and carefully closed the bedroom door. I assumed he would then open the box and show me its contents, but Mr. Fisher wanted to tell me about it first. I had no choice but to listen as he related how he had come to be in possession of the mysterious box.

"I can see I've piqued your curiosity," he began. After observing his interaction with his wife, I realized that he was seldom in control of situations and was enjoying having a captive audience.

"Oh, I'd say that's putting it mildly, Mr. Fisher," I responded. "What's in the box, a treasure map or something?" I asked, making an attempt at humor.

"No. The stuff in that box doesn't mean anything to you or me, but it sure meant something to somebody!" he declared. "Course, Martha thinks I am making a big deal out of nothing!"

"Why do you think it's so important?" I asked, still hopeful, but beginning to wonder if maybe he really was just a crazy old man.

"I found that old box hidden up under some loose floor boards in the back of the downstairs closet about ten years ago. When I found it, I got all excited, because I thought it might have some money in it. I had to break the lock to get into it. When Martha saw it didn't have anything of value in it, just a bunch of old pictures and stuff, she told me to toss it out."

"So how come you saved it all these years, Mr. Fisher?" I asked, a little glimmer of hope coming back alive.

"Like I said, it don't mean nothing to you or me, but I had to ask myself. Why would someone go to all that trouble to hide it like that? It might just be somebody's old memorabilia, but then again, maybe not! I've kept it all these years thinking maybe someone would come by and ask for it back. You know, maybe some lost long relative of those people that got killed. So far, nobody's ever come."

"May I see what's in it?" I asked anxiously. Without thinking, I added, "I grew up right around the corner from here. I might know who it belongs to."

"Is that a fact? How come you acted like you didn't know about the murders?" he asked suspiciously.

Fearing I had lost his trust, I covered my mistake by saying, "I'll be honest with you Mr. Fisher. Yes, I know about the murders. It's just that I wasn't sure how to tell you when you brought it up and didn't want to make a big deal about it. This is your home now. I guess I just wanted to see how much you knew about it. It was a horrible crime and you have to live where it happened. Telling me you had seen ghosts sort of blew me away! I'm sorry if I misled you."

He stared at me for a beat and then deciding to accept my apology, said, "Okay."

He opened the lid and stepped back allowing me my first glance inside. The contents were puzzling to say the least. The first item was a small leather bound book. It was on the order of a daily planner, with each page a day of the week for the year 1967. The first page contained a form for the book owner's name, address, telephone number, etc., but it wasn't filled out. There was a section in the back of the book for addresses and telephone numbers. There had been a couple of entries made, but only initials over the numbers. It was almost as if it was in some kind of code. I flipped through the calendar pages and noted that there were cryptic notations made on several dates, but didn't have a clue as to their meaning.

"This is certainly odd," I commented. "Why do you suppose it was done like this? It's as if the person was afraid someone would find this and figure it out."

"Beats me. Whatever those entries are, the person was sure being mysterious about it. Now do you see why I kept it?" Fred asked. He seemed excited and relieved to finally be able to share his find with someone who could appreciate it and not belittle him as his wife had done.

"I certainly do! I think you have definitely done the right thing!" I said making him smile in gratitude.

I laid the book aside and began sorting through the other items.

"Fred!" Martha shouted from the foot of the stairs, making us both jump again, "Do you want lemonade or iced tea with your cookies?"

He opened the bedroom door and shouted, "We'll take iced tea! Can't a man have two minutes without you pestering? I said we'd be right there!"

"Okay! I'm going to show Kay my flowerbeds out back. It'll be on the table!"

"Okay!" he shouted back, "We'll be down in a minute!"

He walked over to the window and looked down, assuring himself that they were temporarily occupied and signaled that I should continue.

The next thing I came to was a crumbly, yellowed envelope wrapped in a rubber band. Inside was a stack of photographs. They appeared to be amateur snapshots of various family outings, depicting mostly children with a few adults at parks, swimming pools and the like. I expected to see the same people in all of them as you would in a family album, but they were all different. Some of the children were blonde and some were dark-haired. I noticed that they were mostly little boys. A couple of the pictures were of Cub Scout troops. There didn't seem to be any relationship between them. I had expected to see the McCoys among the pictures, but none of them were in evidence. I began to wonder if maybe the box belonged to someone other that the McCoy family.

"Did you see him?" Fred asked excitedly gesturing at the pictures.

"See who?" I asked. He acted as if I was supposed to have made some terrific discovery, but I had apparently missed it.

"Right there!" he said, pointing to a man standing in the background in the picture on the top of the stack.

I looked closer and saw a man dressed in dark clothing with his arm resting across the shoulders of a boy probably six or seven years old. They were watching a little league ball game being played in the foreground.

"You mean this guy?" I asked, pointing.

"Yeah, him. Now take a close look at the next picture and tell me what you see!" he cried.

To my surprise, I noticed that the same man was in that picture as well, only this time he was crouching down in front of a little boy in a bathing suit beside a lake. Again, he wasn't the main focus of the shot, which was of some little ones posing in a rubber raft, but was off to the side of the scene. With the other children in the foreground, obviously the central subjects, I hadn't noticed him. As I flipped through the rest of the pictures, I saw that he was in them all, but always on the periphery, never the main subject. A couple of photos showed him clearly enough to reveal that the reason he was always dressed in dark clothing was because of his collar. He was dressed like a priest.

"Now I see what you're talking about! This guy here! The priest is in all these pictures!" I said catching his enthusiasm.

"I didn't see it at first either," he said, "I just kept looking at those picture trying to make some sense of them and then one day, it just jumped out at me! They are all different people except for the priest. The only one that really shows what he looks like is the one where he is posing with the boy's basketball team. Hand them here and I'll show you."

He flipped through the pictures and pulled it out. This one had been taken in a school gym. It was of a team of boys lined up in front of the bleachers in their uniforms. The boys were lined up in two rows with the boys in front kneeling behind some basketballs. He was on one knee to the left of them. He appeared to be in his early thirties, with short dark hair. His clerical collar was plainly visible. There was no school name on the boy's uniforms only numbers, so there was no way to tell where the picture had been taken.

"What do you make of it?" he asked. When I didn't respond, he continued, "I had to wonder why those pictures were hidden like they were. I never heard about any priest living in this house, did you?"

"No, not as far as I know," I said, flipping through the rest of the pictures.

"I figured that since he was a man of the cloth, I ought to hang on to them. Maybe he's somebody's long lost relative or something!"

"Well it certainly is a mystery to me, Mr. Fisher!" I said.

I laid the pictures aside and took out the remaining items in the box. There was a small gold chain with a crucifix, some brass buttons, a small sized athletic sock and some cloth Boy Scouts merit badges as well as several movie ticket stubs and a torn admission slip for Cedar Point, a local amusement park.

"It just doesn't make any sense!" he said, picking up the sock. "Why in the world would anybody hang on to something like this?"

"I really don't know, Mr. Fisher. But I'm glad you didn't follow your wife's advice. Don't ask me why, but I think this

190

stuff may be very important. Have you ever shown this to anyone else other than your wife?"

"Oh, maybe a couple of people. Everyone thinks I'm full of hot air! I don't even know why I showed it to you! I guess because you didn't laugh at me when I told you I had seen ghosts!" he muttered.

"Well, I certainly don't think you were being foolish! Can I ask something of you?" I said. "I'd like to see if I can help you find out who that mysterious priest might be. Would you be willing to let me take this with me and let me do a little digging? I promise to let you know whatever I find out!"

"Oh, I don't know! I've had that stuff for a mighty long time. What if somebody comes looking for it?" he asked, scratching his head.

"Mr. Fisher, if they were going to come for it, they would have come by now, don't you think? Let me give you my phone number. You can call me any time. What do you say?"

I guess he saw something in my face that convinced him, because he nodded and helped me put everything back.

He started to hand it to me and startled me when he looked me in the eye and said, "you really weren't interested in buying this house, were you? You think this stuff has something to do with those killings, don't you?"

"Would you believe me if I denied that?" I said, afraid he had changed his mind.

"Nope," he said placing the box in my hands, "now let's go eat some of those damned cookies before Martha has my head!"

Chapter Twenty-two

When we got back downstairs, I slipped out to Kay's car and put the box on the floorboard behind my seat. When I went back in the house and entered the kitchen, Martha was glaring at her husband, but to my relief made no mention of what we had been doing upstairs. I had the feeling there would be words exchanged as soon as we left. I nibbled on some cookies and followed Martha and Kay on a tour of the entire house, but I didn't pay much attention, because I could hardly wait to share what I had found with Jack and Andy. As soon as it was politely possible, I ushered Kay to her car.

"What the heck was that all about?" Kay wanted to know, "I thought you wanted to look at the house! You came back downstairs and acted like you couldn't get out of there fast enough! What were you and Fred doing for so long?"

"We were just talking, Kay! Just like you were doing with Martha! I just decided the house wasn't what I had in mind! There was no sense in wasting time everybody's time looking at all the rooms, when it wasn't anything like I imagined!" I explained.

"Whatever! Next time, let's have some sort of signal to let me know you're not interested, okay?" she sniffed.

"You have my word, Kay!" I agreed, hoping that I would never have to suffer her company again.

I knew I was in trouble as soon as we pulled into my driveway. Andy was there, waiting for me in his squad car.

"What's the Chief doing at your house, Ellen?" Kay asked in surprise.

"Oh, I think I may have forgotten to pay my parking tickets, or something. Thanks for the ride, Kay! I'll call you!" I blurted out. I leaped from her car, snatched the box from behind my seat and slammed the door. I could feel her eyes taking it all in but was immensely grateful that she pulled away without asking any further questions.

"Andy! I'm surprised to see you! Lucy told me you would be tied up in court all day! How long have you been here?" I said nonchalantly.

"Only for about ten minutes," he scowled, "matter of fact, I had just about made up my mind to break the door down. Where the hell have you been!"

"Before you yell at me, why don't you come on in and let me show you what I found!" I said, holding up the box for him.

"This had better be good!" he muttered and got out of his car.

He went in the house ahead of me and flopped down on the couch. I set the box on the coffee table in front of him and took a seat in the chair.

"Why didn't you wait for me? I thought we agreed that I would go with you! You went with Kay out to the McCoy house, didn't you?"

"Well, of course I did! Where else would I go with her? I tried to call you, but you weren't by a phone! I figured you wouldn't mind as long as I didn't go by myself!"

"Ellen! I thought I made myself perfectly clear that I didn't want you going anywhere alone! Have you forgotten that somebody is after you?"

"But I wasn't alone! Kay was with me the whole time! You said yourself you can't protect me 24 hours a day! I can't stay locked up in here forever!"

"Oh right! Kay Cornwall would be a big help if some big guy came after you! Ellen, I can't believe you aren't taking this threat more seriously!"

"Okay! Okay! You can dog me for the rest of my days! But please can we change the subject for just a minute?" I whined, doing my best to be charming.

He wasn't buying my act, but let me continue.

I rushed into an explanation about how I had gotten the box and what it contained. By the time I had finished, he had forgotten his anger and was excited about it as much as I was.

"Ellen! We've got to show this to Jack! Grab your stuff!" he cried when I'd finished. I had hoped for an apology for his anger at me earlier, but his enthusiasm was enough for me. We hurried out to his car and sped off to the nursing home.

We found Jack in his wheelchair in the dining room. He was hunched over his lunch trying to chase down some peas with his fork, but not making much headway.

"I don't know why I bother!" he swore, "I hate this slop anyway!" He tossed the fork down in disgust. "You wouldn't happen to have anything decent to eat on you, would you?"

I dug around in my purse and came up with a bag of peanuts I had gotten on the plane ride from Georgia and handed it to him.

"I knew I could count on you, Ellen," he grinned, tearing it open with his teeth and dumping the nuts in his mouth. "So, what's the latest? Did you get a chance to go snooping around the McCoy place?"

"We sure did!" I said quickly before Andy could answer. "Are you done here or do you want us to wait for you to finish?"

"Trust me, I've had about all of this I can take! How about give me a push down to the sunroom, Andy, so we can have a little privacy."

Andy took hold of the handles and I walked beside. We arranged ourselves at our usual table and I set the box in front of Jack. I told him how I had come to be in possession of it.

"Why didn't the old guy just give it to Mark?" he asked.

"I got the impression that he thinks all the McCoys were killed. I don't think he knows that Mark is still around. Lucky for us he kept it as long as he did!"

"I guess that's plausible. He probably bought the house directly from the bank after Mark was in the Army. It stands to reason that with Pat dead, they probably foreclosed on it."

"He did tell me he got a great deal on it. Who knows, maybe he just never associated Mark with the family. Or maybe he just wanted to hang on to it. He thinks the house is haunted, you know!"

"No kidding! There's no way I'd live in that place! With their killer walking free, I wouldn't blame them if they rattled a few chains!" Jack quipped.

I opened the box and began laying out the contents in front of him. The table was big enough so that I could arrange the photographs in rows. I handed Jack his magnifying glass and walked over and stood by the windows where I would be out of the way. I hadn't said anything to Andy about the priest in the photos. I decided to wait and see if either of them noticed, without me telling them. Andy picked up the notebook and began leafing through the pages, while Jack poured over the photos.

Neither of them said a word for what seemed like hours. When I couldn't stand it anymore, I walked around to the seat across from Jack and picked up the little gold cross on its chain. I fiddled with it nervously, watching Jack's eyes as he peered through his magnifying glass at the filmed images. When he got to the last picture, he laid down the glass, removed his glasses, sighed and pinched the bridge of his nose.

"These pictures don't look like they belong to the McCoy's at all! I didn't see any of them in these. Maybe this stuff belonged to someone else!" he said. "Ellen, I think you may have been taken in by that old guy!"

"There's nothing in this book to show that it belonged to anyone in the family either," Andy added, tossing it on the table. "It's just a bunch of scribbling. Ellen, I don't want to disappoint you, but Jack may be right!"

"But what about the priest? Isn't it a little strange that he just happens to be in every one of these pictures?" I asked defensively.

"What priest? I saw the one with the basketball team. So what? Maybe the owner of this stuff was Catholic! That doesn't mean it had to be the McCoy's!"

"Come on, Jack! Look again! He's always in the background, but he's in every one of them! I didn't notice it at first either. Mr. Fisher had to point it out to me."

He replaced his glasses and picked up the magnifying glass and went back over them. When he got to the last one, he looked at me.

"You're right! Andy, take a look at this."

He handed Andy the glass and waited while Andy examined each picture.

"If I didn't know better, I'd think these were surveillance shots, except for the one with the basketball team. It's almost as if whoever took these pictures didn't want the priest to know that he was having his picture taken."

"Maybe the real subject of these pictures is the priest," I offered, "but why be so sneaky about it? And why would whoever took them feel the need to hide them where they did? There's nothing of value here. This necklace isn't even real gold and the clasp is broken. And what about all this other stuff? What would ticket stubs and Merit badges have to do with anything? And a dirty old sock! You have to admit, it does make you wonder!"

"Okay. Let's just for the sake of argument assume this stuff belonged to one of the McCoys. Let's say it was Pat's. And let's really go out on a limb and assume that this is what the unknown person was looking for when they stepped on the table. A box this size would probably fit through a ceiling tile, if Andy's theory about something being hidden in the ceiling were correct. But let's go even farther with this and say that this box had been moved before our unknown person got to it. Why would someone risk getting caught removing evidence from a crime scene for this stuff?" Jack asked, looking from Andy to me.

"You got me, Chief!" Andy shrugged and looked at me.

"What if we were able to learn the identity of the priest? Maybe he was someone the McCoy's knew. I just don't think it is a coincidence that he appears in each and every one of those pictures! There has to be some kind of connection!"

"Wait a minute! I thought you were all but convinced that Rosemary Willowby's husband killed the McCoy's! Doesn't this just muddy the water!" Andy said accusingly.

"I still think he is a suspect, Andy! But I think we need to at least check into this! Maybe the fight he had with Pat was all there was to it! Aren't you the one who is always saying we need to keep an open mind?"

"What do you think, Jack? Do you think we need to get sidetracked with this stuff, or keep pursuing Willowby?" Andy asked.

"There is still the matter of the Mayor's involvement. Have you been able to find any connection between Willowby and Dan Albertson?" Jack replied.

"Not so far. As far as I can tell, they didn't know one another," he admitted.

"You didn't tell me you checked into that!" I accused.

"Well, you're not the only one who can go off on their own, Ellen! Yeah, I'll admit I've made some discreet inquiries," he said defensively.

"In that case," Jack spoke up, "it probably wouldn't hurt to check into it. I guess we could just show this stuff to Mark and see if he knows anything about it. I had hoped we wouldn't have to get him involved, but he's bound to know what we're doing by now."

"What if we showed them to someone at Saint Mary's Catholic Church in town. Maybe someone there would recognize the priest," I suggested.

"I guess it's worth a shot. What do you say, Andy?" Jack asked.

"I say we are probably going on a wild goose chase with this, Jack, but I'll go along with it. I still think Willowby is the best lead we've had so far."

"Yes, and Mark may have been the one all along and we have been doing all this sifting through the mud for nothing!" I reminded him, still angry that he had been doing some checking up on the Mayor without telling me. "Maybe if the police hadn't botched the investigation when it happened, we wouldn't be here!"

They both looked at me in irritation and I realized what I had said.

"Oops! Sorry, present company excepted. I'm just getting frustrated that just when we think we are on the right track, something else jumps at us. Guys, I'm sorry this came up just when we thought we were getting close, but we simply can't ignore it! That's why this case never got solved in the first place. You have to admit they did a pretty superficial job back then!"

"Well all I know is that whenever this thing breaks loose, no matter who it turns out to be, it will be opening a lot of old wounds!" Andy said.

"And someone will finally have to answer for it, don't forget that, Andy! That's why you became a cop, isn't it? To put the bad guys away?" I asked.

"You're right, as always, Ms. Richardson! Now why don't you gather up those pictures. I think it's time you and I went to church!"

Chapter Twenty-three

Saint Mary's is an old gothic church made of age darkened sandstone about a block from the Town Square. I remember thinking that it seemed kind of spooky looking when I walked past it as a child, although many of my classmates were Catholics and attended there. We tried the massive front doors of the sanctuary, but they were locked, so we followed the brick path that led around the side to the rectory in back.

A nun, who introduced herself as Sister Mary Teresa met us at the door. She was a sweet-faced older woman dressed in a modified, modern habit and sensible shoes. She took us into a room off the vestibule to wait, while she went to fetch the current priest, Father Thomas Gillworthy.

While we waited, I took the opportunity to look around having always been a little curious about the place. The wall opposite the mullioned windows contained a bookcase filled with leather bound books, icons depicting various saints and an array of religious materials and artifacts. The winged chairs and small matching settee in front of the windows were covered in deep maroon leather with antique mahogany side tables placed strategically along side. The room's décor featured dark green linen wallpaper and wainscoting to match the bookcase. An intricately fashioned gold crucifix adorned the wall closest to the door over a shrine with candles and a statue of Mary as its centerpiece. The room smelled of rich leather, lemon scented furniture polish and something I couldn't define but was probably incense. Andy and I didn't speak, almost as if it would seem sacrilegious to break the contemplative mood the room inspired.

We both looked up when the nun reappeared, gesturing for us to follow her. She led us to the priest's office in the back and introduced us. We shook hands all around and Father Tom gestured for us to take seats in front of his desk.

"So, Chief Taylor, what brings you by today?" he said smiling over his steepled fingers. "You haven't decided to join the faith, have you?"

He was an elderly gentleman, with a shock of white hair, twinkling blue eyes and a kindly face. His voice belied his Irish heritage.

"No such luck, Father!" Andy grinned. "I'm afraid we're here just to get a little information. We'll have to save my religious conversion for another time!"

"Ah, too bad. I was in the mood for a little soul saving! Things have been a little slow this month!" he laughed. "So, what kind of information did you need?"

"I need to see if you could tell us if you recognize the priest in these pictures. They recently came into our possession and we're trying to find the rightful owner. We thought they might have some personal significance to whoever took them."

Andy handed him the photos and the priest switched on the lamp on the desk and held them one by one under the light. His eyebrows drew together and his lips formed a thin line.

"Where, may I ask, did you get these?" he asked, his voice devoid of the friendly banter.

"I'm not at liberty to reveal that at this time, Father. I take it you know who that man is?"

"Let me just say, I knew him at one time. I haven't seen him in over twenty years."

"Who is he?" I asked, "his identity might be pivotal to an ongoing investigation."

"He came to our parish back in the 60's right out of the seminary," he continued, ignoring the question. "He was assigned to me for further instruction. New priests are sometimes sent to small parishes like ours to gain experience before being sent on to bigger churches in the city. When he first arrived, he wanted to shake things up, you know. He was always trying to change things and I believed, being from the old school, in a more traditional approach to our services. I'm afraid we didn't always get along. After he was here for a couple of years, he seemed to accept my way of thinking and we eventually worked out our philosophical differences."

"So, what happened? Did he move on to a bigger church?" I asked.

"He may have. I really don't know," he said, picking up his letter opener and tapping it on the desk.

"I don't quite understand what you mean. Weren't you informed as to where he was going when he left?" Andy asked.

"He was reassigned by the Church. One day he was here and gone the next. I was never informed as to where he was sent," he said, his voice becoming a little more strident.

"Is that how it is usually done? It sounds as though you weren't expecting him to be reassigned. I mean, you indicated that the two of you had some differences of opinion. Did that play a part in his being moved so abruptly?"

"I really can't comment on that. We were told that he had to go and he went. It wasn't my place to question the Church's authority!" he declared, his face turning red.

I glanced at Andy with an unspoken question in my eyes. Why was he getting so upset? His entire demeanor had changed from friendly to outright hostile in the blink of an eye.

"Father Tom, I didn't come here to upset you," Andy soothed. "I can see this is a sensitive subject for you. So, please, if you don't mind, what was this priest's name?"

"Andy, you know his brother! His name is Francis, Father Francis Albertson!"

"Are you telling me the man in those pictures is related to the Mayor?" Andy asked in shock.

"He is Dan Albertson's younger brother," Father Tom nodded.

"I wasn't aware the Mayor had a brother! Are you sure? He certainly never mentioned that he had a brother who is a priest!" Andy cried.

"If the Mayor chooses not to discuss his family, I'm sure he has his reasons. I'm just telling you what I know. Now if you don't mind, I've got some important matters that need my attention. If you'll excuse me," he said rising to his feet, "I really need to ask you to leave."

Andy stared at the old man, his jaw working as he tried to digest this latest revelation. I stood up and reached out to him.

"Andy, come on. We got what we came for. Let's let Father Tom do what he needs to do."

He dragged his eyes away and glanced at me. I saw a look of shock, confusion, and anger in his face. The old priest looked from Andy to me, nodded and quickly made his exit.

"Andy, let's go." I repeated softly, gathering up the photographs from the priest's desk. "It's obvious we won't be getting any more out of him."

He rose stiffly to his feet and we walked out. I followed him wordlessly back to the car, the shock of what we had just learned weighing heavy between us.

As we drove back towards Shady Oaks, I kept playing back what the priest had said over in my mind. The fact that someone in the McCoy family had carefully hidden photographs of the Mayor's brother, who was of all things a priest, was just too bizarre to contemplate. I hadn't been aware that the McCoys had been a religious family, but I had to admit that I really hadn't known them that well. I kept searching for some logical explanation for the pictures, but nothing came to mind. Even more puzzling, why would the Mayor keep his brother a secret? I really wanted to discuss it with Andy, but I could tell from the way he was acting that he needed time to absorb the information before getting into it, so I kept my comments to myself.

We arrived at the nursing home and found Jack in his bed napping. He awoke as soon as we approached. He turned his head toward us and smiled, but immediately noticed the stormy look on Andy's face and frowned.

"Hey there, Andy!" he said looking to me for an explanation, "what's wrong? You look like you've lost your best friend! Did Father Tom give you a hard time?" he asked teasingly in a failed attempt at levity.

"Andy's a little upset, Jack," I quickly spoke up, "we found out who our mysterious priest was in the pictures. I guess we're still a little shocked at who he turned out to be!"

"So? Don't leave me hanging here! Who was he?" Jack said turning to Andy, who stood looking out of the window with his back to us.

"He is Dan Albertson's brother, Francis!" Andy growled. "I didn't know he even had a brother! Jesus! You think you know somebody and then you find out you really didn't know them at all!"

"Come on, Andy! So the Mayor didn't tell you about his brother the priest! What's the big deal? It's not like he's your closest friend! You just work for the guy!" Jack insisted.

"Jack, don't you see? This Francis person is the connection between the McCoys and the Mayor that Willowby didn't have! Doesn't it seem a little coincidental that pictures of the Mayor's brother are hidden at the McCoy house and the

202

Mayor just up and pays for Mark's defense? Not to mention getting Mark hustled out of town before he can be charged with the crime and then, as if that weren't enough, practically buys him a car dealership! Come on, Jack! Isn't it obvious? The whole thing smells to high heaven!" Andy snarled, hunching his shoulders, the back of his neck turning crimson.

"Well, I agree it is rather an odd coincidence," Jack said reasonably, "but don't you think we need to look at this with a little less emotion? You can't let your personal feelings cloud your judgement, Andy. You know as well as I do that as a cop, you just can't jump to conclusions because someone makes you angry. You need to use your brain, not your heart!"

Jack had said what I wished I could, but knew that Andy would never have accepted it from me. Something passed between them and Andy finally turned away from the window. His shoulders slumped and he shook his head in agreement sadly. My heart went out to him, but I stayed where I was and kept quiet. The two men looked at one another wordlessly for a minute and then Jack broke the silence.

"So! How about putting my sorry carcass into that chair and let's get busy! Ellen, why don't you scoot down to the nurse's station and see if you can get some kind of legal pad. I want you to jot down some notes as we go over all this. We've got some new information and we need to see how it all fits together!"

I was more than happy to have something to do and hustled off on my errand. I also figured that it was Jack's way of giving them some time alone. When I returned, Andy had moved Jack into his chair and was rolling him through the door. I followed them down the hall and we got set up at the table.

"Okay, Ellen," Jack began, taking on a professorial tone, "let's review what we've got so far. You write down the names of our suspects on that pad. We'll discuss motive and opportunity for each of them. Okay with you Andy?"

"Sounds good to me, Jack," Andy said. I noticed that he had resumed his professional demeanor. I knew it was probably due to the conversation he had had with Jack in my absence.

"So, let's start with the most obvious, Mark McCoy. He most definitely had the opportunity. He lived there. He walks in, kills the family, walks out. As to motive, that's pretty obvious. His father was a notorious drunk. According to Mark's uncle, he was also a wife beater so it stands to reason that he probably abused his kids too, although we have no proof of that, but it does seem reasonable, wouldn't you say, Andy?" Jack asked.

"I'd have to say that's likely. If Pat abused his wife, he probably knocked his kids around as well."

"Okay, as to evidence against him, we've got blood on his hands, which was seen by Gerald Yarborough, but doesn't necessarily mean he did it. He could have picked it up when he discovered the bodies. So, what else is there? Anybody think of anything else?" Jack asked, looking from Andy to me.

"There wasn't any gunpowder residue on his hands," I pointed out, looking up from the notepad.

"Yes! Very good, Ellen! You remembered! Andy?"

Andy shrugged and looked at me.

"According to his statement Mark said that his folks weren't happy about him working at the bar. Maybe that could be considered as his motive, you know, he had an argument with his parents about it and things just got out of hand!" I said.

"The only problem with that is the fact that his father was shot while still in his bed," Andy argued, "now I don't know about you, but in my experience most people don't have heated arguments and stay in their bed. There's something about Pat being in his bed. Somehow that doesn't seem to fit. This was more like an ambush, you know?"

"You mean that whoever did it, came in with the gun already in his hands?" Jack asked.

"Well, maybe the argument happened downstairs and then everybody went to bed and Mark just decided to kill his parents. How about that?" I suggested.

"I don't know, if Mark did it, it would make more sense if it was a crime of passion. This killing was just too cold blooded somehow," Andy replied.

"Okay, I see what you mean. The position of the bodies seems to indicate some sort of revenge killing, a sneak attack if you will," Jack offered.

"Yeah, I guess that's what I'm trying to say," Andy nodded.

"Well, why don't we move on to our next suspect. Whom do you want me to write down next?" I asked.

"Let's look at Alice Martinez," Andy said. "She definitely had the motive. Not only had Pat thrown her over for Rosemary Willowby, but she was pregnant with Pat's kid. I'd say that's more than enough reason to off the guy!"

"Okay," I said. "Do you really think this murder was committed by a woman? It seems more like a man's type of thing than a woman's to me."

"Hey, Alice looked as hard a nails to me. She was a pretty rough character. Yeah, I could see her doing it!" Andy insisted.

"Okay," I said doubtfully, "what about opportunity? She wasn't exactly familiar with Pat's house, although she may have gone there when Loretta wasn't home. I guess she could have done it."

"Who knows, she hung out at the same bar where Mark worked. Maybe she drove over to the McCoy's while she knew Mark was at work, killed the family and let the son take the fall for it," Andy added.

"Okay, we've got the Martinez woman. While we're at it, we may as well add Rosemary Willowby too, since we are considering females," Jack said, gesturing for me to write her name down.

"Why her? What possible motive could she have? If Pat had been killed before her husband found out, I could see it, but the confrontation proves that he did know about it. What would she accomplish after the fact?" Andy interjected.

"Maybe she was just angry at the way her husband treated her after he took her back. Maybe he started beating her up or something! Maybe in some warped way she was proving to her husband that Pat meant nothing to her!" I threw in, realizing how unbelievable it sounded.

"There is also the matter of opportunity. According to her, she was doing everything in her power to prove to her husband that she could be trusted. How could she leave her husband in the middle of the night like that? It would have made him suspicious, don't you think?" Jack offered reasonably.

"Which leads us to our next suspect, Mr. Willowby. What is his first name, anyhow?" I asked.

"Brian. His name is Brian Willowby, Jr.," Andy said absently. "I looked it up at work."

"Okay, Brian Willowby, Jr." I said, writing his name on the pad. "We know what his motive is, revenge and jealousy over Pat's affair with his wife. That's pretty cut and dry. We have witnesses that saw him start a fight with Pat."

"Yes, but only Alice was willing to identify him. Don't forget that Dick Chance and Silky Swartz refused to name names," Andy reminded me.

"Yes, but don't forget how they reacted when we asked about it. I thought Dick Chance was going to blow a gasket when you pressed the issue!"

"I'll agree that he probably knew, but that doesn't necessarily mean anything! Maybe he just didn't want to get involved. Maybe he was afraid he'd get dragged into court, who knows?"

"Not to mention the fact, that so far there doesn't seem to be any relationship between Willowby and the Mayor, if there was some sort of cover up," Jack tossed out.

"The same could be said for Alice and Rosemary," I added, "there was no reason for the Mayor to get involved on their accounts. Especially not Alice. I'm sure their paths never crossed."

"Which brings us back to those damn pictures," Andy sighed. "There had to be some reason that they were hidden in the McCoy house."

"Are you saying you think a priest killed the family? Come on, Andy! Just because the Mayor never mentioned him, doesn't mean anything! Maybe they just had a falling out. Things like that happen in families all the time!" I said.

"But why the pictures? And why hide them?"

"Andy, we still don't know that they even belong to the McCoy's! Maybe Fred Fisher is just a crazy old man and set me up! Maybe he got that stuff at a flea market or something! You know how people like to embellish things! Maybe he just did it to get attention!"

"That's what I thought at first, but the fact that the priest is related to the Mayor is just too much of a coincidence. Jack, what do you think?" Andy asked.

Jack had been watching our discussion with a thoughtful expression.

"I think we need to get a little more information. First of all, we need to find out if any of the McCoys attended Saint Mary's. I would assume considering Pat's lifestyle, that he wasn't a regular churchgoer, but maybe his wife and kids were. We might need to talk to some of the older members who were around back then. Next, we need to find out where Francis Albertson is now. I've got a little money saved up, maybe you two could go have a talk with him."

"Father Tom said he left rather abruptly," I told him, "he got really uncomfortable talking about it, almost as if there was a lot more to the story than he was willing to say. He really bristled when Andy tried to get more details, didn't he, Andy?"

"Yeah, he said the church reassigned him just when they were getting their act together. Said it came out of the blue and he wasn't informed about it. Said the decision came from the Church hierarchy. It sounded kind of fishy to me."

"From what you're saying, it almost sounds as if he was removed for some sort of misconduct. Maybe he got in some sort of trouble. That would explain why his brother the Mayor never mentioned him. Maybe he was an embarrassment to the family or something," Jack suggested.

"If that's the case, I'm sure there must have been rumors flying around among the members. I guess that while we're checking into the McCoys' religious affiliation, we may as well ask about that too," Andy said.

"I think it might be worth your time to talk to Silky Swartz again. Didn't he indicate he was good friends with Pat McCoy? He might know something about their relationship with this Father Francis," Jack added.

"Okay. What about the Mayor and Mark? Do you think it's time we went to them? We've been dancing all around them so far," Andy said, though I could tell he had reservations about it.

"Let's save them for a last resort. You've got plenty of other avenues to pursue before you go to them," Jack said and I could see that Andy agreed.

"Well, Ellen, looks like we've got our assignments. Jack, you want to stay here or shall I take you back to your room?"

"Take me back, but grab the box, will you, Ellen? I want to look over that stuff again. Who knows, maybe something will come to me."

I gathered up my notes, returned the photos to the box and we wheeled Jack to his room. The nurse saw us and said she would see that he got back into bed. We said goodnight and drove to my house.

When we got there, Andy checked around as always and nothing had been disturbed. We agreed that we would get together in the morning. Andy reminded me again to keep the doors locked and that a cruiser would be coming by every hour or so during the night. He left me then to check back at the police station and I was glad. It had been a difficult day and I spent the rest of the evening doing my best to think of anything besides the case. At least I tried anyway.

Chapter Twenty-four

I didn't hear from Andy again until the following afternoon. He called to say that he had asked his assistant Lucy, who happened to be Catholic, if she knew anyone who may have attended Saint Mary's back in the 1960's. She told him that her family had moved to Milan in 1979, but she would ask her mother, who was a devout woman who attended Mass several times a week. Her mother had given him the name of a woman who had been a member all her life though she was now in her eighties. Her name was Elizabeth Crowley and she lived by herself just a few blocks from the church. Ms. Crowley had agreed to talk to us and Andy said he would be by to pick me up later in the day.

When he arrived, he seemed to have gotten over his black mood from the previous day. He was back to being the same levelheaded man I had grown to depend upon. I got the impression that he had come to grips with the possibility that there really was something to my discovery and was determined to see it through to the end and let the chips fall where they may. His willingness to put personal feelings aside in order to get to the bottom of what may ultimately incriminate a man he respected was just another reason for me to admire him. He took the responsibility of his position very seriously and was a credit to his uniform.

We arrived at Ms. Crowley's small clapboard bungalow at the appointed time. Her home sat on a tiny lot bordered by flowerbeds in need of weeding at the foundation and a rock retaining wall covered in waves of trailing ivy along the cracked sidewalk by the street. She met us at the door of the screened porch in the front and welcomed us into her doily-draped sitting room. I was immediately impressed with her. She was a tiny elderly woman though by no means enfeebled. She was neatly dressed in a pink print dress, her back was straight and she carried herself like a woman half her age. She proudly informed us that she had reached her eighty-third year, but to me, she looked to be closer to seventy. She added that she still drove her own car, although she admitted she probably shouldn't and Andy laughingly agreed.

"So what brings you folks by?" she asked pleasantly. "I don't get much company, since the grandchildren moved away. My Edward passed away back in 1997, so I'm alone now. Oh my son calls to check up on me, but he lives in Cincinnati, so he can't come to see me that often. I go down there for Christmas and such. He keeps trying to get me to move in with him and his family, but I just can't leave the place where I spent so many years with Edward. His grave is here and I just feel closer to him in my own home. That and my church. Outside of trips to the store and church, I don't get out much anymore. I'd offer you some cake or something, but I don't bake like I used to. There's nobody but me here to eat it and I can't have it anyway with my sugar problem," she said apologetically.

"That's quite all right, Ms. Crowley," Andy said kindly, trying to bring the conversation back on track, "we didn't come to put you to any trouble. Actually we did want to ask you about your church attendance. I understand you have been a member of Saint Mary's for many years."

"Why yes! I don't know what I would do without it! Father Tom has been such a comfort to me since I lost my Edward. He came to the hospital and stayed with me night and day when my Edward passed away. He had a stroke, but he didn't suffer, thank God! Father Tom was there to give him his Last Rites and performed the most beautiful Mass I ever heard for him. Why there must have been five hundred people who came! My yes, Saint Mary's and Father Tom have kept me going, that's for sure!"

"Would you say you've known just about everyone who ever attended Saint Mary's?" I asked.

"Well, some of the younger ones come and go, but I'd know anyone who comes with any regularity. I may not know their names, but I would certainly remember their faces. I'm probably the oldest member still around and I've been going to church there all my life!"

"What about Pat and Loretta McCoy? Were they members?" Andy asked.

"McCoy? You mean those poor people who were killed back in the 60's? Goodness, I haven't thought of them in years! Yes, I do remember Loretta coming to church occasionally, but I can't say that I ever met her husband. She was a pretty shy little person. Poor thing married out of her faith. He wasn't a very nice man as I recall. I remember there was quite some concern about their funeral not being held in the church. They had the services held at the funeral home. It wasn't even a Catholic service! I didn't go but we all felt she would have been upset had she known. At least she and her little girl got their Last Rites, so we can take comfort that they are in heaven now. Father Tom said so. I'm glad you reminded me. I'll be sure to light some candles for them."

"You said Loretta and Becky got Last Rites. Did Father Tom do that?" Andy asked. I knew we both were holding our breath in anticipation of her answer.

"Let me think. No, I think it was that other priest that was helping Father Tom at the time. Now what was his name?" she murmured, searching the ceiling for the memory.

"Could that have been Father Francis? Francis Albertson?" I prompted.

"Why yes! How could I have forgotten his name! My goodness, I haven't thought about him in forever! He was only with us for a few years, you see. Yes, if my old memory serves me right, it was Father Francis who gave the McCoys Last Rites. He was at the house right after the police found them. Father Tom told us they were still alive when he got there, but of course they weren't. I think he just told us that to make us feel better," she said shaking her head sadly.

"What did you think of this Father Francis, Ms. Crowley? Did you think he was doing a good job?" Andy asked. "We got his name from Father Tom in case you're wondering," he added by way of explanation.

"Oh. Well, let me see. Like I said, he was only here for a couple of years. He was quite an enthusiastic young man. He was nothing like Father Tom. Not there is anything wrong with Father Tom, he is a fine priest, but Father Francis just seemed more, I don't know, lively. He seemed especially dedicated to the young people in the church. He was always organizing outings and the like. We needed someone like him to bring the youngsters back to church. I guess it was the times. Most young people quit coming to church in the 60's. You know, what with the hippies, drugs and sex and all that was going on back then. We could use more people like him to breathe life back into the church. I was sorry when he left."

"Were you aware that he is related to our Mayor Dan Albertson?" Andy asked.

"Yes. It always seemed kind of strange that they were brothers. Most priests come from Catholic families and Dan Albertson is Methodist. It raised a few eyebrows, I must say, but I certainly never felt comfortable talking about it. It was just one of those things that you didn't talk about. I had always been taught to have respect for the priests. Their private lives were none of our business and I just didn't ask. Nowadays, everybody knows everybody's business. The world would be a better place if people knew when to keep their opinions to themselves."

"So, were you surprised when he left? Father Tom indicated that his departure came rather abruptly. What did you think about it?" Andy asked.

She cleared her throat and adjusted the doily on the arm of the chair in which she sat. For the first time in our conversation, she seemed at a loss for words. She had been extremely forthcoming up until this point and the change was very noticeable.

"What did I think? You mean when he had to leave? Well, we knew he was only going to be with us for a short time. It was bound to happen sooner or later. It wasn't my place to feel one way or the other about it. When the church says go, the priests go. I certainly didn't have any say in the decision!" she insisted hotly.

She pulled a Kleenex from a nearby box and nervously blew her nose. I got the impression she was hedging. Andy picked up on it and decided to press the issue.

"I certainly don't mean any disrespect, Ms. Crowley, but you seem kind of uncomfortable talking about this. I get the feeling that maybe you didn't agree with the church's decision. Am I right?"

"Whatever the church decides, I abide by. As I said, as a good Catholic it isn't my place to second-guess those in authority! I leave those things to God!"

"But you can at least tell us how you felt about him as a person. Did you like him?" Andy asked kindly.

"I thought he was a fine young man! I never listened to the gossips! It is just shameful the way some people run their mouths!" she declared, balling up the Kleenex in her fist and snatching another.

"Are you saying that some of the parishioners expressed their opinion concerning his removal?" Andy asked.

"Chief Taylor, you seem like a very intelligent young man! You know very well that whenever something unexpected like that happens, there are always some uncharitable people who feel the need to make comments. I find that sort of talk both unpleasant and very unchristian!"

"I can certainly understand your feelings, Ms. Crowley and I admire your stand. I agree with you that people often stick their noses into things that don't concern them."

"You are so right! I never involve myself with rumor and innuendo!" she declared indignantly.

"Well, I am sure you did the right thing, Ms. Crowley! I am sure that Father Francis appreciated your support!" I said encouragingly.

"It was the least I could do for him," she sniffed. "I never got the chance to tell him. He disappeared before I got the opportunity!"

"If you don't mind, I'd like to change the subject for just a minute, Ms. Crowley. Have there been any other young priests that have come to Saint Mary's for a short time the same way that Father Francis did?" Andy asked.

"Yes. Not many, but over the years we've had a few," she responded.

"And when these other individuals left, was it ever announced in advance? Or did they just sort of disappear the same way that Father Francis did?"

"Hardly! There was a going away party held for every last one of them. To be honest, I was hurt that we never got the chance to do the same for Father Francis!"

"And when it was announced that they were leaving, were you ever informed as to where they were going?" Andy asked. I was watching him draw her out with fascination. I felt he would have made an excellent attorney.

"Of course! Some of them still write to us! One of the young man ended up in Rome working for the Vatican!" she said. "Father Tom considers him the son he never had!"

"But nothing from Father Francis?" he asked, raising his eyebrows.

"No. We never heard another word from him," she said shaking her head sadly.

"Didn't you ever wonder what had become of him? You have to admit, he did leave under some rather unusual circumstances."

"Like I told you before, Chief Taylor, it wasn't my place to question the decision of the church," she repeated defensively.

"Now Ms. Crowley, I respect your feelings with regard to rumors and the like, but you know that sometimes you have to tell the police anything you might know if it has any bearing on an ongoing investigation, don't you?" Andy said with just a hint of sternness in his voice.

"Of course, Chief Taylor," she said her eyes opening a little wider, "I would never hold anything back from the police!"

"Well, I appreciate that, ma'am. You'd be surprised how many people don't think a thing of covering things up when I ask them questions!" he said resuming his friendly tone. "Now I'm not asking this out of idle curiosity, I assure you, but I need to know anything you may have overheard at the time of Father Francis's removal from your congregation. You indicated that there were rumors being bantered about, so I have to assume you must have heard what some of the other church members were saying."

"Not that I paid any attention, mind you, but yes, I knew what some of them were saying," she admitted softly, lowering her eyes to the floor.

"And what was it they were saying, Ms. Crowley?" he asked.

"They said he must have done something really sinful. That he must have committed some kind of terrible sin. Some said it was probably something to do with stealing and some accused him of having an affair with one of the members. I can't even say what one person said. I'm simply too much of a lady! It was just plain disgusting!" she said, her face blushing scarlet.

"Now, Ms. Crowley, you have to remember I am a police officer. There is very little in the world that would shock me.

Ms. Richardson here is a colleague of mine and knows that anything you say must be held in the utmost confidence, isn't that right, Ellen?" he asked, turning to me.

"Ms. Crowley, think of Andy here like a doctor. Sometimes you have to tell the doctor things that you wouldn't ordinarily say. It's okay, really!" I said soothingly. "Believe me, we know you would never falsely accuse anyone of anything!" I looked at Andy and we locked eyes.

"Okay. They said he had been touching the little boys, you know, improperly," she whispered, covering her face with her hands and starting to cry.

"Ms. Crowley, I'm sure they had to be wrong! I'm so sorry we had to bring up what is obviously a very painful subject," I said and walked over and patted her shoulder.

"Andy, have we about finished? I think we ought to let Ms. Crowley get some rest."

"Yes, I think you're right! Ms. Crowley, thank you. You have been very helpful. I'm sorry we had to put you through that. Ellen, let's go."

We showed ourselves out. I felt a pang of guilt for upsetting the poor old woman, but knew we had had no choice. As soon as we got in the car, I couldn't contain the questions that were swirling through my head.

"My God, Andy! You don't think there's any chance that the Mayor's brother was a child molester, do you? Could something like that happen here of all places?" I cried.

Andy made no response and we drove to Shady Oaks in stunned silence.

Chapter Twenty-five

We found Jack at his usual spot at the table in the sunroom pouring over the notes from our interviews. When we told him what we had learned from Ms. Crowley, he didn't seem as surprised as I expected him to be.

"You know, after you left, I looked at the stuff in the box a dozen times trying to see the connection each item had to the other, you know, what they all had in common," he said. "I started off thinking that it was just a lot of random things that had been thrown together. Maybe it was just the usual junk that people toss in drawers and the like, but the fact that someone went to the trouble to hide the box, ruled that out. The contents of that box obviously had some significance for somebody. So I tried to put myself in the place of the person who hid it. There had to be a central theme to the items, if you know what I mean."

"And what was the theme, Jack?" I asked impressed with his intuitiveness.

"The main subject of the photographs, the Merit Badges, and boy's athletic sock were all related to children, particularly little boys. While the cross necklace could have belonged to a girl, it could also belong to a boy. The ticket stubs were also places of interest to children. Do you see where I'm going here?"

"Okay. But what about the notebook? That certainly isn't something a child would have," I pointed out.

"I'll admit that that had me stumped," Jack admitted.

"So what did you decide?" Andy asked.

"I really hadn't come to any conclusion, but from what you got from the old lady, it makes perfect sense now. Come on, Andy! Think about it. What if the rumor about the priest being a child molester was true? That would have been some pretty explosive information if it ever came out."

"You can say that again! This town would have lynched a man for that back then! Priest or no priest!" he agreed.

"You said yourself that the pictures looked as though they were taken in a way so that the priest wouldn't realize that he was the actual subject. What does that tell you?" Jack asked.

"That someone was trying to get proof of his guilt?" I asked.

"Exactly! Now, look at the entries in that notebook. See those numbers on the date pages? What if they represent money? What comes to mind?" he asked.

"My God! You're talking blackmail! You're saying this stuff belonged to someone who was blackmailing the priest! I guess we don't have to wonder who that person was!" Andy cried.

"Who else? Pat McCoy! Ms. Crowley said he wasn't Catholic, so he certainly wouldn't have cared that the man accused of child molesting was a priest. He obviously wasn't big on morality. Just look at his lifestyle! Would it be too far of a stretch to imagine that he would have used this kind of information to his own advantage? He could have gone to the police, but why? There is a lot of money to be made if you know something about someone that they would pay big bucks to keep covered up!"

"But a priest? Come on, Jack! They don't make that kind of money! If these entries represent dollars, there's no way a priest could have come up with this kind of money back in 1968! It just doesn't add up!" Andy argued pointing at the day planner.

"You're forgetting that Francis Albertson wasn't any ordinary priest! Where would he go to get hush money?" Jack asked.

"I'd say that's pretty obvious," I said before Andy could answer. "His brother, Dan. He was a wealthy man, he could have given him the money to pay a blackmailer."

"I don't believe it!" Andy shouted. "This is all just a lot of conjecture! These are some mighty serious accusations we're tossing around here! And even if what you're saying is true, what does it have to do with anything!"

"Look Andy, I don't like this any better than you do. But you have to admit if there ever was a motive for murder, this would be right at the top of the list!" Jack insisted.

"But if Francis was paying Pat to keep quiet, why kill him?" I asked.

"Who knows? Maybe the well ran dry. Maybe Pat upped the price and he couldn't keep up the payments. Maybe Pat discovered he had a conscience after all and decided to go to the police. Maybe the guy just got tired of being scared. There's any number of reasons why he felt he had to get rid of Pat!" Jack answered.

"But a priest? That was a pretty gruesome murder, Jack. Even I have a hard time imagining a priest doing that!" Andy said.

"I agree! Priests don't go around blowing people's head off, Jack!" I cried. "And it wasn't just Pat who got killed, don't forget. Loretta and Becky certainly didn't have anything to do it. Why kill them?"

"Maybe it wasn't supposed to go down the way it did. Maybe they just got in the way. Who knows? Maybe he thought Pat would be home alone."

"I still don't think the priest did it!" Andy insisted stubbornly, crossing his arms across his chest.

"Then the only other possible explanation is that his brother either did it for him or paid to have someone else do it. You know as well as I do that people will do just about anything for the right amount of money, Andy. It happens all the time!" Jack said.

"Jack, do you realize what you're saying? You are accusing the Mayor, a man you and I have both known for years and who I might add has been a pillar of the community, of either personally killing three people or paying to have them killed! I just don't buy it! We don't have any solid evidence to support it."

"I have to agree that so far all we have is a theory. I know it sounds crazy, but you have to admit, it is a possibility. This scenario is no more unbelievable than any of the others we've come up with so far," Jack responded.

"Besides, where would Dan Albertson find this so-called assassin. You can't just look up murder for hire in the Yellow Pages. Someone was bound to find out! He's always been in the public spotlight, Jack. He's a politician for Christ's sake!" Andy cried.

"Which unfortunately only adds another reason to cover the whole thing up. Think what a scandal like that would have done to his career in politics. If that had ever come out, he couldn't have gotten himself elected dogcatcher! Like I said, all we have so far is only a theory, but we simply can't sweep it all under the rug! That's been the problem all along. Those three people died, Andy, and we owe it to them not to leave any stone unturned until we uncover who did it. If that means we have to step on a few toes, so be it!"

"So what do you suggest we do? Go charging into the Mayor's office and beat a confession out of him?" Andy growled.

"No, I think it's way to early to tell him anything. We need someone to corroborate Ms. Crowley's statement about the abuse. We have to substantiate the rumor that the priest really was some kind of pedophile," Jack said.

"You mean find out where the rumor started?" I asked.

"Exactly!" Jack said, gesturing in my direction. "If there actually was something like that going on, there's someone out there who knows about it. There may be some grown man who was molested by Francis as a child, but never reported it. The experience would probably have been very traumatic. That's the kind of thing a person would never forget, although getting someone to talk about it might be difficult," he pointed out.

"I would certainly feel a lot better if I knew that the priest really did do something," Andy agreed. "At least then I wouldn't feel like we're going off half-cocked."

"So, how do we find this person?" I asked.

"I guess we'll have to get some names from Ms. Crowley. I hate to have to use her again, but I don't see that you have any choice. Father Tom certainly won't tell you. I'm sure if he was aware of anything like that going on in his church; he would do everything he could to cover it up. Can you imagine the kind of adverse publicity that would create?" Jack said.

"She may decide to clam up on us as well, Jack. It was all I could do to get her to say what she did on the subject! She liked the guy! I got the impression she said about all she intended to on the subject!" Andy complained.

"What about Lucy? She got us the lead on Ms. Crowley from her mother. Maybe Lucy's mother would know some of the men who were members in the 60's. We could focus on men who were of a certain age at the time. Say men who are now around forty to forty-five. That would make them ten to fifteen at the time of the murders. Then we wouldn't have to go back to Ms. Crowley." I offered.

"I guess it's worth a try," Andy said, flipping open his cell phone.

He spoke to his assistant briefly and gestured for me to hand him my legal pad. He wrote down some names, thanked her and rang off.

"She gave me three possible individuals that she felt fit the description. She said she would call her mother and see if she could think of anyone else. She'll call me with any more."

"What about any of Pat's known associates, Jack? Do you think we still need to talk to that Swartz guy? He seemed to be a pretty good friend of Pat's. If Pat was involved in some sort of extortion plot, maybe he started throwing around some sudden cash and Silky would remember. Who knows? Maybe Pat even said something to him about what he was doing."

"I think that is an excellent idea! At least then we'd see if there was any fire to go with all this smoke!" Jack nodded. "What do you think, Andy?"

"Oh, I wouldn't mind pulling old Silky's chain again. I'm sure he's heard about our visit with his buddy, Dick Chance. He might just be shook up enough to spill something."

We decided to try getting in touch with the men on Andy's list before pursuing anything with Silky. We would use him only if there was some indication that our suspicions were based on actual events. If we did need to talk to Silky, we decided we would probably get more out of him if we made a surprise visit, so I wasn't to call him. Andy took me home to set up the appointments while he returned to the station. I wasn't looking forward to talking to these men about such a delicate subject. I was glad that Andy would be the one asking the questions.

As I was making the calls alone in my living room, my thoughts turned to my total immersion into the investigation. I realized that it was getting hard to remember why I had come back home in the first place. It seemed like just a few days prior to the situation in which I found myself, I had been spending time with old friends, laughing, enjoying myself and getting back in touch with my roots. I had been trying to recapture all the good feelings I had as a child and had discovered to my dismay that I had been looking at my birthplace through rose colored glasses. It seemed as though there was ugliness and greed and violence around every corner. For the first time since I had come, I was homesick for my uncomplicated life in Georgia. The village of my childhood would never hold the same fond memories in my heart. I wanted it all to go back to the way I thought it had been, but knew it never would. I knew that no matter what we uncovered, everything I thought I knew about my hometown had been a fantasy. The serene place that I thought I knew had been merely an illusion.

Chapter Twenty-six

It took a couple of days to locate the men on Andy's list. Two of them had moved away from Milan. One of them now lived in Toledo and the other in Columbus. The third still lived in the vicinity, but commuted during the week to Cleveland, so we had to make arrangements to meet with him on the weekend. I set up appointments with the other two for the following week. We decided we would show the men the photographs of the priest and use that as a way to get them to open up.

Andy had to catch up on some work at the police station, so I had some time to take care of some of the chores around the house that I had been putting off. Andy checked up on me every so often, which I appreciated since the person who had written the poison pen letter had yet to surface. The time provided us both with a respite from the all-encompassing focus of the case. By the time the weekend rolled around, I was back on track and anxious to forge ahead.

Andy picked me up at my house on Saturday morning. We drove out to the home of our first contact. To protect his identity, I will call the man we were to see John Smith. We had to drive several miles out into the country to reach his house. It was a large Victorian-style home made of white clapboards with black trim. The property was well tended with at least an acre of mowed grass and four huge oak trees at all four corners of the house. Harvested cornfields on either side bordered the lot. As we drove up the long gravel driveway, we spotted him on his lawn tractor pulling a cart filled with bags of leaves and other garden debris. He waved hello and indicated with a gesture that he would be with us shortly, so Andy and I waited for him by the car.

He parked the tractor beside a large brush pile beside the garage out back and removing his leather work gloves, walked to where we stood. He shook hands with Andy and me and suggested that we join him on the large front porch that wrapped around the front of the house. We followed him up the steps and took seats on the wicker chairs off to one side against the wall while he sat on the porch swing facing us. He was dressed in jeans and plaid workshirt open at the front and was an exceptionally handsome man with short sandy hair, an athletic build and boyish features. I noticed he was wearing some sort of medallion on a chain that hung down on his chest. I assumed it was probably a Saint Christopher's medal or the like.

"So, what did you want to talk to me about, Chief?" he smiled brushing a piece of grass from his hair. "I'm not in any kind of trouble, am I?"

"It's nothing like that, Mr. Smith," Andy assured him, "as Ms. Richardson said on the phone, she and I are working on an old case and just wanted to ask you a few questions."

"Well, I'll do what I can. I pretty much tend to my own business, but if there's anything I can do to help you, I'll be happy to try," he said, looking from Andy to me with an open friendly expression. "Can I get you folks something? A cup of coffee or soft drink?"

"No, thanks. We don't want you to go to any trouble, besides it looks like you've got your hands full. I know you're anxious to get back to your yard work, so we'll try not to take up too much of your time," Andy said.

"Yes, as I told Ms. Richardson, I work in Cleveland during the week for an advertising agency, so I have to make up for it on the weekends. This place is a lot of work, but I like it. It helps me to get away from the rat race of the big city. It's a hassle, but I think it's worth it."

"Well, you certainly have done a great job with it!" I complimented him. "Does your wife mind you being away so much? You are kind of isolated out here."

"Nope, no wife. I live here by myself," he replied evenly.

Since he didn't elaborate on his comment, I left it at that. We weren't on a social call and it wasn't any of my business anyway.

"I understand that you have been a member of Saint Mary's Catholic Church for a number of years," Andy began.

"I don't go to church much anymore, but I guess you could say that. I'm still Catholic, if that's what you mean. I used to go a lot more often when I lived with my mom, but I get so little time nowadays, it's hard to fit church into my weekends. May I ask what that has to do with this case you're working on?"

"Actually, Mr. Smith, I'm not a liberty to discuss it at this time. We are still in the process of gathering information, so we can't comment at this stage of our investigation. I can tell you that it involves an incident that took place in the late 60's."

"That's an awfully long time ago! It must have been important if you're still working on it! So, what do you need from me? I was just a little kid back then," he said, glancing from Andy to me with a puzzled expression.

I noticed that he had begun pushing his feet on the floorboards to put the porch swing in motion. There was something in his body language that seemed to say that the conversation was beginning to make him uncomfortable. I hoped that Andy would notice the subtle change in his behavior.

"We are trying to get some information on a priest that was at Saint Mary's around that time. Ellen, why don't you hand Mr. Smith those photographs we have and see if he recognizes him," Andy said to me.

I fished them out of my handbag and placed them in Smith's hands. We watched his expression as he silently flipped through them. One of them seemed to cause a reaction in him, because his eyes narrowed slightly and his lips formed a thin line. He held it up so that we could see it.

"Where did you get this? That's me standing next to Father Francis. I don't remember having this picture taken!" he said with a slight tremor in his voice. I got the impression that he was struggling to keep his voice neutral.

I walked over and sat down next to him for a better look. It was the picture at the little league game in which the priest was standing by the backstop with his arm draped over the boy's shoulders.

"You mean this little guy here?" I asked, pointing at the picture.

"Yeah, that's me. I don't see me in any of these others. But that's Father Francis Albertson in all the rest. What's this about, Chief?" he asked as he nervously straightened the snapshots and handed them back to me.

"We were hoping you might be able to tell us what you remember about Father Francis. We understand he left town under rather unusual circumstances and that there were some pretty nasty rumors flying around. We are checking with people who may be able to confirm or refute those rumors."

"Hey, I was just a little kid! I don't know anything about any rumors!" he said jumping to his feet and moving to the porch railing in effect turning his back on us.

"What's the matter, Mr. Smith? You seem kind of upset. What is it about that picture that's got you all worked up?" Andy asked quietly, cutting his eyes in my direction pointedly.

He didn't respond but leaned on the rail with his shoulders hunched up while staring at the middle distance. Neither Andy nor I said a word while we waited for him to decide if he would answer Andy's question. After a few minutes, I couldn't take the silence and walked over to stand beside him. It was obvious that he was struggling to hold on to his composure.

"It's okay, John," I said softly, "you don't have to tell us if you don't feel up to it," I said softly. He turned and looked at me, the pain plainly visible on his handsome face.

"We already suspect that the rumors were true, Mr. Smith. We just need some confirmation," Andy said from his seat at our backs.

"Is somebody trying to sue Father Francis? Is that what this is about?" Smith asked, turning back away from us, obviously debating whether he wanted to open up old wounds.

"I can't really comment on that, Mr. Smith. Like I said, we are still in the preliminary stages of our investigation. But anything you tell us will be held in the strictest confidence. We aren't asking out of idle curiosity, I assure you," Andy said.

"I just don't want to talk about it!" he cried, the back of his neck turning red, "all that happened a long time ago and I have done my best to put it all in the past! What possible good would it do to bring it all out in the open now? I've moved on. Can't you just leave it be?"

"Under ordinary circumstances, I would say yes, Mr. Smith, but we really need your help here. Whatever you can tell us could have bearing on another matter that is a whole lot more serious than what may or may not have happened to you!" Andy said sternly.

"So this isn't about somebody trying to bring a lawsuit against Father Francis?" he asked turning toward Andy.

"I can only tell you that we are investigating another matter that could possibly be related to Father Francis. I'm sorry, I can't tell you any more than that."

"Would I have to testify?" he asked in a small voice, "because I don't think I could face that!"

"I have to be honest with you. It may not come to that, but there is a possibility that you might be called as a witness if there ever is a trial," Andy said. "We might be able to keep your name out of it, but there's no way I can promise that it won't come out."

He looked at Andy and then me with a hurt look in his eyes. My heart went out to him, but unless he said the words, we had nothing more than theory and supposition to go on. I had just about decided he wouldn't answer, when he abruptly walked back to the swing and leaned towards Andy with his elbows on his knees.

"I want you to know I have been carrying this around with me for most of my life. This is not something I want the world to know," he said urgently.

"I understand, Mr. Smith. Take your time. You were just a child. You have absolutely nothing to be ashamed of," Andy said kindly, glancing up at me.

"That's easy for you to say. I looked up to the man. I thought he was my friend. See, my dad died when I was six. My mother encouraged me to spend time with him. She thought he would be a good influence on me!" he laughed ruefully, shaking his head at the irony.

"But you're saying that he betrayed that trust, right?" I said taking a seat next to him on the swing.

"Oh, that's putting it mildly! Yeah, he betrayed us all right!" he said, covering his face with his hands.

"So what did he do, Mr. Smith?" Andy pressed.

"At first I thought it was just my imagination, you know? He was always rubbing my back and putting his arm around me, like in the picture. It felt good, you know? I didn't have a dad and I sort of felt like he was a kind of father figure. I really felt close to him, so when he touched me, I liked it. My mom was never big on physical affection, you know. She was always so sad, because of my dad being dead, I guess she just didn't have it in her. She would kiss me goodnight, but never really hugged me that much. And he did. It made me feel loved. God! I was such a fool!" he cried, scrubbing away the tears that had appeared on his cheeks.

"John, you were just a little boy! He played on your need for affection! It wasn't your fault!" I insisted.

"That's easy to say now! But you weren't there! I really loved Father Francis! I thought he loved me!"

"But then things started to change, right?" Andy said.

"It didn't happen all at once. First it was hugs and then kisses on the cheek. And then one time he missed my cheek and kissed me on the lips," he said in a tiny voice. "Of course, I thought it was a mistake. We both laughed about it, but he got this weird look on his face after it happened. I had no idea what that look was all about, but he made me promise that I wouldn't say anything about it to my mom, because she wouldn't understand. It was to be our little secret, he said."

"But that wasn't the last of it, was it John?" I prompted.

"No, things started to escalate from there. He kept inviting me to go on these youth group trips with him and some other boys. But by then I was getting uncomfortable with what he had been doing, you know, touching me where he shouldn't and then laughing it off like it was a mistake, only I knew that it wasn't."

"Are you saying the contact progressed to the point of him touching your genitals?" Andy asked in his most professional tone.

"Yeah, always through the clothing. He'd say things like I was really becoming quite a man and then feel me up like he was some kind of doctor or something! I had this feeling that if he ever got the chance, he would do more than that. I started making up excuses to my mom whenever he called to invite me on one of his outings. Then he came up with this idea for the camping trip. My mother yelled at me because she thought I was just being rude when I said I didn't want to go!" he said shaking his head at the memory.

"So she made you go?" Andy said.

"Yeah, she wouldn't take no for an answer. I wanted to tell her what had been going on, but I just couldn't. She thought he walked on water!" he spat. "So I had no choice. When we got to the park and set up the tents, he insisted that I sleep in his tent. I think he may have been messing with the other kids, because they all looked at me funny, like they knew what was going to happen. Later that night, he, he, well, he took it to the next level."

"Are you saying he raped you?" Andy asked.

"He tried to, but it hurt, you know and I started to cry. He got all sorry and cried and promised it would never happen again. God, I hated him and I loved him all at the same time. If I had been older, I probably would have killed myself. It never happened again, but I just felt so dirty. I almost confessed the whole thing to Father Tom, but I just couldn't do it. I was so confused and ashamed. Why did you have to bring this all up again? It took me years of therapy to get over it. Why do you think I don't have a wife? It left me so messed up I couldn't sustain a normal relationship with a woman! And I'm not gay! Jesus, why couldn't you just leave me out of it!" he sobbed.

"Mr. Smith, I am so sorry we had to bring this up. I know this is very painful for you, but if it's any consolation, what you have told us might be just what we need to put a very dangerous individual behind bars. Thanks for talking to us. We'll let you get back to your yard work. We'll be in touch," Andy said patting his back and nodding toward the car at me to indicate we needed to be going.

"Take care, John. You did the right thing," I added and followed Andy to the car. He was still rocking back and forth on the porch swing with his face in his hands when we backed down the driveway to the road.

"I wish there was something we could do for him!" I said, turning to Andy. He was holding on to the steering wheel so tightly that his knuckles had turned white.

"That son of a bitch! No wonder they whisked him out of town! There's nothing in this world that makes me madder than somebody taking advantage of a little kid! No wonder the Mayor disowned him. Can you imagine having somebody like that in your family?"

"I've heard that that sort of thing is probably more common than most people realize. I saw a television show about a case where the victim had repressed memories of the abuse and confronted his molester years and years later. If we can locate Francis, maybe John will get the chance to tell him what he really thinks of him. Who knows, it might make him feel better!"

"I don't know, Ellen. The guy was pretty messed up. I think he would just rather not have to think about it. I hate that we had to dredge it all up again. I sure would like to have about five minutes alone with the good Father! I'd like to beat the guy to a pulp!"

"Do you think it's some kind of sickness? Maybe he just couldn't help himself!" I asked doubtfully.

"Yeah, he's sick all right! I'd just like to be the one to give him the cure!" Andy growled, pounding his fist on the wheel.

"Well, it did happen a long time ago. Maybe he's gotten treatment and has stopped."

"Ellen, guys like that don't stop! It's an obsession. Pedophiles gravitate towards jobs where they can come in contact with little kids. Especially jobs where they have the trust and respect of the unsuspecting parents. They play on the kid's emotions, like Francis did to John. They make the kid feel guilty, like they asked for it. Either that, or they threaten the kids' families or pets if they say anything. I say prison is too good for these guys. The whole thing makes my skin crawl!"

"So we've got John's story. What about the other two guys? Do you think we need to meet with them as well?" I asked. "Don't you think we've got enough to go on? I hate the thought of making anyone else have to relive such a horrible experience."

"We can't go on the word of one person, Ellen. Francis could deny the whole thing. He could say John is making it up. There were no witnesses to the abuse. If we're going to prove anything, we have to find at least one other person who would be willing to come forward. Then we can take the next step and see if there really was some sort of blackmail scheme and cover-up. I have a feeling we have just seen the tip of the iceberg."

"Andy, I don't know if I'm up to this. Maybe you should just go see those other men without me," I said hesitantly.

"You aren't getting cold feet are you? What happened to that ball of fire that jumped all over me for not getting involved?" he asked turning to me in surprise.

"I just don't know how much more of this ugliness I can take! You've made it your life's work to deal with criminals and the things they do. I've seen more in the last few weeks than I ever thought I would. My whole world has turned upside down! I just wanted someone to care enough to find out who killed the McCoys! I didn't think I'd have to hurt innocent people in the process," I said. I felt sick at heart and turned my head away from him.

"I know this is difficult for you. It's no picnic for me either. Do you think I liked what our questions did to that guy? Let me tell you something. No matter how it makes me feel I am looking for the truth. Sometimes the truth isn't very pretty. If I didn't see this thing through, I would be no better than the people who tried to cover it up! I need you, Ellen. Please don't wimp out on me now!"

His words struck a chord with me. After a few moments of silence, I shook off my self-pity, squared my shoulders and faced him.

"Okay! I'm sorry! Everyone is entitled to a weak moment now and then," I said forcing myself to look him in the eyes. "I've come too far to chicken out now!"

"That's the spirit!" he said, slapping his hand on the dashboard. "Just keep reminding yourself that we are on the side of truth and justice!"

"Yeah, yeah. I'm a regular Girl Scout, now can we get something to eat? I'm going to need my strength for the next ordeal," I replied with a sniff, determined to change the subject.

"Ellen, if I didn't think you'd get mad at me, I'd tell you I love you," he grinned and gave me a mischievous leer.

"I love you too, partner," I said and playfully punched his arm. And I didn't dare mention the fact that it didn't make me mad at all!

Chapter Twenty-seven

We stopped for lunch at a sandwich shop on the way to Shady Oaks. We were both anxious to share what we had learned from our latest interview with the third member of our team, Jack. When we arrived, we found him in his bed asleep. I had expected to find him hard at work in the solarium. He had such a forceful personality, I had forgotten that even though he had a brilliant mind, he suffered from tremendous disabilities. I was afraid that he might have tried to do more than he was physically able to do.

Rather than disturb him, I left a note on his bed stand where he would see it, telling him that our theory had been correct and that we would check back with him later. We stopped by the nurse's station on our way out to check on his condition. We were told that thanks to our visits, his attitude had improved to the point that he was now willing to participate in some physical therapy, which he had always refused to do before. His nurse said he had spent the entire morning working with the therapist and would probably be wiped out for the rest of the day. I told her about the note I had left for him and asked that she make sure he saw it when he woke up. She promised she would and I followed Andy to the car.

"I guess you need to get back to work," I said casually as we drove towards my house. I was feeling a little let down because I had been looking forward to us spending the afternoon with Jack and really didn't want to be alone.

"Yeah, I do need to check in. But I think I may be able to get away later this evening if things haven't gone to hell in a hand basket. It's supposed to be my weekend off."

"Well, I'm glad to hear it! Everybody deserves a little time off, even you."

"I have been pushing it a little hard lately. Just when I think I'm caught up, something else happens."

"I know it isn't easy keeping up with your responsibilities at work and doing the McCoy case at the same time. If I haven't told you lately, I want you to know I really appreciate all you've done so far. There's no way Jack and I could have done it without you."

"I'm doing it because of you, Ellen. If you hadn't forced me to open my eyes to what was going on, I would have just let things rock on forever. I'm the one who should be grateful to you. You've made me realize why I became a police officer in the first place. Thanks to you I have the chance to right a wrong that has been brewing in this town for years."

"Andy, you would have gotten around to it eventually! That's just the kind of man you are! As soon as you learned that Earl's accident wasn't what it appeared to be, you would have started an investigation."

"You're forgetting that Earl may have been killed because he talked to you," he reminded me.

"Oh Andy! You're right! It is my fault that he died. I hadn't thought about that! I feel terrible!" I cried. I really hadn't looked at it that way before and suddenly felt incredibly guilty.

"Hey, it's not your fault. You didn't do anything wrong. If he was killed to shut him up, the person who did it is responsible. You were just the catalyst. It's almost as if you were sent here to get things moving again. If you hadn't come, we would still be living in a fool's paradise around here."

"I know, but a man died, Andy! Probably because he talked to me! I bear some of the responsibility for his death. There's just no way to get around it," I pointed out dejectedly.

"Earl chose to talk to you. He could have just kept his comments to himself like everybody else around here. Think of his death as a sacrifice to the truth. Without him, we would never have come as far as we have!" he insisted.

"Well, we simply have to find out who killed Earl. It's got to be the same person who shot Jack and probably killed the McCoys. Do you think it could have been the priest?"

"I think it's a little too soon to be pointing the finger at anyone. There are still too many other possibilities that we need to explore. Look, do you mind if we change the subject? I think we both deserve some time off from the McCoy case."

"Sure! We certainly can't think about it 24 hours a day. The case has been sitting around for thirty years, I guess it isn't going to disappear. What did you want to talk about?"

"Well, I was thinking. I seem to remember that you graciously invited me over for dinner a while back and I have yet to reciprocate. How about letting me cook you dinner at my house tonight? That is if you don't have any plans!"

"Plans? What plans? I have been pretty much a prisoner in my own home lately, thanks to my pen pal, so no. I don't have any plans. But you really don't have to do that! I enjoyed having you over. Your company was more than sufficient payment!" I insisted feeling a blush begin creeping into my face and praying he wouldn't notice.

"Now Ellen, my mother taught me that if you eat at someone's home, you simply must invite them to yours. You wouldn't want my mother to think I forgot my manners, would you? Come on! I make some mighty incredible spaghetti! What do you say?" he grinned.

"Well, since you put it that way, how can I refuse! She and I probably have a lot in common. Okay!" I laughed nervously. "But I insist on bringing dessert!"

"Great! I'll drop you off and be back to pick you up around six."

As soon as he pulled away after checking out the house, I started having second thoughts. I thought back to when he had said that he loved me. He had said it as a joke, hadn't he? Of course, he had! There was absolutely no way a young, handsome man like Chief Andrew Taylor could have feelings for an old widow woman like me! He should be out with women his own age, not wasting his time off with me. I simply had to stop this foolishness! I should have put that silly comment of his out of my mind as soon as he said it! I felt embarrassed at the thought that he had probably regretted saying it as soon as it came out of his mouth. I had at least made light of it, so maybe he had forgotten about it. I hoped so. I couldn't ever let him know how it had affected me. I would be mortified.

I had just about made up my mind that I would make up an excuse to back out, when he called. He said he was really looking forward to dinner and asked if I would make some more of my homemade salad dressing that I had served him before. He sounded so excited about showing off his culinary skills; I didn't have the heart to disappoint him. I would just have to make sure that we maintained our distance.

I put the whole thing out of my mind and busied myself in the kitchen. By the time I had finished preparing the dressing, showered and changed the doorbell rang. It was still early and I figured Andy had gotten off of work ahead of schedule. When I looked through the peephole, I expected to see him, but there was no one in sight. His car wasn't in the driveway either. Puzzled, I opened the door a crack and looked to see whoever had rung the bell. I looked down to see a small brown paper lunch bag on the front stoop, but no sign of whoever had left it. I had no idea what it might contain, but it seemed pretty innocuous. I didn't know any of my neighbors, but I figured that maybe one of the children had put it there.

I guess I should have been suspicious, considering the threat I had received, but I had so many other things on my mind, I just didn't think about it. Anyway, when I picked it up, it was so light that at first it seemed to be empty. When I unfolded the top and looked inside, I couldn't tell what it was. It almost looked like some sort of small stuffed animal, but one that had gotten dirty and wet. I carefully dumped it out on the cement without touching it and let out a little yelp. It was a dead rat! I whipped around to see who would have left such a disgusting thing on my doorstep, but there was no one in sight. A cold chill ran down my back. I kicked the horrible thing into the grass with the toe of my shoe and ran back into the house. I felt as though my heart would leap out of my chest. Whoever had left it, was giving me a message. I slammed the door and locked it. I was still huddling on the corner of my couch; almost too frightened to move when Andy finally arrived.

"Ellen! What's wrong?" he cried when I jerked open the door, "you're white as a sheet!"

"Did you see it?" I demanded.

"See what?" he said taking me by the shoulders. "I don't know what you're talking about! See what?"

"Outside, in the grass! It was on the step! It's disgusting!" I croaked.

He ran back outside and found the rat where it had landed beside the paper bag. When he came back inside, he was angrier than I had ever seen him.

"Did you see who put it there?" he demanded urgently, grabbing hold of me again and shaking me.

"No," I managed to squeak, "someone just rang the bell and ran away. They were gone before I could get to the door."

"Get your stuff! You're not safe here! We'll figure something out later," he ordered.

I started to protest, but he was in no mood for argument. I did as he instructed and packed a bag. He waited for me by the front door, glancing through the peephole every few minutes. He carried my bag to the car while I gathered up the food I had been preparing from the kitchen. We drove to his house in silence.

I had wondered what his house was like, but I only noticed that it was a ranch-style brick with an attached garage. The grass hadn't been mowed in a while and the hedges were overgrown, but it certainly looked inviting to me. He hustled me inside and had me wait in the sparsely furnished living room while he carried everything from the car. He took my suitcase down the hall to one of the bedrooms and the food into the kitchen. He returned with a glass of wine and held it out to me.

"Will you be all right for a few minutes?" he asked, placing the glass in my hand while he looked at me with concern. "I'd still like to fix dinner, if you're up to eating anything."

"I'll be all right, Andy! You just go do what you have to do. I just want to sit for a few minutes and pull myself together. This wine is just what I need," I said with a shaky smile.

He looked at me doubtfully, but nodded and left the room. I could hear him rattling pots and pans and running water in the sink. The wine calmed my shattered nerves and I looked around the room. It was about what I expected a bachelor's home to be. There was a huge color television that dominated one side of the room, while homemade bookshelves made of planks and concrete blocks were on the other. The room had hardwood flooring and off-white painted walls with large colorful posters of racecars for decoration. The furniture looked as though it had probably come from yard sales and included a fake leather sofa, two mismatched stripes and patterned chairs and a massive dark coffee table with stacks of sports magazines scattered on top. The whole room exuded a male personality with not the first hint of a woman's touch in sight.

I set my glass on the coffee table and walked over to the bookshelves. There were a couple of football trophies displayed among the stacks of paperbacks, most of which were true crime stories and mystery novels. There was also a droopy potted plant that hung over the side of its container in desperate need of water.

"Trying to get a fix on the homeowner?" a voice asked from the doorway to the kitchen. He had startled me and I could only nod, embarrassed that he had read my thoughts so easily.

"Your plant needs water," I said absently, trying to act nonchalant.

"I don't get to spend much time at home. With the hours I keep, I'm surprised it hasn't dried up and blown away. I'm sorry the place is such a mess. I've got a cleaning lady, but she only comes every other week. As you can probably tell, this is her off week."

"Oh I don't know," I said giving the room a mock once over, "I'd say you're holding your own. At least the floor isn't littered with dirty socks and underwear! You should see my son's apartment. You have to follow the paths between the piles of junk!" I laughed.

He didn't share my humor, but looked at me with a serious expression, "Why did you say that?" he asked.

"Say what? I'm sorry, I was trying to give you a compliment! I think you are a very good housekeeper!" I insisted. I couldn't imagine what I could have said that would get such a negative reaction.

"Why did you feel the need to compare me to your son?" he asked with a frown.

"Andy, you're a single man, my son lives out on his own. That's all there was to it. I wasn't trying to insult you!" I said walking toward him. He had been so kind to me; I wouldn't have said anything to hurt him for the world.

"You're always saying things about the differences in our ages. Now you're comparing me to your son! If you think I care how old you are, you are dead wrong!" he said and turned on his heels back into the kitchen.

I rushed after him and stopped just inside the doorway. I was speechless. He wouldn't look at me, but began taking ingredients for the salad from the refrigerator and scrubbing them furiously in the sink.

"Andy, I'm sorry! I had no idea I was saying anything that would upset you. It's just that I'm so much older than you are. I mean, the difference is so obvious. I have the greatest respect for you. You are an incredible police officer! I certainly hope you don't think I would ever belittle you just because you happen to be younger than I am! Why are you making such a big deal about a few off hand comments?"

"You just don't get it, do you?" he said, tossing down the lettuce and putting his fists on his hips in irritation.

"Get what? Andy, I'm sorry, but I just don't see what it is you're trying to say!" I said.

"How old do you think I am anyway?" he said refusing to let it go.

"I don't know! Thirty-five, forty, somewhere around there. You're still younger than me!" I insisted indignantly.

"I'm forty-three years old! And I happen to know that you just turned fifty, so you're not exactly old enough to be my mother!" he spat.

"And just how did you know that, might I ask?" I snapped, stunned that he had gone to the trouble to check out my age.

"That is none of your business, Ms. Richardson! As Chief of Police, I can find out a lot of things!" he growled.

"Okay, so you know how old I am! I still don't see why you're getting so huffy, just because I dared to compare you to my son! Most people would consider that a compliment!"

"For your information I happen to think of you as a woman. A very desirable woman, I might add. Personally, I don't see that age has anything to do with anything. You are the first woman I've met who has more on her mind than how much money I've got to spend on her. I just wish you'd quit all the talk about how you're old enough to be my mother!"

I was so shocked by his admission, I couldn't think of a thing to say. He stared at me another moment or two, as if daring me to contradict him and when I didn't, he returned to his task as if nothing had transpired between us.

"Why don't you stir that spaghetti sauce," he said evenly, pointing at the pot with his knife, "and quit standing there looking like somebody just hit you over the head."

I slinked over to the stove and picked up the spoon.

"I had no idea you felt that way, Andy," I said softly, stirring the bubbling contents of the pan, "I guess I owe you an apology."

"No apology necessary. I meant what I said earlier, Ellen. You can fight me on this, but I intend to take care of you. If anything happened to you, I wouldn't be able to live with myself. Whoever left that rat on your doorstep meant it as a warning. You know what they were saying don't you?"

"That I'm a dead rat?" I said quietly. "Or will be if I don't stop poking my nose in their business?"

"I'd say that about sums it up. If I had any sense at all, I'd make you go back to Georgia and stay as far away from here as you can. Call me selfish, but I want you here with me where I can keep watch over you. You'll let me do that, won't you, Ellen?" he asked, turning towards me.

"I'll do whatever you say, Andy. You know I wouldn't go anyway. At least not until we get to the truth. That's what it's all about, right? Truth, justice and the American way?" I said teasingly trying to lighten the mood.

"Yeah, right. I'll let you off the hook for now, but don't think you've gotten off scot-free. You're going to have to accept the fact that I'm a man who's interested in you as a woman. One of these days, you'll see things my way!"

"Yessir!" I laughed, giving a mock salute, "now can we please eat? The smell is driving me crazy!"

Chapter Twenty-eight

Andy, to his credit, did not push the issue as to his newly revealed feelings for me for the rest of the evening. He was an excellent cook and the meal turned out to be even better than I expected. I got tickled when he actually blushed when I asked for the recipe. We spent the rest of the time together swapping tales of our lives and history and talking about our hopes for the future. I had never seen him so laid back and relaxed. I discovered that he was a man with many facets to his personality. He was not only intelligent, but also funny and charming and I soon found myself telling him things I had only discussed with my closest friends.

He told me about his college days at Ohio State and how he had dreamed of playing football there, but had injured his knee before he ever got to the first game. He said his father had been in law enforcement, so his career choice had been made for him long before he ever entered school. He had majored in criminology with a minor in psychology and graduated in the upper third of his class. I can only say that it was a welcome relief for both of us to be able to talk about anything other than the case.

By the time we decided to call it a day, my fears had been assuaged and I felt as though I knew him better than I ever expected I would. He insisted that I spend the night at his house for safety's sake and I have to admit that knowing he was close by made me feel secure. If I had been anyone else, I probably would have taken our relationship to the next level, as he so obviously wanted us to do, but somehow I wasn't comfortable with the idea. I just couldn't get past the difference in our ages. Not to mention the fact that I wasn't one to hop into bed with a man unless I had some kind of permanent relationship with him. My husband had been the love of my life and I really wasn't ready to make any new commitments no matter how tempting the offer.

Plus, he was still young enough to want a wife and family, while I had raised my children and couldn't have had any more even if I wanted to. I was flattered by his attention, but knew that eventually I would have to go back to my life and he to his. Besides, I reminded myself, we really had to stay focused and any emotional entanglements would only get in the way of our working together. I knew he would insist that we discuss it at some point, but decided to avoid the subject as long as possible.

I woke up late the next morning, wrapped up in my bathrobe and went looking for him. The bed was made in his room and the house was quiet. I spotted him through the front windows in the front yard out by the street. He was hard at work pruning the hedges with an electric trimmer, so I threw on an old sweatshirt and some jeans and went to the front door. He saw me, waved and hollered that he had made coffee and to help myself. I decided to make breakfast and after searching around for a while, found everything I needed to show off some of my own culinary talents. When he finished his chores, he joined me at the kitchen table and we dug in enjoying the companionship we had discovered the night before, but the pleasant interlude didn't last long.

We had barely begun when the phone rang. It was one of his officers calling to say that he was needed at the station and we both knew he had to go. He wolfed down his food and asked me to stay at his house until he got free. I told him I would, if he insisted, but that I would really prefer to go check on Jack. He wasn't too happy about having me out of his sight, but I promised to stay at Shady Oaks until he finished at work. He changed into his uniform and drove me to the nursing home.

We had to pass my house on the way. Everything looked the same as it had looked the previous day. There was nothing to indicate that anything had happened in my absence. I felt a little foolish for reacting the way I had and imposing myself on him. It had taken me a long time to reach my current stage of independence since the death of my husband and I wasn't ready to give that up.

"Andy, I think it would be better if I just stayed at my own place tonight," I said hesitantly, "the house looks okay to me. If somebody wants to get to me, they can do it no matter where I am. Look, I really appreciate what you're trying to do, but do we really want to let whoever it is think that they can intimidate us? If I don't go about my business as usual, they win!"

"Ellen, don't you think I'm a little more qualified to access this situation? I don't think you're taking this threat seriously enough. I don't think they're going to stop with leaving you notes and dead rodents. This guy means business!'

"Well, what would you do if someone was after you? Run and hide like some kind of scared rabbit?" I asked indignantly.

"You can't compare our situations! I'm a trained professional!" he scoffed.

"I asked you a question. What would you do?" I demanded.

"I'd keep my nine mil close by and blow the bastard away!" he sniffed.

"Then that's what I want to do!" I fumed.

"What! Ellen, that's crazy! You don't know anything about guns! Jesus, what will you think of next! You are something else!" he laughed shaking his head at the thought.

"The only reason I don't know anything about guns is because no one ever taught me!" I muttered in irritation. "Lots of women carry guns these days. Why shouldn't I?"

"Are you saying that you could point a gun at somebody and squeeze the trigger? You know that once you aim at someone, there's no turning back, because otherwise you'd just be providing your attacker with a weapon to use against you. Ellen, I don't think you could do it!"

"How do you know I couldn't!" I said, "I might be capable of a lot of things that you're not aware of! Just because I'm female doesn't mean I'm a coward!"

"Is this the same woman that nearly had a heart attack over a dead mouse?" he laughed again, making me grit my teeth.

"I'll have you know it wasn't a mouse, it was a rat! A horrible, disgusting, half-rotten rat! You certainly didn't think it was so funny!" I reminded him.

"Ellen, I'm not laughing at you. It is serious. If I didn't think it was, I wouldn't have insisted that you stay at my house last night. It's just that you are such a prim and proper lady, I just can't picture you as some gun toting hard as nails moll. You have to admit, it just isn't you!"

"Just because I feel the need to protect myself, doesn't mean I can't be the same person I have always been. Maybe it's time I showed a little backbone and quit acting like such a ninny!"

"A ninny? I haven't heard anyone use that term in years!" he cackled.

"Yeah, well, make fun all you want, Mr. Taylor! I want you to get me a gun and show me how to use it!" I said glaring at him.

"Ellen! Come on! You can't be serious!" he said, wiping the tears of laughter from his eyes.

"Either you help me or I will do it myself! It's a free country! I have a constitutional right to bear arms and I intend to do so!" I declared stubbornly.

"Now you're spouting the Second Amendment. Jeez, you're really determined to do this, aren't you?" he said pulling the car into a slot in front of the nursing home.

"You bet I am! Now, are you going to help me, or not?"

"If, and it's a big if, I agreed to this harebrained scheme of yours, I have to have one thing understood," he said sternly.

"And that would be?" I asked blandly, glancing out of the window as if I didn't have a care in the world.

"You follow my instructions to the letter. You don't complain, you don't go off on your own and you absolutely never show the weapon unless you are sure that you are in mortal fear for your life," he said, ticking off the points on his fingers. "And when you do shoot, you shoot to kill, not wound, not threaten, to kill!"

"So when can we start?" I piped up eagerly.

"Do you understand what I just said to you? Do I have your word on it?" he asked, and I could tell that all the laughter was a thing of the past.

"I will do exactly as I'm told. I will not complain. I will not go off on my own. And when that bastard comes after me, I will shoot him full of lead. How's that, professor?" I said, allowing a little smile to creep across my lips.

"I know I'm going to regret this, but I'll do it. You'll just go behind my back anyway and probably shoot yourself in the foot! Say hi to Jack for me. We'll go out to the shooting range when I get off work. You stay put, you hear?"

"Aye, aye, Captain! I'll see you later!" I laughed and kissed his cheek. I hopped out of the car and trotted towards

244

the door. For the first time in my life, I felt that I could handle just about anything. It was a feeling that I will never forget.

Chapter Twenty-nine

"So how's the therapy going, Jack?" I asked. He was back in his wheelchair in the sunroom.

"I won't be doing any handsprings anytime soon, but okay, I guess," he muttered, "I got your note. So the priest was messing around with little boys."

"According to our latest interview he was," I said. "Anything new on your end?"

"I'm still trying to decipher the entries in the diary. If my calculations are correct, Pat McCoy was making a nice chunk of change off of Francis Albertson. I had hoped that there would be some way to verify it by bank records, but it's been so long ago, there's nothing on file."

"How do you know that?" I asked.

"I put in a call to the bank president at his house this morning. He said that since the old Erie County Bank got bought out, there's no telling where the old records are now. For all he knew they were probably destroyed years ago."

"I have to wonder if Pat would have put extortion money in a bank account, Jack. He was doing something illegal, do you think he would want to take the chance of having a record made of it?"

"You're probably right, but we have to get some kind of proof somewhere. Somebody had to have noticed that Pat McCoy, a common laborer with a wife and two kids suddenly had a lot of extra money. If he didn't put it in the bank, he had to have done something with it! You really need to put the pressure on Silky or anyone else who was close to him at the time. Somebody must have noticed something!"

"Remember that Silky said he was a gambler. Maybe he just gambled it all away! Or he could have spent it on his girlfriends. I doubt he would have spent it on his family!"

"You may need to check back on the girlfriends, Alice Martinez and the Willowby woman. I doubt that you would get anything out of Ms. Willowby, but from what you said Alice seemed pretty agreeable. It might be worth it to see her again."

"I agree, but I don't think we'd have to go to the trouble of meeting with her. I think I'll just give her a call. Andy seems to think we'd get more out of Silky if we pay him a surprise visit like we did with the bar owner Dick Chance. I still have to wonder what his problem was. The guy was sweating bullets the last time we talked to him!"

"As I recall, you were under the impression that he was worried about being linked to Brian Willowby. Maybe he was worried for a different reason. Maybe he knew about the blackmail plot and was involved somehow and was afraid you were going to open the whole thing up again. He's covering up something, that's for sure!"

"Well, if that's the case, wild horses couldn't drag it out of him. He's a tough old bird. Silky, on the other hand, impressed me as being a little more pliable. I think Andy might be able to get him to spill what he knows. I think he'd probably say something if we could get him alone. I think he was relying on Dick for moral support. You know what I mean?"

"Well, if anybody can get the guy to talk, I'm sure Andy can. He strikes me as a regular bulldog when he sets his mind to something," Jack said, shaking his head. "He reminds me of me when I was his age."

"You've got that right," I agreed. "I have a feeling he'll have poor old Silky spilling his guts before he knows it. If he actually knows anything, that is."

"We'll just have to cross that bridge when we come to it. So, I take it you and Andy are getting along these days?" he said with a knowing glance.

"I guess you could say that," I said feeling my face get hot at his implication. "He has certainly impressed me with his skill as a police officer, if that's what you mean!" I added defensively.

"Oh I think there's more to it than that, judging by your reaction! Can it be that the two of you have discovered that you might have more in common than this case? I've seen the way he looks at you!" he declared.

"Jack! I'm surprised at you! Where in the world would you get an idea like that! Andy and I are just friends. I'll admit, I really didn't like his attitude when I first met him, but he has really come around. He's been working on this thing as hard as you or me. I admire his determination and his abilities. That's all there is to it!" I insisted.

"Ellen, I may be crippled, but I've got eyes! The guy's crazy about you! Don't tell me you haven't noticed!" he laughed. "And if your red face is any indication, I think Andy must have let you know how he feels."

"Jack, what am I going to do with you? Andy is a super guy. I think the world of him, the same way I care about you, but I didn't get involved in this case because I was looking for romance! There's too much at stake here to be getting sidetracked with that sort of thing! You know that as well as I do!"

"So he put his heart on the line, huh? And you turned him down. Ellen, you're still a young woman. You sure you want to miss out on an opportunity to be with a good looking guy like Andy?" he advised sagely.

"Jack Miller, I don't know where you come up with this stuff! He and I are just friends and that's the way it has to be. I think you are letting your imagination get the better of you! All this exercise you've been doing lately has got that brain of yours in overdrive! Can we please get back to the matter at hand?"

"Boy, he sure got to you, didn't he? What are you afraid of, Ellen? Are you scared people will talk because he happens to be a little younger than you?" he asked, refusing to let it go.

"Look, Jack. I have no intention of divulging what may or may not have transpired between Andy and me, but rest assured that my only interest in him is in his official capacity and as a good friend. That's all you need to know. Now can we please drop it?"

"Okay, okay! I'm sorry I brought it up. It's obviously a pretty touchy subject for you. I just wanted you to know that I think the two of you would make a pretty terrific couple."

"Well, thank you for your vote of confidence. Now, is there anything else we need to discuss about the case? I'd like to go over my notes from the Smith interview with you to get your take on it. You know, see if we overlooked anything."

As I searched through the boxes of files, I could feel him watching me. I should have known that nothing would get past retired Chief of Police Jack Miller. He had an incredible ability to observe and analyze human behavior, which had made him such a good investigator before the shooting had robbed him of the use of his body. I was amazed that he had been able to read what Andy had been thinking all along. I felt sorry for any criminals who had ever had to face him in an interrogation room. I had a feeling that he was pretty good at detecting when someone wasn't telling the whole truth.

Chapter Thirty

To my vast relief, Jack dropped the subject of Andy and my relationship and we focused our attention back to the case files. Even though our investigation had shifted to the Mayor and his brother, we decided not to completely dismiss the other suspects, who also had reasons to see Pat McCoy dead, so we discussed them as well. We agreed that we were a long way from placing the gun in Father Francis' hands. It was beginning to look as though the only way we would ever reach a solution was if we could locate someone who either saw something on the night of the murders or confessed. Both of those options seemed extremely unlikely. Jack and I had gone over everything we had so far again and again and could find nothing new. I was getting frustrated with our lack of progress.

It was late afternoon by the time Andy arrived to pick me up and I was happy to see him.

"So, you ready?" he asked as soon as we got in his car.

"Ready for what?" I asked with a straight face.

"Don't tell me you've changed your mind! You know perfectly well what I mean. I even stopped by my house and picked something up for you. It's in the glove compartment. I called the range and they said to come on over."

His attitude towards my learning to shoot a gun had been so negative that I was taken back by his unexpected enthusiasm. I pulled out the pistol and my stomach flipped. I wasn't prepared for the reality of what I had proposed. The weapon felt cold and heavy and sent a shiver down my spine. I had to wonder if I really would be able to point it at another human being and shoot. It had sounded so easy in theory, but holding the evil looking object in my hands was a whole different story.

"That's a nine millimeter Smith and Wesson. It holds eight bullets in the clip and one in the chamber. It weighs about 28 ounces, so you shouldn't have any trouble holding it. I bought it for my ex-wife, but she refused to have anything to do with it. You sure you still want to do this? It's not too late to back out if you don't think you can handle it."

"I said I would do this and I will," I insisted, "but it still scares me a little. I see you with your gun all the time, but you're used to it. Your gun is a part of your regular day to day life. It's just going to take me a while to get over my fear."

"Think of it as a tool, like a hammer or a kitchen knife. Sure, you could kill somebody with either of them, but used properly, they serve a useful purpose. That gun could save your life. Like I said, the whole point is to give you the knowledge to use it only in the event of a life-threatening situation. Hopefully, you'll never have to shoot it at anything but a paper target."

"Have you ever shot anybody?" I asked in a small voice.

"Nope, I am happy to say. I've had to pull it out a time or two, but so far, I've been lucky. But I will tell you this; if the time ever came where it was between me or some other guy getting killed, I wouldn't hesitate. You just have to sure that there really is a threat. You can't be shooting at people without just cause. There has to be no question about their intent. Otherwise, you'll be the one going to jail."

"Well, hopefully, like you said, I won't be faced with the decision," I said thoughtfully. I put the gun back in the glove box and tried to think of something else to get my mind off of it. Knowing it was in there still gave me goose bumps.

"Jack suggested that we check with Alice Martinez to see if she remembers if Pat McCoy came in to some cash just before he was killed. I thought I would give her a call tomorrow and see if she knows anything," I said absently, watching the scenery go by.

"Sounds good to me. I thought we could run by Silky's place tomorrow after work. Maybe we can shake something loose out of him."

"Don't forget we've got the other two guys that may have some information on Father Francis lined up for Tuesday and Wednesday. Will you be able to get off work to take me?" I asked, trying to keep the conversation going.

"Don't worry, I've already made arrangements to have someone cover for me. By the way, there's something else I've been meaning to discuss with you," he said, checking the rearview mirror as he came to a stop at a traffic light.

"What's that?" I asked, holding my breath, afraid he was going to bring up the subject of us.

"I want you to contact a security company and get an alarm system installed on your house," he said and I let it out with a sigh. When I didn't immediately respond, he turned to look at me. "What'd you think I was going to say? Let's elope to Vegas?"

"No, I didn't," I snapped angrily, "it's just that Jack was giving me a hard time about you and I'm just a little paranoid."

"Oh really? What'd he say?" he asked with a grin.

"You know you can't get anything by him. He said he saw you looking at me and put two and two together. I told him it wasn't any of his business. I'm sorry, I didn't mean to sound so snippy. I'm just getting frustrated that we're not making any headway and the last thing I need is Jack playing cupid."

"Or me putting pressure on you?" he asked.

"Exactly. You made your intentions very plain last night. I'm just not ready to get into it now. We have too many other things that we need to do before we think about any kind of emotional entanglements. Okay?"

"Okay. Not that I happen to agree, but if that's how you want it, that's how it will be. Now, what about that security system. I really think that's a good idea since you are insisting on staying in that house alone."

"I think that is an excellent idea! I'll call first thing in the morning. Maybe I'll be able to get it installed by tomorrow afternoon. I'm glad you thought of it!"

We had arrived at the shooting range. The sign by the road proclaimed it as Barry's Firing Range and Gun Shop. There were several pick up trucks and a minivan in the weedy parking lot. It was located several hundred yards off the road in a wooded area. We could hear the sound of gunfire as soon as we stepped from the car.

"Okay, Annie Oakley, let's see how you do," Andy said with a laugh.

"Very funny. Just remember I've never done anything like this before. I hope you're not going to yell at me. I'm nervous enough as it is all ready!"

"Ellen! I wouldn't yell at you! Relax, I'll have you hitting the bulls eye in no time."

We entered the long corrugated steel and cinderblock building and approached the display case that doubled as a counter for the cash register. All though the building was nondescript, the shop area was decorated like an old-fashioned hunting lodge with rustic barn wood paneling, hunting scene paintings and mounted deer heads gazing down at us with their glass eyes. There were several racks of camouflage pants and jackets and other hunting paraphernalia scattered around the room. It was a veritable gun enthusiast's paradise.

The proprietor, Barry Bradford, was a short, broad shouldered man with a military style crewcut and round rosy face. He was dressed in a tee shirt with the company logo emblazoned across the front, camouflage pants and black lace up boots. He greeted Andy like an old friend.

"How ya doing, Chief!" he beamed, "is this your student?"

"Yep, she's the one! Ellen, this is Barry. He's been teaching gun safety for the county for years."

I shook his hand, and was impressed with the firmness of his grip. A lot of men don't apply much pressure when shaking hands with a woman, but he was the exception. I have always believed that you can judge a person's character by the way they shake your hand and I wasn't disappointed. He looked me in the eye and seemed to be making a judgement of my character as well.

"So, the Chief here tells me you've never done any shooting before," he said pleasantly.

"No, but I'm ready to learn. What do we need to do to get started?" I asked feeling my pulse rate increase.

He reached down under the counter and handed me some ear protectors similar to what I had seen being worn by airport runway personnel.

"Slip these on. It will save your hearing. Andy, I've got you set up at the far end of the range by yourselves, so she won't be distracted by the other shooters," he said handing Andy a pair as well.

He led us through a thick glass door into the main part of the building. We walked the length of the firing range past glass partitioned cubicles on our left occupied by people aiming and firing at targets on the far wall. I was surprised to see that there were a couple of women included in their number. Everyone seemed so intent on what they were doing that nobody paid any attention to our passing.

We reached the last cubicle and Andy laid out my gun and several boxes of ammunition on the waist high shelf facing the targets. I wondered how anyone would be able to tell how well they had done, when I noticed that the targets were affixed to a pulley system. The targets could be placed at various distances as indicated by signs along the ceiling as well as being carried to the opening of the cubicle in order to check for the accuracy of the shots thus eliminating the need for anyone to enter the range itself. I was glad I had on the earmuffs because otherwise the sound of guns reverberating off the walls would have been deafening.

Barry handed Andy several paper targets shaped like a human form with targets printed on the head and chest area. Andy thanked him and said he would take it from there. The owner gave me an encouraging smile, patted my back and left us.

I assumed that Andy would load the gun and I would begin firing away, but before the first shot was fired, he laid out the gun and ammunition and demonstrated to how to load it, unload it, how to release the safety and check that the chamber was empty. I watched him carefully as he expertly handled the weapon and when he was satisfied that I understood what to do, he handed it to me. My hands were shaking so badly that I fumbled around with it, dropping shells on the floor and generally making a fool of myself, but he was extremely patient with my ineptitude and before long I got over my reticence and could complete the exercise as he had done.

I kept reminding myself that it was merely a tool and that in order to use it properly, I had to learn as much as I could about it. Andy proved to be an excellent teacher and before long my confidence level increased to a point that I was actually looking forward to giving it a try. He showed me how to hold it in a two-handed grip for stability and to line up the sight with one eye shut. He had me pull the trigger several times with the gun unloaded in that position so that I would get accustomed to how much pressure I would need to apply in order to fire it. It felt awkward at first, but he stood behind me and kept repositioning my stance until he was satisfied.

With the preliminary instruction completed, Andy attached one of the targets to the cord and ran it out to the fifty-foot marker. He had me load the clip and take aim. My hands started shaking again, so he stood behind me, reached around and placed his hands on mine for support. I lined up the sight as he had instructed and squeezed the trigger. When the gun went off, it made such a loud noise, I instinctually shut my eyes. The recoil caused the gun to kick upward and I didn't need to see the target to know that I hadn't come close. Before I could discuss what I had done wrong, Andy had me try again, which I did. He insisted that I continue firing until I had emptied the clip. Not being accustomed to it, my arms and shoulders started to throb, but I held my tongue. I had promised that I wouldn't complain and I was determined that I wouldn't.

He had me reload and this time hold the gun without his support. My biggest problem was keeping my eyes open, but eventually I got to the point where I could actually take aim, fire and see the target all at the same time. The more I shot, the less intimidated I felt and I found that I actually started enjoying it. I never did come close to hitting the center of the target, but I managed to at least hit the edges of the target three times.

"I guess I'm not Annie Oakley after all," I complained as we packed up to go.

"Hey, you did pretty good for a beginner. Nobody masters it on the first try," he said charitably.

As we passed one of the ladies who had been in one of the cubicles closest to the door, she smiled and congratulated me. She was in her thirties with blonde hair pulled back in a ponytail and yellow-tinted aviator-style glasses.

"If this is your first lesson, you should be proud of yourself. I saw you blazing away down the line. You looked like a natural. It took me three times coming here before I could get up the nerve to pull the trigger!" she laughed. "But I didn't have such an attentive teacher! Do you give anybody lessons, Chief?" she asked Andy flirtatiously. "I'd be more than happy to pay!"

"No, sorry, Ellen here is a friend of mine. I'm just doing it as a favor to her. I'm sure Barry would be more than happy to work with you," he suggested taking my arm, propelling me toward the exit and ignoring her obvious attempt at getting his amorous attention.

"Well, if you change your mind, you can find me here on Sunday nights!" she called after us. "I would definitely make it worth your while!"

We passed through the glass doors into the shop and Andy laid some bills on the counter in front of Barry.

"Sounds like you got another admirer, Chief," he winked as he gathered up the money and put it into the register.

"Yeah, whatever," Andy growled and walked to the outside exit and held the door for me. "I'll call you to set up that same slot later in the week, Barry."

"You got it, Chief!" he replied.

When we got out of earshot on our way to the car, I couldn't contain myself.

"My goodness, Chief," I teased, "you are a regular babe magnet! I thought that woman was going to drool all over you!"

"Woman like that are a dime a dozen! They're crazy about the uniform," he said dismissively, opening the car door for me. "Don't pay any attention to it. I sure don't."

I could tell by the way that he was acting that he wasn't in the mood for ribbing, so I changed the subject.

"So, how'd I do? It was so hard to hear in there, I couldn't hear half of what you said. Did I do okay?" I asked.

"You seemed to be getting more comfortable towards the end, but you've got a long way to go before I can turn you loose on your own. So far you know just enough to be dangerous to yourself and anybody else who gets within range of you. We'll practice some more later in the week."

I appreciated his honesty and found myself looking forward to my next lesson. He insisted that I stay one more night at his house and I grudgingly agreed, but planned to get the security system installed before the next day was out. I was determined to reestablish my independence.

Chapter Thirty-one

The next couple of days were spent on the telephone getting bids on the security system, selecting a suitable company and then waiting around for the installers to arrive. As soon as it was operable, Andy agreed to take me home. He returned to work and I was finally left to fend for myself. I placed my call to Alice Martinez, but the results were disappointing. She said that as far as she knew, Pat may have had some extra money to spend, but he certainly didn't spend it on her. I practically had to drag the answers out of her and I got the impression she really didn't want to talk to me.

She suggested that I ask her rival Rosemary Willowby, because if Pat spent money on anyone it would have been on her. Alice had apparently had time to think about our previous conversation and was having second thoughts about revealing as much as she had. I considered giving Rosemary a call, but thought better of it. Her behavior indicated to me that she had said all she intended to say on our previous meeting. There was no point to antagonizing her.

We had to postpone our confrontation with Silky Swartz because of Andy's work schedule until after our interviews with the remaining two possible victims of Father Francis. Andy kept his word about arranging time to meet with them and we drove to Toledo as planned on Tuesday.

We found the first of our subjects in a rundown apartment building in one of the seedier areas of the city. He was a short, fat, balding man with thick glasses who met us at the door dressed in sweat pants and dirty sneakers and a long-necked beer bottle in his hand. He had a large family that included a homely wife and an indeterminate number of children. From what I could see from the front door, their home was littered with trash. He explained that they had just finished eating when we arrived. His wife was in the kitchen cleaning up, yelling at the children and banging pots and pans. She stuck her head through the kitchen door, gave us the once over and disappeared back into the kitchen. His kids were scattered around the living room bickering over the television. There was so much noise and confusion; we suggested that he meet with us on the front stoop of the building. He followed us there and I handed him the photographs. We waited as he went through them.

"So, Mr. Jones, can you tell us anything about the priest in those pictures?" I asked as he handed them back to me.

"You mean Father Francis? What do you want to know?" he asked noncommittally.

"We know that he left town under some rather suspicious circumstances. We just wanted to know if you had any idea as to why that was," Andy said.

"That was a mighty long time ago. Why are you asking about it now?" he wanted to know.

"There was some talk that he may have taken some sexual liberties with some of the boys in the church. We are just trying to see if you might remember anything that might be useful to our investigation."

"And what investigation is that? Is somebody trying to sue him or something?"

"I'm not at liberty to discuss anything about the case we're working on, Mr. Jones. Anything you can tell us would be greatly appreciated," Andy said politely.

"It must be something important if you went to all the trouble to find me. I haven't lived in Milan since I was sixteen. How'd you find me anyway?" he asked his eyes narrowing.

"We are talking to men who may have had contact with Francis Albertson as children. Your name was given to us by one of the current members of Saint Mary's," Andy explained.

"Is there any money in it? I might be willing to get in on this thing if there's some money involved," he said, licking his thick lips.

"Now why would you think this has anything to do with money, Mr. Jones?" I asked, my distaste for the man growing by the minute.

"Hey! I'm not stupid! One of those guys has decided to cash in on this thing, am I right? Who was it? I'll bet I can guess! Is it John Smith?" he asked, his piggish eyes lighting up like a kid at Christmas.

"Why do you think this has anything to do with John Smith?" Andy asked.

"He was such a pretty little sissy boy, I figured he's the one saying that Father Francis messed with him. If he did and I'm not saying he did! It'd be just like John to carry on about stuff that happened when he was a little kid. Ain't that the way it always goes? He's probably got more money than he knows what to do with and now he's trying to get more out of a poor old crazy priest."

"So you are saying that if Mr. Smith was making an allegation concerning some improprieties made towards him by Father Francis, it would be untrue?" Andy asked.

"Hey, I didn't say that! I never saw anything personally, but who knows? There were others that said the same thing about the guy. He never got out of line with me! All I'm saying is if it happened, Smith should have said something a long time ago. Everyone has moved on. There's no point in digging it up all over again. I say let bygones be bygones. Unless there's some money involved and then I say, go for it!" he chuckled, taking a swig from his beer and wiping his lips with the back of his hand.

"You mentioned that there were other boys who made similar comments concerning the priest. Do you happen to remember any of their names?" Andy asked.

"I don't think that would be such a good idea. I've got all the trouble I can handle," he smirked hooking his thumb towards his apartment. "I don't need some guy getting pissed at me because I ran my mouth to the cops. The right amount of money might make it worth my time, but otherwise, you'll have to get that information somewhere else. Now, if you don't mind, I'm missing my favorite television show. If John is willing to cut me in, tell him to give me a call."

He tossed the empty beer bottle out into the patchy yard where it landed with a few dozen others and slammed the screen door behind him on his way back to his apartment. Andy and I exchanged glances and returned to the car.

"What a positively disgusting man!" I exclaimed. "Talk about a pig! And to think I was all set to feel sorry for the guy!"

"Yeah, he was a real winner all right! I guess it takes all kinds. At least we know there was somebody that didn't appeal to Father Francis."

"Maybe something happened to him and then again, maybe not, although he'd probably say it did if there was a buck to made."

We drove back to Milan with little conversation. The disappointment hung heavy in the air between us. Our visit with the unpleasant Mr. Jones had left a sour taste in my mouth. I hoped the last of our potential victims would give us what we needed. So far all we had was John Smith's word against Father Francis.

It was dark by the time Andy dropped me off. He made sure that I had the alarms set and reminded me to be sure that I kept the gun where I could get to it in an emergency. We were scheduled to go to Cleveland the following day and Andy suggested that we call it a day. I felt drained from the day's activities and gratefully agreed. I called my daughter before I turned in and hearing her voice made me feel better. The night passed peacefully and I got up the next morning ready and eager for our next encounter.

It was late afternoon the next day when we set off for Cleveland in search of potential victim number three. He had requested that we meet him at his photography studio on the outskirts of the city. His place of business was in a strip mall located on a busy thoroughfare crowded with beauty salons, dry cleaners and gas stations. When we got there, he was tied up with trying to photograph a crying baby who was refusing to cooperate. The baby's mother was upset, scurrying around trying to get the child to smile, but the little one was having nothing to do with it. Andy and I took a seat in the waiting area while he dealt with the situation. It was half an hour later before he finally finished the session and he apologized for the wait. He locked the door, flipped the sign on the door from 'open' to 'closed' and took a seat across the room from us on one of the plastic chairs.

"Sorry about that," he said apologetically, "sometimes you just can't make it work no matter what you do. I'm sure she'll be back for another session. There's no way she's going to be happy with what we got today. So, what can I do for you folks?" he asked, looking nervously from Andy to me. "You obviously didn't come to get your picture taken."

He was a small, thin man with long bony fingers and tiny feet. He had short black hair streaked with gray, neatly parted on the side and a wispy mustache. He was dressed in a rumpled white dress shirt and loose fitting dark slacks. He kept crossing and uncrossing his legs, and fidgeting as if he couldn't sit still. His eyes flitted around the room anxiously, his hands in constant motion. He reminded me of someone who was either painfully shy or was only comfortable when he was in control behind the lens of his camera.

"First of all, let me say that we really appreciate your taking the time to speak to us," Andy began kindly, trying to put him at ease. "We just need your help with a case we're looking into. It concerns something that happened over thirty years ago."

"Really? My goodness, I was just a little boy thirty years ago! What could I know that would possibly have any bearing on anything?" he asked in surprise.

As before, I handed him the stack of photographs and we sat back while he flipped through them. He stopped after the first few. His face turned red and a thin line of sweat appeared along his hairline.

"That's me in this picture by the pool. I'm the one the priest is talking to. Where did you get these? I don't remember having my picture taken!" he said, his eyes growing wide.

"We aren't sure who actually took those pictures, but we are especially interested in the priest. He's the one that is crouched down in front of you. Can you tell us anything you may know about him?" I asked.

"That's Father Francis. He came to Saint Mary's in Milan when I was an altar boy. He was only there a couple of years. I haven't seen him since. What more can I tell you?" he asked with a slight tremor in his voice, jumping up and handing the pictures back to me as though they burned his fingers.

"We understand that he left under some extraordinary circumstances. Do you have any idea why that was?" Andy asked quietly as the man resumed his seat.

"I don't know what you're talking about! I was just a child! People came and went all the time! Nobody ever asked me my opinion on anything! I can't see what I could possibly know that would be of any use to you!" he cried.

"We have been told that he may have been doing some things that were not appropriate with some of the younger boys in the church. We just wondered if perhaps he may have done something to you," I said.

"Me? Where would you get an idea like that! Did someone say they saw something? If they did, it's a lie! I would never take part in such a filthy thing! You better tell me what this is all about!" he demanded, leaping to his feet indignantly.

"Relax, Mr. Brown! No one is accusing you of anything! If anything, we consider anyone who was molested by Father Francis a victim. There is absolutely nothing to be ashamed of!" Andy assured him.

"Do you know what that would do to my business if it ever got out? I come in contact with children every day! I can't afford to have the slightest hint of scandal being tossed about. It would ruin me!" he insisted, scrubbing his hands together and pacing back and forth.

"The fact that you may have been molested as a child is no reflection on you, Mr. Brown! What does that have to do with the fact that you photograph children?" I asked.

"You see the news, Ms. Richardson! It's common knowledge that people who were molested as children grow up to become molesters. Mothers trust me with their kids. I have to touch them when I take their pictures. I wouldn't be able to get within a hundred yards of those children if their mothers knew I had been molested! My God, why can't you people just leave me alone!" he exclaimed, dropping back into his chair and covering his face with his hands.

"Mr. Brown, not everyone in your situation grows up to become a pedophile! There's no reason that anyone should think any less of you because of what happened. Unless someone comes forward, this sort of thing never gets reported and the molester is free to victimize others. If Father Francis molested you, he probably touched plenty of other boys. We've already talked to another man who told us his experience with Father Francis. So far it's his word against the priest's. If you have a similar story, that would make it two to one. What do you say, Mr. Brown? Haven't you been carrying this around with you long enough? The man deserves to be punished!"

"You mean like he was after I told on him?" he asked sarcastically.

"You told someone about it?" Andy asked in shock.

"Fat lot of good it did me! At first my father accused me of making it up and my mother refused to talk about it. They didn't believe me! Then when the rumors started surfacing, they went to the older priest, Father Tom and reported it. I never knew what happened, but the next thing I know, Father Francis is out of the picture and my folks made me promise never to bring up the subject again. No apologies, no explanation, nothing! I think the church paid them off or something, because that was the end of it. I was forbidden to ever speak of it again and everything went back to normal. For everyone else, anyway. Nothing was ever the same again for me! I still carry the scars of what happened to me!" he sobbed.

"I'm so sorry, Mr. Brown! I know this isn't easy for you. I wish there were someway to make things better for you. Andy and I intend to see that he pays for what he did to you and the other boys. Don't we, Andy?"

"Mr. Brown, if there is anyway we can bring the man to justice, we will. You have my word on that!" Andy assured him. "Can we count on your testimony if it ever comes to that?"

"I don't know," he responded miserably, shaking his head from side to side, "I just don't know that I would be able to talk about it in open court. It would just be so humiliating!"

"Then he wins again!" I said. "Does he deserve your silence?"

"I'll have to think about it. That's all I can promise for now. Maybe if that other man is willing to come forward, I will too. But right now, I just don't want to think about it!"

"I understand, Mr. Brown. Thanks for your help. You have no idea how much we appreciate your candor!" Andy said, indicating with a nod in my direction that we needed to leave.

"Thank you, Mr. Brown. We'll let you know where things stand when the time comes," I said softly and followed Andy through the door. He didn't look up when we walked away but simply kept his head in his hands. I was both exhilarated and saddened by what we had learned.

"Looks like we hit pay dirt!" I said when we got in the car.

"Yeah, that's a good way to put it. I feel like we've been rolling in the dirt!" Andy said sadly. "I wish this whole thing would just go away."

"I know what you mean, Andy. I know what you mean."

Chapter Thirty-two

It was a few days later before Andy got the time away from work to accompany me on our surprise visit to Silky Swartz. We decided our going there would have more of an impact if we showed up in the morning before he had a chance to leave for Dick's Tavern, which didn't open until noon. Silky lived in Huron, which was a short distance from Milan and we found his address on a back street near the Lake Erie waterfront. It was an old two-story row house badly in need of repair. The paint on the exterior walls was peeling and the front porch had several places where the boards were either sagging or missing. When we rang the doorbell, the elderly lady that answered told us that he lived over the garage out back in a small efficiency apartment. We followed her directions, climbed the rickety stairs and knocked on the door. Several minutes passed without a response and we had almost decided that he wasn't at home, when the door opened a crack. He peered out at us and as soon as he realized who we were, he tried to close the door, but Andy had slipped his foot in the way.

"Good morning, Mr. Swartz!" Andy smiled, "we'd like to have a word with you."

"Go away!" the old man croaked as he tried to close the door on Andy's foot. "I ain't feeling so good. You got no right to come here and hassle a sick old man. Why can't you people just leave me alone!"

"We're not trying to hassle you, Mr. Swartz. We just need you to answer a couple of questions and we'll be on our way," I said in a rush.

"I said all I had to say the last time," he insisted, still trying to shut the door. "I know my rights. I don't have to talk to you people! Now move your foot, mister, or I'm calling the cops. I've had about all I can take from you!"

"You're right, Mr. Swartz, I don't have any jurisdiction here, but I'm here to tell you that you may be considered an accessory to murder. There's no statute of limitation on murder, Silky. You'd never survive a long prison sentence.

We've found out some things about your friend Pat McCoy that are pretty disturbing. For all we know, you were right there in the thick of it. Don't you want to tell us your side of the story? I sure would hate to see you end up in jail, because you didn't tell the truth!"

"Jail! What the hell are you talking about?" he cried and flung open the door. We had only been able to see part of his unshaven face and one rheumy eye, but with the door open we could see that he was dressed in a shabby old bathrobe. His spindly legs were bare and his hair stood on end as if he had just gotten out of bed.

"Like I said, we just want to hear what you have to say and maybe you can convince me that you had nothing to do with the McCoy murders. I guess I could force you to come down to the station to answer our questions, but I'd rather not have to put you to all that trouble. Why don't you go get dressed and Ms. Richardson and I will wait for you right here."

He seemed to think it over, but he eventually nodded and closed the door. After several minutes, he returned, with his hair slicked back, dressed in work pants and shirt.

"Come on in," he growled, "you'll just have to shove stuff out of the way. I wasn't exactly expecting any company."

We picked our way through the cluttered living room and cleared away space on the threadbare couch and chair. The whole place smelled of sour sweat, stale beer and cigarette smoke. Needless to say, Silky's housekeeping left a lot to be desired.

As soon as we were all seated, Andy began the interview.

"We have uncovered some evidence that seems to indicate that Pat McCoy was involved in an extortion plot, which may have ultimately resulted in his death. Of all the people we've talked to, you seem to be his closest associate. What can you tell us about it, Mr. Swartz?"

"What kind of evidence?" he asked suspiciously.

"The current owners of the McCoy house found a box containing some photographs of the person that Pat may have been using for the purpose of blackmail. A notebook with coded entries possibly indicating cash payoffs was also found. We have spoken to some of the other people who were in the photographs who seem to confirm that the target of Pat's attention had good reason to pay large amounts of money to keep Pat quiet concerning his activities."

"So Pat was involved in some shady business, so what? He's dead and buried. There's nothing you can do about it now! That was over thirty years ago! What does that have to do with me?" he asked defiantly.

"In your initial statement at the time of the murders you indicated that Pat McCoy came to you for a loan to pay off his gambling debts. You therefore had intimate knowledge of his need for some quick cash. Since he felt he could come to you in that way, you obviously had a close relationship with the man. If he suddenly came into all the money he needed, it stands to reason that you would have had questions as to the origin of his newfound wealth. Being his close associate, it is logical to assume that he may have told you what he was doing, maybe even offering to cut you in on it. I think you took him up on that and helped him get the goods on the guy."

"That's a damn lie! I had nothing to do with blackmailing anybody!" Silky shouted. "Since you seem to know all about it, what difference does it make now? You can't put a dead man in jail."

"On the other hand, if you knew that Pat had a lot of money laying around, maybe you killed him for it. You have to admit, it is a possibility!" Andy interjected, purposefully ignoring his outburst.

"You are out of your mind! Pat was my friend! I never would have harmed him or his family! I'll admit he wasn't the nicest guy in the world, but I certainly didn't want to see him dead!" he declared angrily.

"But you are willing to confirm that you were aware that Pat McCoy was involved in a blackmail scheme?" I asked in amazement.

"Maybe I am and maybe I'm not. What's in it for me? I'm not going to jail for something I didn't do! So what if Pat was making money off some poor stiff. You can't pin that on me!" he cried, raking his fingers through his hair.

"Whether you were a part of it or not isn't really the issue here. We are looking for a motive for murder. Blackmail could very well be that motive. Mr. Swartz, you say that Pat McCoy was your friend. Doesn't it bother you that the person responsible for his death has never been punished?" I asked.

"It wasn't up to me to find who did it! That was the cops' job, who couldn't have found their butts with both hands as I recall. I didn't want any part of it! I had to take care of my own skin. There was nothing I could do for Pat!" he said defiantly.

"But there is something you can do for him now, Mr. Swartz! You can tell us what you know about his activities just prior to his death. Your cooperation could be what we need to finally put this thing to rest. We have no positive proof that you had anything to do with the extortion plot."

"How do I know I can trust you?" he asked accusingly.

"Look, Silky, there are no guarantees. Either you cooperate and tell us what you know now, or I'm going to find something on you and run you in," Andy snarled.

"You can't do that, that's against the law!" Swartz whined.

"No more games, old man. It's your choice. Tell us what we need to know, or so help me God, you will live to regret it," Andy said threateningly through gritted teeth.

The old man's jaw dropped open, his eyes darting back and forth between Andy and me. I turned to Andy in shock. His tone of voice frightened me. He had always been so kind and soft spoken, he was like a completely different person.

"Come on, Ellen!" Andy snapped, rising to his feet, "We're getting no where with this pathetic piece of crap. I'll come back here later with a warrant. Maybe if he cools his heels in lock-up for a day or two, he'll feel like talking!"

"Wait! Wait a minute!" Silky cried, jumping to his feet and holding his hands out toward Andy, "there's no need for that! If I tell you what I know, will you at least give me a chance to explain?"

Andy stood with his hands on his hips visibly seething and glaring at him with contempt. I shook off my initial reaction to his uncharacteristic behavior and rushed to the old man's defense by taking a position in front of Andy forcing him to look at me.

"Andy," I said in what I hoped was a soothing voice, "Maybe we ought to hear what he has to say! Please? Can't you see he's scared enough all ready?"

Andy broke away from glaring at Silky to look at me and his face softened.

"Ellen, you are too kind hearted for your own good. Don't you see this guy doesn't give a rat's ass about helping us find out who killed his friend? All a guy like him cares about is saving his own hide!"

"That's not true!" the old man whimpered, "I do care! I just can't face going to jail! You have to promise me you won't send me to jail. I'd never survive that!"

"If, and it's a mighty big if, you tell me everything you know, I might be able to work something out. But if you stonewall me, I'm coming back for you, old man! You can take that to the bank!" Andy growled stabbing a finger in his direction.

"Okay! Okay! Whatever you say! Can't we all just sit down and I'll tell you what I know!" he promised.

"What do you say, Ellen? Do you really want to trust this guy?" Andy asked sternly.

"I think we should hear what he has to say," I said softly.

The standoff continued for several seconds before Andy finally backed down. We resumed our places, but there was still tension in the air. Silky slumped in his chair, his shoulders sagged in defeat. He suddenly seemed to have aged twenty years before our eyes.

"Yeah, he told me what he was doing," he began in a quavery voice. "He said he had found out that the new priest in town was messing around with little boys, although he never said how he found out. He said he had proof. All he said was that the priest had a brother that had lots of money and was willing to pay to keep his mouth shut about it. I told him I didn't want any part of it. He made me swear that I wouldn't tell anybody, but if something happened to him, I was to go to the police. As soon as I heard he'd been killed, I went to the Chief of Police, Art Talbot and told him about it."

"What exactly did you tell Chief Talbot?" Andy asked suspiciously.

"Pat said he kept the stuff hidden up under a loose tile in the ceiling and that if anything ever happened to him, he wanted the cops to know about it. I told the Chief where to find the stuff and washed my hands of the whole thing. I did what Pat asked me to do. If the police decided not to pursue it, that was their business. If somebody killed Pat over it, I didn't want to be next. I've kept my mouth shut for thirty years! I

271

should have known this thing would come back to haunt me! I swear I had nothing to do it! Pat was my friend! He didn't deserve what happened to him, no matter what he was doing to the priest! I did what he asked. I figure I've done all I could for him. It wasn't my place to find out who killed him!"

"Let me get this straight. Pat told you he was blackmailing a priest who was molesting children," Andy said, ticking off the points on his fingers.

"That's what I said," Silky responded dejectedly.

"He offered to cut you in on the deal, but you refused."

"Absolutely. I ain't no blackmailer!"

"But he did tell you where he hid his proof."

"Yep. In the ceiling above the tiles."

"And when Pat was killed, you went to Chief Talbot and told him what you knew and where Pat had told you the evidence was hidden."

"I already told you. The Chief knew where it was. What he did from there, is anybody's guess. I just wanted to keep my name out of it. He told me to keep my big mouth shut and he would handle it. And that is exactly what I did. I haven't told another living soul about it in thirty years! What do you people want from me! I'm just a sick old man. Why can't you just leave it alone!" he cried, burying his face in his hands.

"Mr. Swartz, you have no idea how important your information is to our investigation. With what you have told us, we may be able to finally find out who killed your friend and his family. Once it is all out in the open, you'll be able to put the whole thing behind you once and for all. Don't you want to know who the real killer was?" I asked.

"All I know is, I didn't have anything to do with it. You never really suspected me did you, Chief? You just said that to shake me up. Right?" he asked hopefully.

"Maybe and maybe not. All I know is it's long past time that somebody told the truth. You know what they say; the truth will set you free. If what you have told us is the truth, you can live the rest of your life knowing you did the right thing. That ought to make you feel better."

"Whatever you say, Chief. Somehow, I feel worse than I did before!" he said miserably, shaking his head.

"We'll be in touch. Please don't discuss what we talked about today with anyone. It is extremely important that no one find out what you have revealed to us. Do I have your word on that?" Andy asked sternly.

"I've kept quiet for thirty years, mister! I think I can hold my tongue for a while longer!" he said in a small voice.

"Thanks, Mr. Swartz. You did a very good thing today," I said as we stood to leave. "I'm sure that if Pat were here, he would be thanking you as well. With your help, we are closer to solving the crime than we ever thought we would be. You are a very brave man!"

He waved us off dismissively and we showed ourselves out. My head was spinning from the encounter. Everything we had learned pointed to Mayor Dan Albertson, as having been involved in a horrible crime. With Andy's relationship with the man, I knew it had to be killing him.

As soon as we pulled away, Andy turned to me, "I'm sorry you had to see that. I guess I should have warned you, but you wouldn't have reacted the way you did if you knew ahead of time. You did just what I hoped you would. We make a pretty good team, don't you think?" he asked nonchalantly.

"That was an act?" I shouted. "You nearly scared me out of a year's growth! I had no idea you could behave like that! You had that old man about to wet his pants!"

"Desperate times call for desperate measures, Ellen. I could tell we wouldn't get anywhere with him pussyfooting around. I told you I intended to shake him up. What did you expect me to do? Ask him pretty please and thank you?" he sniffed.

"I guess not," I fumed. "I'm just not used to such brutal tactics."

"Like I said, you are too kind hearted, Ellen. That's why I'm the professional and you are the civilian. I have to do things like that sometimes when the situation calls for it. I'm sorry if I scared you."

"Apology accepted," I said grudgingly knowing that he was right, but still put out that he hadn't let me know what he had intended to do ahead of time. "What do we do now?"

"I'd like to talk it over with Jack, see if he has any suggestions," he said and I agreed.

273

We headed off in the direction of Shady Oaks, but before we got there, he got a call on his cell phone. It was his assistant, Lucy from the station. As he talked on the phone, I could see his expression darken. I couldn't tell from his end of the conversation what was making him so upset. As soon as he snapped the phone shut, he filled me in on the latest development.

"I guess you know that was Lucy," he said glancing in the outside rearview mirror.

"I figured it was. What's up? You look like whatever she said was bad news! What did she say anyway?"

"She said Mayor Albertson stopped by the office and wants to see me out to his house ASAP. She said he was mad as a wet hen. I think this may be it!" he said with foreboding.

"Are you ready to confront him about our suspicions? This sure doesn't give you any time to prepare!" I replied sympathetically.

"I knew this time would come, Ellen. What would putting it off accomplish? I have an obligation to the McCoys. As you are always pointing out, it is my duty to uphold the law no matter who is involved."

"I know. I just know how difficult this is for you. I know I can't go into the meeting with you, but would you let me at least go out there with you? I'll wait in the car while you go in to see him. I could be there for moral support if nothing else," I offered hopefully.

"No, Ellen. I have to do this on my own. It's my responsibility. Besides, it may get ugly and I don't want to have to worry about you being in the middle of it. I think I better drop you off at your house and fill you in later."

"Don't you think you might need to take someone out there with you? What if he gets violent? You're going to accuse him of some pretty awful stuff!"

"Don't worry about me. I can handle the situation. I'm just going out there to talk, not get in a fight with the man!" he assured me.

"Well, I guess there's no point in trying to talk you out of this," I said worriedly.

"That's right! I'm the professional, remember?"

"And I'm the civilian," I sighed dejectedly.

"And I wouldn't have you any other way!" he smiled.

Chapter Thirty-three

When we reached my house, as always, Andy made sure that everything was secure and that the alarm system was functioning as it should. As soon as he had satisfied himself that I was sufficiently protected, he returned to his car and drove off for his rendezvous with his boss. I was disappointed that he hadn't let me go along and more than a little nervous about what he was about to do. All the weeks of our investigation had been building up to this defining moment and there I was stuck at home, alone, pacing the floor in frustration. When an hour went by with no word from Andy, my feeling of disappointment turned to concern. What could be taking so long? I didn't dare try to call him on his cell phone, since I knew he would be angry if I interrupted him, but I felt I had to do something. The suspense was eating me alive. I tried to putter around the house to keep my mind occupied, but my thoughts kept drifting back to him.

When another hour passed with no contact, I couldn't stand it any more. The walls were closing in on me and I simply had to do something. The only thing I could think to do was talk over my concerns with Jack. We hadn't had time to tell him the latest development and I was in desperate need of his calming influence. Andy would be upset with me for leaving the house alone, but I pushed those thoughts aside and grabbed my purse making sure my gun was inside and headed off to Shady Oaks. I started to take the rental car, but at the last moment, changed my mind. It was only a short distance. I felt that the walk and fresh air would clear my head.

By the time I had reached the convalescent center, rather than abating, my fears had escalated. I trusted Jack's insight as much as I did Andy's and rushed down the hall in the direction of his room. I found him there, sitting in his wheelchair by the window.

"Jack!" I cried, "it's all coming to a head! Andy's gone to confront the Mayor with what we have! He went to the Mayor's house and could be getting the last pieces of the puzzle as we speak!"

"Whoa! Slow down! What are you talking about, Ellen?" Jack asked with surprise. "You look like you're about to bust at the seams. Why'd don't you sit down and start from the beginning. I've been out of the loop these last few days. What's happened?"

I took a deep breath and forced myself to calm down. Jack needed to be brought up to speed as to what we had learned and he couldn't help me if I didn't fill him in. I dragged the chair over to where he was and gave him a quick rundown of what we had been doing since we saw him last.

"Okay," I began, "you know about John Smith, the first guy we went to see. The one that lives here. He confirmed that Francis had been doing what we suspected."

"Right. I'm with you so far. So what happened when you went to see the other two?" he prompted.

"Well, the guy in Toledo was a real jerk! All he wanted to talk about was the fact that if there was a pending lawsuit and money to be made, he wanted in on it. I don't think Francis ever did anything to him. At least that's the impression I got. He said he knew about the rumors, but wasn't any real help. As far as I'm concerned, he was a dead-end."

"Maybe he was just too embarrassed to admit he had been molested," Jack offered reasonably.

"No, I don't think so. He sure didn't act like he had been traumatized to me! He was a pig, Jack! A greedy, disgusting pig!"

"Just because he wasn't your idea of a victim, doesn't mean that he wasn't," Jack pointed out.

"Maybe, but he just didn't strike me as one. I tried to give him the benefit of the doubt, but there was just something about him that told me he wasn't involved. I may be wrong, but what can I say? He just acted so nonchalant about the whole thing."

"Okay, so the Toledo guy didn't work out," he conceded, "What about the other one? Did you get anything out of him?"

"Oh, Jack. That guy was definitely one of Francis's victims. The poor man was a wreck! We met him at his photography studio in Cleveland. At first he wouldn't open up to us because he was scared that the molestation would affect

276

his business. He had this idea that if his clients learned about it, they wouldn't want him around their children! He was like a scared rabbit!"

"You mean he thought that just because he had been abused as a child, he thought that automatically labeled him as a child molester?" Jack asked in surprise.

"Go figure! He said he'd seen news reports that indicated that most child molesters were molested as children. He assumed that others would think the same of him! Jack, I just felt so sorry for him! He said he thought the church might have paid off his parents to keep quiet about it. Do you think that's possible?"

"I guess that could have happened. The church wouldn't have wanted the bad publicity. Although, all these years later, there's no way to confirm it."

"Well, it really doesn't matter anyway. He gave us enough information so that we at least have a second witness against the good Father. I telling you, Jack, the whole thing makes me sick to my stomach!" I muttered.

"I know what you mean. Using a position of trust and authority to prey on innocent children is an ugly business. That's something that can scar a person for life. I'd like to take guys like that and beat the living daylights out of them!" he agreed vehemently. "Okay, so you got your second victim. Is that why Andy went to talk to the Mayor?"

"No, Jack. I haven't gotten to the best part. We made our surprise visit to Silky Swartz this morning!" I said excitedly.

"You did! How'd it go? Did he tell you anything?" Jack asked with renewed intensity.

"Oh, I'd say that's putting it mildly! Jack, he confirmed the whole extortion plot! He knew all about it! Of course Andy had to threaten him with jail if he didn't fess up. I wish you could have been there. We were having this nice friendly conversation and Silky started balking, you know, refusing to cooperate. Suddenly, out of the blue, Andy gets really hostile. He cut the interview off, said he was going to go get a warrant and come back to arrest him! The poor old guy about had a heart attack! I was so taken back, I hardly knew what to say! Andy was so mad, I thought he was going to deck the guy! I jumped up and pleaded Silky's case, you know, asked Andy to at least listen to what he had to say. The next thing I know, he's spilling his guts!" I said in wonder.

Jack started laughing and I looked at him in astonishment.

"What is so darn funny, Jack? I fail to see what is so hilarious. Andy about scared me to death!" I cried indignantly.

"Ellen, that's the oldest trick in the book! You mean to tell me you never heard of good cop, bad cop? The police use that sort of thing all the time! The first cop gives the suspect a hard time, so that he becomes the enemy. Then the second cop takes the suspect's side and voila, he's the guy's best friend. All of a sudden, it's two against one. The suspect feels he can trust the second cop and tells all. That Andy! He's a real pro!" he chuckled.

"Yeah, well, it would have been nice if he had let me in on his little ploy before hand. I was totally clueless!" I spat, my cheeks burning at the memory.

"Come on, Ellen! Don't be so sensitive. He probably wanted to get an honest reaction out of you. It wouldn't have been as effective if you had known it was coming!" he said in Andy's defense.

"That's what Andy said," I admitted, "but it was embarrassing just the same!"

"Hey, the end justifies the means. You got what you came for. That's the important thing!" he said soothingly.

"You're right, of course. If the worst I suffer is a little embarrassment, I guess I can't really complain!" I agreed begrudgingly.

"So, Andy decided to go tell the Mayor the whole thing, huh?" Jack said enthusiastically.

"Actually, he got a call that the Mayor wanted to see him out at his house. Lucy said the Mayor had a bee in his bonnet and wanted to see Andy right away. I offered to go with him, but he turned me down flat. He said it was something he had to do on his own. Jack, that was hours ago and I still haven't heard from him! That's why I had to come see you! I'm scared that something may have gone wrong. He should have gotten in touch with me by now!" I cried, the fear that I had felt before reemerging in my chest.

"Hey, take it easy, Ellen!" Jack said calmly, "Andy knows what he's doing. I think you're getting yourself all worked up for nothing. I know Dan Albertson pretty well. I don't think he would try anything with Andy. Besides, Andy is an experienced police officer. He can handle the Mayor!"

"But the Mayor has a lot at stake! Maybe he'll panic and pull a gun on Andy!" I cried, visions of Andy lying on the floor in a puddle of blood rising unbidden into my head.

"Ellen! Andy is fine! You're overreacting! They are probably just talking. It stands to reason that this isn't the sort of thing you can handle in a minute or two. Maybe the Mayor is trying to convince Andy that his theory is way off base. Maybe he has some other explanation for his involvement. Who knows? There's any number of reasons why it's taking so long! You've got to quit worrying and relax. Andy will call you when he can," he said.

"Well, he can't very well do that if I'm not by the phone, can he?" I said dejectedly.

"You are absolutely right! Now, why don't you scoot on out of here and go back home and wait for Andy to call. If I hear from him, I'll let you know."

"Okay, thanks, Jack. You're probably right, I'm getting upset for nothing. I just have to have faith that Andy knows what he's going," I agreed despondently.

"That's the spirit! He's probably left a message on your machine by now. He's not going to be very pleased that you weren't home to take his call, you know!" he reminded me.

"You're right! I've got to run! I'll talk to you later, Jack!" I said and kissed his cheek, "thanks for being here for me! I don't know what I would do without you!"

"Same here. Now get out of here!" he smiled jerking his thumb at the door.

As soon as I reached the exit, I immediately realized that it had been a mistake to walk to the nursing home rather than taking the car. During the time I had spent with Jack the sky had turned black and it was starting to rain. I could hear thunder booming in the distance and knew I would be soaked before I got home. There was no sense in running, since the rain was coming down in a steady downpour, so I just hitched up the collar of my jacket, held my pocketbook over my head as a makeshift umbrella and forged ahead through the puddles towards the house.

By the time I got to my front door, I was freezing cold. My clothes were drenched; my shoes full of water and my hair hung in wet strings dripping down the back of my neck. My hands were shaking so badly, they refused to cooperate and it took several tries before I was able to get the key in the lock. It had gotten so dark, I regretted that I hadn't had the sense to leave the porch light on. I had been so intent on unlocking the door and getting into some dry clothes, that I never saw the man who stepped out of the shadows and grabbed me from behind, pinning me to his chest and holding a knife to my neck. He had appeared so suddenly, I had no time to react. He held me so that I was facing away from him. I never got the chance to get a look at his face.

"Hello, Ellen," he crooned, his lips brushing my ear, "it's been a long time. You've been a very bad girl. You just couldn't let it alone, could you?" he said softly in an eerily cheerful voice.

I thought my heart would burst in my chest from the most intense fear I had ever experienced in my life. I was paralyzed with terror. I could feel his breath on my cheek as he spoke and my knees started to buckle. As I started to slide down, he held me even tighter, so tight that I couldn't breathe. I felt the edge of the blade dig into my throat.

"Now, now, Ellen. We'll have none of that," he whispered, "we can't have you fainting on us, can we? That would spoil all the fun. You are going to cooperate, aren't you?"

I was so terrified I couldn't speak.

"Aren't you?" he repeated and increased the pressure of the knife against my neck. I felt it slice into the skin and felt blood start trickling from the shallow wound.

I could only mutely nod my head in agreement.

"That's good, Ellen. I could gut you right here, but we don't need any witnesses, now do we? You and I are going to go where we can have a little privacy. Now, I'm going to let you go, but if you try to run, I'll do it right here in front of the neighbors. You wouldn't want to upset the neighbors, now would you, Ellen?" he asked in that horribly calm voice.

I shook my head to show that I understood and the pressure against my chest was released. When I was able to catch my breath, my first instinct was to start screaming at the top of my lungs, but before I could, he spun me around to face him. I looked up into the eyes of a madman. A madman who I had known since I was a child. I was looking into the eyes of Mark McCoy and he now had the tip of the knife pointed at my heart.

"Mark!" I managed to croak past my parched lips.

"So you do remember me!" he grinned maniacally, his eyes alight with insanity, "I saw you at the class reunion, but you wouldn't even look my way," he said drawing his face into a pout. "And I thought you were such a good friend!"

"I'm sorry I offended you," I said, frantically struggling to think of something to say that would reach him.

Before I could utter another word, he reared back his fist and hit me in the face. I was so stunned by the blow that I started to black out, but before I fell, he grabbed me like a rag doll and began dragging me down the driveway with my heels scraping the concrete and then on across the street toward a car that was parked there. He dropped me in a heap at the rear of the car and I fell over on my side. Through the haze I could hear him working the lock on the trunk lid, which popped open and he yanked me to my feet and pushed me into its dark interior. When I landed inside, I hit the back of my head on the spare tire. He roughly stuffed my legs in and slammed the lid down. I was instantly enveloped in total darkness. My head started to clear and I felt the car dip down as he got behind the wheel and heard him slam the door. The motor turned over and the car began to move.

I was initially overcome with panic as claustrophobia set in. I felt as though the walls were closing in and I couldn't breathe, but thankfully, the feeling passed. I was thrown back and forth as he sped around turns and stomped on the brakes. I became so disoriented; I had no idea where he was taking me. I groped around to see if there was a safety release on the inside of the lid, but the effort proved futile. I was his prisoner and knew that unless I could get through his madness, I would die. I kept trying to think what Andy would do in a similar situation, but I was so terrified, nothing came to mind. Then I thought of the gun. I frantically felt around me for my purse, but to my dismay, I realized that I must have dropped it when he hit me. The hopelessness of my predicament slowly sank in as I contemplated my impending murder. I was at the mercy of a psychotic killer and no one would ever find me. I could only hope that the end would come quickly.

Chapter Thirty-four

Time had no meaning in the dusty black confines of the car's trunk. It seemed to take forever to reach our destination, yet it wasn't nearly long enough for me. I was overwhelmed with dread at the thought of what would happen to me when the lid was finally opened and I came face to face with a psychopath. I desperately tried to come up with some sort of plan for when that moment came, but my initial fear was so intense, no rational thought could get past the panic. Life had become my most precious commodity and I could feel it slipping through my fingers.

As much as I wanted to give in to my hysteria, I forced myself to take deep breaths to quiet my pounding heart knowing that I simply had to gain control of my raging horror. It was obvious that in Mark's current state of mind, I was playing right into his hands. I could let myself be his frightened victim and let him win, or I could use my wits and at least try to save my life.

I decided that I wouldn't go out without a fight. At least three people and possibly four had fallen prey to Mark's murderous rampage and I made up my mind that I wasn't going to make it easy for him. I mentally prepared myself for the battle of my life.

I needed a weapon. My gun was gone, but that didn't mean I couldn't use something else. I crabbed my way into the farthest recesses of the storage compartment and started feeling around in the dark. It seemed hopeless. Other than the spare tire, the trunk appeared to be completely empty. Then my searching fingers came to a long hard bump under the carpeting at the base of the far back wall. I felt blindly around, searching for the seam between the wall and the floor, finally found it, slipped my fingers under the edge and pulled it back. The object was cylindrical, heavy and metallic. I couldn't believe my luck. My groping fingers had found a tire iron that Mark had overlooked. I thought about Andy telling me that an everyday tool like a hammer or a knife could be used for many things, including murder. I wasn't sure I would have the nerve, but if the opportunity presented itself, I promised myself that I would use it. I slipped it up into the sleeve of my jacket next to my body. Thus armed, I laid back and grimly waited for Mark to make the next move.

We finally reached the place that Mark had chosen, the car came to a stop and the engine was turned off. I heard the driver's side door open and shut and after a few seconds, the key being inserted in the lock. The lid popped open and I saw him lean towards me, an ominous dark silhouette backlit by a halo of yellowish light. He stayed there looking down at me for a beat and then obviously deciding that I wasn't going to come out on my own, he reached in, grabbed me by the front of my jacket and dragged me out. Though I was tempted to struggle, I didn't resist. As soon as I got to my feet, he brandished the knife in my face so that the light reflected off its razor sharp edge.

"Did you enjoy the ride?" he asked pleasantly. "We're going to have so much fun together, Ellen! I've been looking forward to this for such a long time!"

I tore my eyes from the blade he held and forced myself to look into his eyes. What I saw there made my blood turn to water, but I forced myself to appear in control, stifling my natural urge to panic.

"You really didn't have to put me in the trunk, Mark," I said casually, dusting off the seat of my pants and running a hand over my damp hair, purposefully ignoring the knife. To my surprise, night had fallen. "Where are we anyway?"

My question and attitude seemed to take him off guard. He gave me a perplexed look.

"That's right. You haven't seen it," he said hesitantly, uncertainty washing over his face. His crazed expression momentarily melted away and he continued, "this is my dealership. People come from all over north central Ohio to buy cars from me!" he said proudly, pointing with the knife in the direction of the huge lot. His demeanor had changed so dramatically considering what had happened before; it took me by surprise.

"I'm very impressed, Mark!" I stammered. As bizarre as it was, I did my best to sound enthusiastic. I felt that as long as I could keep him talking about anything other than killing me, I might be able to talk my way out of the situation without having to resort to violence.

Desperate to keep the conversation going, I asked, "so how many cars have you got here?"

I turned away from him for a better look around. I scanned our surroundings to get my bearings. We had parked in front of the huge glass windows of the darkened showroom. The yellow cast I had seen was due to the security lights scattered about the area over the long rows of shiny wet cars. I could see long strings of colorful pennants strung out between the lampposts hanging limply over them. The wind and rain that I could have used for cover had diminished. I could see a light mist reflected in the glow they cast. I began searching for some avenue of escape.

"I keep about a hundred new and about seventy-five used in my inventory. Course its after hours now. The salesmen and mechanics have gone home for the night. We do all our own repairs. There's a full garage out back. That's one of our best selling points," he bragged, talking as if I were a prospective buyer.

"No kidding! I'll bet you get a lot of repeat customers that way," I commented, trying to determine how far I would get if I made a run for it while his defenses were down. "I saw you driving that convertible in the Melon Festival parade."

"You did, really?" he asked pleasantly, his tone of voice so normal, it was hard to associate the current conversation with the man who had threatened me with a knife and stuffed me in the trunk of his car. "I've been doing that for years. It's good for business. Would you like to see the showroom?"

"Oh, I wouldn't want you to go to any trouble," I said, afraid to go inside where I had no hope of anyone seeing us.

"Its no trouble!" he grinned, "don't forget I own the place! I want you to see my office!"

Before I could protest, he took me by the arm and led me to the glass doors. He reached in his pocket, pulled out a ring of keys, and unlocked the door.

"Ladies first," he grinned as he held the door open for me. I had no choice but to enter the dimly lit area ahead of him. He turned the knob on the door to the locked position and taking my arm once again, hurried over to a security system keypad and punched in a code to deactivate the burglar alarm.

"We wouldn't want to set off any alarms, now would we?" he asked in that strangely friendly tone of voice.

"Don't you want to turn on some lights, Mark?" I asked shakily. Somehow the silence of the darkened showroom was more frightening than being locked alone in the trunk.

"Naw, if I turn on the lights, people will think we're open for business. Besides, I want you to see my office! Come on!" he said playfully, pulling me toward the hallway which was lit by a small security light at the far end.

I was afraid that if I resisted, he would slip back into his madness, so I let him lead me forward. We passed a row of shadowy glass cubicles obviously used by the salesmen to meet with clients on the left to a wooden paneled door on the right. It had a brass plate with his name on it and it too was locked. He unlocked it and pushed it open so that I could enter first. He pulled out a chair for me, so I sat. The only light in the room was that coming from the outside lights through the window. He circled around to the opposite side of the large executive style desk, took a seat in the large leather chair and flipped on the desk lamp. His eyes gleamed in its muted glow.

"So, what do you think? Pretty fancy for a small town guy like me, huh?" he asked, leaning back in the chair proudly and gesturing around the room with the knife. He looked at the implement in his hand as if he couldn't quite remember how it got there. He shrugged dismissively and laid it on the blotter, and looked at me expectantly.

"Very nice, Mark!" I said nervously, glancing around at the expensively appointed space with its raw silk wall covering and dark wainscoting. There was a matching set of floor to ceiling bookshelves and cabinets behind the desk. The room was tastefully decorated in a masculine theme. The wall nearest the door was covered with an array of congratulatory plaques from little league teams, charities and the Chamber of Commerce as well as a variety of photographs in which Mark was posed with important looking people.

"What can I say, Mark?" I asked, pretending to read what was on the plaques in the dim light and trying to come up with something to keep the conversation going. "It's very nice. Did you have someone do the decorating for you?"

"Of course! Nothing but the best for the owner of McCoy Motors!" he crowed. "Course I couldn't have done it without Dan," he said conversationally.

I turned to make another innocuous comment only to see that his calm, rational demeanor had shifted slightly and the menacing gleam in his eyes had returned.

I sat frozen to my seat as he glared at me. "I've got something I'm sure would interest you, Ellen," he hissed, his voice now devoid of its previous warmth, "something you would just love to get your slimy hands on."

"What, what's that?" I choked out past the sudden constriction in my throat.

"It's right here," he said, "I've been keeping it here for just this occasion." He turned the chair in which he sat on its pedestal so that he was facing the cabinets and opened the lower door. As soon as his back was turned, I edged forward in my seat in preparation to bolt from the room, but he turned back around so quickly, I missed the opportunity. I instantly regretted not making a run for it when I saw what he held in his hands.

I was looking down the twin bores of a double barrel shotgun pointed directly at the center of my forehead. It simply had to be the same gun he had used on his family so long ago. The openings looked like the entrance to the Lincoln Tunnel.

"Isn't this what you've been looking for, Ellen?" he spat, drawing back the hammers with his thumb.

"Mark! No! My God, please don't!" I screamed, throwing up my hands in front of my face. I squeezed my eyes shut fully expecting to have my head blown off when I heard a metallic click immediately followed by another, which was then followed by hysterical laughter.

"You should have seen your face!" he cackled, doubled over with glee, "I bet you just wet your pants!" he howled.

I was in such a state of shock, so absolutely horrified; I was speechless.

"Ellen, you are so totally stupid! Did you honestly think I would mess up my beautiful office by spattering that sorry excuse for a brain of yours all over my pretty walls?" he chortled.

"Mark, please don't do that again!" I whimpered when I found my voice, "We've known each other forever. You've got this great business and all going for you. I thought we could be friends, you know?"

"And you have been doing everything you could to take it all away from me, you bitch!" he snarled, spittle flying from his lips. He tossed the gun aside. It hit the wall and fell noisily to the floor. He delicately reached out, picked up the knife and twirled it in his fingers so that it caught the light. "You just couldn't leave it alone, could you? You had to just keep digging and prodding and poking your nose where it didn't belong! You're all the same!" he raged, slashing the knife in counterpoint to his tirade and leaning towards me over the desk. "I thought I was safe when I shot that friend of yours, Jack Miller. But nooo, that wasn't good enough! Then you came to town and got Earl all worked up again after I paid him to keep his big mouth shut about what he saw in the woods that day! I drove his sorry ass into that tree and you still wouldn't quit! I tried to scare you off with the note and the dead rat on your doorstep, but you still wouldn't let it be!"

He suddenly leaped to his feet, charged around the desk, grabbed me by the lapels and yanked me to my feet. He put the knife's point up under my chin and glared into my eyes, his nose mere inches from mine. I let the tire iron slip down a little from my sleeve until I could hold it in my hand.

"Why, Mark? You're going to kill me anyway. Why did you do it?" I asked softly, gripping the cold steel rod tight against my body out of his sight.

"You just don't get it, do you bitch?" he screamed, "I loved him! I loved him and my old man was ruining it for me!"

"Loved who, Mark? Who did you love?" I asked desperately trying to reach past his madness and praying that he would come back to his senses. If he didn't, either I would die or I would have to do my best to kill him.

"You don't know?" he laughed hysterically, digging the knife a little tighter into my flesh, "Father Francis, you idiot! He was the only one who ever treated me like a person! He listened to me, he loved me, and he made me feel special. And my own father was trying to ruin him! I had to stop him. Don't you see? My father was trying to take away the only thing that mattered to me! And you know what's so totally screwed up about the whole thing?" he demanded, nudging my chin up with the tip of the blade.

"What's that, Mark?" I gasped, feeling a trickle of blood begin to ooze down my neck.

"The son of a bitch won. I blew his fucking brains out and he still won! They shipped Father Francis off to some mental hospital and I never saw him again. Can you believe that! I killed my own family for nothing!"

"Mark! I'm so sorry! I had no idea!" I cried, doing my best to reach him.

"Oh right, now you're sorry!" he growled, "Well, say good-bye, Ellen. I haven't spent the last thirty years trying to make something of myself for you to waltz in and ruin it for me!"

"But what about your mom and Becky?" I asked in a rush, hoping to rekindle his humanity, "what did they ever do to you?"

His face twisted into an expression of consummate pain and grief as tears sprang into his eyes.

"I never meant to hurt them," he sobbed, and pressure of the knife under my chin eased slightly, "but they took his side. He beat us all the time and they screamed at me! Screamed at me! Can you believe that? They should have been thanking me! I didn't want them to die! But they just wouldn't stop! I couldn't stand the screaming. I swear I never meant for them to die. The gun just went off. And there was blood everywhere! And then Becky came in and I hit her, you know, to make her stop. I never meant to hit her so hard. I just couldn't stand hearing her scream!" he cried, holding his hands over his ears as if he still could hear the screaming.

"I know, Mark," I said soothingly. "It was an accident! You never meant to hurt your mom or Becky! You need help. You've been carrying this around with you for such a long time. There are people who can help you. Let me help you, Mark!" I said, reaching out to him.

As soon as my hand made contact with him, his face flashed into a mask of rage, the demonic gleam returning to his eyes.

"I know what you're trying to do, you bitch!" he shrieked, slapping my hand away. "You don't care about me! What

289

kind of fool do you take me for? You're just trying to save your own skin! You're not my friend! You want to lock me up just like they did Father Francis!"

In a lightening move, he reached up behind my head, grabbed a fistful of hair and yanked my head back exposing my throat. As he drew back to deliver the killing thrust, I swung the tire iron as hard as I could and connected with the side of his head with a sickening thud. His eyes popped open in surprise, his eyes rolled back in his head and the knife slipped from his hand to the floor. As he started to sink to his knees, I wrenched free from his grasp and ran down the hall to the outside door. I frantically pawed at the knob until it finally released. I ran across the lot towards the long line of cars. About halfway down the row, I ducked down and crawled underneath one. I stayed there panting for breath for a few seconds to see if he would recover sufficiently enough to follow me. I didn't have long to wait.

"You fucking bitch!" he shrieked, as he came bursting through the showroom door, "I was going to make it quick! Now I'm going to cut you up one inch at a time! You're going to pay you bitch! I know this place like the back of my hand! There's no place to hide!"

I could hear his feet slapping on the pavement as he ran down the row of cars in my direction. He would stop every few feet as he searched between the cars.

"Ellen! Come on out, Ellen. It's time to take your medicine, Ellen," I could hear him muttering to himself; one second in a singsong, childish voice and howling with rage the next.

I prayed that he wouldn't have the presence of mind to start looking under the cars. The sound of his footsteps advanced closer until I could see his feet move in front of the car I was under. I held my breath, closed my eyes and laid my cheek down on the wet blacktop. My heart was hammering so hard, I felt as though it would burst from my chest.

To my relief, he continued on past until I could hear him down at the end of the row. I felt terribly exposed and knew it was just a matter of time before he started looking under the cars, so I crawled out and crouched down beside the car. I peeked up over the hood and saw him going from car to car checking underneath each in turn and calling my name in that horrible voice. At the exact moment I saw his head was down, I jumped to my feet and dashed off in the opposite direction, back towards the showroom.

"You bitch!" he screamed and ran after me. I sprinted around to the back of the building, desperately seeking another hiding place, but the area was wide open and the back door was locked. I still had the tire iron in my hand, but knew I was no match for a maniac with a knife. I could hear him coming and knew I couldn't outrun him, but I decided to give it a try. I had no intention of making it easy for him. I thought I might be able to make it to the car out front and lock myself inside. I could blow the horn and flash the lights and maybe, with any luck, someone passing by would stop to investigate before he could get to me. I ran around the other side of the showroom building, praying that he hadn't had the presence of mind to lock the door, dashed to the car, found that it was indeed unlocked, flung open the passenger door and jumped inside. I discovered that the car was equipped with electric locks, so I quickly locked the doors just as Mark reached for the door handle.

He started banging on the glass with his fists, screaming and swearing at me as I slid across the seat in search of the keys. To my dismay, they were nowhere to be found. I suddenly remembered that he had used them to open the trunk and at the same time, so did he, because the banging stopped and I turned to see him grinning triumphantly at me through the glass, waving the keys back and forth for me to see. As he unlocked the passenger door, I exited through the driver's side and narrowly escaped his grasp as he lunged across the seat at me.

I got several yards toward the main road down the long driveway, when he overtook me and tackled me to the ground, knocking the air out of me. As I lay sprawled on the ground, gasping for breath, I felt searing pain in my back and the back of my leg where he was slashing at me. I kicked at him, connected with his head, rolled over to my back and swung the tire iron. I managed to strike some part of his body, because he let out a howl and released his hold on me. I scrambled to my feet, but fell down almost instantly. For some reason my legs refused to support me. The tire iron pinged on the pavement and bounced out of reach. I was trying to crawl towards it on

291

hands and knees, when he grabbed me by the shoulder and flipped me onto my back. He threw himself on top of me, straddling my body with his knees and pinning me to the ground. He loomed over me with the knife up over his head, preparing to plunge the knife into my chest. I closed my eyes in resignation. I had come to the end, but at least I had fought like a tiger. I knew that Andy would have been proud of me.

A vision of my family passed before me and when the fatal blow came, I was surprised that it went off in my head like an explosion. For some inexplicable reason, I hadn't felt any pain in my chest and my ears were ringing. I opened my eyes a crack and saw that Mark's chest was awash in my blood. He was looking down at the gore with a look of shock on his face. I was curiously detached from the experience. I figured my dying brain was protecting me from the full impact of it. I closed my eyes and lay back waiting for death to overtake me. The weight of Mark's body on top of me suddenly went away and I said to myself that dying really wasn't so bad after all.

I heard someone calling my name through the fog that was settling into my brain and I was pleased because that meant that there really is an afterlife after all. I opened my eyes expecting to see some heavenly entity there to lead me off to wherever it is that dead people go, but to my surprise, it was Andy's face looking down at me. He was crying and telling me to hold on; an ambulance was on the way. I reached up to touch his face and was surprised that he was real.

"What are you doing here?" I whispered. "Are you dead too?" I asked in wonder.

He started laughing and crying and gathered me up into his arms and held me to his chest. I felt warm and safe and gradually drifted off to sleep. That was the last thing I remember before I woke up in the hospital the following day.

Chapter Thirty-five

"Good morning, sleepyhead," someone said. I opened my eyes towards the bright light that was streaming through the parted drapes off to my right. I turned my head in the direction of the voice and saw a figure sitting by the window. He got to his feet and stood over me. It was Andy.

"How are you feeling?" he said softly, gently brushing back the hair that had fallen over my forehead.

"Kind of dopey," I croaked. I felt something bulky up under my chin and reached up with my fingers to investigate. There was an IV attached to the hand and I discovered that the wounds to my neck and chin had been covered with a thick bandage. "What happened?"

"You tell me. When I got there, Mark was sitting on top of you about to punch your ticket. If I had been a second later, we wouldn't be having this conversation!"

"I remember that you were there," I said drowsily and quickly felt around the front of my chest in a panic seeking the place where the knife had gone. There was no wound to be found. "Where's the cut? He stabbed me in the chest! I distinctly remember him stabbing me in the chest!" I cried in alarm.

"What are you talking about, Ellen? He didn't stab you in the chest!" Andy said soothingly, taking my hand in his.

"He most certainly did!" I insisted, snatching my hand from his grasp and trying to sit up for a better look.

Andy gently pressed me back down on the pillows and I complied, because not only was I as weak as a kitten, but I felt a sharp streak of pain shoot up from a place near the center of my back.

"You better settle down there, you're going to pull your stitches loose. Now, where did you get a crazy idea like that?" he asked as he dragged the chair over so that his face was down on my level.

"I heard this incredibly loud noise just as he stuck me with the knife. He had my blood all over the front of him, Andy! I saw it with my own eyes!" I told him stubbornly.

"Ellen! That wasn't your blood, it was his!" he informed me. "That noise you heard was my nine mil. I shot the bastard!"

"You mean you shot him? Mark's dead? Andy! You saved my life!" I cried.

"And you nearly scared the living daylights out of me, young lady!" he growled. "Why in the world did you go over there without me?" he demanded.

"It wasn't by choice, Andy! He caught me off guard at the front door! I was soaking wet from walking in the rain from the nursing home and was so intent on getting inside, I never saw him until it was too late." I said defensively.

"Hold that thought," Jack said from the doorway. We both looked up in surprise to see him being wheeled in by one of the nurses from Shady Oaks.

"Jack!" I cried. "What in the world are you doing here?"

"Did you think I could stay away when you very nearly got yourself killed?" he said in irritation. "Thanks, Linda," he said to the nurse, "we can take it from here."

She glanced over at Andy, who nodded, gave me an encouraging smile and left us to talk in private, softly closing the door behind her.

"Jack, I didn't think you were able to leave Shady Oaks. How did you manage to talk them into bringing you by?" I had to know.

"If you raise enough hell, people will eventually pay attention," he growled dismissively and waving off my question, "now, you were saying?"

"Saying? How much of our conversation did you hear?" I asked.

"Andy called me earlier and told me that he found you about to be sliced and diced by that maniac Mark McCoy before he blew him away! You were telling Andy here how you managed to get yourself in that predicament in the first place. You were perfectly fine when you left me!"

"Yeah! I meant to ask you about that, Jack! How come you didn't keep her there with you?" he said accusingly.

"Hey! Nobody ever told me she was being threatened!" Jack said defensively.

294

"Why do you think I insisted on going everywhere with her? Didn't it seem kind of odd that she never showed up by herself?" Andy asked indignantly.

"I thought you had the hots for her, Andy! How was I supposed to know she had somebody after her!" Jack shot back.

"Hey! Boys! Boys!" I shouted and their heads swiveled in my direction. "Cut it out! That's me you're talking about! Andy, Jack's right! We never told him about the threats. It was my fault for not staying put like you told me to. I won't have you attacking Jack for something he had no way of knowing!"

"Yeah! You're the one I ought to be yelling at!" Andy scowled, "what the hell were you doing running around in a thunderstorm by yourself anyway? You knew it wasn't safe!"

"You're absolutely right, Andy! I'm sorry I didn't listen," I said apologetically.

"You can say that again! You very nearly got yourself killed, Ellen!" he scolded me.

"I know. I know. It's just that you were gone for such a long time, I got worried. I needed to see Jack. And for your information it wasn't raining when I left to go over there. It didn't start to rain until I left!"

"That was my fault, Andy. I just wasn't paying attention. I thought she drove over." Jack admitted.

"It wouldn't have made any difference anyway, Jack. He was hiding in the bushes right outside my door when I went to unlock it. It didn't matter that I had walked home. He would have jumped me regardless of whether I was on foot or in a car."

"Whatever. There's nothing to be done about it now anyway!" Andy said in a huff. "Go on. What happened after he got a hold of you?"

"Well, he came up behind me and put a knife to my throat. He said he didn't want to kill me there where there might be witnesses. He knew I wouldn't go with him willingly, so he balled up his fist and hit me. I started to pass out and he dragged me to his car and threw me in the trunk. Andy, he was crazy! He was so consumed with rage! He swore he would kill me! I've never been so scared in all my life!" I sobbed as the memory of my ordeal washed over me.

I had been trying to put on a brave front for my two protectors, but the facade crumbled. I felt helpless and weak and foolish. I berated myself for not listening to Andy. If I had, Mark wouldn't have had to die and I wouldn't be laid up in the hospital with holes punched in various parts of my body.

"It's okay, kid," Andy said patting my hand. "It's all over now. He won't be hurting anyone else, I can assure you of that!"

"I know," I sniffed, "but if I had listened to you, he might have gotten treatment. If I had just stayed in the house, he wouldn't have been able to get to me. It's my entire fault that he's dead. He was insane, Andy! He couldn't help himself!"

"Ellen, come on! If he had wanted to get in, he would have! There was nothing you could do to stop him!" Jack said from the other side of the bed, laying his hand on my foot.

"I lost the gun, Andy," I admitted in a small voice, "fat lot of good that did me!"

"Hey, you probably wouldn't have used it anyway! Don't beat yourself up over it!" Andy said kindly.

"Oh, you're wrong there! If I had only had my wits about me, I would have made sure I had it with me. He had no way of knowing I was armed. I didn't want to see him dead, but like you said, when it came down to him or me, I would have pulled the trigger, I know I would!"

"Okay, I believe you! So, what happened when you got to the dealership?" Andy prompted.

"The strangest thing happened when I was in that trunk, Andy! At first I was so petrified, I couldn't think straight. When I realized I had left my gun behind, I just about gave up hope. I had pretty much resigned myself to my fate, and then something came over me. I made up my mind that I could either go like a lamb to the slaughter or I could use my head and fight for my life. That's when I found the tire iron!"

"The what!" Jack said in surprise.

"I wondered how that got there!" Andy said, "I figured he had used it on you!"

"Nope, the tire iron was mine. I found it under the carpeting in the trunk. I had hidden it up inside my sleeve. I only planned to use it as a last resort if I couldn't get through to him, but he gave me no choice. I hit him in the head with it the first time he tried to slit my throat!"

"Ellen! You are something else! It sounds like you gave him a run for his money!" Andy said in amazement.

"You would have been proud of me, Andy," I said attempting a smile, "when I thought I was dead, I thought about you. I just knew you would have been pleased with my performance."

"So you whacked him, huh? Good for you, slugger!" Jack added.

"Yeah, well I guess I didn't hit him hard enough, because he didn't stay down. He chased me all over the lot, to the car and then out the driveway. That's where he caught me. I hit him again, but I lost the tire iron in the struggle. That's when you came along, Andy. How can I ever thank you for what you did? I didn't stand a chance!"

"I am proud of you, Ellen. There are not many people who could have done what you did! Thank God I came when I did!" Andy said shaking his head.

"Speaking of that, why did you come? There was no way you could have known he had taken me there! What made you come looking for me?" I asked.

"Yeah, Andy. I'm wondering that myself," Jack added.

"Ooh, wow, that is a long story," Andy said, standing to gaze out of the window.

"So, tell us. Was it something you learned from your visit to the Mayor's house?" I asked, glancing with concern at Jack.

"Isn't it strange how this whole thing came together?" Andy said staring off through the window, more to himself than to us. "We were so busy trying to pin the murder on everyone, but the most obvious suspect. All those people whose lives Pat McCoy touched. Alice Martinez, Rosemary Willowby, Father Francis, Becky and Loretta. Even Silky and Dick Chance. We stirred up all those secrets and the real perpetrator was right there under our noses the whole time."

"You still haven't answered the question, Andy. What made you go by the dealership?" Jack insisted.

"Okay," he sighed, and sat back down. "Here it is. I dropped Ellen off and drove out to the Mayor's place. He was

297

just like Lucy had said he'd be. As soon as I walked in, he jumped all over me. He demanded to know why I was wasting so much time on a case that had been dead for years and not focusing on more important things. He accused me of neglecting my duties when I should be concentrating on the present. According to his Honor, every time he needed to speak to me, I was out traipsing around the countryside with my girlfriend!" he laughed ruefully.

"He actually said that?" I snapped. "That's what he thought we were doing? Going out on dates!"

"Don't get your panties in a bunch, Ellen! I'm just telling you what the man said," he replied defensively.

"Well, I assume you set him straight!" I huffed.

"I told him that we were working on some very promising leads in the case and that my personal life was none of his business!" he said.

"Okay, so is that when you lowered the boom about what we knew about his brother and Pat's extortion attempt?" Jack asked quickly before I could mutter a response.

"If I had, Ellen might never have left the house to go see you, Jack. I was just about to tell him everything when I got a call over my radio that there had been a holdup at the convenience store out by the turnpike and the gunman had taken a woman hostage. I simply had to take the call. I told the Mayor that there were some things I needed to discuss with him and told him I would come back just as soon as we gained control of the situation at the gas station. It took a couple hours for the county swat team to get a hostage negotiator there and a couple more before the guy gave himself up. When I got back to the Mayor's house, his wife said he had gone to the store, so I had to sit around making small talk with the missus while I sat on my thumbs waiting for him to get back."

"Why didn't you call me, Andy? I was out of my mind worrying about you!" I had to know.

"Give the guy a break, Ellen! I know how it is! With all that was going on, he had to give the situation his full attention! He didn't have time to call you, just because he felt like it!" Jack spoke up in Andy's defense.

"Well, what about while you were waiting for the Mayor to come back? You could have called then," I pointed out, not willing to let it drop.

"And say what? Excuse me, Mrs. Albertson, I have to call my girlfriend and let her know I haven't had the chance to accuse your husband of a felony?" he snapped.

"I am not your girlfriend, Andy, and there's no need for sarcasm!" I snapped back.

"Will you two just cut the crap!" Jack hollered, glaring at us both. "Go ahead, Andy! Tell us what you found out when the Mayor arrived!"

"Okay! As I was saying, Dan finally got home. We went into the study and I started off by telling him that I knew that Francis was his brother."

"Did he act surprised that you knew?" Jack asked.

"I'm not sure. Maybe. You could have heard a pin drop after I said it. But he quickly recovered, because he demanded to know what business it was of mine who his relatives were. I told him what we had learned about his brother's predilection for young boys and I thought he was going to blow a gasket!"

"I'll bet he did!" Jack chuckled, "I wish I could have been there to see his face!"

"So, did he deny it?" I asked breathlessly.

"You bet he did! Vehemently! Said it was all a lie. His brother was a kind caring person and blah, blah, blah. He cut off his testimonial when I told him that we had located two of his victims! I thought he was going to have a coronary right then and there! He just sort of sank back in his chair and looked at me in total shock. That's when I asked him about the payoff to Pat McCoy. As soon as the words came out of my mouth, he started crying like a baby!"

"So it was all true! He did pay the blackmail money! I knew it!" Jack said, slapping his hand on the bed.

"Yeah, apparently old Pat really put the screws to him and his brother. He swore he didn't know who killed the McCoys, but I wouldn't let up. I could tell he knew more than he was saying. I asked him if he or his brother killed them. I may have even hinted that I had some proof, you know the routine, Jack. He really got scared then. That's when he spilled his guts!"

"Come on, Andy, don't leave us in suspense! What did he say?" I urged impatiently.

"He said that when he first heard about the McCoy murders, he suspected that his brother had had something to do with it. Francis swore up and down that he wasn't involved and he believed him. Then when the police pointed the finger at Mark, he kept quiet. What could be better? The blackmailer's son took care his problem for him. His troubles were over! That's when Chief Talbot got involved."

"What did Art have to do with it?" Jack asked.

"Remember Silky telling us that Pat told him that he had hidden the evidence up under the ceiling tiles, Ellen?"

"Yeah! He said he went and told the Chief about it!"

"And the Chief told him to keep his mouth shut, he would handle it. He did all right! He told the Mayor about it. The two of them were best friends. He went looking for the box of evidence, but apparently Pat had moved it. That was his footprint on the dining room table!"

"Get out of here! Really?" I declared in amazement.

"Yep! The Mayor said he got really nervous then. He kept waiting for it to turn up, but it never did, so he thought he was home free."

"So why did he help Mark? He could have just let him take the fall for it and no one would ever have been the wiser! The whole thing would have died with Pat McCoy!" Jack commented.

"I bet I know!" I piped up.

They both looked at me. Andy put his hands on his hips.

"Okay, Sherlock, why did the Mayor help Mark?" he asked doubtfully.

"Because of Francis," I said simply.

"How do you know that?" Andy said, surprised at my unexpected intuition.

"Because Mark told me!" I cried triumphantly. "Just before he made his first attempt at killing me, he screamed that the reason he had killed his father was because he found out that Pat had been trying to ruin Father Francis!"

"So what? What does that have to do with anything?" Jack demanded.

"Just let her finish, Jack," Andy said, "I want to hear where she is going with this," he said thoughtfully.

"Mark told me he loved the man! He said he was the only person who had ever understood him, cared about him, you know, been there for him. And Pat was trying to ruin his life. Mark killed his father to protect Father Francis!"

"I still don't see where you're going with this!" Jack grunted.

"Don't you see? Francis loved him too! He would have done anything to see that Mark never had to pay for his crime! He did it for him! Remember the missing time? Maybe Mark went to Father Francis and told him what he had done for him!"

"And Francis went to his brother, who was always there to get him out of trouble and talked him into helping Mark!" Jack cried, finally getting the picture.

"Exactly! Am I right, Andy?" I asked expectantly.

"I couldn't have told it any better than that!" he agreed. "The Mayor told me he promised his brother that he would take care of Mark for the rest of his life. And until we came along, that is exactly what he did. Only the church found out about Father Francis and shipped him off to a mental institution where he has been ever since!"

"So the kid killed his folks for nothing!" Jack said, shaking his head at the irony.

"I'm afraid so, Jack. He told me he never meant to hurt his mother and sister. They just sort of got in the way. I think he really felt remorse over them," I said.

"And now he's dead. So, what happens now, Andy? Did you arrest Dan?" Jack wanted to know.

"For what? What he did was certainly morally wrong, but he didn't kill anybody. There really isn't anything I can charge him with at this late date."

"So what made you come to the dealership?" I asked.

"I called your house and you weren't there. I knew that Mark was probably the one who had been making the threats and knowing what he was capable of, I got scared. I decided I'd better locate him as soon as possible. When he wasn't at home, I drove out to the dealership. That's when I saw the two of you struggling in the driveway and him with that knife. I knew I only had a few seconds to act, so I took aim and fired. It's a good thing I followed my instincts. I don't know if I could live with myself if I hadn't gotten there in time!"

"Well, I don't know about the two of you, but this whole thing has wiped me out! Andy, would you mind terribly if you took me back to Shady Oaks? I think our patient here could use some rest," Jack said, giving my foot a little shake.

"Will you be all right for a little while?" Andy asked.

"I'll be just fine, Andy," I smiled, "with you and Jack around to watch out for me, I couldn't be better!"

Andy kissed my forehead and Jack squeezed my hand and they departed. I drifted off to sleep knowing I would never again find two better men than them. I felt honored to be able to call them my friends.

Epilogue

I was glad that the plane heading for Atlanta Hartsfield International was carrying so few passengers, because I had been given a window seat in the back of the plane with no one seated on the aisle next to or across from me. I needed some time to think and didn't feel up to making small talk with anyone. My physical wounds had healed, but I would carry the scars of my experience forever.

My daughter was meeting me at the airport and I looked forward to seeing her. It seemed a lifetime had passed since I had been with my family although in truth it had only been a couple of months. She would have the kids with her and I couldn't wait to hold my two precious grandsons in my arms. My recent brush with death had convinced me that life doesn't come with any guarantees. The priceless kite string of life had nearly slipped from my tenuous grasp. I had almost lost them forever and I promised myself that I would never take my family for granted again.

I braced myself as the engines revved up for take-off. My body was pressed back into the seat as the pilot released the brakes and we began accelerating down the runway. Within moments the jet reached maximum velocity and we were airborne. The grinding sound of the wheels stopped and the noise from the landing gear doors being slammed shut reverberated beneath my feet. We continued to gain altitude and I glanced out of the window at the ground below. I could see the buildings of downtown Cleveland off in the distance to the west so small they looked like the miniatures of a toy train set.

The flight path was taking us out over the sparkling blue water of Lake Erie. Tiny boats were dotted across the expanse below and I had to smile at the memory of my disastrous boat trip to Put-in-Bay with my classmate Emily and her husband. I'm sure they were still chuckling over the sight of me tossing my cookies over the side, but they were the kind of people I expected my old friends to be and I would always cherish the memory of that carefree day.

I had finally broken down and called Betsy from the hospital. She had been very put out with me at first for not letting her know I had stayed in town after the Melon Festival, but once she learned of my narrow escape from Mark, she had rushed to my bedside. How our paths never crossed during the weeks of my stay remains a mystery to this day.

I had been a different person when I had come to Milan for the reunion. There was no way that I could have known how much I would be changed by my dogged determination to solve the McCoy murders. I had come home to Ohio to recapture my youth only to discover that much of what I thought I knew about the place of my childhood had been pure fantasy. The reality of the matter is that evil can be found even in the most seemingly serene settings. The ugly secrets of the town had been buried beneath the surface as surely as the trash had been plowed under the soil of my grandfather's farm. In the innocence of childhood, I just never saw it. I was overcome with an intense feeling of sadness and loss.

I wish I could say that Andy and I made something of our budding relationship, but I just couldn't get past the difference in our ages. In the aftermath of the attempt on my life and Mark's untimely death, Andy stayed with me night and day until I recovered. He did his best to persuade me to stay. He was convinced that it would work out between us. But I knew I belonged in Georgia with my children and the home I had shared with the love of my life, my husband. It's probably foolish on my part, but the thought of being with another man seems somehow disloyal to his memory. Andy is my dearest friend and will always hold a special place in my heart. I can never forget that I owe him my life. I hope someday that he will find someone who loves him the way I loved my husband and deserves such an extraordinary man. Maybe then he'll understand why I had to say no.

As I gazed at the scenery passing below, my thoughts turned to the other man who had come to play such an important role in my brief sojourn in Ohio, Jack Miller. He had remained the one constant during the weeks leading up the end. I'd like to think I had some small part in his decision not to give up on life. His trip outside the nursing home to the hospital seemed to act as the catalyst for his renewed efforts toward recovery. The last I heard, he was making remarkable progress with his physical therapist. The McCoy case gave him back his zest for detective work. After my release from the hospital, he told me he plans to start work in a few weeks on another cold case from a neighboring town. With his brilliant mind and intuition, they could do a lot worse. He is also someone I can never forget.

With Mark dead and the threat that the secrets surrounding the McCoy case were on the brink of exposure, Mayor Dan Albertson quietly retired from office. The car dealership was sold and I heard that he made a good profit. He was honored by the town as having held the office of Mayor longer than any other mayor in the state of Ohio, with over thirty years of public service. A plaque was placed inside City Hall in tribute to him. I found the whole thing a little disturbing, but considering all the other things he did for the town, I guess it was appropriate. Some people seem to be able to land on their feet no matter what they have done.

As to what happened to the other people I came in contact with during the course of the investigation, I never heard. The men who had been traumatized by Father Francis could have pursued it further, but I had my doubts that they would. Too much time had passed and no amount of money would ever take away their pain.

Life goes on, as they say, and the little town of my birth will recover from the scandal. People come and go and memories soon fade. As for me, I've decided to remember only the good times and the wonderful friends I made while I stayed there. Those are things that can never be taken away from me. The town helped shape me into the woman I am today and for that

I will always be grateful.

A sneak peek.....

Where Love Is Not

By Deborah E. Warr

"I would rather live and love where death is king, than have eternal life where love is not."
Robert G. Ingersoll

July 15, 1995 – 6 Miles off the Coast of North Carolina

"This can't be happening!" Teresa thought as she struggled desperately to reach the surface of the water. Only a moment before she had been standing at the railing of her new 32-foot cabin cruiser reveling in how happy and content she felt. In all her 60 years she had never been so much in love. The last thing she remembered, she had been enjoying the feel of the wind in her hair and admiring the view. Then without warning, the railing had snapped and she had tumbled overboard.

When her head finally broke free, it was all she could do to get enough air into her lungs to scream for help before another wave washed over her instantly flooding into her mouth and nose.

"Oh God! Help me! Help!" she choked out, panic seizing her as she frantically tried to stay afloat. She barely got the words out before another wave loomed over her.

"Christoff! Help me! For God's sake, help me!" she cried, her shouts reverberating across the expanse. The yacht had come to a stop and was idling in the distance. Once again the surging swells engulfed her.

When the wave passed, she raked her sodden hair back out of her eyes to see her husband standing in the stern of boat. The distance between her and the boat had stretched to fifty yards. Fearing that he hadn't heard her cries, she waved her arms over her head. No sooner had she done so that another wave took her under and after what seemed like forever, she resurfaced sputtering and gasping for breath.

"Christoff! Over here! Please, you've got to help me!" she screamed.

When she looked again, to her absolute horror, she saw that instead of rushing to her aid, he was standing in the stern, scanning the water in her direction with binoculars. She was sure that he was looking right at her. Yet he made no move to save her, but inexplicably stood mutely watching her. Panic swelled in her wildly pounding heart as she saw him casually let the binoculars hang down on the strap around his neck, reach into his pocket, withdraw a cigarette, cup his hands around the tip, light it and blow a stream of smoke into the wind.

"Christoff! What are you doing? Please! Oh, my God! Help me back into the boat!" she shrieked, "you've got to help me!"

Her husband seemed rooted to the spot; casually flicking the ashes from his cigarette over the side and staring in her direction. She couldn't imagine why he seemed so unconcerned and why he wasn't doing something to save her. She knew he had to see her. Each time she was overwhelmed beneath a wave, she would come back up to see that he was still there, his head tilted slightly to one side with one hand on the railing bracing himself on the rolling deck and holding the cigarette to his lips with the other.

"Christoff, over here! What are you waiting for! You can't just let me die!" she wailed.

She realized with a start that the current was taking her farther away from the boat by the second. Her husband still made no move to come to her aid, so she began awkwardly dog paddling towards the boat doing her best to keep her face out of the water. To her dismay, it wasn't enough. She had never been a strong swimmer and her efforts were useless. For every few feet she gained, she lost even more. The next time she looked, he wasn't at the back of the boat any more. Relief surged through her. He had come to his senses and was finally going to save her. Perhaps he had just been frozen with fear for her she rationalized. Yes, that would explain it, she told herself. People do strange things in panic situations. He had simply been so shocked; he must have been paralyzed with confusion. He simply needed to analyze the situation before taking action. She was sure it was just a matter of time before he pulled the boat closer, tossed her a life ring and pulled her out of the water. Knowing that her young handsome husband was coming gave her a rush of renewed hope and strength. All she had to do was stay calm and it would all be over shortly.

Then she heard the diesels kick over and the boat began a wide arch circling back around in her direction. She wasn't sure how long she had been in the water, but she felt chilled to the bone. The prospect of warm towels and a sip of that wonderful brandy Christoff had brought along was almost more than she could bear. She promised herself that as soon as she was safely back on the boat, she would let him know in no uncertain terms how much his odd behavior had frightened her.

Then the unimaginable happened. Instead of coming right up next to her as she expected, the boat came to rest well past her. Her heart sank. It was closer, but still too far from her position to do any good. As soon as the boat settled back down into the chop, her husband came to the side of the boat, but this time he had his hands cupped around his mouth as he shouted to her.

"Teresa! Can you hear me?" he yelled.

"Yes, I hear you! What are you doing? For God's sake, move the boat closer! Please, Christoff, I begging you! I don't know how much longer I can hang on!" she screamed.

"I'd really like to help you, but you see, I've already got everything I need from you! Remember that million-dollar insurance policy we took out on you? The agent says it'll pay, so I'm afraid, your time's up. I just thought you'd like to know that I'll take good care of your money!" he shouted over the wind.

"What are you talking about? Is that all you care about? My money? Are you insane? Please, Christoff, you can have it all! I don't care! Please! For the love of God help me!" she pleaded. "You know I can't swim!"

"As your grieving husband, I can have it all, Teresa! Don't you get it? Why should I tie myself down with an old bag of bones like you? If you divorced me, I'd get nothing! This way, I get your properties and insurance money with no strings attached! I'm a young virile man, Teresa! Did you really think I enjoyed making love to an old dried up prune like you? I can't wait another twenty years! Can't you even die without that incessant whining? Do you have any idea how hard it's been pretending to listen to you yammer on and on and on day after day after day! Have you any idea how truly boring you really are? I've got a real life to live, Teresa! Do us all a favor! Just get on with it! Good-bye, Teresa!"

With a final mock salute, he flicked his cigarette butt in her general direction, returned to the wheelhouse, revved up the engines, swept around in her direction, flew past her and left her bobbing in his wake. As she helplessly watched her only chance of survival shrink in the distance, Teresa's heart was inundated with shock, outrage and then indescribable despair. His brutal parting words hurt her more than the prospect of her impending death. The enormity of his betrayal was more than she could bear. How could she have been such a fool! Two years! He had been her whole world for two years and it had all been a lie! He wasn't even willing to let her die in peace. He couldn't even give her that! He just couldn't leave without ripping away her last shred of dignity.

"Dear God in heaven," she prayed, "make him pay. For all that is holy, make him pay."

Stoically accepting her fate, Teresa Montgomery closed her eyes, said another prayer for her immortal soul, opened her mouth to the swirling waves, sucked the water into her lungs and surrendered to the pull of the deep. She lost consciousness with her husband's parting words still ringing in her ears.

Be sure to watch for the published novel, coming later this year from Limitless, Dare 2 Dream Publishing.

Author's Bio:

Deborah E. Warr was born in Sandusky, Ohio, but has lived in Georgia since 1970. After twenty years in the banking industry, Deborah retired from the business world in 1999 in order to write full time. Deborah says that books have always played an important role in her life and that she inherited her love of literature from her mother, who was a librarian and poet. Other books include *In the Name of the Mother* and *Where Love Is Not,* a sequel to *Home to Ohio* which is scheduled for release in 2003 by <u>Limitless D2D</u>. She is currently at work on another untitled novel in the Ellen Richardson series.

The Amazon Queen by L M Townsend	20.00	
Define Destiny by J M Dragon	20.00	
Desert Hawk by Archangel	15.00	
Golden Gate by Erin Jennifer Mar	18.00	
Love's Melody Lost, 2ndEd. by Radclyffe	18.00	
Paradise Found by Cruise and Stoley	20.00	
Spirit Harvest by Trish Shields	15.00	
Storm Surge by KatLyn	20.00	
Up The River-out of print **...While supplies last...** by Sam Ruskin	15.00	
Memories Kill By S. B. Zarben	20.00	
Fatal Impressions by Jeanne Foguth	18.00	
	Total	

South Carolina residents add 5% sales tax.
Shipping is $3.50 per book and will be via UPS.

Watch for more and upcoming titles:
Visit our websiteat:http://limitlessd2d.net/index.html

Please mail your orders with a check or money order to:

Limitless, Dare 2 Dream Publications
100 Pin Oak Ct.
Lexington, SC 29073

Please make checks or money orders payable to:
Limitless.

Title	Price	
The Amazon Queen by L M Townsend	20.00	
Define Destiny by J M Dragon	20.00	
Desert Hawk by Archangel	15.00	
Indiscretions **By Cruise**	18.00	
A Thousand Shades of **Feeling** **by Carolyn McBride**	18.00	
The Amazon Nation **By Carla Osborne**	20.00	
Spirit Harvest by Trish Shields	15.00	
Encounters, Book I By Anne Azel	22.00	
Encounters, Book II **By Anne Azel**	25.00	
Memories Kill By S. B. Zarben	20.00	
Deadly Rumors by Jeanne Foguth	20.00	
	Total	

South Carolina residents add 5% sales tax.
Shipping is $3.50 per book and will be via UPS.

Watch for these and more upcoming titles:
Visit our website at: **http://limitlessd2d.net**

Please mail your orders with a check or money order to:

Limitless, Dare 2 Dream Publications
100 Pin Oak Ct.
Lexington, SC 29073

Please make checks or money orders payable to:
Limitless.